THE
TERMINAL
STATE

JEFF SOMERS

www.orbitbooks.net

Copyright © 2010 by Jeff Somers
Excerpt from *The Final Evolution* copyright © 2010 by Jeff Somers
All rights reserved. Except as permitted under the U.S. Copyright Act of 1976, no part of this publication may be reproduced, distributed, or transmitted in any form or by any means, or stored in a database or retrieval system, without the prior written permission of the publisher.

Orbit
Hachette Book Group
237 Park Avenue, New York, NY 10017
Visit our website at www.orbitbooks.net

Orbit is an imprint of Hachette Book Group. The Orbit name and logo are trademarks of Little, Brown Book Group Limited.

Printed in the United States of America

First Edition, August 2010

10 9 8 7 6 5 4 3 2 1

The grunt put his face in mine, wrapping his arms around me and squeezing with excruciating, surprising force, making my ribs bark and trapping the shredder between us.

Blood had spilled out over his mouth and chin, making him look suddenly older, more dangerous.

"Still got the thumbs, old man," he panted at me. "You gonna break 'em with your mind?"

I liked this guy. I liked the troops better than the cops—the cops were all fucking attitude, dandies in their rich suits, even before they'd all been forcibly turned into avatars, Droids with digital brains. They had more metal in their brains than I liked, sure, but we all had faults. I tended to kill everyone I met, more or less by accident.

Before I could tell him about my growing affection toward him, Remy rose up in the air and attached himself to the back of the soldier, his skinny arms locking around the grunt's neck. Before I could even blink, he'd leaned in close like a fucking lover and bit the grunt's ear, a savage, tearing bite.

The guard screamed. It was a high-pitched, boyish scream. He staggered off me, his arms slapping up at Remy, and I smiled, thinking, *That's my boy.*

Praise for the Avery Cates novels:

"Somers just might be the genre's best-kept secret."
—Pat's Fantasy Hotlist

"An exhilarating example of powerful and entertaining storytelling." —*The Guardian* (U.K.)

BY JEFF SOMERS

To my darling wife, whose surplus of good judgment makes up for my near-complete lack of it, for ass-kickings richly deserved, and for love I'm not nearly worthy of.

PROLOGUE

IT ONLY GOT DEADLY WHEN
YOU STOPPED

"Evry'ting fallen apart," Dingane groused, rubbing his dry, cracked hands against his unshaven chin. "T'whole fuckin' world, yeah?"

I raised the wooden cup from the wobbly table and held it in the air between us, steeling myself. I'd tasted some terrible things in my life, but the moonshine Bixon made out back routinely tasted like it had been filtered through corpses and it felt like it was taking a layer of your throat off as it went down to boot. I was a murderer, Plague survivor, and wanted man, and I still had to steady myself before each shot.

"Quit your fucking bellyaching," I advised Dingane, "and tell me if you got my stuff."

He was right—the System was cracking open—but that was no reason to encourage him. After years of plotting against each other, the System Police and the civilian government had been in open civil war for a year, piling up bodies and destroyed cities, burning through yen and bodies, building up these sudden fleets of military-grade hovers and weapons, things that hadn't existed for decades, since unification had ended war for fucking ever, didn't you know. The whole world, bound together for a while, one government, one police force, no armies in sight. And now we didn't have police anymore, just armies, and it didn't matter who won. You just wanted them to get it over with *fast*, before they killed everyone.

Dingane paused, nasty, and then thought better of it and smiled. I immediately wished he hadn't, green teeth and black gums, and I tipped the shot into my mouth to distract myself from his grin. My throat tried to close up in instinctual defense, but I was ready for that and just worked it on down. I breathed through my mouth.

"Ohkay, ohkay," Dingane said, affecting a jolly expression. "Av'ry is impatient today, uh? Av'ry's in the *revenge* bidness, huh? You lis'n to Dingane, m'friend, an' be happy. Fo'get these two men made you so fuckin' angry."

I gave him a frown, a steady unhappy expression. "There's a reason you're crawling the fucking earth trading in junk and reclaimed ammunition, and I'm sitting here *hiring* you. When someone sells me out"—Wa Belling, handing me over to Kev Gatz and the Plague—"lies to me and leaves me for dead"—Michaleen, staring down at me from the hover as it drifted away, leaving me to be bricked in Chengara—"I don't fucking *forget*."

You're small, a voice whispered in my head. I blinked, ignoring it.

Suddenly he was grinning, happy to oblige. Just like everyone else, if you were polite you got static. If you showed them your fist, they got polite. "You pay'n the bills heeyah, so ohkay," he said hurriedly. "I got mos' de stuff you ask. Not easy t'transport heavy shit, t'big shit." He spread his chalky hands. "No 'overs any mo', Av'ry. From here t'Florida you can't get no 'overs. An if you *could*, the fucking armay be shoot'n your ass *down*, trust. So I can't get the big items. And bullets is hard. Ammo. Hard. No one makin' any'ting anymore. Nowhere. Mexico, sheeit, usesta be, Mexico you get *any'ting*, now, no. Nothin' *in* Mexico 'cept armay and cops, armay and cops, shootin's at every'ting, bombing t'cities back to fuck."

It was my fate to listen to Dingane bitch and moan every now and then. I'd pulled his ear a few times to discourage him, but Dingane was one of those leathery fellows who looked a fucking century old and acted like pain didn't mean shit to him anymore, which maybe it didn't. Easier to let him talk. I wasn't going anywhere anyway.

That didn't mean I couldn't move things along. "Hell, Dingy, can't you shut up for one fucking minute?"

He gave me the grin again. "Sho' can, Av'ry, but I thought y'wanted news of your order, huh? You wanted clips, mag'zines, for what'ver caliber I could get. I got some, I got some, but it ain't cheap or easy. N'one down south makin' 'em up an'more. I gots to go *far afield*, you dig? And the Geeks—oh, fuck, the fuckin' Geeks, Av'ry. Dey band t'gether, you know that? SPS? All these fuckin' Techies, throwin' shit down."

I let Dingane talk. It was good cover. I closed my eyes and pictured the place, Bixon's uninsulated shack with the long bar made up of crates in the back, the wobbly tables lashed together, the big ugly metal stove in the middle of the room glowing red, pulsing with heat, making the whole place smell like my own armpit, and stinging the eyes with soot and smoke. Better than outside, where snow was howling—the weather was fucked up. You never knew what you were gonna get these days. Rumor was it was all fallout from the war screwing up the climate, but who the fuck knew. I'd never been in this part of the world before. Neither had most of us.

I thought of Old Pick, long dead now. I thought about everything that fat old bastard had known, the data of lifetimes, the oral history of every criminal worth remembering in New York since Unification. And who knew what water he'd carried across the line from pre-Uni times. All of it gone now, like they'd never happened. And there'd never be another Pick, ever. Not these days.

The tables, six of them, arranged randomly in the tight space beyond the bar, more or less around the stove that stood in the middle. Me and Dingane, the Mayor and her cronies playing dominoes, Tiny Timlin and some of the other kids looking puffy and sick on their fourth or fifth dose of Bixon's poison. Bixon himself, behind the bar, a man who had never washed once since I'd known him, more beard than human at this point. All of them just flotsam, people fleeing the war and dead cities abandoned by one side or another, showing up here. For the most part, if you could lend a hand, you were pretty much welcome.

If you couldn't lend a hand, or didn't want to, and stuck around anyway, that's where I came in.

"And this utter t'ing you ask me to look into, I t'ink I got you something."

I popped open one eye and put it on him. The black bastard was grinning again, pleased with himself. I shut my eyes again. "Yeah?"

I pictured the place again: one door in the front, a heavy

piece of wood on crude but solid hinges, one in the rear of the room that led out to the back where Bixon created his horrible juice. I didn't know how he made the stuff, and I didn't want to know; if I went back there and found him milking some terrible giant green worm, I wouldn't be surprised.

Behind me, the band was chicken pickin' their way through a complex series of chords that managed to sound pretty good even though they had ten strings between the three of them. They were old guys, fucking ancient, but everyone here did something. If you couldn't work the fields or make booze or kick the shit out of people when the *Mayor* told you to, you played a bass line on a single string and made it sound snappy.

And then, bellied to the bar and examining his cup of booze dubiously, the Badge.

Not a badge *anymore*, but certainly an old System Pig. I didn't recognize him.

Me either, the voice whispered faintly and was gone. Not a ghost, since Dick Marin was still—well, alive wasn't the right word for it, but still in existence.

But he had the look.

"Yeah," Dingane said, leaning forward so I could get a real good whiff of him, a courtesy. "Europe, I 'ear. Amsterdam. Both o' dem. Solid source, uh?"

I shook my head, opening my eyes again. I didn't hear from my ghosts much anymore, but they still popped up once in a while, still there, still complete and whole. Amsterdam. *Both of them.* I figured Michaleen would be in Europe—I wondered if Belling was working with him again. Knowing a city was a good start.

"Why you lookin' to leave, eh, Av'ry?" Dingane shifted

and spat into the sawdust on the floor. "Y'got a good thing here. Roof, food, friends. Should not walk away from dis, I don' think."

I looked past Dingane. "I got unfinished business. Debts to settle."

The cop—ex-cop—turned to survey the place, sizing us up. He was tall and heavy, a gone-to-fat heaviness encased like a sausage inside a heavy leather overcoat, which looked battered and salty, and a dark-blue suit that had seen better days. His shoes were woefully unprepared for the mush outside, with a noticeable hole in one through which I could see his bare toe, pink and squirming. You didn't need to see his credit dongle—assuming he still carried one like a totem—to know this ex-cop had seen better days.

He still had that gloss, though. That cop arrogance. He'd somehow escaped Marin's avatar purge, and he'd somehow wriggled away from the civil war to go adventuring, but even without backup or a discretionary budget or fucking *shoes* he still thought he was going to run the show here. His hair was bright red and thin, a halo around his pink head. His cheeks hung from his face like they were full of ball bearings and sagged with weight, and his eyes were watery and red.

As I watched, the cop picked up his cup without looking at it and delivered it to his wet mouth. Tipping it back without hesitation, he swallowed the shot whole and returned the cup to the bar without comment or visible reaction. My respect for the man went up a half inch. Anyone who could drink Bixon's poison without wincing or coughing or bursting into flames had something going on.

Glancing to my right I found, as always, Remy staring at me. Remy had lost *his* gloss; he was starting to look like a normal human being. I didn't know how old he was or why I always had squirts running after me like I was fucking Santa Claus, but Remy was coming along from the spoiled little brat in his shiny shoes screaming about his daddy. He was firming up, and I even had hope he'd someday stop calling me *Mr. Cates.* Then we had to work on the staring, but to be honest it came in handy. I nodded my head slightly, and the kid was up off his crate immediately and out into the storm.

"Listen up!"

The ex-cop's voice was booming, deep and smooth, the voice of a man used to being obeyed. His eyes, though, roamed the space nervously, and his hands were curled into fists. The music stopped on a dime.

"My name is Major Benjamin Pikar," he shouted, turning slowly to make sure we all got the benefit of his jiggling jowls. "And I am here to protect you!"

Major. I eyed him up and down and decided he'd given himself a promotion. His coat was captain, if that.

Our mayor, who'd been elected by dint of referring to herself as the Mayor until we couldn't stand it anymore, behaved herself and kept her eyes off me. Gerry was an amiable old hag who'd been a banker before the Plague. She'd lost her family during that little fun ride and had been in Chicago when the friendly folks of the System of Federated Nations Army had sent in five hundred thousand single-use bomb drones armed with F-90s, field-contained armaments. Wandering south out of the wreckage, she'd found us here in Englewood. She was skinny, with a huge triangle of a nose that bobbed up and down whenever she talked and gray eyes permanently squinted from years peering at holographic data streams. The last time one of these ex-pig entrepreneurs had shown up to save us from the big bad world, Gerry'd leaped up to announce she was the mayor and would speak for the town, and I'd been forced to knock her unconscious.

"I have been assigned by order of Richard Marin, Director of Internal Affairs for the System Security Force, to take administrative charge of this settlement, bring it in line with the laws and customs of the System of Federated Nations, and organize your defense against both the insurgent forces and...criminal aspects seeking to take advantage of you," Pikar said with a straight face. I wondered, briefly, why Marin never just cut the cord and promoted himself to director of the Whole Fucking World or What Was Left of It After the F-90s.

Can't, the man's outdated ghost whispered in my head. *Programming limits. They thought by limiting my position they limited* me.

Pikar looked around to see how well his shit was floating, and he didn't look pleased, his red face getting darker, his knuckles white at his sides.

"Perhaps you have heard," he managed to say calmly, putting his hands on his hips in a practiced motion that pushed his coat back to reveal the twin guns under his arms and the battered badge clipped to his belt, "rumors of SFNA Press Gangs in the region." He nodded crisply. "I can confirm this."

I glanced at the two windows, small and cloudy, set into the front wall. Against the snow, I could clearly see dark forms gathered at each, and I put my eyes back on Pikar to make sure he hadn't noticed. He hadn't; he was caught up in the pitch. I knew what was coming next. I could have written the script for him.

"There is no reason to fear, however, as I am here now to organize your defense against these dangerous rebels." He was all business now. He'd given us the scare, showed us the cannons, and now came the offer. He turned to signal Bixon for another drink. Bixon, as wide as he was tall, was all beery muscle without a hint of augments. He just stood there behind his rotting makeshift bar, hands hidden and caressing, I had no doubt, his prize possession: a personally restored 10-09 shredder, original SSF issue and held together, literally, by tightly wound strands of silvery wire. It had seven rounds left, and odds were it was going to explode in his hands if he ever dared fire it, but it still made grown men who knew what it was shit their pants when they saw it.

"I will require the following items in order to fund and organize my office here," Pikar boomed, tapping his fingers on the bar. "First—"

I'd had enough. "First, shut the fuck up," I said. I didn't say it loud. Everyone heard me anyway. This was what I got paid for, if you counted a roof over my head and enough tasteless gruel to keep me alive—not to mention a bottomless tab at Bixon's—as pay. I hadn't received any better offers, so I'd stayed on, kicking asses and running shitheads along.

The ex-cop looked at me, and to his credit all his nervous tics were instantly gone, replaced with the careful stillness of someone trained to handle himself. "Excuse me, citizen?"

I stood up, wooden cup in one hand as I slid my other one into the oily pocket of my raincoat. Waving the cup around, I pushed my hand through the slit cut into the pocket and put my palm on the butt of my prized Roon—the best handgun ever made—oiled every night and cleaned every other, gleaming and smooth like there was no such thing as rust, decay, or death. I made for the bar, working hard to keep the pain and stiffness in my leg from showing. "I said shut the fuck up. You're making this place smell worse than it normally does with that bullshit, and that's saying something." I placed my cup on the bar. "Sorry, Bix."

Bixon nodded, his eyes still locked on Pikar. "No worries, Avery."

Pikar turned his head slightly toward Bix, but kept his eyes on me. Logging the bartender as a combatant, marking his position, probably noting for the first time the absence of visible hands. He shifted his weight and angled his hand from his belt to tap the badge.

"You don't want to fuck with police, friend," he said. "This is official business."

I nodded, leaning with my back against the bar. The badge had shorted out and didn't have the cheery gold glow of the holograph anymore. "From what I hear, the System Pigs' business these days is tripping over themselves retreating from the army. You ain't the first asshole to wander in here out of the fucking snow with holes in his fucking shoes trying to shake us down. You're looking for soft touches. Keep walking until you find some."

That was his one chance, I decided. Fair was fair. Couldn't blame a man for trying to score. Only for pushing his luck.

He kept his flat little eyes on me and his hands perfectly still. His jowls, though, were quivering, rhythmically, bouncing slightly with every thudding heartbeat that kept his face purple. Then he smiled.

"New York," he said, jolly now. "The accent. You're Old Work from the island, right? Spent a few weeks in some Blank Rooms here and there, uh?"

I shrugged. "You don't know me." He probably knew of me, my name, but it didn't matter.

He nodded. "Maybe not. I know your type. Strawman, stuffed with shit. You all think this piece of turd is your hero?" He suddenly asked the room. "You're betting on the wrong man."

My own heart pounded and my stomach was complaining about Bixon's swill. A cold sweat had popped out on my face too, and I wondered if there was any way to turn puking my guts out into an advantage in a gunfight.

"Look out the windows, *friend*," I advised. "We've called out the militia."

He squinted at me. I almost felt sorry for him: Every cop in the System had been transformed into an avatar, usually against their will. He hadn't. That meant he'd been in some backwater post, a fuckup out in the middle of nowhere, or else he'd been running a lot longer than I'd imagined. Desperate. Shot on sight if the army found him, packed into a data brick for leisurely debriefing whenever the immortal Dick Marin felt like it if the cops picked him up—he was screwed. He wanted to look, but he didn't want to be stupid, didn't want to *look* stupid. That was all he had left. The aura of a cop.

Everything falling apart, sure. Dingane had it right. Even the System Pigs were just ghosts these days.

The shadows in the windows looked good. Menacing. Remy and his friends had balls, sure. They didn't have any *guns*, but you couldn't tell that through the windows. It didn't matter if Pikar looked or not, if he saw men with rifles or kids pissing their short pants—it made him think, it fucked him up, and that was all it was meant to do.

He snorted. "I'm taking control of this settlement," he said slowly. "I am ordering you to hand over whatever it is you're fondling in your pocket and take your seat."

I had everyone trained by this point, and I was pretty sure I could count on them to stay still and not do anything I'd regret. Except Bixon. I struggled to keep my eyes off the barrel-shaped asshole and contented myself with hoping he didn't move. The whole place was still and quiet, narrowed down to Pikar and me, my aching leg and stiff back. I wondered, for a second, if Pikar was aching too, how old he was, what he'd been through.

And then he moved.

It was good, too. He'd taken the windows seriously and realized that with me and Bix standing across from him we were nailed in crossfire, so he went low, crouching down and yanking his guns out beautifully, both clear and in his hands in a blink as he duckwalked to put his back against the front door, out of the imaginary rifles' sightlines. Jerking the Roon up and out of my pocket, I put two bullets an inch or so from his left ear and then threw myself up and back onto the bar, giving myself a million tiny splinters as I pushed myself across, dropping behind it like a sack of wet cement.

As I righted myself on the floor, I saw Bix heaving the shredder up with a yell, and before I could stop him he depressed the trigger and the familiar headsplitting whine filled the room, the 10-09 barked and jerked up out of Bixon's hands, spluttering six rounds into the ceiling before it smacked Bix in the nose hard enough to break it.

I hedgehogged up, poking my head over the bar just long enough to take in the room and then dropping back down, braced for the *pop pop pop* of a trained shot. There was nothing, no noise at all. I heaved myself back up with a grunt and let the bar support me for a moment, the Roon pointed at Pikar, who was slumped in front of the door, his belly a swamp of blood, one arm still up, holding his gun on me. Everyone else was still sitting, frozen, like this was all just the fucking floor show.

Pikar grinned blood. As I slowly walked the length of the bar to step around, his gun followed me, inch by inch. Just as I cleared the crates, his finger twitched, sending me to the floor with a choking grunt. Instead of the thudding bark of a shot, there was just a dry click. I pushed myself back up to put the Roon on him. The cop was just laughing, still holding the gun on me. As I got to my feet, he pulled the trigger a dozen more times, getting the same dry click each time.

"You shot me with a fucking *shredding rifle*," he sputtered, flecks of bloody spit spraying from his mouth and landing on the floor, where the dry wood soaked them up forever. "You fucking *rats*. I don't even have any fucking *bullets*."

I stood up and kept the shiny Roon on him. My ass burned like someone had stabbed a million tiny pieces of wood into it. "What kind of asshole pulls his piece if he can't do anything with it?" I hissed. I was angry. I wanted to slap his face for being a fucking asshole. "Were you going to throw it at me?"

"Fuck you." He sighed, deflating. He was still holding his useless gun on me, even though his arm shook with the effort.

"Avery," Gerry suddenly said, her voice a scratchy whisper. "Okay, man, the situation's calmed. We'll take care of him from here."

I nodded without looking at her. Pikar was still smiling at me. "You were a cop," I said. "You know how this works. You pull a gun, you take the consequences." I'd learned a lot about the human race over the years. I'd learned that the dead didn't stay dead. I'd learned that no good deed ever went unpunished. And I'd learned that trying to have a code of honor got you a lot of people telling you how much respect they had for you while they were beating your head against the floor.

Ignoring the dull pain in my leg, I took a bead and put a shell in Pikar's face. Then one more in his chest just to be safe, making him twitch and flop. I turned and stumped back to the bar, slipping my Roon back into place and then putting my shaking hands flat on the bar. The only cure for Bixon's rotgut was more, and fast. It only got deadly when you stopped.

I

I DIDN'T HAVE TIME FOR IT.
I HAD PEOPLE TO KILL

"What are you smiling at?"

I turned away from the darkness and the wind and focused on the trooper. I still hadn't gotten used to the *dark*. There wasn't a light anywhere, and no moon in the sky, and the whole world was just wind and the creaking, shaking truck bed, just a single uniform so white it seemed to glow with its own energy and fourteen other assholes who hadn't been fast enough. The truck was ancient, a rust bucket being driven by a Droid on a programmed course. Distantly, I could see other trucks streaming across the desert, just bouncing headlights.

The trooper was a fucking kid, but everyone was a fucking kid these days. His face was dirty, but he sat with the shredder on his knees like a man who wasn't afraid of fifteen shitkickers who hated him and wished him dead, even if the shredding rifle bucked like a wild hog and took three seconds to warm up from cold metal—a crowd-control weapon only an asshole would use. Three seconds was a long time in my world. Or the world that used to be mine.

I inched the smile up a notch. "In a couple of minutes I'm going to break both your thumbs, and I'm looking forward to it."

He studied me for a moment, his face blank. Then he smiled, ten years dropping from his face just like that. "Talk to me again and I'll hook you to the back and drag you to the Recruit Center."

I laughed, nodding, and looked back at the desert, replaying my favorite memory: me on the ground, watching a hover rise into the air with a sudden jerk, Marlena's face peering over the edge down at me. Sometimes I saw Michaleen's face leering down instead of Marlena, cackling. *Mocking* me.

I turned back to the interior of the truck bed for a moment. No one was looking our way, afraid to be associated with me, except Remy, who was still staring at me like I might pull Nutrition Tabs out of my ears. We were all just biological resources—the army needed manpower. They weren't too picky about the quality of it—they had augments to make you stronger, faster, sharper—so they just went around scooping up every asshole who couldn't run fast enough, pushed them into the grinder, and out came shock troops on the other end. It was a beautiful system.

At least the army had resources to tap. The System Pigs, under the reins of Director of Internal Affairs Dick Marin—the King Worm, as he used to be known when he was just the top cop in the System—had converted every cop in the world, practically, into avatars. Droid bodies with digital brains. The avatars were expensive and required rarefied materials, and under the strain of a civil war, they'd lost their last avatar factory and were suffering severe manpower shortages as a result.

The wind was exhiliratingly cold, and I was, against all odds, still alive. Feeling strangely cheerful, I looked back at the trooper. "Fuck you," I said, still smiling.

He thought about it, but after a moment he smirked and looked away. It would have been good if I'd gotten him up, off-balance, and pissed-off, but the kid had more on the ball than that. So I took a moment and went over my resources. Since I had a whole moment, I did it twice.

Our silicon bracelets had been put on sloppy; I'd been out of mine for half an hour. That was one. I looked around the truck as the wind tore my hair—longer than I'd ever had it before—and considered my fellow presses. It was pretty much the entire population of Englewood who had survived the raid. Gerry, our unelected mayor, sat on the opposite side of the truck, up toward the cab, slumped over with her head down. Bixon, bleeding from his scalp and looking pale, stared straight ahead and moved with gelatinous ease every time the truck hit a bump, vacant. Remy, staring at me. Our eyes met and he blinked once, deliberately, and looked down at his lap and then back at me. I moved my eyes down, and he spread his hands slightly, flashing me his bare wrists. When I looked back at the kid's face, he was smiling at me. I gave him a little smile back. Fucking Remy. He'd been following me around for months, telling the other kids he was my *deputy*, a word I'd never heard before. I liked the kid.

So, I had me and a fourteen-year-old kid who'd grown up with a Droid nanny wiping his ass. I looked back at our guard. Soldiers were humans; they weren't avatars with control chips like the cops, so you could negotiate with them, sometimes. I'd had some success bribing army grunts in the past—escaping from Chengara Penitentiary, I'd paid out millions of yen for a pair of parachutes and the right to jump out of a hover—but I didn't think my yen was worth enough anymore, and I'd seen the grunt taking his marching orders from his commanding officer right before we'd pushed off. He might not be impressed with *me*, but he was scared shitless of the tall, skinny colonel with the white hair and perma-tan skin. Both of the colonel's eyes had glowed softly, the left iris a cold silver and the right a warm orange. He didn't smile. I had an instant impression that he had never smiled, that he might in fact lack the necessary muscles.

"Cheer up, citizen," he'd bellowed. "You gonna remember this day as the happiest day of your life, the day you joined the System of Federated Nations Army, an' rejoiced."

Thinking of Chengara made me think of Michaleen. The Little Man was unfinished business, and here I was being kidnapped into the System of Federated Nations Army. I didn't have time for it. I had people to kill. If I'd gotten moving three days ago like I'd intended, I wouldn't have been scooped up with the rest of Englewood's ridiculous population.

I looked back at the kid and nodded. We had some pretty reliable sign language; the kid had attached himself to me and followed me everywhere, my fucking valet, and I'd taught him a few things. He nodded back, and I turned to study the guard, still sitting there at the back, shredder across his knees, looking about as fearsome as a daydream.

The SFNA soldiers were fast, filled with augments that made them faster and stronger than nature had intended, with a host of extra little abilities like night-vision and such—one-on-one, they probably weren't a match for the cop avatars they were waging this civil war against, but they still had bad motherfucker as a *baseline*. Me, I felt pretty good. A few months of eating steadily and taking it easy, with just an occasional head to crack, and I felt better than since before the Plague. My leg still ached and I wasn't as fast as I'd once been, but I was in decent shape.

I didn't think I'd be able to handle the trooper on a level playing field, but I didn't intend to play fair.

There was nothing good about getting pressed, from what I'd heard. Aside from the fact that most of the people being pressed were going to be shock troops without much value to throw against entrenched positions or other suicidal missions, rumor had it that a lot of the officers sold people out of the army if someone wanted you badly enough—or sometimes wholesale, in big groups to anyone who had the cash. I could think of a few folks who might not mind getting their hands on me, and I didn't want to find out if any of them were still interested.

I signaled the kid, and he nodded again. He let the bracelets drop silently to the floor of the truck, stared at his feet for a few seconds as we bounced along, and then stood up.

"I want to go home!" he shouted, putting some screech into it.

The guard was already on his feet, shredder in his hands—fast. But he didn't toggle the shredder into life. He held it on Remy as he balanced on the balls of his feet, but he didn't regard the kid as a threat.

"Sit the fuck down," he ordered. "You make me say it again and I'll smack you."

"I want to go home!" Remy shouted again. I kept my eyes on the guard, watching, and when his jaw locked and his weight shifted, I leaped up and jumped at him, putting my hands on the shredder and smacking it up into his face, breaking his nose easily. I launched myself into him and let gravity take us down, cracking his back over the tailgate and pinning him there with my weight. I smacked the shredder into his face one more time because it felt good, and then I pushed it down onto his throat, hard enough to choke him a little but not hard enough to do any real damage.

"About those thumbs—"

He surged beneath me and I was thrown backward— the kid was *strong*. I kept my grip on the shredder and tore it from his grasp as I staggered back, crashing into the crowd. They shoved me away like they were afraid I might get some balls on them, so I popped back up in time for the grunt to bury his head in my stomach, knocking my breath and what felt like my kidneys out of me and shoving me back into the crowd. There were a couple of high-pitched screams and hands were on us, pushing us away frantically, all of them too terrified to see twenty seconds into the future, which was us scattering into the desert, free. Most of them had come from comfort, from money, some even from power—old power, power that wasn't there anymore. None of them truly believed they were fucked. They still thought an angel was going to swoop down and collect them, apologize for the inconvenience, and make it all go away. Including me, who'd been keeping them *alive* for the past six months.

The grunt put his face in mine, wrapping his arms around me and squeezing with excruciating, surprising force, making my ribs bark and trapping the shredder between us. Blood had spilled out over his mouth and chin, making him look suddenly older, more dangerous.

"Still got the thumbs, old man," he panted at me. "You gonna break 'em with your mind?"

I liked this guy. I liked the troops better than the cops—the cops were all fucking attitude, dandies in their rich suits, even before they'd all been forcibly turned into avatars, Droids with digital brains. They had more metal in their brains than I liked, sure, but we all had faults. I tended to kill everyone I met, more or less by accident.

Before I could tell him about my growing affection toward him, Remy rose up in the air and attached himself to the back of the soldier, his skinny arms locking around the grunt's neck. Before I could even blink, he'd leaned in close like a fucking lover and bit the grunt's ear, a savage, tearing bite.

The guard screamed. It was a high-pitched, boyish scream. He staggered off me, his arms slapping up at Remy, and I smiled, thinking, *That's my boy.*

I straightened up and spun the shredder before me, feeling good. I kept my balance as the truck swayed and bounced under me. The gun's ammo readout glowed red and plump, a full clip. But I didn't want to turn the guard into a fine red mist, even if Remy got clear; he was just doing his job. Swallowing the ice ball of nausea and pain in my belly, I flipped the rifle around and grasped it by the barrel with both hands. It was top heavy, but I didn't need it to be a *good* weapon. I just needed to knock him off the truck, leave him behind in the night.

Remy wasn't giving up easy. The grunt had both hands on the kid's head, trying to tear him off, but Remy wasn't going. I took three steps forward, swinging the shredder back behind me. Just as I got within range, the guard got a grip and tore Remy off of him, throwing the kid down onto the bed, where he skidded along the slick metal floor, crashing softly into the cab.

I swung the rifle, but the guard's arm flashed up faster than I thought possible and intercepted it, like smacking into an iron bar. He wrenched it violently and I let him have it, diving forward and using his own trick, putting my hands on his throat and pinning the gun between us. This time, I squeezed for all I was worth.

"Sorry, chum," I panted, winded suddenly. "The army just doesn't suit me."

He grinned at me, and I fell in love with the bastard. "Fuck, man, I don't blame you. If I'd been bought out by Wa Belling, I'd get the fuck off this truck too."

I froze. "What?"

The grunt nodded. "The CO told me. You set a fuckin' record on the price. If a fuckin' Gunner like Belling wanted *me*, I'd lie, cheat, and steal to get away, too. I heard stories about him—he's all over our watch lists. Got a standing 909 order—if we press him, we shoot him."

For a moment, I was outraged. Wa Belling. He'd been a founding member of the Dúnmharú, sure, one of the original hardcases. He'd been a personal fucking failing of mine, though. He'd fucked with me in London on the Squalor case, first pretending to be Canny Orel, the most famous Gunner in history. He'd killed people when I'd ordered him not to. Then he'd pretended to be my ally in New York, killing cops because I thought it made a difference. He'd sold me out during the Plague, though, when a madman had unleashed a trillion nanobots on the world, with me as Patient Zero with Belling's help.

I hadn't see him since then. I'd cooled my heels in Chengara getting fucked over by his boss, Canny Orel—aka Michaleen Garda, my bestest pal in prison, who'd lied to me and used me and left me for fucking dead after fucking me over. I'd spent the last six months contemplating revenge against Michaleen, but Belling—Belling would be a fine way to start. Wa Belling had played me for a fool for fucking *years*. Why not?

"If he's got a standing kill order," I said, "how can he do business with you?"

The guard snarled. "The CO deals with anyone who can pay the price," he spat. "Dick Marin could make him an offer and he'd make the fucking arrangements. Anners is a fucking pig."

His outrage was touching—a true believer. There were more of them in the System than I'd have imagined. I eased back from the guard. We stared at each other, him frowning suddenly. I held out the shredder.

"Here," I said. "Let's call it a wash."

The soldier stared at me, the bottom of his face a mask of blood. His hands were slack on the shredder for a moment and then firmed up as he straightened up. He studied me for a moment, and then smiled. I almost thought he understood. Or maybe he was just relieved to bring in the full head count he'd been entrusted with.

"Take your fucking seat then," he said warily, watching me and finally toggling the rifle on. The squeamish hum was torn away by the wind and barely seemed to be there.

Wa Belling. I turned and found my seat again. I had plenty of markers Belling could pay off, and if this truck was bringing me closer to Belling, then fuck it, I was going to ride my way to him and then shove my fist up his ass as far as it would go.

I sat down and the two people on either side of me tried to shrink away. I looked around and saw Remy up by the cab, staring at me. I glanced at him and looked away, flushing.

"Shut up, kid," I whispered. "I'm working."

II

WE GONNA SET THINGS RIGHT, MR. CATES

I was being wheeled down a corridor again, fear bubbling at a low simmer. When I finally died, my life would flash before my eyes and it would just be scenes of me strapped down to something with wheels, being transported from one hell to another. I remembered being sucked into the Abbey, going after Squalor and his Electric Church, dead and suffering. I remembered being carried around like luggage by Hense and her squad during the Plague. I remembered being wheeled into the bricking labs by the German cunt, ready to have my brain sucked clean. And here I was, upright at least, strapped to a handtruck so tightly my hands and feet were numb. My bum leg, obliging as always, had spiked its familiar ache deep into my bones, and the desire to shift its position was like having ants under my skin, tunneling through nerves.

Avery Cates the Gweat and Tewwible, I thought. *He'd be a fucking scary man if he wasn't always tied up like a side of meat.*

Corridor was the wrong word: The walls were canvas, just the outside walls of large tents set up six feet apart, with canvas stretched above for a ceiling and a pathway of rough planks laid on the dirt. The System of Federated Nations Army was a mobile force that had no permanent bases; even its processing and recruitment centers were designed to be rolled up and moved in a matter of hours. I was being wheeled by a skinny tan kid named Umali, a corporal, who was running down a report on me based on data extracted from me while I was unconscious. My new friend the Palest Man Alive marched purposefully next to us.

"...but I'd say about fifty, based on his physical condition and stress results on bone and ligaments. Let's see, above-average reflex reaction, excellent muscle development, excellent day-vision but night-vision is now suffering from age-related degeneration. Multiple scars on...well, just about everywhere, though few are noticeable in normal light. Including your standard-issue Plague scars on his throat and chest; man's a survivor. Teeth are a nightmare. Several missing, the rest in various states of rot. Good balance, above-average IQ, slight chemical imbalance that looks to be natural and probably not much of a problem aside from temper and socialization difficulties."

I couldn't move my head, so I rolled my eyes, trying to get a good look at them. My hands twitched as I tried to break my arms free, teach the skinny fuck a lesson in politeness.

"Now this is interesting: He has a standard AV-79 procedure scar on the back of his head."

I rolled my eyes over to the officer in time to see him turn a frown on me. "What?"

"Clear as day. He must not have finished the process, obviously."

The officer stared down at me for a few more steps and then looked forward again. "Not necessarily. Word from the Mountain is they've got new avatar procedures, nonlethal. Though they still kill the poor fucks anyway, or so I heard."

Umali cleared his throat. "Yes. So, let's see...brain function is very unusual, which may be connected. Off the charts, though he tests out normal on the Amblen Rating. But every other test redlines."

"But he's not a g'mp?" the officer said. It was like he spit out pieces of the words. "E's *funk'tional.*"

"Oh, yes." Umali sounded pleased to be able to confirm this, his voice soft and gentle, not at all what I'd expected the army to have in its ranks. "For all outward appearances he's completely normal. His brain waves are very strange, however, and we may need to prepare for unexpected reactions to augmentation and—"

"Who gives a fuck?" I was getting used to his accent and processing it faster. "A few hours, he's not our problem anymore."

"Yes." Umali sounded annoyed, but after a moment he continued. "As for background, he's got several *dozen* entries in SSF databases. Several flagged at high-level clearance; several we actually can't even access because they're not even on the SSF cloud *at all*. They're just symbolic links to an off-line server. He's only got two stints in holding, though one of those was Chengara Pen, which may be where he got his skull fuck." Umali ran through the rest as if we'd arrived at the steep slope of diminishing importance. "Let's see...quite a lot of yen in dormant haven accounts, though not worth much these days. Other than that, I find almost no record of him at all. No employment files, no logs in old Joint Council records, nothing."

"'Course not," the officer said. "The man's a criminal. Don' matter. All that matters is someone wants his carcass, see?"

"Yes, sir." Umali sounded unconvinced. I tried to force myself to relax, waiting for the moment when they took off the straps and I actually had options.

We rounded a corner and approached a doorway formed in the walls by the expedient of cutting a long slit from top to bottom. Standing outside was a short black girl in what may have been the most expensive suit of clothes I'd ever seen. Bright green, the fabric shimmered and flickered as she shifted her weight, and against her dark skin it seemed like controlled fire, always in motion. Her face was broad and flat, and her skin was flawless. Her hair matched her suit perfectly, a bright, nauseous green, and I imagined she had an augment that allowed her to set her hair color with every wardrobe change.

Her eyes, on the other hand, were a bright, glowing blue—a wireless data augment. I'd seen them before, though rarely. Allowed her to connect with whatever available nets were in the air and transfer data directly.

"Colonel," she said, her accent subtle, like she had a tiny stone in her mouth that made her curl every vowel too much.

The officer waved a hand at her. "Not *now*, Mardea, dammit," he growled. "You wan'ta talk *bulk*, y'wait a fucking minute."

She opened her mouth again, then thought better of it

and nodded. "Very well, Colonel. I'll wait until it is *convenient* for you."

She turned and strode away. She had no identification or rank on her coat, but she didn't seem concerned or out of place. For a moment, the three of us just watched the rhythm of her walk, all of us, I thought, having the same sexual fantasy simultaneously. Then the officer grunted and they wheeled me through the slit into an adjoining tent that sported a cheap-looking plastic table and a few chairs. A tall pitcher of water was on the table, surrounded by a small farm of metal cups; my eyes latched onto it and stayed there, my mouth suddenly dry as a desert.

Umali wheeled me to the table and made sure I was stable, and then stepped away, reappearing in my peripheral vision as he moved quickly to stand behind the officer. He appeared to be about seventeen or eighteen years old, all sinew and back-aching posture in his plain black uniform. His nose was broad and his eyes were sleepy, making him look dull and dense. The officer was the one I'd glimpsed when I'd been pressed. He slouched in his chair, flipping through a digital file with impatient, imprecise gestures. His hair was silvery in the shaky light rigged to the tent's central pole, his nose long and thin and angled downward with a shift to the left that looked like an old break.

I looked from him to the pitcher of water.

"All right, Mr.…Cates," he finally said, tossing the thin sheet onto the table and leaning back in his chair. "How's it feel to be in the greatest fightin' org'nization in history?"

For a few seconds we stared at each other, and then he suddenly closed his eyes, his face firming up into anger. Umali suddenly jumped as if he'd been goosed and skittered over to me and with a practiced flick of his hand unsnapped the chin strap that held my mouth shut and rushed back into position behind the officer as his eyes opened.

"Thank you. Mr. Cates, I am Colonel Malkem Anners. We're gonna hava little talk."

When helpless, it was always good policy to make idle threats. It amused everyone in the short term, and if you ever managed to cash them in, you looked like the most dangerous bastard ever known. I ran my tongue over my lips. "Tell you what, Colonel. Give me a cup of water, and it'll go in your favor when I come back for you."

Anners's smile was immediate. "Hell, sho' you can have a drink." Umali immediately stepped around him again, poured water into a mug, and brought it to me. He held it to my lips and expertly tipped it for me, cool, clean water pouring into my mouth in an ecstatic wave. After a few seconds, he took the mug and placed it on the table in front of me, stepping back to his position. I looked up and Anners was studying me.

"I'm a reasonable man, Mr. Cates. The SFNA *breeds* reasonable men. The SFNA does not want robots or *avatars* or men afraid t'speak their minds. The SFNA wants intelligence, compassion, and leadership."

I concentrated very hard and decided to my horror that Colonel Anners was being perfectly sincere.

"Now, you have chosen, as all good citizens of the System of Federated Nations would, to enlist in my forward unit. That speaks well of you, Mr. Cates, and you have the thanks of a grateful world." He leaned forward and tapped a calloused finger on the table. "We gonna set things right, Mr. Cates. We're gonna push that digital asshole and his toy cops into the fuckin' ocean, Mr. Cates. And you chose to be part of that glorious effort. And I congratulate you."

I wanted to say something. I wanted to tell him to fuck himself. But I *couldn't*. He was mesmerizing.

He leaned back, putting that finger against his chin like a thinker. "It woulda been good timing, too, Cates. I'm gathering forces for a major operation at Hong Kong to cause a ruckus, and you woulda been right there in front, chargin' into those silicone motherfuckers."

I forced my mouth to work. "Sounds like fun. Absorbing bullets so you and your fancy boys don't get hurt."

He grimaced and paused for a moment. The outer tent flap suddenly stirred and a fourth person entered, bowing down to fit under the low entryway. She was a very tall, broad-shouldered woman with a coffee complexion and wiry, stiff-looking black hair that exploded in a wild cloud on top of her head. She was in the same black uniform as Umali, but sported two small silver pips in the broad lapels of her overcoat. Her face was round and young, with full cheeks and big, wide eyes that somehow conveyed distaste.

I glanced back at the colonel and found him on his feet, at attention. I wondered if this was yet another asshole come to kick my balls for a few hours, for fun.

"Sit down, Anners," the woman snapped, waving her hand at him. "I hope I am not intruding."

The colonel relaxed and dropped back into his seat. "No, of course not. Just doing a postrecruit interview." His accent had faded so suddenly I wondered for a moment which was the put-on.

She raised an eyebrow. "You do all your PRIs in person?"

As she said this, she extended a hand toward the water pitcher, and it rose from the table, accompanied by a single mug. I watched them float across the space to her. *Psionic*, I thought. *Telekinetic*.

Dolores Salgado piped up faintly in my head. *We structured the army this way: one political liaison to each unit, with certain authorities over the CO. Keep our hand in. Discourages officers from deciding their units are* theirs.

I blinked her away. I'd gotten a dose of ghosts—people's digitized brains—when they'd tried to make me into an avatar back in Chengara Penitentiary. I'd lost most of them, but the three people I'd known somewhat in real life still lingered. Salgado had been a system undersecretary, and she had some secrets left. I wished fervently the last three would go the hell away, but so far they seemed more or less permanent, like brain damage.

Anners shrugged. "I pull a few, Millar. These folks are gon' be under my thumb, I like t'know a bit about them. Umie here screens 'em and feeds me the interesting ones."

Umali offered up a sick-looking half-grin at this as Millar took possession of the water pitcher, poured herself a dollop, and floated the pitcher back to the table. She took a sip and shrugged. "Fine," she said, and turned away, ducking under the flap and disappearing.

"Fuck, I hate the goddamn Spooks." Anners exhaled softly, his accent thickening up like magic. We both turned to look at each other, and he raised a pale eyebrow at me. "Now, I jus' lied to a superior officer, Mr. Cates. I only talk to the *valuable* folks who enlist in my beloved army." He leaned back and steepled his fingers, his bicolor eyes locked on me. I wondered what the augments showed him, if I glowed with body heat or if he could see ghosts inside me, hollowing me out, if he could see the dull ache of my leg. "Some folks just don't appreciate the army, y'see. An' while it saddens my heart to think a ruthless piece o' trash like you will never know the joy, companionship, and discipline of a true gatherin' of siblings—brothers an' sisters, see—sometimes it's best to cull out the unfortunate few before they become a poison in my unit."

I smiled at him. "Way I hear it, the life expectancy of your *brothers an' sisters* is measured in days."

Anners slapped his palm down onto the table, which promptly collapsed with a whine of cheap metal between us. He pointed a manicured finger at me. "You best watch yo' mouth when you're talkin' about shit you don't unnerstand, yes?" He slowly lowered his hand into his lap and continued to sit there as if destroying furniture and threatening recruits was all in a day's work. This motherfucker was crazy, and I had no doubt he could order his creepy little man standing behind him to put one in my ear and no one would care, or protest. Or even think about it.

"I never woulda imagined," he continued in a softer tone, "that a piece a trash like yourself would have any value on the market, but damn if you didn't sell right away."

I kept my smile on my face. I wondered about Remy and Gerry and the rest—were any of them valuable?

"What do you do, just upload a list of names you've pressed, wait and see if anyone puts in a bid?"

Anners nodded and stood up, plucking his digital sheet from the floor with a graceful bow. "Somethin' like that. Now, I've been enjoyin' our conversation, but you're a rush order, Mr. Cates. Gotta get you into surgery."

Umali stepped forward as Anners headed for the exit.

Before the slim aide could snap the chin strap back into place, I managed to bleat, "Surgery?"

The colonel paused and tapped one long finger against his temple. "For the augments." He turned and called over his shoulder. "Don't worry. The bots is the best in the business. Hardly evah kill anyone at all."

III

YOU'RE NOT GOING TO LIKE ANY OF THEM

I loved the System of Federated Nations Army.

I floated on a warm, deep ocean of narcotics, listening to ghosts. I heard people I hadn't thought of in years—Kev Gatz, slurringly telling me he just needed to sleep, Gleason telling me they didn't make bar stools big enough for my ass anymore, Dick Marin telling me I'd fucked everything up, Pickering rumbling out data about something, his voice like lava seeping up from the ground.

"You're falling apart."

Slowly, I opened my eyes. This seemed like a terribly difficult thing to do, but also a completely voluntary one, without pressure. A kid in a loose-fitting blue outfit and a slouchy white coat sat next to me, gesturing idly at a clipboard. He was very tan, with dark, curly hair that was surprisingly thick and long hanging off of him.

I blinked rapidly, trying to clear my vision, and suddenly realized my vision was fine—but there were readouts imposed over my sight. In the left bottom corner of my field of vision were a stream of numbers stacked up on top of each other, constantly changing, and in the bottom right was a name I didn't recognize: HUGO H. GONZALEZ. Under that was a static string of numbers: 009987-562.

Idly, I ran my eyes over my surroundings, old instincts telling me to gather data about my location, even though I felt wonderful, without any anxiety or fear. The overlays were just there, with no blurring or clipping, the letters and numbers constant and bright. I was in a narrow cot, just wide enough for my body. Wires and tubes sprouted from under the rough gray blanket wrapped around me in a disturbing way I flagged for future investigation. One transparent tube ran directly up into my nose, and once I noticed this I could feel it snaking its way down my throat, and I had to concentrate for a moment to suppress my gag reflex.

I wasn't alone; it was a large tent, and at least ten or twelve other cots were occupied. Running my eyes over the other patients, I decided it was a good thing I couldn't see myself. My eyes jumped back to a bed across the space from me and I went still. I couldn't be sure it was Remy; his face was turned away from me, but he was the right size and the hair matched. I stared, trying to will him to turn over and let me see him. Fucking kid. I'd *told* him to run.

"What?" I said, my voice sounding gummy and hesitant, the tube in my throat tickling. Under the drugs, I felt tired. I felt like breathing was almost too much effort.

The tan kid glanced up. "You're falling apart, Private Cates. I doubt you'd have lived five more years if you hadn't been pressed." He looked back down at the clipboard and gestured. "Microfractures everywhere, at least two compounds that healed…unfortunately. Your blood pressure was through the roof, your liver function is, uh, not good. One kidney looks dubious to me based on preliminary tests. Your brainwaves are fucking *bizarre* although you appear to have complete function and I detect no decline in reflexes or coherency—though there is evidence of *several* major concussions that probably caused some swelling in their day." He looked up again. "You're old for your age, is the point. Hell, man, when was the last time you saw a doctor?"

I closed my eyes again and rummaged the few memories I had as a child. "I don't know. Maybe never."

"Well, the fucking army is the best fucking thing that ever happened to you, Cates. I think we just saved your life." He paused. "For now."

"Who's Hugo Gonzalez?" I asked. The numbers and letters burned in the darkness for a few seconds and then dimmed, still visible but shadowed.

"Huh? Oh, your heads-up display, your HUD. Probably the initial draftee we implanted the neural augment into. We recycle them as often as we can. They don't make enough new ones."

Another ghost! Marin cackled faintly. *Avery, you're a walking graveyard these days.*

"Okay," the tan kid said with an explosive sigh. I opened my eyes again and the readout flared up immediately. "What's your name?"

I licked my lips. "Avery Cates. Who are you?"

As I asked the question, a small window flared into life on my vision, reading EMIL J. GUPTA, CAPTAIN (COURT.), MEDICAL CORPS.

He nodded. "Dr. Emil Gupta," he said without looking up. "Where are you?"

I considered the fact that whatever they'd stuffed into me ID'd people I looked at. "This readout with your name," I said hesitantly, not knowing what to call it. "What—"

"Part of your augment array," he said briskly, irritated. "Only pulls ID on military personnel when you're in range of an SFNA network. Now, follow me, please: Where are you?"

"Fuck if I know. I was unconscious during most of this."

He glanced up at me from under his bushy black eyebrows and sighed. "Sure, sure, but these are standard questions to make sure we didn't lobotomize you by accident." He shrugged. "Happens. About one percent of all recipients just can't handle the augments. You want to pass this test, Cates, because if you fail we'll need the implants for someone else and you don't survive harvesting. So, where are you?"

I was too tired for anything else, so I decided to be cooperative. "In a tent, doc. I've been pressed."

He nodded, gesturing sharply with a finger. "And who am I?"

I grinned. "You're Dr. Gupta, who saved my life."

He actually smiled slightly as he gestured again. "Not me personally. I'm purely post-op review."

"How'd you end up here?" I asked. A faint stinging had suddenly bloomed, everywhere. Every joint seemed to burn just slightly with something that wasn't quite pain yet. I figured whatever they'd spiked me with was wearing off, and a hint of dread rippled the placid waters inside me.

He shrugged, working rapidly on the clipboard. "It's a job. Yen's worthless. A lot of the cities are fucking nightmares." He looked up at me for a moment. "These guys have a mess tent, three squares a day." He looked back down at the clipboard. "Okay, you're conscious and reactive, and your scans are all green, although I think you're in the very early stages of scurvy. Don't you ever eat any fruit?"

I wanted to laugh, but the faint stinging was coalescing into a burning pain. "You're fucking kidding, right? You notice what's going on out there?"

He grimaced slightly. "We'll take care of it, don't worry. At any rate, you're clear, so we're going to remove your hookups and get you up out of bed." He frowned, staring down at the clipboard. "Well, looks like you've got a conditional civvie release-and-retain order." His eyes were back on me. "You've been sold. Your commanding officer put your name on a darknet somewhere and someone put a bid in for you, processed and pinned to a remote."

I nodded, flexing my hands. *Processed* and *pinned* stuck in my head. I felt like I was slowly waking up. "So I hear. Does that happen a lot?"

He nodded, standing up. "Yep. I see about four or five a week. Illegal, of course, and if any of the political liaisons see it, there'll be shit flying everywhere and a couple of officers turned retards overnight, but they always bury this shit in paperwork. And there's a lot of money to be made from it, so almost all the officers do it. All you do is hold back the pressed IDs for a few hours and upload the list to an agent. The agent runs the names by his brokers, and if anyone's interested, they negotiate a price. A lot of folks like the idea of having servants with military augments they can control—CO status is transferable. It can even be assigned to nonbiologics like avatars, Droids, any AI that can be set to beacon a unique frequency. If you sell, your name gets deleted from the official manifest, but we don't check manifests when we process—no need—so you get the works even though officially you're not in the army. Then we hand you over, transfer CO status, and you're someone else's slave." He laughed, stepping around to the other side of my cot. "Shit, I've seen a couple of folks, bigwigs, come through here three or four times." He paused. "You know anyone might want to shop around for you?"

I shrugged. I wanted to go back to sleep. "Too many to even try to figure it out."

He gave me a look, one eyebrow up, and then looked down again. "All right, let's take a look."

Without another word he yanked the blanket off me. I shivered, naked, in the sudden chill. I looked down at myself; tubes and wires sprouted from my skin in three separate patches. There was no blood or obvious incision—the tubes just sprouted from me like they'd been there since birth. I was skinnier than I remembered, ribs showing, veins lacing around my arms like buried worms. My belly was a pale skein of scars; I'd forgotten how I'd gotten most of them.

He grunted to himself in professional satisfaction and reached into one pocket, producing a small square piece of black plastic. He aimed more or less in my direction, and after a moment the stinging sensation rocketed up to searing pain as the tubes and wires suddenly began to pull themselves out of me, worming like living things. I could *feel* them squirming inside me, moving under my skin, pushing aside muscles and nerves, sliding up my throat and making me choke. It was all over in a few seconds, and I lay there shivering and coughing, with no

scars I could see—I lurched up onto my elbows and pat-
ted my abdomen, laced with thin white scars from years
past, but showing just some red, irritated areas where the
wires had been.

"Most of the augments are in the form of nano-
devices in the bloodstream," Gupta said distractedly as he
switched his eyes from me to the clipboard. "The hookups in your brain—"

"*In* my brain?"

"—are larger by necessity."

I looked down at myself—I was still me. Still the
same body with the same windburned tan from wallow-
ing in Englewood all these months, still the same slightly
crooked leg. I slapped my hand up to my neck and found
the familiar Plague scars, and I felt my heart beating—
maybe stronger and steadier than I remembered, but
still *beating*. Suddenly conscious of the people around
me, I slowly forced my hands away from my body and
sat up straight, fighting to control the shaking. The only
thing that kept me alive sometimes was my reputation.
No matter how far from New York I got, that much was
universal—people knew only what they heard about you.

You're an idiot, Dolores Salgado whispered.

I felt *good*. I hadn't even realized how much pain I'd
been in, day in and day out. Not agony, nothing I'd even
noticed. Just constant aches and stitches I'd gotten used to,
compensated for. Most of them gone, all muted. My leg
didn't ache. When I took a deep breath, my chest didn't
twitch into the beginnings of a coughing fit. I felt alert,
rested, *healthy*. It was like somone had rolled back my
clock a decade or so, before the Plague that had almost
killed me and half the fucking world.

I put my eyes on the doctor. He was skinny, and he had delicate hands that moved elegantly over his clipboard, summoning information and entering data. He had the look of a man who'd never been hit, never held a gun, never had to experience any real pain or trauma— and a valuable man, too; they weren't making too many new doctors these days. I saw the layout of the tent in my head—no guards inside, fucking trivial to put hands on the man and make him a hostage. I thought of Remy, thought of another smug, disinterested doctor visiting him. Had to be something in here I could improvise with, and then count on them not wanting to lose a sawbones. Was I worth more than the doctor?

I eyed him for a second. It probably depended on how much Belling had paid for me.

And I could do it. Maybe he had the same augments as I, but I'd been making do without them for a long time. I had skills you couldn't implant. But I discarded the idea. I had no idea what the layout of the complex was, or what was outside the interlocked network of canvas. I was fucking *naked*. Stumbling around with an uncooperative hostage, unarmed, fresh out of surgery, with Spooks lounging around—the odds of one of *them* being a Pusher were pretty much one hundred percent, meaning I'd end my day sucking my thumb and rocking back and forth. I figured, if nothing else, I should wait until I got some fucking clothes. I didn't want to die with no damn pants on.

Besides, every step was a step toward being in the same room as Wa Belling.

The first time I'd met Belling, he'd claimed to be Canny Orel, the best killer for hire in the System, rumored dead. Belling was a liar, but a fucking *good* liar. Then for a while we'd worked together in New York, but he'd just been keeping his hand in while he helped set me up for Kev Gatz and the Plague, so he'd been a liar then, but still a top-of-the-line liar. I hadn't seen him since he'd left me for dead in New York. I hadn't thought of him as much as his old boss, Orel, aka Michaleen Garda, because Garda had been the most recent asshole to fuck me over. But Belling still counted, and I felt good enough to maybe try and strangle him with my bare hands. I felt good enough to get in close and do it old-school.

When Gupta looked back at me, he startled for a moment like *he* could read my mind. Then he smiled.

"I know this isn't an ideal situation for you, my friend. I am sorry—I am, believe me or not. But for the next few minutes, I am your best friend, and I advise you to treat me as such. Because I am all the orientation you are going to get." His smile broadened. I realized that this skinny fuck had spent who knew how long processing people like me, and he had something going on if he was still grinning, untouched and unafraid.

Just my luck. For years the cosmos had been feeding me patsies, and I'd wasted them by twisting their noses and bullying them. Now I needed a patsy and the cosmos sent me someone with half a ball.

I nodded. "All right. You said in my *brain*—am I a fucking puppet now?"

He shook his head. "Doesn't work like that." He grinned, plucking a pile of white fabric from a peg on the wall behind me. "Haven't you already heard the speech: The System of Federated Nations Army does not want robots or avatars or men afraid to speak their minds. The SFNA wants intelligence, compassion, and leadership."

He laughed a little. "That's boilerplate around here. So, no, you're not a puppet—no mind control. If they wanted that, they'd just build themselves avatars, like the cops are." He grimaced. "Fucking mind rape, that's what *that* is. There's coercion, sure—we'll get to that in a minute— but if you die, Private Cates, you die *you*. At least there's that."

I grimaced in turn. "*That* ain't worth much, doc."

"This," he said immediately, shaking me off and holding the pile of white fabric out to me, "is your uniform. It is the only clothing you will need, going forward." He paused, tossing it onto the cot and then cocked his head, hesitating. "Of course, this is a standard script. Normally, you're off to your short unhappy life in the infantry. You probably won't need it very long. Still," he resumed in his brisk, practiced manner, "let's observe protocols. Sit up, stand up, and put on your standard issues."

I picked up the pile of fabric, and it seemed to move in my hands, squirming. I remembered breaking out of Chengara, stealing the uniforms off the corpses' backs, the way the suit clung to me, shifting and tightening onto me. Slowly, I swung my legs over the edge of the cot and pushed myself up—aside from the whole-body sizzle of pain, I felt pretty good; my leg felt almost normal. I stood there naked for a moment with the uniform in my hands.

"I'll apologize in advance for the smell," Gupta said, standing there unfazed. "We recycle the uniforms a lot, too."

I grimaced. "Thanks, doc." Since I didn't see my old clothes anywhere, I shook out the uniform and stepped into it. As I pulled it up and on, I could feel the material flowing around me, tightening in the right places and giving around the joints. It practically formed around me, the slit down the front joining together into a tight seal with no apparent adhesive or other mechanism. I instantly felt warm and dry, about as comfortable as I'd ever felt in my life.

The smell, as promised, was pretty terrible, like someone had been using the suit as a toilet for a few weeks.

The HUD in my eyes flashed briefly, and suddenly a new window appeared in my left eye, transparent and fucking annoying. Data began streaming through it, making me blink.

"It'll fade. Just booting," Gupta advised. "You're lucky—the first generation of those suits had to be hardwired in through the skull. Now it's all implanted chips and wireless protocols." He studied his clipboard for a moment.

Looks good, I heard his voice in my head. I was used to people's voices, and I just stared at him. After a moment he glanced up. *Can you hear me?*

I nodded. "Yep."

Think it, please.

My hands twitched. Gupta was fast running out of my goodwill. *Keep it up*, I thought. *I'm this close to slapping you.*

He grinned. "Very good. All systems seem to be a go. Although your communication systems won't operate once you're mustered out; you have to be in-unit in order to communicate silently. You're scanning out green and you've adapted to the implants remarkably fast. Now, listen up. I doubt anyone's going to take time to answer questions once I deliver you to your new owners, so I'd take notes if I were you. I'm going to skip most of the script here because you're mustering out, so why bother. You won't get the full effect of the augments. You'll notice better vision, better hearing, more stamina and strength, and your augments will have some automatic effect on your perception, but generally you might not even notice them."

I studied his smiling face. "Anyone ever get tired of your shtick, doc?" I asked. "Knock you down?"

He nodded. "At least once a day. But I have *this*." He held up the small black square.

I studied it. "Okay, I give. What is it?"

"Your remote control." He turned it around in his hand as if he admired it. "Tuned to your CO—your commanding officer—or whomever it needs to be tuned to—it's a pretty simple piece of equipment. It has, basically, three functions. You're not going to like any of them."

"I haven't liked anything in twenty years, doc."

He smiled. I liked his smile. It looked like he was really amused. "One, this thing can make you feel the most intense pain you've ever felt. I'm not kidding when I say that. It's been calibrated. Take the worst thing you've ever felt, then imagine it all over your body. Worse by far. Whoever's got your remote can inflict that on you whenever they want. And your CO will do it a lot, at first." He shrugged. "They like to make sure you know who's in charge." He paused and looked down at his clipboard again. "Whoever's buying you will get it. It's also used to set the anti-frag settings."

I smiled. "In case I get ideas about slitting throats?"

Gupta didn't smile or look up. "You think any officer would survive a week out there with all of you pissed-off shitkickers if they couldn't fuck you?" he whispered. "The AF setting means you can't get within a perimeter of your CO or you'll be terminated. Just like that. Cross the line into the red zone and the implant in your brain goes pop. The actual distance is a custom parameter the commanding officer can set—some of them like a lot of room around them, but it can go as close as they want, or even zero if they're feeling lucky. It also sets a *minimum* distance, in case you decide to desert. I've got it toggled off right now. Makes examinations kind of awkward when I have to stay a foot away all the time."

This kept getting better. Suddenly the System Pigs with their robot bodies and regular, old-fashioned beatings didn't seem so bad.

"The remote can also invoke your Berserker Mode." He looked up at me again. "I advise you to avoid that if at all possible."

I tested out the uniform, seeing how it moved and stretched. The holster at my side was empty, and there was no other gear attached. I wanted to *move*. I wanted to run and jump and climb shit. I wasn't naked any longer, but unless I was going to use Gupta's clipboard to very slowly bludgeon everyone to death, I wasn't noticeably less screwed than I'd been a few moments before. I paused. "What the fuck—"

"Berserker Mode puts the subject into an artificial state of consciousness. Your heart rate skyrockets, your brain dumps adrenaline and dopamine, your muscles' pain receptors are turned off, and aggression is maximized. For a short period of time, the combination of all this makes you pretty fucking badass. Your reflexes will approach avatar levels, you won't be fazed by any injury that does not cripple you, and you won't feel tired no matter what you're doing."

I felt exhausted just listening to that shit. "And?"

Gupta raised both eyebrows. "And you pay a *price*, Mr. Cates. Go into Berserker Mode more than twice within, say, six months, and I think you'll probably die from internal stress. Stroke out. Have a heart attack. Kidney shutdown. Get me? If your CO puts you into BM, he's basically taking decades off your life each time."

"You sure got a great benefits package here, doc," I growled. I made a show of stretching out one arm, then suddenly leaned forward, gave Gupta a little shove that put him off-balance, and snatched the little black square from his hand.

Immediately there was a roar in my head and a lance of sharp, burning pain shot up my forearm. My hand snapped open and the remote dropped to the floor. My whole arm had gone numb and throbbing, and I clutched it with my free hand, struggling again to control my breathing. My HUD flashed, streaming data about my injury.

Gupta didn't seem bothered. "Won't work," he said, bending down to retrieve it and then holding it up in front of me. His fingernails were clean and trimmed neatly. I suddenly felt stupid and dirty standing there. "It's attuned to whoever's your CO. Right now, *I'm* your CO. In a moment, I'll transfer it to your owner, and it'll only work for *them*."

I hesitated. The pain was already gone, like it had never happened. But if Belling got my remote, if he was made my CO—shit. I felt like I could run all fucking night and break Gupta in two with my bare hands, but if Belling got my remote, I wasn't going anywhere.

"All right," Gupta said as if this shit happened to him all the time, and gestured at his clipboard in a declarative, final manner and it went dim with a soft chime. "You ready?"

I looked around again. The kid across the room still hadn't moved, and I weighed the risk of trying something against the probability that it *wasn't* Remy. My options hadn't gotten any longer since I'd stood up, so I shrugged. "You've got the fucking button, doc."

"This way."

He took off down the aisle between cots and I lurched after him, feeling energy vibrating under my skin, my joints oiled and smooth. As I passed his bed, I turned my head to stare at the dark mass of hair four beds from the entrance. The kid never turned, but I kept my eyes on him and just before Gupta led me out into the maze of canvas corridors, the little box blazed up in my HUD again.

EVENS O. REMY, PRIVATE (I), SMALL INFANTRY.

I stopped, letting Gupta exit the room. I stared at the kid's back, hands twitching at my sides. I didn't know what to do. I was unarmed and I wasn't even sure where I *was*, and the kid had been implanted with tiny, invisible strings just like me—if we left the camp, would we just end up stroking out after a mile? A half mile?

Gupta reappeared, frowning, my remote held up by his chest. "Private Cates, I *do* have a schedule to keep."

I'd reached the end of Gupta's humanity, and with effort I turned and followed him out of the tent, back into the weird canvas hallways. *Kill Belling*, I thought. Kill Belling before there was any official transfer and then worry about the kid, if you could. After just a few seconds of walking, he turned left and we entered another of the large tents. This one might have been the one that Anners had interviewed me in; it had the same cheap table, the same cheap chairs, the same pitcher of water.

"You're waiting on Cates, Avery?" Gupta said briskly to the man sitting at the table.

"I am. I paid an exorbitant fee for him." Wa Belling leaned back in his chair. "Hello, Avery," he said. He ran his eyes up and down my uniform. "Dapper as always, I see."

IV

YOU SURVIVED *ME*. NOT MANY HAVE

Gupta gestured at one of the frail-looking chairs.

"Have a seat, Cates. Mr. Belling, if you are satisfied that this is the cargo you requested, you can indicate your agreement here." He rudely thrust the clipboard and the remote control at Belling, making the old man straighten up sharply and scowl, taking the remote and immediately pocketing it.

Belling looked...young. His hair was darker and his face had tightened up, smoothing out decades of wear and tear. He looked like an approximation of Wallace Belling at age fifty, a sketch done from memory years after the fact. His eyes, though, were the same: yellowed but bright, cunning, and mean. Behind him, I noted two soldiers, their sidearms in their hands and pointed at me.

"Have a *seat*," Gupta repeated. "Transfers are tricky moments, and those two will shoot you the moment they don't like what they see, okay? We've found having guards on hand makes these transactions go easier."

Belling glanced at the clipboard. "And the final install-ment?" His voice was melodious, seductive. Educated. I always wanted to believe Belling.

Gupta shrugged. "That is between you and the trans-acting officer. All I do is deliver the cargo."

I eyed the two guards. I had the feeling they'd shoot me if I sneezed. Slowly, I let myself sink into the chair.

Belling looked at Gupta with a sunny smile, then held his thumb out. My eyes flicked from the guards to Bell-ing's thumb and back again. I curled my hands into fists. After a moment, Gupta's clipboard chimed, and the doc-tor flipped it around and nodded. He glanced up at the two guards and jerked his head slightly. They instantly holstered their weapons and exited the room in sync.

"Is that it? He's mine?" Belling asked, still smiling.

Gupta nodded without looking at him. "Yes, Mr.—"

Belling reached up with one hand and took hold of a healthy shock of Gupta's thick hair and yanked the doc-tor's head down, smashing his nose into the table. This table didn't collapse, though it vibrated like a musical instrument as Gupta dropped to the floor. Belling leaned back a little to run his eyes over the prone form.

"He'll live," Wa said with a smile, looking back at me. "But perhaps he'll be more polite next time some-one comes in to transact business." He cocked his head. "Why, Avery, you look like you're not happy to see me."

I took a deep breath. Instantly, my HUD showed my heart rate slowing, and I felt myself relaxing in quick increments, helped along by my new wiring. I'd missed my chance; Belling had the remote and if I tried for him, I'd just end up twitching on the ground. "You look refreshed, Wa," I said. It was important to not react. Belling had betrayed me too many times for us to be friends, but we were peers. Or at least I thought so; Belling himself probably still thought of me as second-rate. I wasn't going to give him the satisfaction of surprising me. "You're fucking *beautiful*. I think I'm getting a little excited over you here."

He shook his head. "Homophobic humor from you, Avery? Very disappointing." He spread his hands. "Pockets of civilization remain, for those of us who have the influence. Not just plastics, though, Avery. I have had a full process. Artificial ligaments, skin therapies, artificial hormone emitters. I am, in a very real sense, younger than when you last saw me." He shrugged. "I do not intend to die like some pathetic old cat, whimpering in a darkened corner."

The eyes were freaking me out. The eyes were *old.*

"You, on the other hand," Wa said, squinting at me. "You look *terrible*. Older than your years."

I rewound Gupta's assessment of me from a few moments before. "So I'm told, Wa." I rolled my shoulders. "But I *feel* great."

I kept my eyes on the old man and pictured the tent, everything in it, assessing the situation with old, undying instincts that had kept me alive beyond all probability. The pitcher looked like glass, but it might be a polymer or even cheap plastic, something that wouldn't shatter into a satisfactory edge. The chairs would make decent bludgeons but they'd be clumsy to work with. And there was the fucking remote control; if Wa Belling had bought me to drag a knife across my throat, to eliminate a loose end from his past, I wasn't going to be able to stop him— especially with lab-grown ligaments under his hide—but I wasn't going easy.

A few seconds of silence wound around us, pulling tight.

"So," I said, "what's the going rate for old Gunners these days?"

Belling studied me calmly, the remote control being spun around in his deft, piano-player hands. These, I noted, had also been left untouched by the surgeon—they were papery and mottled with age spots, the original issue. He reached out and pulled one of the metal mugs toward him.

"Well, Avery—"

He snapped his arm up and sent the mug screaming right at my head. My arm popped up and I snatched it from the air, surging to my feet.

"What the *fuck*—"

"I apologize, Avery," he said, waving a negligent hand at me. "Sit down." He reached into his coat and I tensed up, but his hand emerged with a large flask that he unscrewed slowly, watching me. "Your reflexes are still good. Have you been working?"

I blinked. I felt very strongly that I'd lost control of the conversation. "What?"

He took a long pull from the flask and then extended it toward me with a nod. "This reminds me of our earliest conversations," he said cheerfully. "Me speaking clearly and simply, and you saying '*What*?' over and over."

I hesitated, and then stepped around the table and reached for the flask. I considered taking his wrist and breaking his arm instead, but he would be ready for that. I considered him taking *my* arm and breaking *my* wrist, but Belling had never been one to crack heads when he could simply shoot you from across the room—he'd see that as a waste of energy. So I pinched the flask between two fingers and took a sip: whiskey. Good whiskey.

I turned and walked back to the other end of the table with the flask. When I sat down again, I put my feet up and took a second swig, even though whiskey had never been my thing. Belling's expression was one of annoyance, and I enjoyed it, since it was all I was going to get by way of revenge. For now.

"Working," I said. "If you mean taking contracts, no. I've been in the armpit of the fucking System watching the troops march past. If you mean *killing* people, I've kept my hand in."

He sat forward. "Glad to hear it, Avery. I've seen your medical reports, and with the standard-issue SFNA augments plugged into you, I must say you're in better shape than I would have imagined."

I wondered if that was an insult, considering what Gupta had told me about my physical state. "Let's cut this bullshit short, Wa," I said, setting the flask down on the table in front of me. I watched his eyes flick to it. "Why do you care what kind of shape I'm in?"

Belling gave me his billionaire smile, spreading his hands. "Because we want you to work for us, my dim-witted American friend," he said. "The Dúnmharú has been reformed, and you're being recruited."

I frowned before I could stop myself. The Dúnmharú— Canny Orel's contract murder mill—was legendary. The best Gunners in the world banding together during Unification to take contracts from governments. The biggest money, the toughest marks. I knew Belling had been a charter member; Belling was *old*, despite the best work of his surgeons. "You just bought me, Wa. You've got that fucking piece of black plastic in your pocket, can make me sizzle. So cut the bullshit about *recruiting* me and tell me what it is you want me to do or else I get a zap, okay?"

He shook his head and stood up, pushing his hands into his pockets. His suit was expensive looking and cut nicely, with a stiff back collar that was popped up behind his ears. I still marveled at the new Belling, younger looking now than when I'd first met him, all those years ago in London, when he'd been trading on Orel's name. "You'd rather hump it in a suicide squad? Get assigned a shredding rifle and a date of death, running across some field already muddy with the blood of insignificant morons?" He shrugged. "Too bad. We've got a job, and we need someone with experience to run it for us."

Still, I looked at the cocksucker's smug, smoothed face and I couldn't just give in. I leaned back in my seat and pointed at him, letting him squirm a little. *"Experience?"*

He shrugged again. "Avery..." He paused and looked at his hands appraisingly. "Avery, the System is not operating at peak efficiency."

I snorted. "That's the fucking understatement of the year."

"Yes. Civil war—the front line shifting back and forth hundreds of miles in a week, cities bombed to pieces, whole populations displaced, press squads denuding the world of labor forces, breakaway states, ruined communication lines, restricted travel." He looked up at me from under his eyebrows, suddenly and obviously casual. "Hong Kong is days away from declaring independence. Did you hear that?"

I thought about telling him what Anners had said about taking his unit to Hong Kong, wanting to one-up the old bastard. Instead, I just shook my head, and he sighed.

"Avery, thirty years ago, during Unification, we made a fortune taking on contracts from governments, playing them off each other. Those times are here again, and there's an opportunity to not only remake those fortunes, but to shape the world. To take command. To shift the course of things." He leaned back, satisfied with himself as usual. "The problem is, there's a lack of individuals with the talent level we require."

I raised an eyebrow, and he jabbed a finger in my direction, his face comically enraged.

"Don't bring up old news, Avery. I live in the present. You can't just skim through the slums anymore and find some talented kid who can be trained. They're all dead. Or in the army, which is the same thing." He scowled. "You're, what, forty now? Old, but you have *experience*. You've organized large-scale jobs. You've survived global emergencies—you survived *me*. Not many have."

I nodded. "I'm all you've got."

"*Yes*," he hissed, unhappy. He stood up, shooting his expensive cuffs. "Money doesn't mean anything, anymore. Power *always* means something. And the Dúnmharú means power." He paused and gave me what he probably imagined was a friendly look. "You were once powerful, in your way. In New York, after Squalor. You remember it, I am sure."

I sighed. I needed to stay with him, needed to get out of the army's sphere and wait for Belling to make a mistake so I could kill him. It didn't matter what line of bullshit he thought he was feeding me.

I thought of Remy. "I was scooped up with some other—"

"No, Avery," Belling said and shrugged. "We're here for you. No one else. I don't want to hear your bleeding-heart bullshit. In or out, that's it."

I scowled. "Listen, goddamn—"

"In or *out*, Avery! There's no room for anyone else."

"I'm in," I said quietly. Let Belling think he'd beaten me down. Let him think I was too tired to go after him. I felt like a fucking newborn. "So how much *did* you pay for me, Wa?"

He dug through his coat and produced the plastic remote control, appraising it. Then he looked up at me. "Oh, for god's sake, Avery, *I* didn't buy you. Michaleen did. He's Canny Orel, after all. He *is* the Dúnmharú."

V

THE MAN'S A *HERO*

Stepping onto the hover that Belling had somehow gotten permission to haul through SFNA airspace was like going back five years in time.

The hover was first class. Even five years ago it would have been first class, and these days, when just getting a hover into airspace without seeing it shot down was impossible, it was like some sort of miracle hover. The interior was luxurious, with polished wood everywhere, thick carpeting, and soft leather seats that moved any way your body shifted, always offering maximum support. A tiny Droid roamed up and down the aisle, offering cocktails and food, clearing away trash the moment you set it down, and humming a soothing little tune that made me want to smash a fist into its tiny plastic face. But I didn't want to be rude so I contented myself with obstructing it with my foot every chance I got, making the thing vibrate in frustration until I moved.

Belling had a suit of clothes waiting for me in the

hover. At first, I'd been angry, but the clothes I'd been given on our way off the army base weren't mine; they smelled like someone's sour cologne and were two sizes too big, handed to me from a huge pile in the processing tent where Belling signed me out. The suit from Wa was beautiful: black, quality, and close to a perfect fit. The moment I'd peeled off the creepy military issue and had it on, I felt like a human being again and decided to forgive him. Until I managed to kill him.

I sat in my ass-hugging seat sipping a glass of gin that was absolutely perfect except that it was completely unlike any gin I'd ever tasted. It was perfect: chilled, with a curl of something green and fragrant hooked onto the glass— and I hated it. I hated Belling, I hated Michaleen or Canny or whatever the fuck his real name was. I stared at Belling while he made a show of strumming a small handheld, his elegant hand swirling around in lazy patterns, data glowing in bright clumps. He looked like a dandy, like a rich old man who'd been eating well and drinking well and fucking well his whole life. I knew better. I watched his hands and knew that Belling was better than me, and always had been: faster, dirtier. Crueler. Even as an old man, Belling would beat me, with or without his remote control.

I hated him even more for being better than me.

For a moment, I was filled with so much hatred my hands shook, and I wanted to try and strangle the bastard despite the bleak odds.

I closed my eyes and imagined my globe of glass, everything else on the outside. Inside, just peace and quiet. I realized my hands were clenched into fists, and I forced myself to relax them just as Belling spoke.

"Avery, I can almost *hear* you plotting from over here."

I opened my eyes. The Old Man was looking at me, calm and relaxed, the plastic remote held idly in one hand. I put my eyes on it for a moment and then smiled back at Belling. "Why would you think that, Wallace? Because you sold me out to Kev Gatz? Because you made me *Patient Fucking Zero* in the Plague? Because you're a fucking liar? Because you're working for Michaleen?" I shook my head and offered him a smile. "Wallace, you're not afraid of *me*, are you?"

He smiled back, shaking his head. "No."

His finger twitched, and I almost bit my tongue off.

Pain like I'd never felt before flooded into me like liquid being pushed through a needle directly into my nervous system. White hot and corrosive, it shattered my imagined inner peace and in the second or two that I remained conscious, it taught me that whatever I'd been defining as *pain* before was just a shadow of the possibilities.

Cold, wet, and awake.

I surged up to consciousness, still twitching on the floor under my seat. I was damp everywhere; I'd pissed myself and the carpet around me. As I lay there, shivering, a huge snot bubble inflating and deflating on the tip of my nose, I could feel gravity tugging on me; we were in descent.

"Behave yourself," I heard Belling say cheerfully, his voice muffled by the leather upholstery between us. "You're now a wholly owned subsidiary of the Dúnmharú. Fuck up and I'll stroke you out."

My whole body ached like a shallow echo of what Belling had just done to me, softly vibrating. I squirmed to get my hands under me, my fingers sinking into the damp pile, and pushed myself over onto my back. I lay there gasping, legs still twitching every few seconds. The ceiling of the hover was smooth white, with small round lights set every two feet or so, making me blink. After a moment, Belling's weird, smooth face swam between me and them.

"Up and at them, boy," he said, giving me a little tap with one shined boot.

"Where are we?" My voice came out rubbery, soft and stretched.

"Amsterdam. That's where the man is, so that's where we have to go." His upside-down face scowled at me. "Michaleen does not do any kind of electronic communication. You want to talk to him, you go where he is. Now, get the fuck up before I get irritated. This is probably the last hover flight we'll sneak out; our usual contact with the System Pigs can't help us anymore, having been shot to death in the recent Northern Europe campaign. The army's in charge up here now and we don't have any contacts with the Europe Central Command."

I gathered myself slowly and pushed up onto trembling arms, finally maneuvering my way around so I could hook an arm onto the seat and support myself sitting up. A shock of adrenaline hit my bloodstream; I was going to see Michaleen. I was going to be in the same fucking airspace as the little fucker, and I would have a window when the remote was still hooked to Belling. A window when maybe I could take a shot at Michaleen, aka Canny Orel, aka the greatest Gunner in history. And me, piss-soaked and shaking. I squinted at Belling, who was primping, smoothing himself down like a peacock. The Old Man would slit someone's throat for a better view of a Vidscreen; I didn't see him diving in front of a bullet to save Mickey.

I struggled to my knees. I felt about as quick as a corpse, but I was going to be within arm's reach of Michaleen for the first time since escaping from Chengara, and I was going to make it count.

"Come on," Belling said, smoothing down his white, short-cut hair. "We're landing. Time to meet your coworkers." He paused and looked at me, grinning with barely contained humor. "Avery, I can tell you still hold some sort of grudge against me."

I pushed myself onto my feet and stood for a moment with clenched fists. "Wa, you've got me all wrong. All I ever needed to know, I learned from you."

He laughed, pushing his hands into his pockets and rocking on his heels. "Avery, I know you too well. Never could let things go in favor of good business decisions, could you?" He leaned forward. "I'll make you a fair offer at penance, Avery. When Michaleen approaches you in a few minutes, you're likely to have one of those Cates-brand lapses of judgment, yes? I'll be a little slow with the remote. Give you a few seconds." He nodded. "If you can do something with a few seconds—and any Gunner worth his rate could—consider it a gift."

I concentrated on breathing, trying to figure out Belling's play here. There was no risk here for him—if I somehow killed Michaleen, he had my remote and could disable me immediately, and Cainnic Orel would no longer be around to give him orders. If I failed, he would just shrug and apologize for being unfamiliar with the remote. Michaleen no doubt would know better, but if Belling's lack of loyalty surprised him I'd eat my shoes.

I swallowed bile. I felt like I *had* eaten my shoe already. I had no weapon. My eyes roamed the cabin for a few seconds and finally lit on the glass tumbler I'd dropped when Belling'd zapped me. I crouched down and snatched it up, slipping it up into my sleeve and holding my hand bent at the wrist to keep it in place. Then I stepped behind Belling, fighting my inner ears as they tried to tip me sideways into the seats again, and followed him to the hatchway just as the hover touched the ground with a thump. I twisted my neck around until I got a satisfying pop.

I knew him, a little. I remembered Michaleen telling me, about my father. *Not long and not deep.*

I didn't like being lied to.

As the hatch opened, a set of tiny stairs automatically lowered, and Belling stepped down easily, throwing back his coat as a blast of cold wind hit us, lighting me up and making my damp clothes burn unhappily. I ignored the fresh coat of shivering that descended on me and concentrated on stepping off the hover without checking my footing, my eyes open and sweeping the scene.

It was a large airfield, old, ancient. The open space reminded me of the wilderness at first, just grass and weeds and the occasional skinny young tree trunk. A second glance showed the broken concrete and asphalt, the buildings in the near distance, the accumulated trash and collapsed fencing of a long-abandoned complex being slowly swallowed by the world. I felt instantly exposed.

As I stepped around Belling, I saw Michaleen immediately. He was wearing a suit badly, everything cut wrong, his tie undone, a ridiculous wide-brimmed hat set on an angle on his head. He was at least two feet shorter than each of his companions, both young. One, a leggy girl, with bright, unnaturally red hair done up in a complex set of braids and sweeps, wore a pair of skintight pants of tough-looking material that shimmered slightly in the pale sunlight and a tightly zipped leather jacket. The other was a boy, dark skinned and hollow cheeked, with a shaved head that was like half an egg set on top of his artificially thick neck. His legs were skinny, trembling little sticks popping out from under a thick, leather longcoat that looked hot and uncomfortable, but his neck and chest and arms were huge, heavy hunks of meat, almost throbbing with their own alien intelligence.

He wasn't the type for stupid augment-junkie security assholes. Therefore the kid wasn't security. I ignored him. The girl, maybe. She looked fast and mean, her face all angles and shadows, her eyes set too deeply into her face for beauty. Both of the kids looked too clean and scarless, which was either an expensive surgery habit or they were two jumbo softies who'd never scraped a knuckle.

I was careful: I contained my body language and followed Belling slowly, nonthreateningly. The weight of the glass was comforting in my sleeve. I asked myself what Michaleen would expect from me; he'd expect anger, so I stared at him and ground my teeth—that was easy. He'd expect something reckless and immediate, so I had to stutter the timing, try to throw him off. This was the man known as Cainnic Orel, I reminded myself. He'd had weeks to case me, and he'd done it well enough to play me like a fucking child back in Chengara—I had to go random, try to shock the fuck out of him, and count on Belling to be the unlovably selfish piece of shit he'd always been in the past.

Physically, Michaleen hadn't changed at all. He was

the same short, powerful-looking fellow, old as sin with
a craggy, leathery face that was always screwed up into a
fantastic expression that resembled either incredible pain
or incredible amusement. His nose was long and rounded,
his eyes bright and young in that tanned face, framed by
thin, ghostly threads of white hair. He looked prosperous,
like *he* hadn't spent the last six months drinking paint and
eating wild rabbit, shivering with the fumes over Bixon's.
Like he hadn't even thought of me once since leaving me
to be *processed* into an avatar in Chengara.

As Belling and I approached, unbelievably the little
man smiled and threw his arms wide.

"Avery Fucking Cates as I live and breathe," he
shouted. "I told these pups here that a great hero from the
past was comin' to lend a hand to our li'l enterprise. Pups,
you're lookin' at the genuine article, a man who has *done*
things."

Belling stopped a foot or two away, and I stopped too.
"Hello, Mickey," I said. "Got a cigarette?"

His eyes were merry, on me at an angle. His tiny hands,
his plump middle—it was immediately unbelievable that
this man was the most dangerous Gunner in the world.

He roared laughter, a good, natural sound pouring
out of him. "Cigarettes! You fucking ballbuster. Sure, I
got—"

A split second of peace settled on me. I'd been thinking of Michaleen for months, kicking ass on spec in
Englewood, plotting, sending out my feeble feelers. Here
he was, the cosmos rewarding me for a change, for years
of steady service. I unkinked my hand and the tumbler
dropped into it like gravity had been designed for that
express purpose. I swung my arm up and leaned forward,

and when the glass actually shattered against Mickey's tiny head I was fucking *shocked*.

He staggered to his right, absorbing the impact, and as blood splattered everywhere he ducked under my arm and drove his bleeding skull into my stomach, knocking the breath out of me. I hung onto the broken glass desperately, the edges digging into my skin and peeling the flesh away from my fingers, but it was the only weapon I had and I wasn't going to fucking drop it.

Michaleen was heavier than he looked, and he put me off my feet and we fell as a unit to the broken asphalt beneath us. My head smacked into the ground and I heard Gupta for a second, distant, telling me how many fucking concussions I'd had. Then I dug my elbow into the ground and pushed off, rolling us until Michaleen was under me. I raised the lump of raw meat and shattered glass that had once been my hand into the air, and Michaleen squirmed under me, suddenly yanking his arm free, swinging his hand up between us. In his hand was the world's smallest gun. It was an old Roon model 56—a peashooter, small caliber. At a distance, it was like setting off a firecracker— the best you could hope for was to annoy your target. Two inches from your face, it would do the job.

For a second, we were frozen like that, panting, dripping blood, my hand in the air, his tiny gun aimed at my eye.

Then my whole body lit up again, white fire snapping everything rigid and making rigidity a torture. This time I bit down on my tongue hard, blood flowing into my mouth as I tried to scream. Michaleen pushed me off of him like I was an inconvenient piece of scenery and I just rolled away, the shattered glass dropping away, forgotten.

As my consciousness narrowed down to a dot, I heard the little man laughing breathlessly. "I told you, pups," I heard him say, fading fast. "You been working wit' me six *months*, you take whatever the fuck I hand you. He's here two goddamn *seconds*, he's trying to kill me. The man's a *hero*."

Turned to cinder by Belling's remote, I disappeared into darkness, and was glad for it.

VI

THE MIDDLE FINGER OF GOD

Hot, stiff, and awake. I opened my eyes and had a distorted view of a well-used tabletop, pitted and scratched, covered in endless layers of varnish. A glass of something brown and transparent loomed directly in front of me, a giant's glass, everything receding from there. A heavily tattooed pair of hands were folded far away, impossibly tiny. Stamped on top of everything was the tiny text and graphics of my heads-up display, which was going fucking *insane*. Text was streaming from bottom to top at a furious pace in the left of my vision, and status bars were jigging and jiving in my right, going from red to green, one after the other. My HUD distilled everything about my physical state into a stream of numbers, code words, and unexplained graphics that didn't mean much to me beyond a few basics.

"Better be careful. The Middle Finger of God. Give you brain damage."

I lifted my head from the table and squinted at the

freak who'd been with Michaleen at the old airport. He'd
taken off his jacket to reveal a sleeveless black shirt, his
arms lying on the table in front of him like heavy burdens
he'd just dropped, lifeless and ridiculously humongous.
His right arm was heavily inked starting at the elbow,
bright, animated tats that moved constantly, a flickering
horrorshow of colors and movement that I didn't want to
see. I shifted my eyes to his face, trying to wet my lips,
but my tongue had turned into a swollen toad living in the
dark cave of my mouth and didn't want to do anything
except make breathing difficult. I managed a grunt.

I was seated at a dark wooden table next to a huge
plate-glass window that had been starred pretty badly
and was held together now by a complex system of gray
tape. It was dark inside and raining outside, a muddy river
creeping up a crumbling bank. Evidence of an old paved
road and a concrete sidewalk could still be seen, slowly
being sucked into the brown water, an inch a year. Across
the river was another strip of crumbling pavement and a
row of narrow, neat-looking buildings, rough stone, and
peaked roofs. A line of trees adorned each bank, twisted,
overgrown roots bursting from the ground, undermining
the bank further, everything working together to destroy
everything else.

I glanced down at the table and found a glass of whiskey. I picked it up, staring at it. The weight felt wrong.
Everything felt wrong. Gravity was pushing me up, and
my tongue was a toad lodged in my mouth. The whole
place smelled, a sweet, heavy scent that was pleasant at
first but became sickening pretty fast. We were the only
people in it aside from a terrified-looking blond girl
behind the bar, hugging herself on the far end, as far away

from us as she could get without leaving her post, her eyes fixed in our direction.

"Old man is out back," my minder said with a grin. "Taking Belling's confession. This is Amsterdam."

"I know where I fucking am," I said, leaning back. The bars in my vision suddenly stabilized and turned green, and I realized that I didn't feel bad at all. I even felt *good*. I raised the glass and paused with it awkwardly in the air, and nodded in his direction. "Nice work. Expensive?"

He nodded. "Very expensive." He jabbed a finger at his neck. "One for each person I've killed. They still live on me."

I raised an eyebrow. As I squinted at the freak, my vision suddenly zoomed and the tiny, animated tattoos came into sharp focus. They were very detailed, the faces contorted into masks of horror as they were murdered over and over again: a fat black man in a suit was garroted, his eyes bulging, his tongue popping out of his mouth; a slim woman with graying hair was shot in the forehead, the wound appearing suddenly, her eyes popping wide and staying that way; a dozen others endlessly replaying their deaths.

This was amateur hour. Maybe the cops weren't interested in arresting anyone these days, sure, so wearing your own evidence wasn't so terrible, but bragging and giving your enemies information for free, this shit was worth punishing. I swirled whiskey around in the glass, looking over the rim at him. His arms were . . . I wasn't sure if I knew of a bigger word than *fucking humongous* and looked like good augment work, the muscles not twitchy or taut, but slow as fuck. He was sitting at Michaleen's table, though; that meant something.

Michaleen. I knew I was going to have to table that bastard for the time being, and the thought of waiting another year to make him pay for playing me made my stomach sour.

"You proud of yourself?" I asked, swallowing the whiskey. It tasted like shit, paint thinner burning all the way down, which was a huge improvement over Bixon's slush back in Free Failed State of Englewood. The thought that the *good stuff* out there in the world was now shit was depressing, and all these kids who'd never had a pre-Unification cigarette or a decent glass of gin, they thought everything was fine. The standards had slipped, and people like me who knew better weren't long for the world.

He nodded. "I am quality. I do work needs to be done. They call me the Poet."

I raised an eyebrow theatrically. "Bullshit. I'll bet you anything you like not one person has *ever* called you the Poet unless you had a knife up their ass." I pointed a finger at him. "I will call you Nancy."

He flushed, color coming in black on his cheeks. I felt good; I was running this meeting.

I smiled and raised the glass over my head. "Sweetheart," I shouted. "Another one of these, and a pack of cigarettes, on the Old Man's tab!" As I set the glass back on the table I marveled for a moment at my hand: The cuts were still painful and visible, but they looked like they'd been healing for days, and I found I had full movement without too much discomfort. These army augments were fucking first class. I felt like doing push-ups. I put the smile on him and set myself, feeling an old dark joy filling me up—feeling this good was eroding my good sense, and I felt like a kid again, having fun, swinging my dick around.

"Tell you what," I said, leaning forward. "I think being proud of sneaking up behind assholes and strangling them with your freakazoid monkey arms stitched onto your shoulders is nothing to fucking be proud of. And I think having your crimes tatted on your neck is flash. And I think *the Poet* is maybe the dumbest fucking name I've ever heard."

He actually moved his arms, flipping over his hands so he could spread them wide, smiling back. "It is a good thing," he said and paused, "that I don't value your thoughts. Feel like teaching me?"

My HUD suddenly flashed and I knew someone was creeping along my peripheral vision, a silent little twitch in my head. The girl, eyes wide and hands trembling, was approaching our table like it was a bomb that could go off at any time, which in a way I supposed it was. I turned my head to look at her.

"No one's gonna hurt you," I said slowly. "Don't worry."

"I give no such word," the Poet said easily. "Take your chances like the rest. See if *he* helps you."

I looked at him and we stared at each other. Slowly, she stepped between me and the table and set a bottle down, along with a dull metal cigarette case. My eyes lingered on the case; I hadn't had a fucking cigarette since before I was fucking born. My mouth was watering. She smelled like shit, like someone who hadn't been near water in a long time.

She scurried away as if I'd goosed her and my hands were opening the case before I was even conscious of them.

"I have heard of you," the Poet said, relaxing his hands and shifting his weight. "More lucky than talented. That is what I think." He pushed his chin at me. "You would not save her," he added, his face comically serious. "You would kill her like the rest, if you felt you must."

I nodded, cigarette between my lips, my attention on the case. It had a built-in lighter, and I traced my fingers over it, trying to figure out the mechanism. "You're absolutely right, but I wouldn't be fucking *proud* of it."

His voice was a shrug as I finally produced a bright blue flame. "Your bullshit bores me. I suspect I'm not the first. You're a chatty man."

I sucked in smoke and decided I was ready for the cosmos to kick me off the rail and send me to hell, as long as I could smoke this cigarette first. It was the worst fucking cigarette I'd ever had. It tasted like ashes that had been wetted and molded back into the shape of a cigarette. I didn't care. It was heaven. It put me into a better mood, and I sent the smoke back into the air and looked at my newest friend.

"All right," I said. "Tell me about Amsterdam." I looked around. "Doesn't seem like the war has hurt it too badly."

He cocked his head and smirked. "This is Old Man's bar," he said. "Not much left in this city, but it's not dead yet." He licked his lips. "The army bombed it, everyone moved underground; the streets are rotting."

I looked back out the window at the crumbling street, the dirty canal.

"Then the cops show up, a couple of Spooks in tow, proclaim city free. Gathered up leaders, shot the lot dead in Dam Square, no time to brick them." As I looked back at him, he spread his hands again. "Then army came back, dropped more bombs, re-took city, not much left for us."

I grunted, picking up the bottle and pouring a few fingers into the glass. I felt wonderful. No pain—even my leg wasn't throbbing—drinking and smoking in a bar. I held the bottle out toward my new friend. He held up a hand, a languid, majestic movement of his arm. "Thank you, but no thanks. I do not dull my senses." He inclined his head. "Professional pride."

We stared at each other in silence. Wearily, I wondered why it was always a pissing contest. This kid had his fucking credits animated on his *skin*, and I was an old man filled with nanotech, with someone's boot up my ass directing me. Still, this asshole with the speech impediment thought he had to sit on me and make me like it. I knew I was going to have to make a demonstration for my peace of mind, and a wave of sullen heaviness swept through me.

I lifted the glass to my lips and tossed it back. It was wonderful to be in sin again. Holding the glass up, I made a show of studying it and smacking my lips, keeping the freak in my peripheral vision, which had suddenly become crystal clear and precise. "Do you know why I'm here, Nancy?" I asked. "Does the Old Man have something lined up?"

The Poet nodded, frowning. A sensitive lad. You could call me names all day and I wouldn't care, but assholes with vanity arms and their exploits in cartoon form on their skin didn't like being made fun of. "Oh yes, he has job. Big pay, but competition." He shrugged. "You are our ringer. To me, you look old. Methuselah in the flesh. Not worth the money."

I nodded. "I *am* old." I cocked my head and grinned,

bracing. "How old are *you*, anyway? Did you know your mom? Who knows, I might be your daddy."

It had been my experience that punks with sensitive egos always had sainted mothers.

The way he went still, frozen for a second, I knew I'd hit him where he lived, and tensed myself up, counting the seconds. I had the timing, and when he surged up from his seat, I shoved the table at him, putting my weight into it, slamming him back into the window, which groaned under the impact, the tape popping as the shards snapped free. Ridiculously, he leaned forward and slapped his huge arms at me, a few inches short. I thought of his skinny, neglected legs under the table, useless.

"Lesson one, asshole," I said, keeping the grin in place and giving the table an extra shove for the hell of it. "When someone insults you to your fucking *face*, they're trying to bait you. Get that shit under control."

From behind me, the sound of clapping. I waited a beat, winked at him, and with an extra little shove stepped back from the table, grabbed the bottle, and spun around. Michaleen was standing there with the red-haired girl, both of them grinning.

"Avery, Avery," Michaleen said. "You're entertaining as always, ain't ya? Never imagined you as the patient tutor for the Lost Generation. Ah, so you've met the Poet here, who's better in the field than perhaps he's given the impression of. This is Mara, our Taker."

He gestured at the girl, who looked past me for a second at the Poet, smirked, and looked back at me. "Welcome to the team, Mr. Cates," she said in a rolling accent similar to Michaleen's. "You'll do well."

VII

JUST THE WORST THING THAT HAD EVER HAPPENED TO THESE POOR PEOPLE

"Thank you, darlin'."

The blond girl stared at Michaleen in terror for a moment, and then she managed a jerking, horrifying curtsy before spinning and walking away with tight, awkward steps. I watched her go while Mickey inspected his cup of tea and wondered where he'd found her and why he kept her around as his personal waitress. Why he *thanked* her.

I was seated between the Poet and Mara, the Taker. She smelled nice, and her hip was warm against mine under the table, a girl of maybe eighteen with milk-white skin and a tense, uncomfortable sense about her, like she was always in slight pain. The Poet was calm again, quiet, with his shovel hands folded in front of him. The window behind us was letting in the wind now and the sour smell of Amsterdam, like all of the canals had gone stagnant, like the sewage system had backed up and spilled the guts of the dead population back into the air.

Michaleen picked up his dainty cup and smiled around at us, his whole face folding up and crinkling into lines. "Avery," he said with a nod. "Walk with me, eh?"

I cocked my head. "You sure I won't jump you again?"

He chuckled, standing up, and with a subtle movement of his hand produced the square remote control. "You can try, boyo," he said, and with another flexing of his hand the remote disappeared.

I stood up. "All right," I said. I didn't mind the pain, or even the inevitable blackout, but there was no point in going after Michaleen if it was just going to end with me pissing myself again while he shook his head and chastised me. He'd set the anti-frag to a couple of inches, so unless I thought I could kill him with one smack, I was going to have to play along with him until I figured out a way around the augments the army had stuffed into me.

He led me out into the cool, curdled air. My eyesight adjusted to the new brightness automatically, a flash of information giving me the temperature, the humidity, and my position in a series of numbers I didn't completely understand. The status bars in the corner were green, but they'd faded to a pale transparency that I found easy to ignore. We went a few steps along the broken pavement, which narrowed in places so that only one of us could walk at a time. I was conscious of the raw earth underneath it all, ready to give way at any moment, the hungry water lapping at it endlessly, patient. I amused myself by hopping one-legged from spot to spot, one hand out casually to brace myself against the building facades we passed.

Something in the canal caught my eye. I watched it resolve into a corpse, bloated and green, floating slowly

by us. I paused to watch it for a moment as it passed, bob-
bing peacefully, the eyes in the blackened face open and
staring, yellowed and syrupy. I didn't like bodies. I usually walked away from people the moment they died.

"Been hard," Michaleen suddenly said, sipping his
steaming tea. "Amsterdam was pretty safe for a while,
a cop stronghold with a lot of space around it. But it got
swollen up with refugees and such, people running away
from the front. Got so big the army decided it needed
reducing, eh?" He shook his head. "But I like it here."

Amsterdam looked peaceful. I realized the line of
buildings across the river was just facades, the outline of
buildings attached to each other. Behind the empty windows and scorched rock of the fronts was nothing but
rubble, as if somehow the SFNA had a bomb that carved
off the fronts of buildings, leaving them intact. If you
squinted and didn't pay attention, it was beautiful: the
storefronts and old buildings, the water slipping past, a
few trees still hanging on along the edges of the pavement.
The smell was horrible, sour-sweet, rot, and something
else, something scorched and burned and unpleasant. But
the sky was blue, and everywhere. I didn't remember seeing the sky much, back in New York. It always seemed
gray and clouded, and it had always been full of SSF hovers, waiting to rain Stormers down onto us.

The sky was empty above us, and it suddenly made me
feel naked. I *missed* those hovers.

"I won't pretend," Michaleen said, "that you're a part-
ner in this, Avery. You don't have any choice—you're
gonna do what I want and help us with this."

I didn't say anything. After a moment he spat into the
canal.

"So there's that. But I will offer you an incentive, yes? I'll offer you a deal, from the goodness of m'heart. Here it is: Run this for me, take lead and get it done, an' I'll cut you loose with jus' your word not to come bother me."

I shook out another cigarette, feeling prosperous to suddenly have a bellyful of decent booze and a fresh pack of cigarettes, even if they were synthetic and tasted like fuck. Sticking one in my mouth, I fiddled with the case lighter again, the trick of it mysterious once more. "Tell you what, if I don't find a way to fuck you over once we're out in the field, I'll take you up on that."

He chuckled. "You're a fuckin' card, ain't ya. But that's why I'll be signing over the remote to my girl while you're out and about, right? She'll be ridin' herd on you, keepin' you on point."

I considered this as a bright blue flame suddenly appeared from the lighter in response to a mysterious gesture I'd managed and couldn't re-create in my head. I lit my cigarette before it could change its mind and fade away. "So this is the fucking famous Dúnmharú, huh? Two old men, a fucking freak, and a girl who looks like she traps spiders and sets them free."

He winced around his teacup. "You've got a mouth on you, boyo. If I didn't have this endless affection for you, and a sense of having wronged you—"

I choked, sending out a premature cloud of blue smoke. *Wronged* me. He'd gotten me to help him escape prison, and my reward had been watching him rise into the air while I got dragged down to an underground lab to have needles shoved into my brain. *A* sense *of having wronged.*

"—I'd set this cup down and teach you some fuckin' manners." He took three steps in silence, chewing his tea.

"Try it without the remote, since you're such a fucking *legend*," I said, studying the coal of my cigarette, "and I'll pull those ridiculous ears off of you like they're a fly's wings."

He waved an impatient hand at me. "The Poet—his name's Adrian, by the by—he's skilled. A bit of a fuckin' weirdo, o'course, but the man has credits. He's a *thinker*, like you. And you'll need the muscle on this. If I'd had time to recruit five more people, I'd have given them all to ya, Avery, but time's short—you were kinda a lucky find for us, at th'last minute. And Mara is a pro. Not a killer, maybe, or maybe she is, but she kin find anyone, and get plugged in—even in these sad times—anywhere. Trust me. These are the best available."

"I expected more, Mickey. You're a fucking legend. This is . . . not legendary."

He grimaced. "Fucking hell, Avery—you think it was back in the day? Shit, you think we were sitting around in fucking tuxedos, smoking cigars and what, slitting throats from across the room with our fucking Psionic powers? Me and Wallace and Turnby and Tracy—we were just men and women."

Eoin Turnby, Gwendolin Tracy—I'd heard the names. Dim and dark, just names.

"We killed people. It was fucking messy and it took effort, but that's all we were. We just killed folks who were supposedly too well protected, too rich, and too powerful to be killed. And the fucking world was shaking down around us, so when it was all done, all that was left was bullshit and such." He laughed. "Hell, Avery—if you met Eoin Turnby on the street thirty years ago you would've given him the shoulder out of principle. He looked like a

fucking shabby Pick." He paused. "Died with a fuckin'
ice pick in his throat, hands tied behind his back. Bled
out over four fucking hours. No way for a killer to go."
He looked at me sideways and let that ring for a moment.
"Your problem is, you've had too much Wallace Belling.
That fucking dandy's always liked playin' the part. Likes
playin' it more than he likes *livin*' it. He's a fuckin' *actor.*
Enjoys fuckin' with people." He sighed, sipping tea. "Still,
Wa's the best I ever saw with a traditional pistola, y'know?
Could shoot the tits off a pigeon a mile away."

We took a few steps in silence. The city wasn't entirely
quiet, though, I realized; my augmented ears were picking up some crowd noise not too far off to my left. As we
passed a large intersection, I turned and saw a smoke-
stack-shaped hunk of stone thrusting up into the air in
the middle of a large, empty square. There were people
dotted around it, sitting, standing, moving about, the first
natives I'd seen so far. Michaleen turned and we headed
toward it.

"Fuckin' war," he muttered, tossing the rest of his tea
out onto the street and shaking the cup. "This is fuckin'
worse than Unification. At least you had countries goin'
at it, back then, organized countries. Now it's just these
fuckin' armies running back and forth tramplin' everything, the whole world going to shit."

I shrugged. "I heard some places are going independent. Breaking away."

"Sure, sure," Mickey said sagely. "Half the fuckin' System is going to think about it." He looked at me sideways.
"Way I hear it, Hong Kong's the test case. They're gearin'
up for an official declaration, tellin' the cops and the army
to stay the fuck out. Way I hear it, a bunch of old cops

who gave Marin the slip and never got turned into fuckin' androids are there, ready to be the city's security."

I sucked in smoke. "I doubt the people with the guns are going to let that just happen." The sun suddenly peeked out from behind some clouds, hitting me with a pleasant warmth. One of the status bars in my vision flashed briefly. "Why give me the current events, Mickey?"

"Y'know I've asked you not to call me that, Avery. I do you a courtesy and use your proper name, don't I?"

I smiled. Michaleen Garda, aka Canny Orel, legendary killer, miffed that I had a nickname for him. "You want to trade with Adrian? I'm calling him Nancy."

I felt his eyes on me for a moment. I thought of him in Chengara, in his prison scrubs, the fast way he moved, the secret strength in those short arms. I saw in a flash exactly how he'd been so good as a Gunner: Michaleen could walk into any situation and no one would look at him twice. And then he'd move so fast you'd be dead before you could startle. Michaleen was always hidden in plain sight. I could *feel* my body tuning up; hell, I could *see* it in my HUD, which suddenly clarified, brightening up, giving me an adrenaline dump graph and a spiky endorphin readout. Everything seemed to slow down just slightly, the whole world getting bled of color and tightening up.

Then it passed. Michaleen's posture softened and he spat onto the street. "You with the needle, all the fucking time. All right, I wouldn't have this little bit o' tech in my pocket if I expected you to have warm feelins for me, eh? All right." He stopped walking.

"Let's be clear, Avery," he said quietly. "You ain't an employee and you don't get a share and I know you'd shiv me in the belly and leave me to bleed out as soon as you'd wish me a good mornin', and I don't give a *fuck* 'bout you either, pup." His eyes were roaming the street, calm and clear, his whole posture relaxed, like we were talking about the weather. "Know this: I will punish you if you fuck with me. I will punish you until your brain leaks out of your ears, copy?"

A wave of intense, white pain slammed through me, shattering my bones and turning my blood into sand. I dropped to the freezing pavement and jittered there, eyes popping slowly out of my head, throat swollen tightly shut, my hands out above me in a ridiculous pose, the fingers curled into claws.

Slowly, with a lazy grunt, Michaleen knelt down next to me. His eyes were still everywhere.

"So listen good, eh, Avery? I am your *boss* on this. I leave this on you for a few minutes and you don't come back from it. This shit is how they get all the chaff o' the world to run directly into shredder fire, eh?" He sighed, sounding almost sad. "So, your choice: You can do what you're told and play ball and you walk away at the end. Or *this* is how you end, pissing yourself on the street. Understood?"

With a private nod to himself he stood up and held the little remote out in front of me. "All right," he whispered, and the pain stopped, just like that. He made another minute gesture with his hand and a sudden soothing warmth flooded in behind it, scraping away the acid marks and embers. Seconds later, I almost felt *good*.

"All right," he repeated. "On your feet, boyo. You keep in mind I will be watching. You play by my rules, and we have ourselves an agreement."

Slowly, I sat up, still feeling shivery and weak despite

the pleasant rush of endorphins. I climbed unsteadily to my feet and Mickey started walking again, forcing me to limp after him, hatred smoldering, hidden, almost as bright as the memory of agony he'd flashed at me.

He cleared his throat as we entered the square. It was dominated by the huge monument in the center, a glorious fucking waste of concrete that jutted up into the air for no reason at all that I could detect. A few dozen people were standing around chatting in the damp air, but as we moved through the square they all stepped away, leaving us with a bubble of space that traveled with us as if it was invisible foam attached to us. The wind suddenly swelled up, pushing around us, whipping our coats up into fluttering chaos. Michaleen turned and tossed something at me.

My HUD flashed in my eyes, and the little data cube seemed brighter than everything else as it flashed in the air. I snapped my hand up and grabbed it from the air, holding it up in front of my face.

"Our mark," Michaleen said, looking away and stuffing his hands into his pockets in a gesture I recognized instantly from Chengara. "Techie. You'll work this with Mara and Adrian." He snorted. "Can you fuckin' believe it? That's how low we've sunk. Thirty years ago I was hired to kill presidents and prime ministers. Now it's *Techies*. Fuckin' grease monkeys." He shook his head. "We are in low times, indeed."

I slipped the cube into my pocket. "Techie," I said, squinting around. The square, I noted, was emptying out, people leaving in their clumps, twisting their heads around to stare back at us. I wasn't worried; usually when places emptied out like this it was a warning, the hairs on the back of my neck rising up in alarm. This time it was just Mickey, I was sure. He was just the worst thing that had ever happened to these poor people.

I cleared my throat. "So, low security, if any. But tricky. You can get me my own technical advisor?"

He snorted. "Avery, you got bigger problems. This one is hot, and you're gonna have competition."

I frowned. "I've worked jobs against other Gunners before, Michaleen," I said, shrugging. "It's an easy problem to get past. Who's it gonna be?"

He turned and stepped past me, patting me on the shoulder. "Everyone."

VIII

I WILL BE IRRITATED. YOU WILL ALL BE DEAD

"We're being boarded."

I glanced up from the reader screen; Mara's plain, round face was just a foot or so away. She had warned me that she'd set the anti-frag perimeter of my remote to three inches—though she'd included the Poet in the speech, which made me wonder if I was the only recent army recruit suddenly working for Michaleen. Three inches. Enough to make a physical assault problematic, but not enough to stop me from shooting her, if I had a gun. Which I didn't.

She looked out the cloudy window of our compartment, the sun making her red hair look brittle and fake. She wasn't bad looking, I thought. No beauty, but young and tall. But her face was blank and her skin rough, her nails short and her hands covered with tiny spider scars.

Next to me, the Poet's hip pressed against mine. He was snoring, his head back against the metal seat back, his eyes hidden behind his mirrored glasses. Every few minutes his hands twitched like he was strangling something in his sleep.

"Where are we?" I asked, my voice rough and phlegmy.

"Maybe outside Antwerp," she said without looking at me.

I squinted out the window, my augmented eyes instantly adjusting. I'd heard of Antwerp, and I knew it was vaguely on the way to Brussels, our ultimate destination. I felt the same; the idea that I'd been wired up seemed impossible, as if I should feel the wires pinching my ribs and the cables crowding my throat. The train had stopped in the middle of a forest, or what had once been a forest. As many trees were cracked and on the ground, charred black and rotting, as were still standing, and huge scoops of earth had been carved out of the embankment here and there where shells had exploded. A small crowd of troops stood almost directly outside our window, their uniforms dingy and torn, their shredders bright and polished. One short little woman with a single, angry eyebrow had two dark pips on her shoulder, and she sent the others scurrying with silent looks.

"For us?" I asked. We had boarded without weapons on Mara's advice. Against twenty-five soldiers, we had fists and shoes and whatever else we could throw at them, unless the Poet could manage to annoy them to death, which I thought possible.

She shook her head. "No, no, not for us." She sighed and shifted her weight in the seat. Mara was always fidgeting, always stretching her long limbs like they pained her. I filed it away for future reference if we ever got into a scrape; being able to stay still for at least a few minutes was an important skill. "Standard inspection." She looked at me, her eyes green and perfectly white. "That's why we came on naked, Mr. Cates."

I nodded; I didn't like having no weapons, but I accepted her logic. I didn't know if I could trust this Taker, this kid who'd probably just gotten her boobs the year before, but it made enough sense, especially since nothing in the fucking world made any goddamn sense anymore. I was on a fucking *train*. We were comparatively rich, so we'd managed to acquire a small private cabin—private in the sense that we were not smashed in with fifteen or twenty people, like just about everyone else. Standing room only, no toilets, no restaurant, and a sixteen-hour trip not counting the endless delays. In a hover, while sipping something nice and maybe getting some sleep, it was a half-hour flight. I was on a *train*. I kept wondering at it. I'd been on trains before—being shipped to Chengara Penitentiary like a side of beef—but those had been fast, and sleek. This was a bloated tube trundling along at a fast walk, smelled like garbage and smoke, and hit gaps in the tracks every few miles that stopped us cold while the crew scrambled out to fix the problem, which sometimes took hours.

Michaleen had said that getting a hover clearance when you were paying freight for a colonel in the SFNA was one thing; getting clearance to fly over battlefields for private business was fucking fantasy. So, the train. I'd traveled worse ways.

I looked back at the screen in my hands. Our mark was named Alf Londholm and his photo made him exactly like every other Techie I'd ever seen: skinny, squinty, and with a puzzled expression I'd come to associate with them as a class. His hair was black and plastered against his skull, drooping over his left eye like a scar. He was twenty-three years old and prior to the civil war had been a technical associate with the Joint Council, working with one of the undersecretaries in a support role. No one had suspected a genius in their midst; his performance reports—which Michaleen had acquired somehow—were mediocre and unenthused.

Just prior to the war, he'd been terminated from employment and his name had been handed over to the SSF for detention and interrogation. He'd never been arrested.

Six months later, while the army's tanks were rolling into Belgrade, he'd appeared in Hong Kong, where he'd somehow arranged a meeting with several rich and extralegal personages who viewed a single presentation and proceeded to shower Londholm with yen and resources, including a lot of muscle, and Londholm had been set up in Hong Kong ever since, working. There was nothing in the report about *what*, exactly, he'd been working on. Recently, something had gone wrong and his protection had dried up, his funding vanished, and his lab disappeared—and a bounty was placed on his head, with one stipulation: A complete body had to be presented in order to collect. No parts, no damage. Pristine except for the mortal wounds, the fewer the better.

This last requirement had narrowed down the talent capable of taking on the job, but probably hadn't affected the number of complete assholes who would step up and try anyway.

I glanced to my left at the Poet.

I puzzled over the report. Big money, sure, even in these days, but Michaleen had money—shit, in the middle of a civil war, he had a major city under his heel. The legendary Cainnic Orel didn't scramble after yen. It didn't make sense that he'd come halfway around the System—the world—to buy me out from the army just to round out a team. Cainnic Orel, the legend, didn't do things this half assed. Not for *yen*.

I turned my eyes back to Mara as shouts and ominous banging noises filtered into the cabin from the corridor. "Where's Belling?"

Her eyes leaped to me instantly. "Wallace is working another angle."

I held her eyes for a moment. A first-name basis. A strange feeling stole over me, like I'd met her before, held this gaze before. For a second my HUD tightened up again, everything getting suddenly and perceptively clearer, status bars quickly flaring into life and spiking, like I was about to scrap with this kid. I couldn't know her.

Then it flicked off, everything settling down. "Okay," I said, and the door to our cabin banged inward, old varnished wood splintering into our laps. The narrow doorway was crowded with dingy white uniforms, with Little Mother I'd seen through the window in front.

"Thumbs, or we cut them off," she screeched, her whole little body vibrating with the volume. Her accent was pure New York; I'd heard it a million times, in better days. "On your fucking *feet* and thumbs out or we shove 'em up your asses."

We all hesitated, of course. We knew how this was going to play out: We were going to stand up, present our thumbs like obedient citizens, and eat the shit sandwich. But we didn't have to be *enthusiastic* about it. It was like being in Pickering's during a raid, the good old days, except I wasn't drunk and Kev Gatz wasn't snickering next to me, making ridiculous stoned jokes. As I stared at her, the little box bloomed in my vision again.

ANGELINA R. ROCCAFORTE, LIEUTENANT (2), SECURITY INFANTRY.

Little Mother Roccaforte's eyes were bugged out and watery, and they jumped around the cabin in jerky, outraged leaps. I figured the army wasn't assigning its top rank to train inspections. I thought of myself and all the rest of Englewood being prepped for fucking urban assault; how fucking terrible did you have to be to get *train* duty?

She suddenly stared hard at me, and I pictured one of those little boxes blooming in her own HUD: *Avery Cates, Shitkicker, Deserter.*

"I said *on your feet!*" she screeched, and this time we all stood up, slowly, slouchingly. One by one we held out our hands, and with a curt nod Little Mother sent one of her grunts, a tall black kid whose knees were too high up on his legs, into the cabin with a small DNA scanner. At the same time, one of the other uniforms began working a larger handheld. The skinny guy waved the scanner at each of us in turn like he was afraid we'd snatch it from him. I came up green. The Poet and Mara got a yellow.

"Not in d-d-database," the skinny one said like the word had been taught to him recently, and at great cost.

Little Mother nodded, still staring at me. "And *you* are—"

"I have a safe passage from General Icahn," Mara said immediately. "If I may reach for it?"

I blinked. I'd never heard of Icahn, but if Michaleen was drawing that kind of water, I wondered again why in the fuck my card had been pulled for this.

Little Mother had transformed at the name Icahn, suddenly getting quiet. After a moment, she nodded, and Mara reached into her jacket and produced a data cube, which she tossed at the short officer, who caught it with a lightning move that reminded me that even the shitheel of the SFNA had some serious tech stuffed inside their skins. She didn't even glance at it, just held it in her hand for a moment and then nodded, tossing it back. Mara snatched it from the air with equal ferocity, dropping it into her cleavage with flair.

"They're clear. Weapons?"

The soldier in the corridor looked up from his handheld. "Clear."

Little Mother nodded, and the whole lot of them walked off without another word, leaving us alone in the suddenly spacious-seeming cabin, the door swinging weakly from one hinge. In the hall outside, a crowd of people three deep was crushed up against the far wall, miserable and sweaty. I stared back at them for a second or two, feeling that static electricity that preceded mob action, but just as I was convinced we were about to be rushed, the Poet stepped into the doorway, leaned against the broken hinges, and studied his nails.

"Anyone enters," he said, "I will be irritated. You will all be dead."

He waited a beat, still making a show of looking at his own hand, the tats dancing and spinning on his neck, and then he turned and sat down again. I found myself looking at a filthy little kid, his eyes the only white part of him, clutched to the legs of a woman not much taller than him and looking dirtier, which didn't seem possible. After a moment, I stepped forward, causing a sudden rustle to sweep through the crowd, and pushed the door back into place, trusting to friction to hold it shut. I glanced at my feet. It didn't take much to threaten fucking civilians. It didn't take much to push around people who'd never held a gun or killed for survival. That was easy. And cheap.

I didn't look at the Poet as I took my own seat. Time wasn't right, but I was keeping an invoice for him, and I planned to collect on it someday.

More shrill shouting from Little Mother down the corridor. I looked at Mara again. "Why Brussels?" I asked. I felt good. I'd *been* feeling good. Aside from the new suit, my second in two days—this one blessedly free of piss smell—I looked like the same broken-down bastard, my hairline a little higher, my nose a little more crooked. Inside, I felt fucking fifteen again. My leg still ached, but it was a distant, impersonal thing that I could easily ignore. I felt light and sharp, relaxed but energetic, like I could go to sleep in an instant or stick to the walls, whatever the next moment required.

She had closed her eyes and feigned sleep. "The eternals, Mr. Cates," she said without opening her eyes. "Weapons and information. You can't just hit the nets and ask questions—either the army or the cops are gonna pick up your feed and backtrace you. Keyword recognition—I hear they even have a box that analyzes keystroke patterns and gives 'em a good shot at guessin' who you *are* just based on what you type into a terminal." She shrugged. "So, we go to a friend of mine."

I grinned. "You're pretty useful, for a Taker."

"It's a job requirin' multiple talents, Mr. Avery." She opened one eye. "I wouldn'a be expectin' a fucking gunmonkey to understand the complexities." She sighed and shut her eye. "You can't shoot information."

"We need less talking," the Poet suddenly said, "and a lot more listening. Tell me what you hear."

Mara's eyes opened again, and we looked at each other for a long moment.

"I hear nothing," Mara said.

The silence was perfect. My HUD snapped into bright clarity and I was on my feet. The Poet was smiling, nodding at me.

"Yes," he said.

IX

THE DOOR CAME, AND THE DOOR WASN'T HAPPY

For a second, the silence vibrated inside me, coming up from the floor and burring into my legs. Five hundred desperate bastards squeezed in like cargo, two dozen pissed-off soldiers doing fucking humiliating train duty, and none of them making a noise. I looked at Mara and heard Michaleen's voice in my head: *everyone*.

"Someone crashing the party?" I whispered.

She shrugged her whole body and her eyebrows and then nodded her head a little. She looked like she would close her eyes and take a nap. Movement behind me made me spin, but it was just the Poet, jacket off, flexing his huge arms, twisting his torso this way and that.

"Anyone outside?" I asked, staring in wonder at the Poet, muscles rippling under taut, oily-looking flesh. It was fascinating, like snakes living inside him, maggots squirming to get out—like the cells were eager to start throttling people. I imagined myself in a fistfight with the Poet, and augments or not, it wasn't pretty for me.

"Clear," Mara said. "Why—"

I spun back and stepped to the window, throwing it open as far as it would go, which wasn't too far. I studied it for a second, cocking my head, and then turned halfway, bent my arm, and smashed the window out with my elbow. I felt wonderful. My augments were smoothly managing my adrenaline, endorphins, blood oxygen—everything. It felt good to be able to do the work again I'd always done.

"Give me some room to work," I said to Mara as I levered myself backward out through the opening. I leaned out and held onto the rough corrugated exterior of the train. The wind tore at me as I looked around; the grassy embankment was empty. To my right was a rusty metal ladder attached to the car. Taking hold of a rung, I pulled myself up and out easily, bracing for the ancient metal to give way and send me sprawling to the ground.

All the bars in my HUD were bright green, pulsing with my heartbeat, which remained slow and steady, unconcerned.

I took a deep breath and pulled myself up, crawling on top of the car while my blood oxygen levels scrolled past in an unobtrusive gray font. I hoped someone got an award for that font; it was a work of fucking genius. Thinking about the millions of little details that went into shit like my hand-me-down augments, I flopped over onto my back and stared up at the sky, blue and white and gray, and then rolled onto my knees and pushed myself up onto my feet, facing back toward the rear of the car where the soldiers had been headed. Whatever had shut the train down had come from that direction, and the best tactic I could come up with was to get behind it.

I stepped carefully, taking it slow—which was hard. I wanted to run. I wanted to sprint through everything and just kick everything's ass. When I reached the back end of the car, I got down on my belly and slipped my head over the edge and quickly scanned the link between us and the last car of the train. No one in sight, and no sound except the wind, the whole world just dead and empty. I paused; you had to know your space, where people would come at you, where your exits were. I pushed back up onto my feet and leaped over the gap between the cars, a sudden feeling of exhilaration shooting through me and making my status bars flash.

I landed softly on the next car and trotted down to the butt end of the train, dropping back onto my belly for a quick peek over the edge. I waited a few heartbeats and then swung myself over the edge, letting myself down slowly until I was a few inches from the small platform just outside the door of the car. Dropping the last few inches, I crouched down and peered in, my eyes adjusting instantly to the light difference.

The car was crowded with people. Most of them were in narrow, cramped bunks nailed up against the walls of the car, but some were seated in the aisle, on top of each other, bundles and boxes piled up between them, on top of themselves, everywhere.

They were all perfectly still, staring. I counted to ten, watching, and when no one had so much as blinked, I twisted the latch on the door slowly, grimacing, and eased it open, the metal-on-metal grinding sounding loud and disastrous to my ears as it eased into its pocket. I kept low, duckwalking into the car, but no one even glanced at me, their eyes fixed on some distant invisible object, their lips slack. *Pusher*, I thought to myself. Fucking Psionic freaks, making you dance from across the room just by thinking hard at you. I'd known way too many of them, and a knot of sour anxiety bloomed in my belly.

As I slowly crabbed my way forward, I cast my eyes around, looking for anything that could be a weapon. Spotting a decent-sized walking cane clutched in the slack hand of one of the passengers, I pulled it from his grasp and weighed it briefly in my hands. The balance sucked, but it had decent weight to it and felt like good, solid, synthetic wood. It would cave in a skull as well as anything.

At the forward door, I crouched down and peered through the cloudy glass, ducking down in sudden shock; the five soldiers, including Little Mother, were all standing just outside the next car. I counted three and eased up again, getting a better look: They were frozen as well, locked in postures that looked surprised and awkward, their weight on their back feet. I eased the door open just enough to slip past, easing it back into place while staying as low as possible, my legs starting to burn a little with the effort. The soldiers remained perfectly still. I turned my head and found Little Mother's sidearm an inch from my nose, snug in its white holster. Instead of the standard-issue military sidearms that were linked to the soldier's augments, refusing to fire for anyone else, this was a skinny-looking monster I'd never encountered before, superficially resembling the Roon 87 but obviously cheaper, with a longer barrel. I reached up and lifted it carefully from the holster, brought it down into my own gravity, and checked the chamber.

I dropped the clip into my hand and glanced at it: full and plump, thirty-two shots.

"You're a naughty one," I whispered as I pushed the clip back in until it clicked home. "Swapping for a non-regulation piece, you little minx." I ran my eyes over Little Mother one last time, wondering where she might hide extra clips. I didn't see anything obvious and I didn't have time to do a proper search. I pushed through the soldiers and inched myself up onto the balls of my feet, squinting into our car.

There were no cots in this one, purely semiprivate berths with the corridor running between the tiny rooms, the crowd packed tightly against the wall across from the berths. Three women were grouped outside our door, each wearing a long black coat, their uniformly dark hair tied up in tight buns sitting on their heads like crabs. Cocking the hammer with my palm, slowly, I reached up and unlatched the door. Sliding it open just far enough, I carefully shouldered my way through it. Once inside the car, I raised the gun and paused, taking a deep breath, steadying myself. I needed surprise; the moment the Pusher became aware of me, it was over.

I started the duckwalk again.

They were listening at the door, whispering. The whispers were formless, wordless, just a hissing noise drifting back toward me, a buzzing in the air. I moved the gun as I walked, ticking it from one to the other, getting a feel for the distances and the speed. Halfway to them, I stopped, steadied myself, and took a bead on them. They were standing in a close group—one with her ear almost comically pressed against our broken door, one off slightly to her side, and one behind them, leaning in toward them. I settled on the one in the rear; when she dropped, she'd fall into the other two, slowing them down.

The door exploded outward, knocking all three to the floor in a sudden outburst of noise. The Poet, shirtless and barefoot, leaped into the hallway, the fake, sentient muscles of his arms and chest writhing as he took a moment to preen, flexing the tree trunks he called biceps and howling.

"You gonna creep out here all fucking—"

"Shut up," I whispered to myself, for my own amusement. "You're about to go for a ride."

When he shot up into the air, I just smiled. When he somehow snaked an arm out and sank his fingers into the hair of one of them, taking her with him to the ceiling of the corridor, I blinked in surprise. For a moment, they were a blur of limbs up above, screeching and kicking. Putting the gun on them, I closed one eye and thought about letting both Mara and this idiot go, just letting the Spooks crush their skulls with invisible fists and walking away.

I took a deep breath. I couldn't do it. Even ignoring the remote and the fact that I'd drop dead if I got too far away from Mara, even a turd like the Poet was a brother in arms. Even Mara—we were all making our way and if I was on Michaleen's hook, they were too, probably. I didn't think Mickey inspired a lot of affection and loyalty.

I opened my eye and took in the scene again, trying to judge which one was the Pusher. The Telekinetics were tough, throwing you around like a puppet and making heavy things slam into you, but they could be dealt with. A fucking Pusher could have you doing dance moves with a fucking glance.

It wasn't the one currently getting to know the Poet
better than she—or anyone—would have wanted up at
the ceiling; she would have had him barking on the floor
in a flash. I gave a second to the other two. One stared up
at the ceiling intently. The other stared into the cabin, a
still-life. Ticking the gun over, I took a bead on that one
and squeezed the trigger. The cheap auto bucked in my
hand like I'd kicked a dog, and the Spook's head jerked
forward and left, splattering the wall red, with flecks of
yellow.

The second triplet whipped her head down, big round
black eyes on me like magnets, and then I rocketed backward, my feet lifting off the floor, my arms dangling in
front of me, everything shrinking.

I thought, *Shit, here comes the door.*

The door came, and the door wasn't happy. I managed
to close my eyes just before impact, which was good, seeing as I didn't want to spend the rest of my life searching
for them on my hands and knees.

I snapped awake with a jolt—one second, darkness; the
next, my HUD flaring to life, my chest heaving with sudden anxiety, conscious. My status bars flared emerald—
except for one in the middle of the pack that had yellowed
a little—and then dimmed. A faint sense that something
was wrong, something out of place, licked at the edges of
my thoughts without forming into anything solid. I turned
my head and a sharp pain stabbed up my neck, making
me wince. I blinked, looking down the corridor. The Poet
was struggling with one of the triplets, his huge hands
clamped murderously around her neck, his own eyes

bulging from a face far too dark with blood—even though the woman hung in his grasp like a rag doll, her eyes were locked on him, choking him right back. They were pasted up against the wall like they'd been glued there. I squinted, trying to see if there was anyone else, another Spook doing the heavy lifting, but there was no one. Something was flashing in my HUD, a tiny dot, and as I concentrated, it swelled up, firming into a gyroscope that was slanted dramatically off-kilter. The wall had become the floor; I was sitting on the pocket door between cars. I could hear, dimly, screaming below me, and I pictured all those frozen people, suddenly awake again, smashed in together with gravity plucking at them.

Wincing again, I turned my head until I could squint out the cloudy plastic window. My stomach lurched as the world reset itself, the ground rolling some ten or fifteen feet beneath us, the train car at a crazy angle, still connected to the rest of the train, the other cars hanging on like tin sausages. I was suddenly aware of a groaning metallic sound, continuous and irritating.

On the ground, near the tracks, a man stared up at me.

He was old, with thick gray hair hanging down to his shoulders, but his face had the same familiar roundness to it—a Spook. And since he was staring up at me while the whole fucking train was floating into the air, I had the sudden brilliant intuition that he was a Telekinetic, and the most powerful fucking Tele-K I'd ever imagined. *The whole fucking train.*

I was sweating. The screams below just went on and on, like animals howling.

I rubbed my hands on my coat and looked down at myself; my stolen gun was in my lap, held in place by gravity. I grabbed it and twisted my head around again to look out at the freak below. I had no shot. Even if I could angle my arm, the glass was thick enough to queer me, and if the Spook was good enough to get the whole train in the air, chances were one shot was all I was going to get.

I turned my head again and looked at the door's latch. Tightening my grip on the gun, I took a deep breath, reached up behind me, and yanked.

The door rolled into its pocket with a mean-spirited suddenness, and I dropped down onto the next car, catching my leg on the coupling as I fell, doing a half spin and landing awkwardly. I spent a second making sure I wasn't sliding, and then I rolled to the edge, hooking one foot into the coupling and swinging my arm around. I put the gun on him, reminded myself of the way the piece of shit barked, and braced for impact.

Just as I squeezed the trigger, the motherfucker looked right at me and the train lurched under me. I lifted up for a second and slammed down, rattling my teeth and knocking the gun from my hand. Before I could contemplate the ways in which this train hated me, I felt something like gravity grabbing onto me with invisible wet fingers and trying to pull me off the train. My foot was lodged pretty firmly in the coupling; I felt my leg being stretched as I snagged. Blood rushing to my face, I craned my head up to look down at the Spook, who stared up at me without expression. The screams and the metal grinding had blended together into one formless blast of noise, and a rushing howl in my own ears joined it as the little status bars in my eyes started to wither into yellow.

Behind him, creeping down the embankment, was Mara.

She looked tiny—tall but thin, her limbs too insub-
stantial to be any threat. She looked rough—red hair a
mess, a deep scratch across her forehead, her nifty leather
pants torn across one thigh—and she had a long, black
stick in one hand, one of those collapsible beat-downs that
telescoped from something you could hide in one palm.
How she'd gotten off the train and circled around was a
mystery, but I tabled that thought, shifting my eyes to the
cold, rocky ground below me. I had a sudden vision of my
future. It involved the ground, gravity, and sixty tons of
fucking train right behind me.

I looked back up in time to see her plant herself behind
the old Spook and rear back. My heart pounded into overdrive and the little bar that represented my adrenaline levels skyrocketed, and then everything suddenly...slowed
down.

I watched Mara raise her baton as if she were enveloped
in syrup, her face contorted in a mask of red violence that
ruined the delicate lines of her unpretty face, the baton
rising so slowly I had time to look at the old man's face in
detail: unlined, red skin, with hideous eyes that were dark
pools of shadow surrounded by yellow-black bags, swollen and unhealthy looking. His mouth hung open slightly,
revealing teeth that looked likely to be even worse than
his eyes. I stopped looking at him, preferring Mara's ric-
tus of rage to the Spook's grooming. She'd only managed
to get the baton cocked behind her by then.

My HUD had turned a shade of pink, like a haze had
been smeared over everything.

Before I could think too hard about all of it, the gentle
pulling sensation disappeared, leaving me limp against
the warm metal of the train. The old Spook spun with

surprising agility to face Mara, his hands flying up between them, but she took the opportunity to angle the baton and catch him on the chin with an upstroke, sending him spinning backward, feet off the ground, in a slow-motion ballet.

Beneath me, the train jerked and for the longest moment I'd ever experienced, it seemed to float in the air, my stomach flipping over. When we started to fall, it was beautiful: slow and graceful, a sudden wind around me, my body lifting off the train slightly, the ground drifting up like a dream. A stream of numbers flashed across my vision, tiny and fast, obviously not meant for me, really; a dump for the field technician who would retrieve my corpse, I supposed, a record of how I went down to make sure it hadn't been any kind of technological malfunction.

Gripping the edge of the coupling with my hands, I pulled my feet under myself, crouching on the side of the train as it rolled slowly toward the ground, my own heartbeat a distant, mournful drum, and when the ground was still a few feet away I launched myself horizontally, my HUD suddenly streaming calculations concerning wind speed, inertia, mass, and velocity I ignored. It was easy, like I had all the time in the world. I planned on a dramatic tuck and roll, to come up like an acrobat smoking a cigarette and impressing the only lady in view. Instead, I hit the ground like a bag of shit, scraping some of myself off on the rough ground, and time snapped back to normal speed as I dissolved into a rough, unbalanced roll, bars and numbers flashing across my vision in jagged little spurts until an obliging rotten log on the embankment stopped me.

I stared up at the clouds above, feeling and hearing

the impact of the train as it smashed back into the earth. Half the little bars in my HUD had gone an alarming shade of pus yellow, and a mean-spirited adrenaline dump was keeping me conscious despite my intense unhappiness about it. And then Mara's face, back to its serene, flat-nosed expressionlessness, floated above me, looking down at me like I was a bug tied to a pin, crawling around endlessly.

"You still alive, then?" she said.

I blinked and moved my dried-up tongue around. "If you call this living," I croaked, and with a flash in my eyes I passed out.

X

A LITTLE LOVE AFFAIR MADE UP OF LONGING GAZES AND UNREQUITED VIOLENCE

I studied Mara's face. Lit by the fire, she was almost beautiful—almost. I tried to imagine her smiling, as an experiment to see if that would push her over the edge, but I couldn't manage it.

"So, are we gonna talk about this?"

The Poet danced into view behind her, holding a solar cell up over his head, trying to find a final ray of sunlight to get a little extra juice. We hadn't been able to get in touch with anyone since the attack, and none of us wanted to hoof it through the wilderness. Mara didn't seem worried and had said arrangements had been made, though she'd declined to explain further, which was becoming her trademark. If we'd been able to just use straight, aboveboard nets we'd have been fine, but if you used the mainstream networks, you popped up on a dozen watch lists and sooner or later got a visit from someone you didn't want to see.

He looked fucking ridiculous, but I replayed the scene of him snatching one of the Weird Triplets as he was smashed up against the roof of the train car, and gave him a little more slack. The kid was a freak, but he could kill.

Mara could kill too. The old Tele-K had vanished, she said, after the dust had settled, but I'd seen her work him and was pretty sure he would have been dead if she'd had anything better than a lightweight stick to work with.

"Talk about what?" she asked, settling herself on the damp ground in stages, like she didn't know what to do with her limbs.

I smiled. "You've got that Stupid Disease, huh?" Leaning forward, I plucked up a stick from the ground and thrust it into the fire. "I'm a Carrier—everyone I meet comes down with it. That's okay. I've got therapy for that. For starters, we've been on this job for what—two days? And already we've got major static."

I glanced through the darkness at the shadowed hulk of the derailed train, lit up by dozens of small lights. The other passengers had elected to use the train as shelter, which made sense, except for the fact that just a few hours ago it had been bait for murderous psionics, which was why we were out in the fucking bush freezing our asses off.

"It's a high-profile job," she said, shrugging as I put my eyes back on her. "High-profile jobs get static. That's why you're *here*. Because you c'n handle the static."

"That's just it. The little man, he tracks me down, pays me out of the army, flies me all the way over here for this—we don't have competition, babe. We've got people *coming at* us." I leaned back again and wiped my hands on my filthy coat—I'd managed to be clean and neat for about five minutes, which was a new land record for me.

"So, you want me to believe Michaleen Garda—Canny Orel—is going at this blind?"

We stared at each other over the fire again. The Poet dropped to the ground next to Mara, letting out a long stream of creative curse words. "We are abandoned." He sighed, arranging himself in a ludicrous pose of idleness, stretched out on his side, elbow bent, head resting on one palm as the fire reflected in his ridiculous sunglasses, which he still had on as if there was sun glare only his sensitive eyes could detect. "The modern world has moved on—we're in a dead zone."

He always sounded like he was singing, somehow, when he spoke, and it got on my nerves. "Maybe you should go try again," I suggested.

He oriented his shades on me and smiled, and with a jerk of his free arm he sent the solar cell flying toward me. I twitched, but stopped myself, and let it sail over me with a mask of something approaching calm. Then we had a little love affair made up of longing gazes and unrequited violence. I was beginning to warm up to the Poet, stupid name and all. If we ever got a chance to beat the shit out of each other, I'd probably have to propose.

"If he's boring you," the Poet said, shattering our moment and turning to beam those blank glass eyes on Mara, "I am more interesting. And close to your *age*."

Mara's expression of almost unrelieved contempt would have had me crawling into a bottle, but the Poet just grinned into the maelstrom and flexed his biceps a little, as if certain of their hypnotizing powers. She gave him the withering stare for a few seconds, and then cocked her head. "Where you gettin' the Spooks tatted, boyo?"

"The back of my head," he said immediately, giving me

the creepy feeling he planned where he was going to ink you before he actually planned on how he was going to *kill* you. A pragmatist. "Any Spook tries to sneak up, they see what awaits." He capped this off with a little superstar grin, and I thought, with an echo of disbelief rattling in my head, *This bastard thinks he can bag her.*

Of course he does, the ghost of Dick Marin suddenly whispered. *You're the only Gunner I ever met who didn't think the fucking sun set on his ass, Avery.*

I startled. The ghosts in my head had been quiet for so long I'd almost forgotten them.

Mara turned to face me without a word for the Poet. She flicked her eyes at him and then back at me. "What're you circling around to, Mr. Cates?"

I had my answer ready. "Why are Spooks hot on our trail? What did Alf Londholm do to get the whole god-damn world hepped up about him?"

She shrugged. "The Psionics weren't here for us. As for Londholm—if—if Mr. Garda chose not to tell you, maybe I should take that as a guideline to follow."

"Londholm's a tinker," the Poet suddenly said, stretching his whole body out with a grunt, his massive arms reaching behind his head as he rolled in the dirt. "Made himself the God Augment. Now he's a dead man."

I kept my eyes on Mara. Unpretty as she was, she was better looking than the Poet. "What the fuck is a God Augment?"

"Where you been hiding?" The Poet laughed, rolling onto his back and folding his arms behind his head. "I forgot: in the suburbs. Land that time forgot."

Mara pursed her lips. "The so-called God Augment, Mr. Cates, is an implantable piece o' neurotechnology that stimulates a portion of the brain now known to be associated with Psionic abilities." She stood up and stretched her thin, toned body, shadows making her face hard and demonic. "Once installed, someone who previously did not have any such abilities suddenly has them *all*—Tele-K, Push, limited precognition."

"Plus a few new ones," the Poet said happily, eyeing her body up and down like he was in the tug joints down on Bowery. "Ones we don't have names for yet. Scary magic stuff."

Mara frowned in his direction for a long moment, shaking her head slightly. "What's *wrong* with you?" she said quietly, turning to me. "So, if you're tired of bein' tossed about by the Spooks, you can pay Mr. Londholm to cut you open and turn you on, eh? Sure, sure. Half the fucking world is trying to buy it from him." She shrugged. "The other half hired us to kill him before he can sell it."

I could hear, in the distance, a rumbling sound that put my nerves on alert. I pushed up onto my feet, thinking about the implications of something like that. I'd met only a few Spooks in my time, and only had to go up against them briefly. The idea of half the world suddenly gearing up to make me think I was a butterfly didn't sound appealing.

"And that's why half the world's comin' at us," she added, turning and taking a few steps away from the fire. "All right? Any more questions?"

"Has he built a prototype? Done any tests on humans?"

She closed her eyes for a moment, and I had a sense of a woman gathering the frayed ends of her patience. My hands curled into fists and my HUD suddenly sharpened and brightened up. If Mara was going to try and teach me to shut up, she was going to find out why I hadn't learned a goddamn thing my whole life.

Instead, she opened her eyes. "All right, Avery. I can see I won't have any peace until we have our conversation." The rumbling noise had resolved into the throb of an engine. She didn't seem concerned, although I somehow sensed the Poet rising from his position to stand behind us, turning my head to find him with his arms up like he was spoiling for a fight, his head moving as he literally sniffed the wind.

"He built three working units," Mara said, and I turned back to her, feeling grit in my boots and on my hands, the sandy, cold dirt getting into everything. "And implanted two. To demonstrate viability, you see. Both subjects are now dead, their units destroyed. His funding, lab, and safety have disappeared; he has been relying on paid mercenaries for survival, and from what we understand, his cash is running out." I realized with a start that I could see her face a little better, and I spun to look along her sight line, finding a pair of bright lights approaching, bouncing crazily up and down as they did.

I looked back at Mara. She was obviously not surprised at this, and a sour feeling of irritation spread in my belly. It was bad enough I'd been sucked into this by Michaleen, bad enough to be on the Rail again, pushed along by the hateful cosmos. It was something else to have a goddamn teenaged girl pulling my strings along the way. "How'd you call for transport?" I asked, gesturing at the approaching headlights. "Hamhocks back there danced around for half an hour trying to get a signal."

She smiled without looking at me. "You think Mickey just lets us wander out here *unsupervised*? Count on it, Avery—the Little Man's eye is on us always, like a fucking guardin' angel." Her eyes slid in my direction slyly. "I'd like to see you run, boyo, I really would. Just to see the fuckin' hand o' *god* reach down and flick you away."

I clenched my teeth. Mara, I decided, was my problem, not the Poet. The Poet and I were practically best friends by comparison. Mara was Michaleen's girl.

With a belch of acrid pollution, a vehicle shimmied from the darkness, almost rolling itself as it crested a ridge, slamming down and roaring toward us. It looked gerrymandered, odds and ends fused together through a combination of rough black welds and old-fashioned machine screws. It was a big square hunk of metal with four swollen rubber wheels, bouncing along erratically, black smoke pouring out of the rear. It skidded to a halt just a few feet away from us and sat there, humming and vibrating like a living thing.

"Come on," Mara said, walking toward it. "We got work to do."

I stood my ground. "Hey!"

She paused and then slowly turned to look at me. Her face was blank. The Poet stepped past me, shoulder nudging me as he did so. I had a quick vision of grabbing one of his skinny legs and giving it a savage yank, but resisted.

"What, you goddamn rash on my ass?" Mara demanded, putting her hands on her leather hips and pushing her non-existent tits at me.

"You said the Spooks weren't after us," I said. "What the fuck did *that* mean?"

Avery's grown attentive, I heard Marin whisper at me.

Mara sighed, pursing her lips. "They weren't," she said, turning again and stepping around to the front passenger's door and climbing halfway into the transport. "They were almost certainly here specifically for *you*."

XI

MUCH RATHER HE DIES FOR *ME*

"They like to call themselves Angels," Mara shouted over the murderous bouncing of the vehicle. "Psionics. Not under anyone's control, untrained, wild."

I thought of Kev Gatz, who'd come close to killing the world not too long ago—he'd been a Psionic, too, a Pusher. "Okay," I shouted back, "before my kidneys start to bleed, what the fuck do free-range Spooks want with me?"

The ride was not smooth in the four-wheeler, tumbling over the broken and occasionally bombed-out countryside. Sometimes we were almost vertical, scaling an impossible crater wall and apparently trusting to momentum to get us over the lip, and sometimes we were on two of the wheels, wobbling alarmingly for a few seconds until we crashed back down onto the chassis. I'd peered into the cockpit when I'd first climbed in behind the Poet—who'd been a few days without a bath now—and I wasn't sure yet if I should be alarmed or relieved at the fact that the vehicle was completely automatic.

She didn't look at me. "You've been convicted, *in absentia*, boyo, of being a fucking danger to humanity as a whole. *Angels* ain't a *metaphor* for them, follow? They think they're the next step in human evolution. They think they're here to set things right. Part o' that is gettin' rid of the tyranny of evil men, see? So you're on a list." She turned and winked. "Our boss is on the list, too."

I considered a band of Psionics bent on tearing me into small pieces. It didn't feel appreciably different than my every day. As I considered it, we took a rock under one wheel and the whole cab went bouncing. The Poet hit his round, shaved head on the roof and howled in protest.

"Sorry," Mara shouted back over her shoulder from the front. "We didn't have time to arrange nothin' fancy."

We hit another huge bump that sent the whole god-damn thing into the air, and a second later we slammed back down to the ground. I'd learned the hard way to clench my mouth shut whenever this happened. Traveling by train was bad enough, but this was fucking ridiculous. When I'd been a kid, the only hovers I ever saw the inside of were System Pig bricks, taking me to various beatings around New York. Then I'd had a brief taste of the good life. The good life was better. Flying in hovers everywhere was better. My offices in the Pennsylvania in Manhattan seemed like another man's life, so long ago it looped back and became my fucking future. I'd been rich. I'd had people on salary. I'd been independent for the last time in my life, doing what I wanted.

I thought of Wa Belling, who'd betrayed me and put my feet on this road, strapped me into the Rail. I thought maybe I hadn't been giving Wa the proper attention over the last few years.

The Poet and I were crammed into the backseat of the vehicle ass to ass. He'd helpfully put his huge arm around my neck to make some room, giving me an intimate view of his swampy armpit. I was hungry, my stomach clawing away at my ribs, and I felt dirty and unrested, although my HUD had gone green across the board again and I felt that still-alien sense of being limber and strong. I turned and stared at the Poet, putting my eyes on his ear and leaving them there, hoping he'd notice and look at me so I could twist his nose. I'd never wanted to twist someone's nose more.

The Poet turned his head finally and stared back at me from behind his huge mirrored glasses. He was unshaven and greasy looking.

"Do I remind you," he said slowly, "of someone you used to know? Or am I just pretty?"

"You remind me of a lot of people," I said with a smile. "It's a common type."

He pursed his lips and then reached up to his face, removing the glasses. His eyes were sunken and tired looking, a dull brown. They made him look a lot older than I'd guessed him to be. He didn't look at me; he looked down at my knees, squinting. "You do not know me. What I am capable of. The place I come from."

"Where do you come from?"

"City called Belgrade. It is not there anymore." He shrugged awkwardly. "This is not a loss. But it was my home. I knew every stone there, and now I'm an orphan."

I thought about that, fighting against an upswell of weird emotion. I knew what that was like, walking down a street and knowing something was wrong because a tiny detail was off, knowing where you could get whatever you needed because you knew everything there was to know about the city you lived in. It had been taken from me, too. Before I could start squirting tears like an old woman, I turned to watch the wilderness flash by at a terrifying speed.

"You getting paid for this job, Adrian?" I asked suddenly. "You with the Little Man?"

He snorted. "With the Little Man? Is anyone *with* that prick? I am owned by him."

A question I should have asked right away, from the beginning, instead of comparing balls like I was fifteen again. I turned back to him and leaned in, making the decision to throw caution to the wind. What was I being cautious about, exactly? I was a fucking biological prisoner, a puppet dancing. It seemed obvious that Mara was Mickey's girl and the Poet was just a dim bulb like me who'd gotten fetched up by the great Cainnic Orel, trading under the equally ridiculous name of Michaleen Garda— which meant that to feel really smart, I had to figure it was the other way around, and to be fucking *brilliant* it had to be *both of them*, playing me. That was okay. I'd been a fucking moron for so long I was getting used to it.

It all swirled back to the simple fact that if I was wrong and trusted the wrong person, I lost nothing. They'd laugh at me and press a button, and I'd sizzle like a beefsteak while they explained everything to me. So fucking what. That was how this was going to end anyway. Or with me dead.

"I'm not dying for Michaleen," I said in a low voice.

"Brother, me neither," he whispered back. "Much rather he dies for *me*." He slipped the glasses back on and turned a mild grin on me. "You get pressed as well?"

I nodded. "First Platoon, Shitkickers Division."

Looking ahead again, he nodded once, curtly. "All right."

I found myself waiting a few beats for him to say more, and then I looked out the window again. The world streamed by in jerky, sudden leaps, something to look at while I thought, trying to see a way to get out from under. I considered the situation: Michaleen had my remote, which he'd passed on to Mara, which meant she could knock me down anytime she wanted, fuck with me on a core level I had no defense against. Sitting in the tight, hot interior of the four-wheeler, my hands clenched into fists. A direct assault on Mara was useless; I couldn't do anything with the remote and assumed she had a backup unit as well. And none of it mattered, because without a gun or at least a nicely weighted knife, I couldn't get close enough to her to do anything without invoking the anti-frag mode of my augments. And even if I *could* kill her, the moment she flatlined I'd be dead, too, something going *boom* inside my head in protest.

With the Poet on my wing, though, there was a shot. Two of us. Neither of us could get close . . . but still, it was one more slim piece to work with.

I shifted my eyes to the Poet again. Assuming, I thought, that he was playing me straight.

Forty minutes later, the four-wheeler slowed to a crawl.

"This is out," Mara announced. "We can't drive up to the city. It's copland, an SSF stronghold, and they will be pretty fucking curious about this thing. So from here we walk."

The door to my left sighed open. The wind grabbed hold and snapped it wide in a blink, a howling world of dust tearing into the cabin and pushing me out. I stomped my sleeping legs on the hard, scrabbly soil and looked around; not too far off to the east were the jagged outlines of a large city. A half mile or so north of us was the remnant of an old road; I'd seen similar ones in Paris and elsewhere, old wide slabs of broken pavement and twisted metal, faded signs. This one had been pounded pretty hard in bombings, torn up into islands of serene whole road in an ocean of raw earth and twisted metal.

"All right," Mara said, pulling off the slim backpack she carried everywhere and placing it on the four-wheeler's hood while the thick black exhaust swirled around us. "N-tabs, ID cards, and a quick primer. Either of you speak French? Dutch?"

The Poet and I exchanged a quick glance, and then we both shrugged simultaneously. "Nope," I said. The fact that there was a language called Dutch was news to me.

"Good. Don't. Easiest way to get fucked with local bullshit in this burg is to be one or the other. This is still a big population center; the cops have had it in their tiny little fist all along, and held it against some serious work from the army, so there's been some stability. Comm lines with Moscow are still open, too, so the Prince of Fucking Darkness Marin can still get his way here, anytime he wants. Keep it in mind: lots of people, lots of cops. You can pick 'em out easier, though, 'cause they're all struttin' around in fucking *uniform*." She scowled. "Didn't even know the fucking Pigs *had* dress uniforms, but there you go. Step light."

She handed us each a shiny new ID card, stamped with

the familiar globe-and-stars of the System of Federated Nations. The hologram was a decent image of me, popping up when the card was held flat, my tiny face scowling at nothing in pale, transparent red. I squinted at the tiny name displayed beneath me.

"Hugo?" I said, glancing at her as she counted out N-tabs for us. "Do I fucking *look* like a Hugo Gonzalez?"

"Matches the ID print on your augments," she said immediately. "Just in case you get snagged by a deep scan."

"I am Tomas Pisk," the Poet said thoughtfully. "I knew someone named Pisk, once. Of course, he's dead now."

Mara tied off two small plastic baggies of N-tabs and tossed them to us, one after the other. I snatched mine out of the air with one hand without thinking and stuffed them into a pocket.

"We'll try to get some real food, of course," she said briskly, pulling a nice-looking Roon auto from her bag and checking it over with a casual ease that indicated great familiarity with the weapon. "But if Brussels is like every other fucking city in the System these days, we'll be lucky we brought our own N-tabs."

By the scorched-metal look of the grip, it was an old Roon—a 73 or 74. Both of those guns were outdated before she was born, so the way her hands moved over it and found the hidden safety without trouble was strange— but you could always come across old guns when you had to buy them on the black market. I remembered having a fucking revolver, once, afraid it would explode in my hands the moment I pulled the trigger. If I'd happened upon a Roon 73 for cheap from a clueless broker, I'd have bought it, too, and polished it like it was a diamond.

My hands twitched. As it was, I would be happy to have

any kind of gun. Even that heavy, pre-Uni revolver from London. I'd searched for Little Mother's piece around the train, but had come up empty.

"All right," she said. "We walk. You boys won't have any trouble humping it, I'm sure, with your special hump augments doing half the pull for you. Keep your eyes peeled. There's no fucking law outside the city, and there are Press Gangs out here, too. We don't want to have to fucking buy you out *twice*."

"How far?" I asked, falling in step behind her, conscious of having no weapon. How in the fuck Michaleen expected me to fucking assassinate someone like Londholm with just my bare hands and whatever clever gadgets I could make from shoelaces and N-tabs was a mystery to me. It was strange to think that the world I'd once known, the fucked-up System with its fucked-up police, was *civilization*, something to be *longed for*.

"Quarter mile," she said, striding off. "Keep up. The anti-frag setting has an outer perimeter too, you know."

I looked at her ass for a second, and then shared another look with the Poet. After a second, we both set off after her.

It didn't take long; Mara had been right about the augments; I fell instantly into a steady, muscular pace that didn't feel like work at all, a tiny bit of my HUD suddenly lighting up and reporting how far we'd walked and what my average speed was. My legs felt strong and I didn't even start breathing any harder.

The city crept up on us. We scaled a steep wall of grass and were in a neat pile of concrete rubble, a minefield of sharp edges and rusty points out in the middle of a wild field of long, swaying grass, enclosed by a sagging, rotten wood fence. Another five minutes of walking and the road on our right began to resemble a road instead of the surface of some distant moon, and Mara stepped over the rusted, paper-thin guardrail and led us onto the wide, six-lane road, choked with weeds and riddled with cracks, meandering through the thinning woods. After another few minutes, we were no longer the only people in creation; we caught up with a small band of tired-looking folks pushing small carts laden with what I assumed were their possessions, all of them wearing about seven layers of clothing, everything they owned.

The crowd thickened as we approached the city proper, people of all shapes and looks just tramping along. By the time we came across a makeshift SSF checkpoint manned by one bored-looking officer and five grubby Stormers whose Obfuscation Kit was malfunctioning, leaving them wearing what amounted to stained and torn off-white scrubs, we were just three people in a large crowd. The Stormers looked about as terrifying as kittens in their sad uniforms, but everyone fell into line like sheep.

Mara suddenly stopped. "Shit," she said. "Mr. Cates, you're popular—we should put out trading cards of ya. Looks like the cops have figured out you ain't dead anymore."

I followed her gaze to the Vidscreen, which suddenly had my face on it. I didn't understand the language it was pumping out, but I could read. Above the photo—an old one, enhanced to make the shadows on my face deeper and more ominous—were large, bold letters: REWARD LIST: INFORMATION LEADING TO THE CAPTURE

OR ELIMINATION OF THE FOLLOWING CRIMINALS IS PAID FOR BY THE SYSTEM SECURITY FORCE!

Below my photo, smaller but still clear as day:

AVERY CATES. NO KNOWN ALIASES. LIST CLASS: AAA. DOA. MURDER, SEDITION, ASSAULT OF FEDERAL OFFICERS, CONSPIRACY, GRAND THEFT, KIDNAPPING, WEAPON POSSESSION, AND TRANSPORT. DO NOT APPROACH. REWARD PAID OUT DEAD OR ALIVE.

"Congratulations," the Poet said in a friendly tone, slapping my shoulder. "You are real fucking famous. Hope it don't kill you."

XII

DEATH AIN'T WHAT IT USED TO BE

The Poet handed me my glass and shifted his eyes pointedly over my shoulder. I nodded. "The creep with the blinkers? Yeah, I saw him."

The noise of the tavern closed over us again. I'd never been in a quiet bar, but this one was the noisiest damn place I'd ever been in. My HUD indicated that my auditory augments were turned all the way up into the red just to make sense of what the Poet, standing a foot away, was shouting at me. It was strange to think that tiny circuits were inside me, feeding off tinier batteries, molecule-thin wires spidered through my veins. I didn't feel anything. I just felt better.

Every now and then my auditory augments captured a single line of the roar and brought it to me in perfect, noise-removed clarity.

"In een box enkel van Steeg Taitou, vraagt tweede van de linkerzijde, om Shen."

I held the glass up to my face. It was small, but thick

and heavy, and filled with the cloudy, dark, sweet beer they were serving. It was flat and warm and was dispensed from a huge, leaking barrel behind the bar. Two large, pale guys with flabby, natural muscle stood blank-faced guard over it. It was cloudy, but I'd already observed the locals letting their glasses settle for a few minutes before drinking.

"Vijftig aan u, maar als wij don't vertelt Gerry over het it's zeventig aan u, volgt?"

There were several large Vidscreens bolted to the walls, dark and useless. There was no power. The city's grid was still up, but it was damaged and spotty, with constant blackouts rolling through the neighborhoods, and the System Pigs stole the power they needed without warning, just rerouting it on an as-needed basis. There was no heat, so we were all bundled up against the cold, crushed in together. While Mara had disappeared into the crowd to locate her contact, the Poet and I had gotten seats at the bar simply by asking for them; their prior occupants had taken one look at us and thought it best to occupy different space.

It wasn't a big place; one story, with a flat, leaking roof that was bare to the rafters, gaps in the ancient shingles wide enough to stick your fingers through if you got up that high. Like the whole fucking city, the place smelled like sour deodorant. You didn't mind at first, maybe even thought it was pleasant, and five minutes in you wanted to cut off your own nose.

"Seize à vingt-deux, treize à cinquante et un."

Brussels felt like a small city; every block was the same: narrow, winding cobblestone streets, tall, narrow buildings of old, bleached stone, skinny, ghost-pale citizens talking like they had rocks lodged deep in their throats. It felt damp all the time, as if the city were built on a swamp. And everything smelled like no one had taken a shower in a long time, and a thin, invisible sheet had been placed over the city to trap the odor. After getting past the bored and overwhelmed Pigs at the checkpoint simply by putting my head down and walking briskly—a tactic dumbasses throughout history had always disdained—I'd fallen in hate with Brussels immediately.

The fucking sweet, flat, warm beer was just the icing on the hate cake.

"So what do you think?" the Poet said, downing his cloudy beer in one heroic and probably ill-advised gulp. "About old Blue Eyes back there. A Spook? Augment? What?"

The Poet's speech patterns were fucking hypnotic. Every time he spoke, I wanted to slap a beat on my thigh, tap my foot. I was starting to like the bizarre mother-fucker. He was my only hope. I hated having Michaleen's thumb on my head, hated having his proxy following me around, and hated the fact that even when she'd taken a powder I didn't even think about making a break for it. The remote had a long range, and I didn't want to collapse into red agony just as I was hitting the open country. I was resigned to being on the Rail for the universe. I wouldn't be on Michaleen's rail.

I turned around in my seat to look right at Blue Eyes. He was a blob, a fat boulder of a man in a heavy-fabric coat that had seen much, much better days. It had so many food stains on the front it looked like you could boil it up into a nice soup, as long as you didn't mind the fingernails and neck hairs that had probably gotten lost in it years ago. His eyes glowed a bright, neon blue, bright enough to light up a dark room, I thought, and they were fixed on me in an unblinking stare.

"Augment," I said. I knew the type. A Broker, selling information. Wired up to the nets—legal and otherwise—with an always-on connection, eyes sending images of everything he saw upstream and getting back data on the downstream, all stored on a data cube, kept in his pocket if he was cheap and embedded in his skull if he was rich. Did the same job Pickering used to do, except Old Pick hadn't needed augments. Pick had just done research, and remembered.

As he stared at me, my face was being processed by his offshore servers and a full report was coming back to him. The SSF was offering a reward for me, dead or alive, and this bastard was going to know it in a second or two.

I looked at my glass of beer and considered: Did I feel lucky? My augments weren't going to do much against invasive microorganisms. Hoping the alcohol would kill whatever lived in that barrel, I downed the whole thing in one swallow, warm and off-sweet. Wiping my mouth, I stood up. "Let's say hello. See what kind of trouble we can get into before Mara gets back."

His hand appeared on my shoulder like a slab of cold fish, restraining me. For a second my HUD flashed red as I had the sudden, urgent desire to grab his wrist, twist hard, and spin him around. I swallowed bile and forced myself to stay calm.

"Mara is absent," he whispered to me, my augments catching each word with a sizzle of noise reduction. "Perhaps we take advantage, and absent ourselves."

I shook my head, settling my coat onto my shoulders.

"How far do we get before she knocks us on our ass—what did you call it? The Middle Finger of God? No, we're stuck with Mara for now." I nudged my chin at Blue Eyes. "Him we can scrape off."

The Poet shrugged, removing his hand and falling in behind me. I had to push a few people aside to make my way to the Blob's table, sharing a few stares until word got passed on and a narrow tunnel opened up for us. You didn't have to speak the language. The same process happened in New York back in the old days: You shoved, you sized each other up, and someone grunted and stepped aside. Or shoved back. The results varied, but the opening steps were always the same.

When we were looming over Blue Eyes' table, he looked up at us serenely as a kid scrambled into position next to him, a short, runty kid who resembled a monkey in just about every aspect you could think of. I glanced at the kid as the Poet shoved a thin, white-haired old man from a chair and spun it around so he could sit with his arms crossed on the back, putting himself level with Blue Eyes, who didn't even glance at him. After a moment, Blue Eyes said something I didn't understand. Immediately, as he was still speaking, the monkey kid began screeching out an English translation.

"You're gonna have a harder time pushing *me* out of his chair," the kid shouted. His teeth were tiny black pebbles. I didn't like looking at him. "Mr. Cates out of New York, and Mr. Panić out of Belgrade."

The kid's English was perfect, with an accent, but clear. Before I could say anything back, Blue Eyes was growling out syllables again, and the kid began overlapping him immediately.

"It's funny. The SSF database still lists you officially as dead, Mr. Cates, but there's a reward on your head. I'd say that was strange, except these days death ain't what it used to be."

I didn't know whom to look at when I spoke—the kid or the Blob. "I know you can upload a report just by blinking your pretty eyes in code," I said, looking at the Blob. "But I wonder how you imagine you'll spend it after I inspect your cranial implants by hand."

The kid translated in the chunky language they shared, and the Blob smiled at me.

"As I said, Mr. Cates: Death ain't what it used to be." The kid grinned at me. "And here is your associate."

I turned and was startled to find Mara at my side. A flat slab of self-contempt dropped into my stomach, letting her creep up on me like that, a fucking *kid*. A kid with skills, though, I had to admit—Mara knew how to handle herself. She wasn't even paying me any attention as she smiled blandly at the Blob.

"Hullo, Goren," she said.

"Ms. Mara," the kid said, translating so fast I almost thought he was just making shit up as the Blob rumbled. "Regards to my dear friend Mr. Garda."

She nodded, once, regally. "We need weapons, intel, and sundries."

The Blob grinned. "Luckily, your credit with me is good."

Mara's smile vaporized. "It better be, you fat fuck, or I might give Mr. Cates *permission* to inspect your augments, right?" She nodded once, smirking, as the Blob's shining eyes flicked to me in a sudden change of mood. "Right. To business, then."

The word *permission* hung there in the air, and I clenched my teeth.

Mara tossed a data cube onto the table. The Blob moved with surprising speed and snatched it up. "Londholm," Mara said.

The Blob nodded, talking. The kid chattered away like he had a cable up his ass feeding him his lines. "Of course. Still in Hong Kong. Trapped. Hong Kong is going to declare independence from the System of Federated Nations any day now. Officially. The System Pigs"—here the kid paused to spit viciously onto the floor, immediately resuming his duties—"still claim the city, but word is a number of officers have gone over. Mutiny. The army sits outside like a spider, waiting to go in for the kill. Londholm normally would be long gone, but there's no easy way in or out of Hong Kong these days." The Blob inclined his head at us. "This is why Garda has resurrected Avery Cates, I assume, a man known for getting *in* places he is not supposed to."

Mara nodded. "We need everything you have on the city. *Everything*. Sewage plans, building plans, SSF assignments, water approaches, defenses, cultural synopses. Everything. Everything on Londholm, too, though I doubt you have anything we don't."

The Blob raised an eyebrow, but said nothing to this.

"We need better papers," Mara continued. "Too many checkpoints out in the open these days."

The Blob pointed at me, rumbling, and the kid jabbed his sharp, bony chin at me. "He's famous. Papers won't help much if he gets OFR'd. I can recommend a good sawbones to give him a new nose or something."

I touched my nose before I realized it. "No fucking way," I said. I'd had enough surgery to last a lifetime.

Mara studied me for a moment, and then shrugged. "No go. Papers, then. Best you can do. We'll hit a price when I see what you can come up with. We ain't payin' premium for simple forgers, follow?"

The Blob nodded, smiling. The kid said for him, "You know, you are officially dead, too."

There was a beat of bar noise, and then she leaned forward and simply slapped him across the face, a full-on, open-palm, roundhouse slap that jerked his head all the way around. She turned to glance at the kid, and then reared back and slapped *him* just as hard, sending the kid flying three or four feet in the air, crashing into a group of lanky men with unfortunate facial hair. When they turned to scowl in our direction, I stared back until they looked away and bent to help the kid to his feet. He pushed them away with a growl and scrambled back to the Blob's side, just in time to translate the flood of consonants pouring from him.

"No need for that, now. We're all—"

"Spare me the fuckin' *professionals* speech," Mara snapped. "You ain't here to *talk*, boyo, follow?"

The Blob nodded, composing himself. "All right," the kid said. He'd lost his snarl, though; a bright red imprint of Mara's hand was on his face. She didn't like him talking about her situation, and I decided to take some time later and wonder why.

"Weapons," she said, giving him back his space and brushing imagined dust off her shoulders. "I need army-issue, remote-safety equipment with burnable chips—"

I moved my jaw until the joint cracked. "No."

Mara paused and looked at me. "No?"

I shook my head. "I'm not going into a job like this

with a fucking gun that can be fucking *remotely turned off*." I looked at my chest and shrugged. "You want to pop a vessel in my head, fucking fine. Do it. Do it now." I looked back at her. "If not, step back and let me make my own fucking arrangements, because I am *not* going into this with a piece of shit, remote-controlled, blow-up-in-your-hand military piece, goddammit!"

I hadn't realized I was shouting until the silence around us washed in. It lasted only a second, and then the Poet whistled appreciatively behind me. The noise rushed back around us, and Mara smiled.

Energy bubbled through me, fire in my arms, my heart steady but rapid. Every surface and opening had been calculated—I could leap up onto the table with just a thought, spin and bury a fist in the little kid's hair, yank him down, smash an elbow into Mara's face hard enough to dislodge some teeth, and roll off her holding onto her wrist, spin her off-center to the floor with a snap. The augments made it possible. The augments made it *impossible* with Mara's finger on my button.

"All right, Avery," she said, sweeping her arm in front of her. "My brief is to let you run this job. If you've decided this is your moment, by all means, make your arrangements. Goren, attend to Avery now."

The Blob turned his shining eyes on me and licked his lips. I watched my HUD bars slowly shrink back into the green, and licked my lips.

"What can I get you?" the kid said. I kept my eyes on the Blob.

"I've got a long list of heavy items," I said. "But we can start with a Roon 87a, series three or earlier," I said immediately. "Two."

The Blob blinked, and scowled, putting his hands up and rumbling away as the kid chattered. "87a no good, Mr. Cates," he said. "Prone to jamming."

I shook my head. "Not if you shim the chamber." I held up two fingers. "Two. Plus ammunition, of course— as much as you can get. Three shredders, standard SSF issue, and a series-16 fuel-injected SLR snipe." I looked up at the Poet. "What do you want?"

"Hamada two nine," he said immediately. "Cut barrel, with sanded stock." He winked. "And a steel garrote."

I grinned. "Hamada. How old are you? I never met anyone under a hundred that still went for Hamadas." The Hamada corporation had disappeared thirty years ago, sinking under the waves of Unification. "Besides, it's a piece of shit gun."

He frowned, hesitating, but quickly recovered and looked almost happy. "Three series, yeah sure. Two series will punch through walls, never jammed for me."

"So you consider 'exploding in your hand' a feature, huh?"

Before he could formulate his response, there was a sudden wave of noise at the front of the tavern, following a ripple of commotion. My HUD flashed as all three of us spun around. Someone shouted from behind us.

"Politie!"

"Fucking cops," I muttered, turning my head slightly as my eyes scanned the room. I looked at the Blob and smiled. "How fast can we get those guns?"

XIII

A SURGE OF BLOODY JOY

In an instant, the bar was turmoil. The Blob suddenly seemed to rise up into the air; I blinked and saw that the group of bearded men behind us had stepped forward, laced their arms together under his bulk, and lifted him up. I watched them carry him back through the crowd and he stared back at me, the glowing circles of his eyes fading.

When I spun back around, the scene was so familiar I almost forgot I was in Brussels. People struggled back from the entrance, shitkickers in a panic and a few pros staying calm, standing their ground. The world around us melted into a blurry noise I knew well and felt at home in. The cops at the front looked like officers, but who the fuck knew these days: Everything was mixed up, and I wouldn't be surprised if the quality of your average System Pig had dropped a little—although I reminded myself that being able to run fresh units with old brains out of a factory probably reduced brain drain. I pictured the interior of the tavern in my head as my eyes roamed the chaos. If this were a typical raid, the rear was already cut off and the roof was going to get popped in a few minutes—the cops at the front caused a rush, and all the fish swam right into their net in the back, and the smarter or slower ones would get plucked up into the air.

My heart pounded; everything suddenly slowed down like it had back on the train.

Suddenly at leisure, I looked over at the bar; the beefy guys were gone, and I hadn't seen them vaulting over the bar or heading for either of the exits. If they knew their business, there was a way out right under them, a way to skip the crush of assholes and just slip under the radar. The cops would know about it, too—or *would* have, back a few years, when the System Pigs raiding the joint would have been locals who made it their business to know.

My hands twitched, empty.

While bodies surged around me like they were trapped in syrup, I smiled, feeling limber and energized, almost happy. I turned back to Mara and the Poet in time to see Mara break a big blond Viking's nose, just slamming her flattened palm up into his face and sending him staggering back into the crowd, blood floating in the air in tiny droplets. It cleared a little space around us, but we were about to get swamped by the shitkickers and then we'd be sitting ducks when the cops eventually got the situation organized.

The Poet suddenly leaned down and grabbed hold of the table the Blob had been sitting at. He flipped it over and with a savage kick freed one of the thick wooden legs from it, the broken, bent screws and the remnants of a cheap metal bracket like spikes at its far end. He tested the weight in one hand and looked at me, suddenly tossing the make-shift club my way. I snatched it from the air and it was a nightmare: top-heavy, too wide for an easy grip, splintery and brittle feeling. Mara leaped forward and they each kicked a leg free. For just a second, we eyed each other, twitchy little disbelieving grins on our faces—three professionals amazed that we were we really going to club our way past System Police with *table legs*—and then it was the crowd, everywhere, the only thing in the universe.

The Poet hefted his stick, planted himself, and with a loud animal growl stretched out in my ears he spun around, sweeping his perimeter with it and planting the rusty end in the neck of a tall, bald man just trying to scamper toward the back. The Poet tore the club out immediately, sending a spray of blood everywhere, and immediately swung back the other way, grunting with the effort, ignoring the blood dripping down his face.

"Head for the bar!" I shouted, just as the roof blew, a nicely synchronized series of charges that sent the whole thing crashing down on us, the rotten joists and slats vaporizing, turning magically into Stormers, Obfuscation Kit swirling as they slid down their drop wires, masks giving them one blind eye. I moved easily to avoid having any of them drop on me, my brain operating at clock speeds. The lights blinked off and we were in darkness, lit only by the cops' swinging nova lamps, a confusion of spotlights. My vision immediately snapped into a sick, bad shade of green that outlined every edge in sharp detail, turning everyone and everything into nauseous shadows.

A Stormer landed right in front of me, dropping into a combat-ready crouch, slow enough for me to choose which

ear to smash my table leg into. I dropped with him, both
of us hitting the floor in a frenzy of legs and boots, mud
and sawdust. I leaped onto the Stormer, pinning his arms
and preparing to smash a fist down into his face mask, but
the body beneath me was limp, and as I stared he seemed
to fade subtly, appearing to go dark. I shifted my weight
and clawed at the holster strapped to his hip, tearing the
piece of shit auto from it and squinting down at it. After
a second, I made out the telltale red dot on the grip—the
gun was linked to the Stormer and wouldn't fire for anyone else. This was a new policy for the SSF, since up until
a few years ago the thought that some shithead would nick
a piece from a System Pig was ridiculous. I tossed the gun
aside and jumped back up to my feet, table leg poised.

The Poet had jumped up onto one of the tables and
was liberally swinging his club around, his big reflective
glasses askew and his face split into a smile, almost beautiful, his arms rippling, his teeth perfect and white. I'd
known people like him, psychos who enjoyed it, liked the
taste of blood. They usually got sloppy because they tried
to turn every situation into a brawl, chasing death until it
finally turned around and caught *them*, but they were usually pretty fun to watch from afar. Mara was on the floor
behind him, ducking down to stay below his swings, and
together they owned a small spot of clear floor.

"The bar!" I bellowed. "You can't just *stay* there!"

Mara nodded at me, her eyes on the crowd, and she
shouted something over her shoulder at the Poet. It was
strange, everything was *slow*, but I moved at will and
didn't *feel* slow. It was like I saw and heard everything
a second before it actually happened, the future rear-
projected for me.

I took one step toward the debris-strewn shadow of the bar in front of me, and right on time the back exit of the place blew inward, a soft charge that knocked half a dozen assholes to the floor as more officers crammed into the place. The System Pigs had lost some of their style, but they still knew how to take down a dive when they wanted someone.

A broad-shouldered ape of a cop swam up in front of me, a jolly sort with a big red face, his necktie too tight, his hair sweaty and chaotic on his balloon head. "Cop cheerful" was an expression—that crazy light in their eyes that told you they knew they could kick you in the balls and get away with it—and this guy had the classic version lighting up his face. The whole place smelled like beer, a sweet, rotting smell that made my stomach roll as I swung the table leg hard at his face; he ducked fast, but I had spidery wires laced through me these days and I caught him on the forehead, a solid impact vibrating up my arms.

He popped up with balletic slowness immediately, but I *expected* it, had foreseen it. He had a very believable contusion on his temple, and he grinned at me. *Avatar*, I thought. A fucking android with a cop's brain downloaded to it, fifty of the same cop scattered all over the place. I tried swinging my club back around, but my momentum was all wrong and the cop knocked it aside with one arm, shooting its other hand in and grabbing hold of my throat and squeezing, instantly choking me.

"Avery Cates," it said, grinning, cheerful eyes shining at me in the sudden night inside the bar, and then it convulsed, letting go of me and dropping to the floor. I spun away, finding the Poet at my side, crouched low, having just swept the cop's legs out from under him with his own club. We locked eyes for a second, his ringed in blood splatter and crinkled at the corners from his wide, crazy-ass grin, and then we leaped onto the cop, smashing our clubs down on it three, four, five times, its arms and legs leaping into the air comically with each hit.

The Poet stood up and shouted, "One goddamn cop down, five hundred thousand to go!" Another wink that almost made me flinch. "We make a good team!"

Mara was somehow in front of us, making room as she went, heading toward the bar. We arrived almost simultaneously, dodging chaos and putting our backs to the old wood, a glorious stretch of bar I regretted having to use as a shield.

I scanned the dim space; it was just bodies moving, lit up green by my sudden, involuntary night-vision. I was a goddamn freak too, just like these cops, just like every other little ant with god's magnifying glass trained on them—I stared around at the slimy-looking green bodies and wanted to hit them all, wanted to hit *everything* and just keep hitting it. Some skinny mope with a long, curly beard crossed into my sight and I flicked the leg out at his face, knocking him backward with a spray of fluids, white in my night-vision. A surge of bloody joy swept through me, and I wanted to stand there all day cracking skulls, punishing the world for my situation.

Mara leaped up onto the bar as I noticed a group of SSF officers closing in, tossing aside tables and shoving their own Stormers out of the way as they approached. I pushed myself up onto the bar and swung my legs around the back, running my augmented eyes along the floor behind it, spotting the faint outlines of the trapdoor almost immediately; as I looked, the outline of it seemed to glow suddenly, making it clear and easy to spot. The crooks in Brussels did it the same as we'd done in New York: The trap was there to give you a head start, not to confound the Pigs forever. I pointed my table leg at it.

"There!" I shouted. "We can—"

I glanced up, something catching hold of my augmented vision. Through the crowd and the dust and the gloom, a flash of white that froze me for a moment, everything getting impossibly *slower*. I stared at the spot while Mara shouted at me, while the population of the bar squirmed away from the tattered arm of the cops. After a few long, stretched-out seconds, I saw it again: a white, fake-looking face staring at me from across the bar. *Staring at me*, not just looking around. Staring at me and grinning.

Without a word to Mara, I leaped back down to the floor and started carving my way toward the rear. Mara screeched behind me, ordering me to hold the fuck up. Everyone else was swimming down toward the rear as well so the going was easier at first, but everyone clogged up the doors and windows as the cops streamed in, so about five feet from the door, I had to start swinging my club freely at about neck height. I didn't care about Mara; I didn't care about the System Pigs. I wanted to know why a Monk, fully operational after all these years, happened to be in the same bar as me in fucking Brussels, staring at me like it could hear my thoughts.

As I clubbed my way closer, sweating freely, arms burning, it was gone. I stared around wildly, trying to spot that white face again. I worked my arms, shoving the crowd away savagely, and then a hand slapped onto my shoulder, and Mara's voice was hissing in my ear.

"Boy, you don't fucking—aw, now here's some fine bullshit."

A clump of Stormers forced their way through the door, backing the crowd up with their shredders held out stiffly in front of them, the fucking macho assholes. In the middle of them, like a queen, was a short female officer, wearing a sumptuous-looking leather coat with four shiny pips gleaming on one lapel. She was tiny, but she moved like she was floating on air and stared at me with a bland, disinterested expression I suddenly remembered well.

The officer held up her hands, palms outward, stepping forward through the Stormers, who spread out and formed a tight ring around us.

"Everyone calm down," Janet Hense said in that same flat voice. "I just want to talk."

XIV

WITH A HEADSHOT, IF POSSIBLE

As she walked, flunkies kept sprinting to catch up with her and hand over razor-thin digital pages that glowed text up at her; she carried on a profane one-way conversation with her earbud without missing a beat.

Janet Hense had moved up in the world. Or at least this version of her had. She was still tiny, loomed over by her entire entourage, but I doubted any of them realized it, the way she flicked them away with little waves of her hands. She was the first avatar I'd ever met, as far as I knew, and I still remembered being left for dead in Bellevue Hospital, the touch of her dry palm on my cheek. *I see no reason to kill you, Avery*. She could have, of that I was certain.

"How have you been, Janet?" I asked, forcing a smile and some volume into my voice. Every System Pig I'd ever known was sensitive about rank, so I used her name. It was petty, but you used what you could. And here I was days in on this little adventure and I *still* didn't have a fucking gun.

She'd led us just a few blocks through the strangely deserted narrow streets of Brussels. Fires burned in barrels on every other corner, sending black smoke into the air, the flames not casting much light in the dark, dirty city. There was almost no noise at all once we turned a corner and left the bar behind, but here and there as we passed the massive, weather-stained stone buildings you caught a flicker of light behind a blacked-out window. Brussels was a secret city, underground and behind walls. The streets had been abandoned.

"Pleasantries, Avery?" she said over her shoulder, exchanging one digital reader for another from one of her aides, a sour, yellowed man in a dark suit, cigarette dangling from one corner of his thin mouth. "I thought you would be at my throat, vowing revenge."

"One asshole at a time, Janet," I said.

Hense was a major now, an SSF demigod, and her personal HQ was set up in an old hotel that sat like a rounded box on a corner. An old, tattered awning declared it to be HOTEL PLAZA. All the windows—dozens on each side—had been busted out, stationary shredders set on pivots, surrounded by sandbags. Getting in looked hard, with dozens of officers and Stormers at the entrance, which had been ripped out and replaced with a bulkhead of welded metal. Hense didn't even bother waving an ID; she just charged past them all, daring someone to quote protocol, and I would swear they all took a half-inch step backward as she passed.

"You're a hot property, Cates," Mara whispered without looking at me. "I'm walking into a Pig Nest without a struggle. Oy, the humiliation."

I glanced behind me at the Poet. He swaggered through

like a star, glasses back on, his table leg still held in both hands across his belly like it was a magic charm that would get him out of stir if need be. He didn't say anything, just kept that dim-witted grin on me, so I looked forward again. The lobby of the building had been huge, all high ceilings and arches and marble floors—completely empty, without a stick of furniture anywhere—but here on the third floor it was a maze of narrow hallways and closed doors. A thick, ruined carpet muffled all the noise, making it seem like we were gliding along an inch above the ground.

Hense stopped at a nondescript door, nothing particularly heavy or secure. It had once had numbers nailed to it, but these had been pried off, leaving just a pale spot in the wood. She turned and looked at Mara for a moment.

"Disable his frag settings," Hense said. "And wait out here."

Mara didn't move; she put a smirky little grin on her face. "I'm afraid I canna *acquiesce* to your request, Major," she said, playing up the accent. "It's set wide. He'll be fine unless y'take 'im to fucking Moscow."

Hense nodded as if this was reasonable. "Disable them or I'll have you shot in the head."

The words were soft and had been spoken without any dramatic emphasis at all. For a second we were all still, and then Mara shrugged, pulling out the tiny black square of the remote. "You get 'im killed or let him loose, my boss'll come to claim damages."

Hense didn't react, her brown eyes watching Mara's hands on the remote. "Your *boss*," she said, "is a cunt, and he wouldn't show his little ferret face within a *mile* of me."

Mara nodded, putting the remote away. "You fucking

Pigs, always so sure of yerselves. Don't forget your team of ass-wipers here when you go out for a smoke, Major. He's all yours."

"Thank you," Hense said as if the previous forty seconds hadn't been filled with insults and veiled threats. She turned those horrible blank eyes on me. "Mr. Cates?"

"Do I have a choice?"

She nodded. "Yes. This is a *request*, Mr. Cates. You are not under arrest."

I decided to push the limit a little. Why not? This was like a dream anyway: Janet Hense the asskicking robot cop shows up in fucking Brussels and asks me politely to have a conversation with her. Under these circumstances, I thought I might ask for a unicorn, or a carton of pre-Unification cigarettes, or some other impossibility.

"You have rewards posted for me all over the fucking place," I said. "Dead or alive. You're encouraging people to *slit my throat*. But I'm not under arrest?" I shook my head. "Janet, give me a fucking break."

Watching her impassive face, I thought I could see a slight twitch under one eye. The avatars were *built*, that was for sure—they looked and smelled and felt human in every way. I amused myself by trying to guess how many times I could call her by her first name before she smacked me. My guess was four, and I'd used up three.

"It's just a conversation, Mr. Cates," she said, turning and opening the door. I settled my coat back onto my shoulders and followed her in. The door swung shut automatically behind me, and as I heard the click of its latch, the silence that crowded in was a familiar, buttoned-up atmosphere. The room had been gutted—the walls torn off, the floors pocked with open holes, out of which thick cables and wires spilled, snaking around the edges and into the walls, wrapping around studs until they exploded into a huge web in the exposed ceiling. Flat panels of dull metal were fixed into the corners, top and bottom, facing each other perfectly.

"This is a Blank Room," I said. My voice made it three feet and then dropped to the floor, absorbed.

A crude plywood desk and a surprisingly expensive-looking rolling chair were set up where the windows had been; the whole wall had been plated with metal. Hense moved to the desk and sat down, leaning back and crossing her legs at the knee. "Yes," she said. "We had to gut half this tech from old installations. No one's making some of this stuff anymore."

I nodded, looking around. The Blank Rooms of my memories were clean, white places, antiseptic and mysterious. This looked like something a hobbyist had built over decades, collecting junk from the local dumps. Still, it worked—I could *feel* it working. I knew what it was like to be in a Blank Room, and this was it. Nothing we said would be recorded or even heard outside of these walls. No record whatsoever, aside from my memory and Hense's redundant data storage. I was tense, my HUD lit up yellow and my heart racing; most of my visits to Blank Rooms had ended with me picking pieces of myself up from the nice, clean floors.

Looking down into the gloom of the exposed subfloor, I didn't think I'd ever find my teeth if they got knocked out.

"All right," I said carefully, looking back up at her. There was no seat for me, of course. "Here I am. Talk."

"This is," she said slowly, "an *unofficial* contact,

Mr. Cates. On Director Marin's authority. Officially, you're a wanted man and we're offering a serious payout for your capture or execution." She took one tiny hand from her lap and pointed a finger at me. "You're going after Londholm."

I didn't say anything.

She sighed. "Fuck, Cates, of *course* you're going after Londholm. Half the fucking talent in the System we haven't bricked, killed, or penned is after Londholm. There are sixteen contracts on him *simultaneously*, twelve to kill, three to protect and retrieve, and one to make sure he stays in Hong Kong either way, which frankly we can't figure out."

I shrugged. "That's fascinating."

She went still, and I knew that under different circumstances—a few years ago, or a few hours ago, before she'd gotten her newest orders—I'd already be on the floor with her knee in my neck, reconsidering my attitude. After a few seconds, she visibly relaxed. She was an android, but there was a messy human intelligence calling the shots. She was faster, more precise, stronger—but she still had to master her impulse to strangle me. That made me feel good, and a wave of good cheer bubbled up within me.

"All right," I said. "So what do you want from me? Let's say for sake of argument that we're humping across your fucked-over System to go after this asshole in Hong Kong—instead, as I maintain, for our health and education—why the soft-shoe? If you wanted me off the project, I know the fucking SSF—you'd just pop me in the head and walk away."

She nodded. "Are you going to kill him?"

I blinked. "What?"

"You're not working a contract, Cates. Your little team is freelancing it to Hong Kong. So I want to know if you're freelancing there to kill that Techie motherfucker, or if you're going to snatch him, or do gutterball surgery on him in the middle of the street, or ask him to dance, okay?"

Not working a contract. I struggled not to react. "Because why, Janet?"

The *Janet* made her eye twitch again, and my cheer rose up to new levels. One more, one more time I didn't call her Major and I knew she would fly over the desk and knock into me, weighing a lot more than she looked, and we'd find out how much my military augments were worth.

"Because," she finally said, leaning back in her chair, "it is the unofficial policy of the System Security Force and Director Marin's office that Londholm *be* killed. The sooner the better. With a headshot, if possible. With a cranial retrieval if not possible." She leaned forward suddenly. "That augment he's devised is the fucking *end of the world*, Mr. Cates. You've had some interaction with Psionic Actives, yes?"

I nodded, thinking of Kev Gatz, long dead and mostly forgotten, thinking of Bendix and his mean little smile back during the Plague.

"There were a couple of 'em after me on my way here, actually," I said. "One of them lifted a fucking *train* into the air, trying to shake me out like I was stuck to the bottom."

She nodded curtly. "Old man, wild white hair?" I nodded back, trying to look wise and clued-in. "We're aware of that crazy fuck," she said. "Angels. Putting everyone in the world on trial because they're taking over." She smiled thinly. "Pretty much every officer in the SSF is on their list of criminals. We've got plans for *him*, though. Don't worry."

I raised an eyebrow. "I'll bet," I said.

"The other PAs you've encountered have been, for the most part, *ours*," she continued. "We trained them from youth, from birth if possible. We put the fear of *us* into them and made them worker bees. They were *controlled*." She leaned back. "What Londholm has done is make anyone a Psionic. And not just a Psionic, a meta-Psionic, with every ability so far encountered in the wild and a few we haven't. Imagine everyone having these abilities, Cates. Imagine every psychotic criminal, every megalomaniacal undersecretary, every rogue cop in the System able to tear you apart from a hundred feet away, able to make you sing and dance with a glance." She nodded firmly. "Londholm has to die. And Garda doesn't want him dead, no matter what he's told you."

I paused, angry at myself for not even once wondering if Mickey had been lying to me—we were Gunners, we killed people for contract money, it made sense. But Michaleen Garda, who'd built the name Cainnic Orel into legend, wasn't *just* a Gunner, and I should have known better.

"He wants the God Augment."

She nodded again, a precise, prerecorded movement. "Among many other things, but yes."

I spun away, my hands bunched into fists. "I don't have any goddamn choice. I've got a head full of tech and that fucking midget has the strings on me. You want me to guarantee I kill Londholm? Free me up. Tear this shit out of me and set me on it, freelance, on my own. *Pay* me, goddammit."

For a few seconds she just stared at me like I was slowly crawling across her desk, leaving a thin trail of slime behind me. Then she smiled. Her smile was the most horrible thing I'd seen all day. "I cannot, Mr. Cates. The SFNA implants are specced to be one-way. Removing them will almost certainly kill you. I also cannot turn them off—your friend out there will simply turn them back on again." She spread her hands. "I am sorry, Cates," she said, sounding pretty much the exact opposite of *sorry*. "The army's tech is a different gauge."

"Fucking liar, Janet," I said without thinking, angry. "Put some *resources* into it."

I expected an explosion, a demonstration of violence. Instead she just shrugged. "Cates, does it look to you like I have a lot of spare resources for shitheads like you? I blew my wad shaking down the Poechenellekelder to carve you out. We've got the Seventh Army just fifty miles away, the supply lines into Brussels are razor thin, and..." She stopped, looking down at the desk for a moment.

"Fine," I ground out, feeling suddenly desperate. "Hong Kong's yours. Why not just order a couple officers to take him out?"

She was still looking at the desk, her hands very still in front of her. "Hong Kong's ours on paper only. It's surrounded by the Eleventh and Seventeenth Armies and portions of the Fourth. We can't get in or out in force, and the native cops in the city have..." She looked up at me, her face as impassive as ever. "They're unprocessed biologics and they've basically told us to go fuck ourselves. We don't have any authority inside the city, and we can't break

through the forces surrounding it to reestablish ourselves."
She shrugged. "So we're left with freelancers. Small units,
individuals. If Orel hadn't gotten to you, we'd have hired
you. We have our own solo agents in the field, too. Since
Orel *did* get to you, all I can do, privately, is offer you
resources."

I snorted, staring at her. I hadn't seen Janet Hense in
three years. She looked exactly the same. I figured she'd
look exactly the same a century from now. She wasn't
human. I didn't know what that made her.

"Resources?" I said, shaking my head. "You just said
you didn't *have* any resources."

She didn't say anything. She just stared at me.

I smiled. I was tired. I felt like lying down on her floor
and taking a nap. "All right. You've put a price on my
head, but unofficially you're a member of the Avery Cates
fan club and you want me to take Londholm's head off so
he can't become god. You can't give me anything useful
toward that goal except a chuck under the chin and a fucking 'attaboy.' Is that about it?"

She sighed and gestured at her desk. The wall behind
her suddenly formed the outline of a door and swung
inward. I marveled for a moment. For all the rough-
shod construction, the wires everywhere and the dry-rot
debris, the System Pigs had found a Techie somewhere
who knew what the fuck he was doing. The hidden door
swung inward, revealing a deep shadow.

In the distance, a faint, keening siren began wailing.

"Your augments cannot be removed or disabled,"
Hense said blandly, staring at me as a figure shuffled for-
ward from the secret hallway. "But they can be *hacked*,
Mr. Cates. At least, in one important way."

A Monk stepped into the room.

It was dressed in street clothes—baggy, tough-looking pants, black boots, a heavy, hooded short jacket. Its plastic face was still spotlessly white, twisted into one of their limited pre-programmed grins, and its tiny, fragile camera eyes flicked this way and that with delicate precision, but its hands were blackened and charred. It entered in complete silence, and for a moment the only sound was the distant siren.

I looked at Hense and tried to beam *What the fuck?* at her. She just stared back at me, her face impassive. When I looked back at the Monk, it had produced a small handheld LED screen. Smiling silently, it held it out toward me at chest level. I looked from the screen to its face and back again; I hadn't seen an operational Monk since the Plague. I didn't think any had survived.

Bright yellow words began streaming across the screen.

HELLO, AVERY.

I blinked, my hands twitching, and the message changed.

I AM TECHNICAL ASSISTANCE.

XV

SILT OF THE FUCKING EARTH

I sat with my legs up on what was probably the last intact table in the Poechenellekelder, which was what Hense had called the place, smoking cop cigarettes and drinking cop whiskey. Where the cops fucking got it from was a mystery Hense wasn't willing to part with, but they had it in spades; Hense had given me a carton of unmarked coffin nails and a flask without blinking an eye. Back in Englewood I could have bought half the fucking town for what I sucked down greedily, and I regretted not a goddamn moment.

My head still ached, and the flashing red exclamation mark in the corner of my HUD was annoying. I glanced at the Monk, who stood silently next to me like a statue, which is what most existing Monks were these days. After I'd destroyed Dennis Squalor—except for the ghost still living in my head, sometimes deigning to speak to me—and the Electric Church, the resulting Monk riots caused by several million Monks around the System suddenly being free of the Church's control and able to express the sizzling horror and pain they'd been feeling had ended with most of them shot in the head by the cops, who for once were good for something. The few who'd survived *that* got erased after my old pal Kev Gatz had tried to murder the world with the Plague—after that, I don't think more than a few dozen operational Monks remained. You still came across a rusting one in a dark place now and then, but even the ones that had survived all of that had succumbed, mostly, to incidental damage, faulty power skeins in their chassis, or dumb luck like brain tumors.

This one was in decent shape. I wondered if it was the last working Monk in the System. It seemed impossible— there had been millions—but it was certainly the first I'd seen since the Plague.

Around us in a loose circle were no fewer than four Stormers, guns drawn and held at the ready at their sides. The Obfuscation Kit these wore still worked, and the stormers kept fading into the ruin and debris of the bar, stoking my headache.

A noise at the door made me look up in time to see Mara and the Poet duck under the ruined header of the rear entrance where we'd run into Hense the night before, followed by a trio of Stormers with sidearms drawn, shredders hanging from their shoulders. Mara's eyes were everywhere as she took her long-legged strides, hands hanging ready at her sides, elbows bent. The Poet was wearing his sunglasses and smiling his dim-witted grin. They both looked dirty and tired.

Mara stopped at the table and stared down at me. She looked like her head was about to explode. I was setting records for pissing off women, and that was saying something for me. She jabbed her hand at me, the tiny remote pointed at me, and gestured. Glancing at the piece of black plastic, she nodded once to herself and then turned her snarl back at me.

"What the fuck," she said slowly, as if biting the words off of a hunk of rock and spitting them at me, "happened to you? And what the *fuck*," she added with a sharp tick of her head toward the Monk, "is this bullshit?"

"Hello, Mara," I said back pleasantly. I found I enjoyed annoying the women in my life, and wondered, briefly, what that meant, exactly. I'd been with Hense and the Monk for hours, and when I'd finally emerged, Mara and the Poet were gone. I'd been *escorted* back to the bar.

The Poet whistled softly. "You are a brave man," he said, shooting the cuffs of his long coat. "I'm in awe of your courage. You are on your own."

She opened her mouth again, but suddenly our minders snapped as one to attention, holstered their weapons, and marched out of the bar as if we'd suddenly ceased to exist. We watched them silently, and when Mara looked back at me I gestured at the tiny projector on the table and it sprang to life, a flickering holographic representation of a city floating in the air between us.

"Hong Kong. City plans, straight from the SSF servers. Got everything they have: sewer plans, grids, specs, census information, dossiers on the cops still inside the city. Turns out the System Pigs want Londholm dead as much as everyone else."

She stared at the floating city, a sprawl of buildings and veinlike roads sitting on the ocean. "So all this, this is you workin' fer the fucking *cops* now?"

I smiled. I tried to project confidence, cockiness. I

tried to play my part, even as my heart pounded and my HUD edged into yellow despite my attempts to control my breathing. You couldn't talk it over; you couldn't *discuss* shit. Discussion was for pussies, and pussies got fucked over. The world might be falling apart but there were rules that lasted forever. "They like my work. We're old pals."

She looked back at me, her eyes murderous little coals. "Don't you be forgettin' who *owns* your ass, Avery."

I nodded. "The Little Man brought me in to run this show. From now on, I'm runnin' it. You want to pop a vessel in my head, show me who's boss, do it now, because from this moment forward this is *my* show."

She stared down at me for a moment, squinting one eye a little more than the other, and for a strange moment I felt like I knew exactly what she was going to say. She was going to smirk, kinking her mouth up in one corner and say, *All right, boyo, if that's the way y'want it.* I concentrated on the flashing exclamation mark and it expanded in my vision slightly, throbbing there. I wondered what would happen if I went ahead and triggered it. It was strange to finally have some control over my own augments.

"All right, boyo," she said, smirking. "Play it like that, if y'like."

Close enough. I kept my eyes on her for a moment, a strange feeling of been there, done that leaking through me.

The Poet made a big show of sniffing the air. "My friends, that's pungent. And really kind of boring. A pissing contest."

I glanced at him. Fucking kid. Everything was funny to kids. "All right, Mara," I said, with my eyes still on Adrian. "We still have a go with your contact here? Guns? Transport?"

Her nostrils flared. "Guns, yes. Intel, yes—though y'seem to have that part covered, huh? Transport—not on your fucking life. There's no such fucking thing anymore. There are refugee trains still railing out, people herding out before the army drops the hammer. That's all we got."

I relaxed slowly. "All right. Last reports the cops had put Londholm...here." I touched a flickering building with one finger and it swelled up, expanding to fill the whole virtual space. It was a tall, triangular-shaped building rising from a narrow stump, all bluish glass on one side. "A luxury hotel, the Shannara or some shit like that. Five hundred forty-three rooms, and he's the only occupant."

Mara ran her eyes over it, all business. "At least it's on the fucking coast. Security?"

"Private, freelance," I said. "Talent—they say Japanese mercenary, which means—"

"Takahashi," Mara interrupted.

"Dai Takahashi, yes," I agreed. There were a dozen or so well-known mercenary outfits, ranging from a half-dozen assholes with a FOR RENT sign on their chests to big-time operators, and Takahashi was the biggest. I'd heard a hundred soldiers, big weaponry, high-class tech. "He's running out of cash, and there's a possibility his team will just try to kill him if he can't pay their wages anymore."

She snorted. "Like hell. They'll truss 'im up and sell 'im. Probably already thinkin' on it, actually."

I shrugged. "Whatever. The cops aren't up to date, really, because the whole fucking island is pretty much in rebellion. Local cops told SSF HQ to shit in their hat a few days ago, so no one's taking orders over there right now." I gestured and the hotel sank back down as the city rose up again, everything tiny but crisp. "The army's got control of the mainland, and it looks like they're going in soon, like within a few days. Most of the civilian population's gone, with maybe a few thousand people left in the whole goddamn city."

Mara nodded. "The shit left at the bottom. Silt of the fucking earth," she muttered, eyes roaming the model. "A few thousand well-armed, starving assholes with prison tats and infected, roughhouse back-alley augments, huh? Shit, even the ones not being paid by Londholm are gonna be gunning for us. It's gonna be a fucking *gauntlet*."

I didn't know what else to say, so I shrugged again. "Yep."

She squinted. "What's to stop someone—us, someone else, shit, anyone—from just bombing the building, knock it down and everyone inside?"

I shook my head and stuck my cigarette back in my mouth. "The cops were all over that. Hong Kong's got air defense matrices, and so far nothing's been able to get in—the army's even given up trying to bomb the place because everything gets shot down—that's why they're diving in, get some boots on the pavement and take some installations, open the air up. So you'd have to hump explosives to the site. It's a pre-Unification building, okay, but it was a complete gut job ten years ago, bringing it up to modern code—earthquake-rated, intrusion-hardened, designed to resist collapse and preserve property—that'd be a *lot* of fucking explosives." I shrugged. "Nothing for it but to get up close. Do it the old-fashioned way."

"Guns," she muttered. "We're going to need..." She looked back at the Monk sharply. The Monk just sat there smiling. "All right, Avery, what the fuck is this bullshit, then?"

I winked. "That's technical support. You ever hear of something called SPS?"

Her expression clouded up a little. "Sure, sure. Superstes per Scientia." She shrugged. "Heard of 'em. Bunch of fucking hippie Techies, think the world's ending, trying to gather data and tech to preserve it, who fucking knows how." She pointed at the Monk. "It still functioning?"

I nodded. "It's a *member*." I tapped my head. "It doesn't talk, but it's still got a brain up here."

She squinted at it, leaning forward. The Monk just stared back at her, motionless, its creepy little camera eyes like pebbles. "I never liked these fuckin' dummies. Why's it here? You lookin' to keep a pet?"

I studied her for a moment, wondering how old she'd been when the Electric Church had been "recruiting." Ten? "She's *resources*. Courtesy of the cops."

Mara straightened up and spat on the floor. "So let me get this: The System Pigs have been crackin' heads trying to bury these SPS freaks for months now...and suddenly they're partners? They got a price on your head big enough to fund our retirement, and now you're acceptin' help from 'em?"

It was my turn to shrug. "Wouldn't be the first time the SSF dug down into the sewer for some help, huh?" I sat forward and pointed my cigarette at her. "Relax, kid. It's disarmed, mute, and I've killed more motherfucking Monks in my time than you can imagine."

"Relax?" she said, staring at me. "Kid?" She started laughing. "Hell, Cates, you're half smart. You want a *Monk* starin' at you while you sleep, fine, fine. But what's it *for*?"

I looked down at my hands. "For starters, she hacked me. Jailbroke my Berserker Mode."

The little flashing exclamation point beat in time with my heart. I remembered the doctor back at the recruiting center telling me that I didn't want Berserker Mode. Berserker Mode would blow my fuse in three, two if I was particularly unlucky. I didn't care. I concentrated on the exclamation point again and watched it bloat up. I *wanted* to do it. I wanted to find out what it was like.

Mara raised an eyebrow and looked back at the Monk. "Well, ain't that impressive. How'd you manage that, then?"

The Monk suddenly moved, pulling its little LED screen from within its coat and holding it up:

THERE IS A VULNERABILITY IN THE EHA AUGMENTATION SYSTEM THAT CAN BE EXPLOITED, RESULTING IN THE SECURITY FLAGS BEING RESET TO 0. THIS HAS THE END RESULT OF GRANTING YOU DIRECT CONTROL OVER YOUR EHA OVERDRIVE SYSTEM.

"Bully," Mara said, "for fucking you." She looked back at me, then at the Monk. "And I suppose you broke his anti-frag settings, too, huh? Set the bastard free?"

There was a hint of violence about her, suddenly, the sense that she might go for her gun or my throat. My HUD suddenly brightened as my augments went through what was becoming a familiar wind-up to action. But the Monk's response was instant.

THE BIOLOGICAL CESSATION HOOK-INS ARE SECURE AND CANNOT BE DISABLED OR ADJUSTED WITHOUT TERMINATING THE SUBJECT. THIS IS BY DESIGN. ANY ATTEMPT TO FLASH THE SETTINGS OR REMOVE THE TERMINATION THREADS WILL RESULT IN SUBJECT DEATH. HIS ANTI-FRAG SETTINGS ARE PRESERVED.

Mara nodded, and then looked back at me, appraising me for a second. I thought, *She's wondering if that's a lie,*

*if the Monk is lying about it. If I'm going to bide my time
and make a move and then she's shit out of luck. That's
what* I'd *be thinking.*

After a moment, she nodded. "Okey, Mr. Cates, you've
got an ace up your sleeve now, huh? Bully for fucking
you, too. So, if you're in charge, what's next?"

I flicked my wrist and the map of Hong Kong disappeared. "Get in touch with your guy. Tell him we need
some heavy weapons." I fished in my pocket and tossed
her a dented, charred-looking data cube. "Then we figure out how to get near Hong Kong. Then we figure out
how to get *into* Hong Kong." I stretched, raising my hands
high above my head and grunting. "Don't worry about the
details. If the universe wants me in Hong Kong, we'll get
into Hong Kong." I looked at the Poet, who appeared to be
practicing his badass poses for the Gunner trading cards
I'd been hearing about. "You got an opinion, Adrian?"

He shook his head. "I am a Gunner," he said. "Show
me someone to be killed, and I'll speak to it."

She snorted, popping the cube into her reader with a
little difficulty. Her eyes widened. "Heavy weapons—
fucking hell, Mr. Cates. What, are we going to take the
whole damn city by force? And what the hell is *this*?" she
added, thrusting the reader at me and pointing to my one
moment of genius.

I grinned. "That's a surprise. And we might need every
bit of it," I said, stubbing out my cigarette and reaching for
the dregs of my drink. "According to the cops, Londholm
implanted the God Augment into himself two days ago."
I raised the shot glass and toasted her. "The man's a god
now."

XVI

A TRIUMPHANT MOMENT OF
BAD DUMB LUCK

We had come down in the world. The train leaving the "station"—which was just a big open space of blasted remnants of walls out of which rusty tracks sprouted like corroded veins—was so packed with people and their possessions it was hard enough to push our way into a car before we even tried to find a place to sit. Our tiny private cabin on the way in seemed like a dream, suddenly, even with the Poet's body odor and random Psionics attacking us.

The crush of folks trying to get out of the city was unbelievable. These weren't the dregs, either, these were more or less prosperous-looking folks with some belongings and a soft look about them, getting harder all the time. Where the fuck they thought they were escaping to was beyond me, but I supposed when you started to suspect the army was coming to rain hell down on you for a few weeks straight, anywhere was better. The train had no listed destination; Mara told us that the trains just left, went as far south and east as possible on whatever track was still undamaged, and then put everyone off when it couldn't go any farther.

After a few minutes of jostling, I got tired of it and pushed my way to one side, where narrow bunks were bolted to the walls. Every bunk had been claimed and people sat cheek to cheek in them, like pigeons. I picked a spot randomly and grinned up at a thin, young man wearing last year's suit, his coat sleeves a little frayed and his shoes beyond hope. A pretty blond girl sat next to him, clutching his arm; her face was pale and without makeup, but she'd made an effort with her hair. For some reason her energetic DIY hairdo made me hate her, so I kept my eyes on him.

Avery, you're an awful person, sometimes, Dolores Salgado suddenly whispered in my head, making me twitch.

"Funny thing, friend," I said briskly. "My ticket guarantees me a seat, and I don't seem to have one."

His nostrils flared. *"Non Inglese,"* he said, a low, fluttery mutter. But he kept his eyes on me, which I gave him credit for. I eyed his hands, the stupid grin still on my face. They were soft and manicured—the man was fleeing the city for his life, but his fingernails were *perfect.* I reached up, took his nose between my forefinger and thumb, and squeezed.

"Friend," I said. "Would you mind?"

Immediately, the woman next to him released his arm and began screeching, beating her tiny hands against me. The Poet suddenly enveloped her, wrapping his arms around her and lifting her off the bunk bodily, holding her dangling in front of him as she continued to screech and beat her fists against the air.

"Go for the wife first," he said as a surprisingly large space opened up around us—I hadn't thought it physically possible for the people in this train to make any more room. "It is a good rule of thumb. Women are vicious."

The man put his hands up and made a squeaking noise I took as compliance, so I released him. He grabbed two small leather bags from the bunk and dropped to the floor, expertly intercepting his wife as the Poet released her and she tried to lunge for me. The crowd swelled back into place around us, and the pair disappeared into it, muttering to each other as I pushed Mara up onto the bunk, liking the feel of her weight in my hands. I handed up our one large, heavy duffel bag, and then pulled myself up next to her.

The Poet waved off my hand. "I'll remain down here," he said, turning his back on us and rolling his shoulders. "Stand first security watch. You just lost friends, huh?"

I nodded. I *was* a terrible person. I knew it. Everyone on the train knew it by sight. The Monk, wearing a heavy hood over its gruesome white head, took up a spot next to him. I looked around the bunks. A dozen people stared blankly back at me, with another dozen or so on the lower bunks below us. The bunks were just rough canvas, sagging dangerously under us, about as comfortable as being stabbed in the armpit. I looked down at the Poet for a moment and watched his flickering tattoos, a blur of color around his neck. I was hungry, but otherwise still buzzed with the unnatural energy and lack of pain of my augments. I'd thought the train insufferably hot when we'd first pushed our way in, but sitting on the bunk with Mara I felt fine, cool, and numb.

I wondered if this was what it was like to be a machine. I was halfway there, after all.

With my foot I nudged the Monk's shoulder. "Tell me something. Why are you—your group—going after Londholm? Why work with the cops?"

The Monk didn't turn or move its head. It immediately reached inside its coat and held the LED screen up behind it, more or less in my line of sight.

WE PROTECT THE TECHNOLOGY. THE MOMENT HE USED IT ON HIMSELF HE LOST OUR PROTECTION.

Immediately, it lowered its arm and stuffed the screen back into its coat.

"And the cops?"

The screen came back out in one smooth motion.

WE ARE AGNOSTIC CONCERNING RESOURCES.

I grinned as the screen was hidden away again. Everyone thought they were using everyone else—I was the only honest man in the fucking room. I knew *everyone* was using me. "I like that," I said to the back of its head. "I'm going to use that." I shut my eyes and tried to imagine myself inside a clear glass bubble. For a while, when I'd had voices in my head constantly, I'd gotten pretty good at summoning the image, and it had helped, trapping everything outside of me and leaving me alone in a silent bubble, at peace. I was out of practice, but it didn't take long.

I thought about Michaleen.

Cainnic Orel, Michaleen Garda—whatever his real name was. I pictured the Little Man back in Chengara, small and tight, leathery and cheerful. He'd played me in prison and he'd played me into this bullshit. I'd been sleepwalking, but my session with Hense and the Monk had left me feeling more in control than I'd felt in weeks. I had *something* under my control. A resource I might be able to leverage into turning my course back on the Little Man and making him eat it.

My hands twitched. I concentrated on the bubble, on shutting everything, even my own thoughts, out. I hadn't slept in days.

"Avery."

My hand shot out and took hold of her wrist as my eyes opened. My HUD went from a pale, almost-invisible gray to bright.

Mara made no move to snatch her arm back or fight me, so I relaxed, looking around. We were moving, the train car vibrating with speed. It was dark and at a glance everyone else looked to be sleeping.

"My turn at guard duty?" I asked, trying to stretch without jostling my neighbors too much.

"I think we have a problem," she said, gently pulling her arm back. She held out her tiny card-sized handheld, which she'd tuned to one of the few government Vids still operating on a regular basis. It was useless for real information; I hadn't bothered tuning in even when I'd found myself back in civilization. I squinted down at it and saw the same picture of me the SSF had been using at the border crossing.

"Your price has gone up," Mara said. "You're fucking *valuable*."

The reward had doubled, and now resembled a fortune, even if you needed a bag full of yen just to buy a cigarette these days. I gave Mara a grin calculated to be the sort of half-proud bullshit she'd expect from Avery Cates, Destroyer of Worlds, and winked.

"I'll kill myself and we'll split the proceeds."

She put her blank eyes on me. "I *suspect*, you stupid fucking slab o' beef, that we're not the *only* people on this train who've noticed you're worth more than all the crap everyone's carting in their goddamn rucksacks combined."

I paused, my HUD immediately lighting up as the gloomy train car seemed to brighten up, clarifying. Almost everyone appeared to be asleep, their heads in their chests like birds, the standing-room-only section on the floor remaining upright apparently through friction and surface tension.

Somewhere, nearby, there was whispering.

The moment I noticed it, a hissing noise filled my ears and I could just make out every other word, my own name popping up three or four times in quick succession. I turned my head to the right and there they were, an entire bunk of people, staring at me. They weren't rough; their coats were too new and too conservative, their collars popped up in the current style. And they were too old; I was the exception to the rule, but most people from my sort of neighborhood died young. These were just people, a little dirtier and hungrier than they were used to, but just civilians. I gave them a hard stare, carefully calibrated, and one or two looked away. The rest stared back, leaning this way and that to whisper at each other.

I counted. There were fifteen men and six women crammed onto that row of bunks.

Word was spreading, too, leaking downward to the bunk beneath them. It was strange to watch it happening, people being shoved awake, something whispered directly into their ear, two sets of eyes on me. Then again, with the next person, sometimes with a handheld like Mara's held up for confirmation. I looked back at Mara; we were all armed now, and I had no doubt any one of the three of us could handle a half-dozen shitkickers—assuming, of course, that Mara and Adrian would be bothered to step between me and a mob. But there were sixty, seventy people crammed into the car, and sixty or seventy more in the next.

The exclamation point in the corner of my vision beat in time with my heart.

I shut my eyes and took a deep breath. These were just civilians. Before the System started unspooling around them, they'd had jobs, families, dinner dates, and the idea of sharing a train car with someone like me had been ludicrous. I didn't want to do any more damage here than I had to.

I opened my eyes and was fully awake, humming with a slight adrenaline edge. I put my hand inside my coat and closed it over the butt of my Roon auto, not new but well-loved, its grip glossy from use and sweat. I looked across the aisle at the first group of people and stared at them until one of them, a kid with a scum of gingery beard on his face, stared back.

"You don't want this, junior," I said loudly. "Stay alive."

It was too fucking late; I saw that immediately. He had too many people at his back, pushing, and I'd fucked him by singling him out. Or he'd fucked himself by meeting my gaze—it didn't matter. I felt an icy black ball of nausea in my belly, realizing that this chump had no fucking chance here and I'd invited him up onto the chopping block. I looked around the car, quickly, trying to see how we could get past this without killing half the fucking world. I couldn't see a way; if I backed down, it would just encourage them, make them think this reward was the easiest thing they'd ever done.

"Can't do that," the man said, shaking his head. "We've already contacted the police."

My HUD told me otherwise—I could see pretty plainly from the tiny icon in the upper right corner that there was no connection with the grid. A few years ago you could have gone to the fucking south pole and gotten a signal, but things got sketchy away from the cities these days. I didn't know how far out we were, but if someone had sent the cops a note, it wouldn't get there anytime soon, and if it did, I wondered if Janet Hense or someone like her might not do some unofficial voodoo on it, since the System Pigs were playing against themselves on this one.

I shook my head. "No, you didn't." I wanted to give him—all of them—every chance.

They looked around at each other, flicking their eyes up and around. Counting. Crunching the odds. I was doing the same thing, trying to figure how many would take a chance, how many would crowd to the sides of the car, heads down, eyes shut. How many would follow five seconds in if enough of the others made a move. How many I could take on. Nineteen rounds in the Roon, and the possibility that Mara and the Poet would have my back. It was tiring, doing the math.

Shoot him in the mouth, Dick Marin whispered in my head, the ghost of a...brain still clicking and whirring somewhere, a multitude of somewheres, a ghost outdated and gamy from seclusion. *They'll all calm down, then.*

I gritted my teeth. It had been so long since the ghosts—introduced when I'd been halfway bricked in Chengara, my brain sucked into a mainframe—had bothered me, I'd lost my touch at ignoring them. Silence had settled into the tiny spaces between us; I kept my hand on my gun inside my coat and slid the safety off, looking slowly around. No one moved, but most of the car was staring at me. If these had been my sort, from my neighborhood or its like, we'd already be trading body blows—I was valuable. As I looked around, I could almost see the backbone draining out of them. It was one thing to plot over a reward while the subject napped a few feet away. It was something else to read the list of things I was wanted for—murder, kidnapping, conspiracy, treason—and be the first to come at me. The System Pigs had made me sound dangerous.

"All right," I said, and suddenly a man who'd been standing in the press of people on the floor pulled himself up onto the side of the bunks, hooking one arm into the supports and hanging there. He was wearing an expensive coat, but his clothes underneath were grubby and torn, and his silvery beard was mangled and knotted. His eyes were shock white in the midst of his dirty face, wide and fierce.

"This man," he shouted, pointing at me, "is a murderer! And a thief! A piece of human shit! And every person who puts a hand on him right here, right now, gets a goddamn share of the reward!"

The train rumbled on, the steady rhythm and sway so fast and constant as to be silent and still.

He stared around with wide, frantic eyes. He drew in a deep breath and pointed at me again. "This man—"

Next to me, Mara's hand flew up. In the tight space of the car the sound of her gun was intensely loud, louder than anything most of these people had ever heard. The whole train seemed to duck as the shouter's face exploded into a spray of blood, revealing a grisly lump of bone and flesh that had been hiding within, and for a moment the Poet and the Monk were the only things standing upright.

Someone grabbed my arms from behind, and I was jerked backward. I let them pull me, and I got my feet up onto the edge of the bunk, giving myself a powerful push and slamming back into them, their hands snapping loose. I yanked my Roon from its holster and jabbed it up at the ceiling, firing two more booming shots. It should have been enough. It should have scared the shit out of them all.

They swarmed us.

A small figure in a big coat leaped from the bunks to my right, landing on top of me in a triumphant moment of bad dumb luck, and before I could remind myself that these were just people, just civilians, I'd shot her twice through the chest, sending her sailing backward into the suddenly surging crowd. I had no headroom and squirmed up on the bunk trying to position myself on my knees; I wanted the high ground. Whirling around, I found the rest of our bunk cowering behind us, arms up over their heads, people just hoping that if they stayed very still and didn't get involved, it would all pass them by.

How's that working out for you? I asked them silently. I wondered when trains had gone fucking sentient, and when they'd decided they hated me.

Forcing myself back around, I lashed my gun hand out at a tan, oblong head as it rose up over the edge of the bunk, crunching a nose into pulp with a shout, the jolt disappearing up my arm, absorbed by augmented nerve-suppression and circulation monitoring. I felt light and fast. I was a machine, and being a machine was turning out to be kind of fucking cool.

Everyone was shouting. Mara and I were still side by side, kicking and firing and pushing them back. I was amazed—we'd shot three with some prejudice. *Desperate*, I thought. With something akin to panic, I realized we weren't going to intimidate them. We were going to have to kill most of them.

Another head popped up over the edge of the bunk, a sweaty mass of dark hair; as I tried to snap my arm back someone grabbed it, and then another pair of hands joined them, slamming my arm painfully backward. I kicked at the head I'd seen and made some contact, and then someone crawled on top of me, putting a foot on my neck so precisely right I almost thought there might have been a pro or two in the crowd. Choking, I reached back in desperation, hoping for a lock of hair or an ear to grab onto, but instead my free arm was seized, and two more people pulled themselves up onto me. I heard Mara's gun go off twice, three times as my HUD swelled into a red sea of flashing icons and data streams. Then there was a volley of shots, suddenly cut off.

I was being smothered. In the corner of my vision, the flashing exclamation point seemed to grow with every steady, augment-regulated heartbeat. Then I was sliding, being pulled down from the bunk by my shoes, suffocating. I mashed my finger down on the trigger, the Roon barking out fifteen shots in rapid succession, and I stabbed at the exclamation point in my HUD just like the Monk had explained it to me.

XVII

SHE AIN'T THE FIRST

They were like paper in my hands.

Everything got slow, but crisp. So fucking crisp, like everything was being run through a filter before it got passed on to my brain. I pulled the gun up toward my face and my arm tore free from the three people holding it down. It was effortless, my arm popping up in front of me, bruised and scratched, the coat torn. One of the figures that had been sitting on my arm, trying to wrestle the gun free, was sent rolling off the bunk, smashing into the crowd below us in slow motion.

Frowning, I decided to experiment, and I tore my other arm free with the same easy effort. Two people leaped onto my back, but it was easy to time their spastic, wave-like efforts and flick them off of me with my gun-heavy hand, tearing the thin skin of their faces, a tooth flying like a bloody comet through the thick air.

It was *easy*.

Mara was pinned on the bunk next to me, wriggling

and kicking but trapped. On the floor, the Monk had thrown back its hood and revealed its waxy fake head, and a discernible circle of empty space had opened up around it as people recoiled from the first monk they'd seen in years. Next to it, the Poet was struggling with three women, his fist slowly connecting with the chin of one, her face screwed up in a comical grimace.

I didn't feel anything.

I was empty, clinical. My HUD was bright and fully operational, showing my heart rate at the top of the red zone, my blood pressure off the scale, brain activity jagged and spiky—I felt none of it. I was steady and serene, and even when four more hands latched onto me, pulling at me, fingers digging into my skin, I felt nothing—no pain, no irritation. Just a stream of data to analyze, a reaction to calculate. Lazily, I rolled my shoulders and twisted out of their grasp, and decided the time had come to get this over with.

Taking my time, I pushed up and got my knees under me. I dropped the empty clip from the Roon and fished a fresh one from my pocket, slamming it into place and racking a shell into the chamber with my bloodied hand. I turned, swinging the gun out in front of me, and every face that got between the gun and the floor, I put a bullet in. It was beautiful, in a way, the perfection of it, the precision of my own movements. It was like I thought of something and it happened without me having to make any of the intervening calculations or movements.

A young woman in a nice, ridiculous fur coat pulled herself up, face locked in a snarl, rising slowly from the floor as she leaped for my throat. I slashed the gun down onto her head, bones crunching in both my hand and her head, her graceful backward slump gorgeous, ballet.

Rolling to my side, I freed my legs, twisting my back beyond its limits, and popped up into a crouch on the top of the bunk. I scanned the roiling crowd, eyes stopping on a young girl almost directly across from me, her red hair limp and greasy looking. Her coat was nice enough, and her skin was healthy and pale; she looked like a rich kid who'd gone to seed, like the occasional narcs who stumbled downtown in Old New York and never made it out again, sucking their credit dry and slowly absorbed by the neighborhood. She was probably not yet twenty, middle aged and didn't know it, her eyes wide in terror as she stared around. I found I had the time to just crouch there and stare at her for a while, studying her. Gleason, I thought, would have been about her age. The thought seemed to come from outside of me, beamed in, as if the cosmos suddenly wanted me to remember her for some reason, to remember that she'd still be alive if she hadn't hooked up with me and my fucking crazy ideas about making the System hurt, about staying off the Rail, about training her up to be just like me.

That was before the Plague, before I'd been cut down to size. Taught my lesson.

I'd paused long enough for the good citizens of what was left of the System to get their second wind; they'd come this far and if a few of them were dead and a few more sputtering blood onto the floor, all the more fucking reason to tear me apart. I felt hot, and realized with a start that I was perspiring heavily, sweat running off of me in slow, syrupy rivulets. My HUD was a dark, angry red, every status bar slammed into the top of its scale.

There was a determined group of six men and one woman, all soft looking, well dressed and white skinned.

One of the men already had a broken nose and swollen eyes, but he came with the rest of them, rushing me all at once, advancing on me with mouths open, screaming something too slowly to make out. I leaned forward slowly, shifting my weight to absorb the shock of their impact, but movement behind me, a wavelike bounce shuddering through the bunk, made me spin, one hand easing out and taking hold of an offered calf, a half-inch of brightly tattooed skin showing between the heavy hem of the pants and the cracked leather of the sturdy boot. I rolled myself forward, timing it out with ease, letting momentum and gravity pull me down toward the floor as I yanked on the leg, pulling a dense, heavy figure up and over my head as I landed, slamming him into the approaching group and knocking them all on their asses. My projectile tucked and rolled into a passable landing, and when he popped up on the balls of his feet I realized it was Adrian, glaring at me, a fresh scrape along his forehead oozing blood into his eyes. He had a jagged knife in one hand but had lost his piece of shit Hamada.

He was shouting, but I couldn't hear him and just smiled as I absentmindedly stiff-armed a broken-nose asshole who'd spun and rushed at me as best as you could rush in the crowded car.

It was so *easy*. I didn't even fire the fucking gun, I just punched and slapped and pushed. I felt like I could have kicked their collective ass all day long—every face that got close enough, I smashed a fist into it, every flicker of movement behind me, I spun easily and hit low. When I got tired of it, when it had gone on for long enough— though I didn't know how long it had been—I took hold of a convenient body and lifted it up, tearing fingernails

and sending a fresh sheet of sweat streaming down my
face, and threw it into the remaining crowd of screaming,
huddling people. I spun, and had a split-second image of
Mara scowling at me before she smashed the butt of her
gun down on top of my head.

Full of fucking surprises.

Something smelled terrible, and I regretted everything
I'd done in my life, ever, the endless subtle trail that had
led to me smelling this. I tried to flinch my face away
from it, but the moment I tried to move, my head pain
bloomed...everywhere. My right hand throbbed, my left
arm was seared deep with something hot and sharp, my
ribs ached and my neck was frozen stiff. I felt weak and
dehydrated, and immediately I began shivering, which
hurt even more.

I opened my eyes, and the dim red light of the train's
interior burned my eyes and set fire to something in my
head, which joined in the general throbbing. Mara's face
pushed into my vision, filling it as she frowned down
at me.

"You don't look good, you fucking psychopath," she
said.

I tried to say something. My mouth opened and a thin
wail dribbled out of me.

"That was not too smart," I heard the Poet say. Suddenly, my head was pounding. All of my HUD bars were
yellow and well below normal. The fucking exclamation
point was blinking in the corner again, but I flinched away
from it. I never wanted to fucking do that again. "You
almost killed *me*, you fuck. It was...disturbing."

"Disturbin'?" Mara spat, moving away from me. "We got sixteen fucking corpses here he killed with his *bare fucking hands.*"

I turned my head, sharp stabbing pains shooting down my back. The car had been transformed into a slaughterhouse. Most of its former population was gone, but the vibration under me told me the train was still in motion, speeding along. Bodies rolled on the floor around me, limp and bloodied, and the whole space smelled like blood.

"Where..." I whispered, hoarsely, my throat seizing up in pain. "Where—"

"Herded 'em into the next car," Mara snapped as the Monk suddenly knelt next to me, lifting my limp arm in its cold, plastic hands, its face still frozen in that unfortunate grin I'd started to assume was a malfunction. "They didn't need too much encouragement."

The Monk began an efficient examination, retrieving a small handheld from its coat and running it lightly along the perimeter of my body with one hand as it prodded and poked me with the other, getting some weak moans and grunts from me in response. Satisfied, it pushed the handheld back inside its coat and produced the LED screen again.

AS EXPECTED: YOU ARE IN SHOCK, AS IF YOU HAD SURVIVED WEEKS OF DEPRIVATION AND ABUSE. YOU WILL RECOVER WITH FLUIDS AND REST, BUT BE WEAKENED. YOUR AUGMENTS WILL NOT FUNCTION AT FULL CAPACITY WITHOUT SERVICE; YOU WILL EXPERIENCE DEGRADED FUNCTION. I WOULD GUESS THAT ONE MORE INVOCATION OF THE EHA ENHANCEMENT MODE WILL EASILY KILL YOU.

I nodded slowly, feeling like my brain was softly bouncing up and down inside my skull. "You think so, huh? You're fucking brilliant."

I slowly forced my way up onto my elbows, sweat popping out on my brow again. The Poet ambled over and held out a single N-tab and a small canteen to me. I took the tab in a shaking hand and swallowed it, then took the canteen, intending to just take a sip. When I handed it back to him, gasping, I'd drained it, water running down my chin, my whole body shaking. My stomach instantly seized up and tried to send everything right back up again, so I clamped my mouth shut and took some deep breaths, swallowing rapidly until it subsided.

Michaleen Garda had done this to me. I wouldn't be on this fucking train, wouldn't be crammed full of augments, wouldn't be sitting here feeling my internal organs turn into cheese if not for that stump of a man. I ran my dry, swollen tongue along my lips and smiled, sitting up and trying to balance myself so I wouldn't slump over.

"It got a little sloppy," I said, pushing hard to make my voice steady and loud. "So fucking what? You don't look like a girl who cries herself to sleep at night about innocent victims."

I had to play my role. I was going to fuck Mickey over, and to do that I needed his resources. I was going to get into Hong Kong, I was going to find Londholm, and then I was going to take the fucking augment. I was going to pull it hot and throbbing from Londholm's head. And Mickey could come after me, or I would go after him, with the augment as leverage. I hadn't figured out how to deal with Mara and the frag settings, the tiny bomb inside my head, but I still needed her anyway so I could afford to wait for inspiration.

She threw her hands in the air. "Sloppy? He has the fuckin' gall to call it *sloppy*. And now look at you. Gray and shivery. What happens, we get a call from those friendly Psionics now, shakin' the train about, and you like a piece of greasy paper there?" She squatted down on her haunches in front of me. "Mr. Cates, no fuckin' offense, but I could kill you with some harsh words right now, the way you look."

I smiled. "You've got a heart of gold, Mara, worrying about me like that."

She snorted. "You're an *investment*, boyo."

I cocked my head a little. Something about Mara again made me feel like I knew her. It was elusive, and I couldn't make her stick anywhere, but the feeling stayed with me.

"I'm fine," I said slowly. I gathered myself and pushed up onto my feet, rushing into it to get some momentum, terrified I'd lose my balance and fall over. I found I still had my empty gun in my hand, and I slipped it into a damp pocket. "We were outnumbered and I took care of it. We're still headed in the right direction, and if this is the first time you've had to ride with corpses, I'll eat my fucking gun, so stop bellyaching."

I worked hard to stop the shivering. I shuffled forward to the pocket door leading from the car and squinted through the cloudy plastic window across the gap to the next car coupled to us. Faces were pressed against the opposite door, staring back at me, calm and unblinking. I stared back. I imagined the story they'd tell as they fanned out into what was left of the world.

She smiled. "Naw, ain't t'first time I've ridden with the dead, Avery," she said. She shook her head, turning away. "You clean this shit up a little, though. No reason we have to bathe in the gore like some fucking savages, eh?"

I sighed and turned around, holding my shaking hands

in front of me. I froze. Against the rear wall of the train car, staring at me with wide, sightless eyes, was the red-haired girl I'd spotted earlier. The icy white skin of her throat turned mottled and bruised. My hands twitched and my breath turned solid in my throat, choking me.

Stop crying, Dick Marin's ghost whispered to me. *She ain't the first.*

XVIII

IF I WANT SUICIDE, I'LL JUST SLAP YOU IN THE FACE AND CALL YOU NAMES UNTIL YOU CRY

When the train stuttered to a stop, I was jolted awake from a black sleep, dreamless and perfect, like being smothered in myself. I came back online immediately and remembered everything, the rotten smell in the air all I needed as a prompt. My head was pounding and my mouth dry and gummy; I fought the immediate urge to dry heave. My heart lurched in my chest, heavy and staggering, and I wasn't sure if I could stand up without letting Mara know how weak I was.

The Poet sat next to me, putting his Hamada back together more or less without looking at it. He'd taken off his coat, and his metallic tattoos squirmed and flashed on his neck and arms, tiny people in elaborate inks being killed over and over again. He grinned at me, his sudden, thick beard and big reflective glasses making him look like an alien, something not human.

"Welcome back, my friend," he said cheerfully. "We have all arrived somewhere. Not where we wished for."

I licked my lips and tried to swallow. We'd pushed the bodies off the car hours ago, the wind slamming past us with enough force to make it difficult to breathe, but the car was still a swamp of jellying blood and sweat. I felt listless and without energy, and immediately wanted to go back to sleep.

Forcing myself to move, I sat up and made a show of stretching luxuriously. "Well, let's get out there and see where we are."

"No reason to rush," the Poet said, waving one hand negligently. "Take a moment and relax. A long walk ahead."

I stared at him for a few moments. The smile lingered as he reassembled the gun with long, nimble fingers. He was, I realized with a start, being kind to me. I wanted to punch him in the mouth. I wanted to make him eat his pity and regret it. Kindness got you fucking killed. You weren't afraid of people you felt pity for.

After a moment, I looked away. If Adrian Panić smelled blood in the water and started throwing his weight around, let him. I was tired of playing the fucking game. No one had played it better than I. Decades of acting, decades of staying a step ahead of every piece of shit swimming in the same pond as you—no one had been better at it. And where had it gotten me?

I started shivering again. To hide it, I surged up, letting momentum carry me upright. Once there, my vision hazed and I got light-headed for a moment, my legs going noodly, but my HUD flashed yellow and suddenly I felt better, my military augments adjusting my chemistry. I didn't know if I was actually better or if it just felt that way, and I wasn't sure if it made any difference.

"You're feeling better?" Panić said, glancing up at me. "That relieves my mind, my friend. We need you on this."

I fished for my Roon in my pocket and inspected it for a moment. It was slick and sticky with blood. Looking up, I saw Mara lying on one of the bunks, roomy and luxurious now that we had the whole car to ourselves. "Any idea where we are?" I asked.

"No," Mara said without moving.

The Monk was seated on a low bunk under Mara's. It produced its LED screen and held it up for me.

I WOULD GUESS SOME MILES NORTH OF SHENZHEN. ARMY ACTIVITY NORTH OF HONG KONG PREVENTS THIS TRAIN FROM MOVING ANY FARTHER. ALL OTHER PASSENGERS HAVE LIKELY DEBARKED.

Feeling groggy and sick to my stomach, I checked my gun one last time and walked to the door, making sure to keep my gait steady and brisk. The Roon needed cleaning, but I reloaded it anyway and hoped for the best. The Poet might find some morsel of pity for an old broken-down Gunner, but I was pretty sure Mara would put me down like a sick dog if I couldn't do my part.

I slid the door open and stepped between the cars. It was warm and humid compared to Brussels; a brisk wind pushed at me and smelled rotten and smoky. Facing south, I could see the previous population of the train fanning out into the tall grass and scrubby trees, rain falling in a steady, depressing drizzle. On the horizon was an immense plume of thick, black smoke, actively curling up into the air like a column of shifting gray stone. At its base was a soft orange glow.

The people were all carrying luggage and were headed generally eastward. I had no idea where the fuck they thought they were going.

Mara climbed out behind me, stretching her lithe body, her eyes clear and sharp on me. "All right, Mr. Cates. You're in charge of this fucked-up situation, eh? Y'made that clear back in Belgium. And we achieved our current state of *world-record* fucked-up-ness due to you, eh? So now what?"

I gestured toward the column of smoke, the biggest I'd ever seen, like someone had snuffed out a star somewhere on the coast. "We start walking."

She sniffed. "Walk," she said slowly, as if trying the word on for the first time. "*Where*, for fuck's sake?"

I gestured again. "South. Toward Hong Kong. Toward the army."

The column of smoke didn't seem to be appreciably nearer. My head was fuzzy, the headache having spread to envelop my entire brain in a sour pulsing cloud. Despite the humid heat, my teeth chattered in my mouth. I'd been concentrating on putting one foot in front of the other, a slow, ponderous process that had kept me moving so far.

We were walking through the outskirts of what had once been a large city that had been all but erased. The ground beneath us was smooth and warm, like something recently melted, and nothing was standing taller than three or four feet, jagged remnants of foundations. Nothing—*nothing*. It was impressive, a flat field of rubble as far as you could see, not a single building spared. I didn't know if it had been the undersecretaries and their shiny new army or the System Police, but someone had studied up on salting the fucking earth.

The air smelled like metal, and I felt like radiation was soaking into me, even though my HUD showed rad levels as nominal. I just kept swallowing my stomach and staring at the smoke, making sure I was more or less aimed toward it at all times.

"This is impressive. I have seen Berserk before. Grown men were crying."

I squinted but didn't look at the Poet. I hadn't noticed him stepping close to me. This was how broken old men got killed, but I couldn't even summon up panic or fear, outrage or anger. I just didn't want to turn my head.

"Do not be a fool," he suddenly whispered. "I prefer you do not die. Let me be of help."

I licked my dried lips. "I'm fine, Adrian. Go the fuck away."

I heard him snort. "The great Master Cates," he said with a sigh. "I know the need for image. Trust no one, of course. Trust only yourself." He laughed softly. "I've heard Cates stories."

Even though we were just walking, I was gasping. "Like what?"

"You survived the Plague. You killed cops as a *hobby*. Survived Chengara."

I nodded. "I'm the next stage in evolution, sure," I panted. "Can't kill me." I was almost a fucking machine now, anyway. Even when I closed my eyes, I saw the faint outlines of my HUD, electrical impulses fired directly into my optical nerves.

Suddenly the Poet's hand was on my chest, pushing me to a halt. "Stop a moment, please." I looked around;

we were standing in what had once been a large square, where a perimeter wall still clung to existence around us, limestone still clinging to the cinder-block bones beneath, creating shadows. I blinked, ancient instinct struggling up through the haze with a payload of anxiety. He looked back at Mara and the Monk, which moved with the subtlety and quiet of an avalanche. "Despite our silent advance, we are being watched."

Mara stepped forward to stand with us, hands on her slim hips, scowling around. She'd gotten a bend in her back that made her look old, shortened, and worn down. "Fuck me swinging," she muttered. "I think you're right." She turned and spat on the melted ground. "Well, Mr. Cates, I think we've found your army." The Monk, carrying our heavy duffel on its back, stepped next to Mara with its serene, infinite smile on its plastic face and stopped.

I nodded, taking a deep breath and stepping forward, shaking my head, trying to snap some clarity into myself, eyes roaming as I noted the spots I'd have placed snipers and scouts if I'd been in charge. I stood for a moment, swaying a little but unable to stop myself, and then I raised my arms. They felt like someone had tied weights to them, and after a few seconds of standing in silence, just the soft wind and the damp air in my ears, I muttered a curse under my breath and breathed deeply, gathering myself to yell.

"We're four assholes on foot," I shouted. "You waiting to see if we're radioactive?"

There were another few beats of silence, and I thought, *Fuck it, I'm putting my arms down. Let some trigger-happy simp blow my head off for it.* As I dropped them, they all suddenly appeared, stepping out from behind every possible hiding place I'd spotted. Their white uniforms were brilliant, perfect, impossibly clean in the dusty, half-melted city. They all stepped out from their locations simultaneously, but only three or four had their long-barreled sniper rifles trained on us. They all had their cowls up, plastic visors glaring in the dimmed light.

As we stood watching them, detachments trotted around, circling behind us.

"You better know what the fuck you're doin', Mr. Cates," Mara said in a low, unhappy voice. "Some might say this smells like fucking suicide."

"If I want suicide," I said slowly, keeping my eyes on the small group of snipers in front of us, "I'll just slap you in the face and call you names until you cry, okay? Now shut the fuck up and let me handle this."

A few more seconds and then one of the white uniforms stepped forward and pushed its cowl back. A pudgy-faced blond woman stared at me, her face flushed, short hair damp. My vision was suddenly filled with the tiny text boxes, blooming on top of each of the soldiers for a second and then fading to transparency. I ignored them all. I didn't need names.

"Deserter!" she called out, crooking one hand at me. "Step forward. The rest of you don't move, or we'll erase you."

This was said with a curious lack of bravado—it was simply said. She sounded bored and tired and in no mood to actually threaten us. I started walking, trying to put a little pimp roll into it, trying to look dangerous, confident. I kept my eyes on the blonde, feeling every other set of blank, visored eyes on me. As I got closer, I realized she was speaking into a microphone embedded in the collar of her uniform.

"...due respect, you fucking monkey, we are in our assigned *position*. There's nothing fucking *here*, except some fucking vagrants we're going to rub in a minute, okay? So get on the fucking horn and tell your CO we're just standing here with our dicks in our hands and after I get done putting some bullets in some ears we're gonna get *bored*."

She cut the connection with a savage flick of her wrist and turned on me.

"Gonzalez, 009987-562, I got your beacon in my HUD like a fucking stone in my boot, but you're not assigned to a unit or detach service, which makes you a fucking runner. I don't know how you ran or which incompetent piece of shit *let* you run, but I am hereby putting you on trial and I'm about to condemn you to fucking execution. You got five seconds."

I nodded. "You know Colonel Malkem Anners?"

She stared for a moment, then nodded, once. "Yup."

I smiled. "Tell him Avery Cates has a business proposal."

XIX

AIN'T EASY MEANS IT AIN'T CHEAP

"A new Cates story," the Poet whispered next to me. "The great man slept just before his execution."

I kept my eyes shut. The cell smelled like piss that had been fermented, imbibed, and pissed out all over again. "They're not going to shoot us," I said. Then I opened one eye. The Poet—I realized I had gotten perfectly used to his ridiculous nickname and used it even though I knew his real one—sat at my feet on the hard metal bench I was stretched out on, looking grimy and peaceful in his glasses. "Well, they're not going to shoot *me*."

I closed my eye again and was instantly in a drifting, fuzzy place that wasn't quite sleep. It was sheer physical exhaustion.

I heard the creaking of his leather coat. "You also are calm," he said. "You can be shot as well, as far as I know."

Mara's voice was irritated. "They can shoot me a hundred times. What do I care? It's the fucking *delay* that bothers me, follow?"

Her voice echoed in my thoughts. Something about Mara bothered me...I couldn't put my finger on it, but every time she opened her thin little mouth, I wanted to grab hold of her neck and choke her until she explained it to me. She was young; I wondered if I'd known her as a kid and forgotten, maybe one of the rats who had run underfoot back in Pick's, trying to pick up a tip or two, trying to lift a pocket. We'd always tossed a few of them out on their ass every night. I'd never gotten too upset—more power to them if they could snatch a credit dongle off of that crowd.

That didn't feel right, though. She didn't have the look. She always moved like she didn't like her body, awkward and tight. She walked like she was angry with the ground, and her accent, broad and vaguely Gaelic, varied. All of which was perfectly normal, except it wasn't.

The fucking Monk, with its eternal smile and rotting brain, freaked me out less than Mara did.

We were in a small holding cell, a cube of stainless steel apparently formed out of a single sheet of metal, escorted into it with firm but polite insistence by the soldiers after making contact with Anners's staff and relieving us with horrible efficiency of our weapons, even finding Adrian's garrote. In the absence of clear authority to shoot us all in the head, the squad leader had become suddenly polite and businesslike, wondering, I was sure, how a runner like me had any pull with a colonel. She'd even offered to round up some freeze-dried rations for us. I knew that if Anners decided to be rid of me after all, the blonde would shrug and pop one in my ear without hesitation, but until then I might turn out to be a major pain in her ass, and she was playing it safe.

"I don't like the army," the Poet groused. "I do not like uniforms. Men who take orders."

"*You* take orders from our girl over there," I pointed out.

"She has the black button," he said with a verbal shrug. "The Middle Finger of God. This is common sense." The soldiers had allowed Mara to retain our tiny remotes; I guessed that under Anners's command they knew pressees got sold out of the army sometimes, and allowed for it.

"Shut the fuck up, both of you," Mara suddenly said, sounding cheerful. "*That's* an order."

"If they come for us," the Poet said with sudden ferocity, "I'll ask if I can kill *you*. Save them the trouble."

The heavy door to our little cell began grinding open, and I sat up just as Mara said, "Dream on, *cailín báire*."

The blonde pushed her way into the cell, trailed by three other kids in uniform. Their cowls were down, and she looked fresher than before, cleaned up and cooled off. The uniforms were eerie—they shimmered and *flowed*, and I didn't want the material to touch me ever again.

She put her blank, heavy-lidded eyes on me and jerked a thumb over her shoulder. "A'ight," she said. "Colonel wants you."

We all stood up, but the blonde pointed at me. "Just him, eh?" she said. When the Poet and Mara hesitated, her cheeks suddenly bloomed red. "Sit the fuck *down*," she said, snapping her fingers once. The three grunts behind her instantly raised their modified shredders. Mara and the Poet sat down, hands up in placating gestures. The Monk sat down like it had just remembered the maneuver and wanted to try it out.

I smiled around the cell. "Set me wide," I said to Mara, and winked.

*   *   *

The army had built a temporary base a quarter mile outside of what had once been Shenzhen. It was temporary
in the sense that they had built it in a few weeks and its
erosion from natural forces might possibly predate the
sun's going supernova. I followed the blonde down a corridor that felt tight and sealed, underground, with power
lines snaking their way above us, the air sterile and crank.
Everything else might be falling apart, but the grunts still
had a way with resources.

We'd only been on the move for a few minutes when
she stopped outside another impressive-looking metal
door with a spray-painted series of numbers on it. She
knocked once, crisply, and then stepped aside as the door
sagged inward and she gestured me inside. I sketched her
a little salute as I pulled out a crushed pack of cigarettes,
feeding one into my mouth, and entered.

I'd expected an office, a small tight room with Anners
behind a desk, so I was startled at the sudden sense of
space. It was a huge room carved out of a natural cave,
lit from above by several banks of bright white lamps,
giving everything an unnatural crispness, the shadows
sharp enough to cut. It was filled with the buzz of people,
white uniforms moving around talking to themselves,
trading stacks of paper and barking orders. I stood for
a moment, watching and wondering why everyone was
bent over staring at their feet, until I noticed the huge map
of the System on the floor, the whole world stretched out
and distorted so it could lie flat. I'd never seen the whole
fucking thing laid out like that. The cities were marked
with black and white dots, and the whole deal was carved

up into red and green overlays indicating who held what. Just a few feet away from me was Shenzhen, glowing army green. Inches away, Hong Kong island was burning red. Hong Kong was marked with a white dot, Shenzhen with a black one—based on what I'd seen of Shenzhen, I assumed black meant the city wasn't there anymore.

There were a lot of black dots.

"Over here, Mr. Cates."

I glanced up. In the middle of the room—and of the map—was a long table. It was a lazy oval, and in its center were a dozen large Vidscreens, about half black and empty, the rest flashing a rainbow of colors as coded data sped by. A knot of uniforms were standing and sitting around the table, and at the far end I could see Anners, silvery hair close-cut and perfect, nose still as crooked as the Hudson River.

I started walking toward him. He stared at me the whole way, looking hungry. If anything, Anners looked better than the last time I'd seen him, as if reducing a city to sludge and organizing an army or two around Hong Kong was feeding him instead of draining him. He watched me all the way, those bright bicolor eyes locked on, and I slowed my pace deliberately. It wouldn't do to act scared or intimidated.

When I stood in front of him, he pursed his lips and looked me over. "You look like somethin' I left in the latrine this mornin', Mr. Cates." He winked. "You shoulda stayed with army life. No life like an army life. You'd be like a shiny bright penny if you'da stuck with it."

I raised an eyebrow. "The SFNA's been in existence for, what, two, three years? What the fuck do *you* even know about army life?"

His face darkened, and his gray eyes got hard, losing their humor. Suddenly he grinned, shaking his head. "Mouthy bastard. But you crossed fuckin' hell just because you wanted into my unit, and that speaks well of you, Mr. Cates."

I shook my head. Every muscle in my body ached; I didn't have the energy for bullshit like this. "I've got a business proposal for you, Colonel."

His smile flashed away. His eyes, too white, fixed on me for a moment and then he was up. "Umali, with me," he snapped, striding past me. "This way, Cates," he hissed as he stepped past me. I saw the short, tan Umali stand up from the crowd of white uniforms around the table and scamper to join us.

Anners led me to an unmarked door that swung inward as he approached and snapped shut behind me. It was the small room I'd expected, with just a cramped-looking desk of charred metal and nothing else. Anners spun and sat on the desk with his arms—bulging beneath the shiny, creepy white fabric of his uniform—crossed over his chest, staring at me, while Umali walked around with a small black device held out in front of him. After a moment, the smaller man nodded and looked up.

"Clear, sir," he said.

Anners nodded once without taking his eyes off me. "You tryin' to get me *shot in the fuckin' head*, Mr. Cates? Talking about business proposals in the clear like that?" He shrugged his silvery eyebrows. "I got a Spook CO, see?" He sighed, looking down at his shiny black boots. "Fuckin' reading *minds*."

I shrugged. I didn't give a shit if Colonel Anners got fragged by his superior officers, and it was good to let him know that. "I want to contribute to your retirement fund. Since you're a man who doesn't blush at selling people out of his service, I figured there's plenty of other things you won't mind doing."

Anners studied his boots, arms still crossed in front of himself as if he were afraid they'd go rogue and wanted to keep his hands trapped under his armpits. Then he looked up. "All right, Mr. Cates. Whoever bought you out paid a nice sum, so you got yen behind you. All right. Let's hear it."

I nodded. "I need to get into Hong Kong."

He smiled. "So do we. I've got a hundred thousand men and six armor divs, and we're still sitting here pullin' our puds."

Putting a cigarette in my mouth, I fought every nerve in my body in order to appear calm and relaxed. Everything hurt. My thoughts were slick and syrupy, and every time I moved without thinking, I had to fight the urge to gasp and wince. "I'm not talking about a hundred fucking thousand assholes in bright white uniforms," I said, miming a request for permission to reach for a lighter. "I'm talking four people and a duffel bag. Don't tell me you're not getting people on and off the island."

Anners nodded, waving away my request. "Sure, sure, we gettin' people in and out. Ain't easy. Only one tunnel left usable. The cops, or whatever y'call 'em *now*, sit on the other side and step on anything come out from our end." He smiled again. "Ain't *easy*."

I lit my cigarette and sent a plume of smoke into the air. I'd been smoking the terrible cigarettes they made these days for so long now I'd forgotten what good tobacco tasted like and almost enjoyed these. "Ain't easy means it ain't cheap," I said. "Fine. Let's get past this bullshit and talk about it."

Anners stood up suddenly, arms loose. "All right, let's *do* that, huh?" He glanced at Umali, and the little soldier suddenly sprang into action, pulling a larger palm-sized device from his pocket and slapping it down onto the desk. He gestured over it for a moment and a tiny flickering representation of Hong Kong flared up in the air. Anners walked over to it, eyes suddenly smart and focused.

"No one fucking owns this city," he growled. "The cops—rebels—say they do, but that's bull. Everyone owns a *part* of the fucking island, and they're all poundin' each other trying to push the others into the water." He gestured, and a thin line lit up green, leading from the edge of the island into space. "The cops *do* own the tunnel, though, and that's their blue chip. They collect the toll, anyone wants in or out." He gestured again and a multicolored overlay of irregular blotches appeared. With another gesture, he made the green ones flash. "The cops own some property—they grabbed whatever they could. The Geeks"—he glanced back at me as he gestured again, making a series of red blotches flash in unison—"that's SPS, y'ever hear?"

I thought of the Monk. *We protect the technology.* I nodded.

Anners kept looking at me for a moment, and then turned back to his map. "The Geeks own parts of the city too. Who the fuck knows where they came from or what they're *doin'* here, but there they are. And this"—he gestured again and blue patches, smaller and less common, flashed into life—"is the huge empire of the *shitheads*, all the fucking criminal shit that wasn't smart enough to get out before we shut 'em down out here." He sighed, turning to me and looking momentarily tired. "We've been starving them for weeks now. Nothin' in, nothin' out. My orders are to preserve the city. If I could *reduce* the fuckin' place, we'd have moved on by now."

I nodded. "You keep reducing cities like Shenzhen, won't be much System left to worry about, will there?"

He grinned. "Maybe, Mr. Cates," he said, his accent dropping away with startling speed. "We are exceedingly *good* at our jobs." He gestured and the map disappeared. "That was a *gift*, Cates. A little intel for ya. All you need is for us to get you *in*, right?"

I nodded. "Once we're in daylight on the other side, you turn around and go back to sitting out here, scratching your bellies."

He nodded. "All right. Seein' as yen is measured in the ton these days, let's say five hundred million gets you through that tunnel, complete with honor guard."

I blinked. "Honor guard?"

He nodded. "The tunnel ain't *empty*, Cates."

I considered this, and nodded. "Done. Let's go see my banker."

XX

THE ONLY WAY OUT IS FORWARD

I stood next to the Poet in the rain in silence for a few seconds.

"I do not want to go in there," I said.

The entrance to the tunnel rose up out of the melt like a sculpture, a wave of metal and concrete that still had the huge sign affixed to its top: CROSS HARBOUR TUNNEL. A wide swatch of broken asphalt sprang up from nothing, as if torn off of a road somewhere else and dropped here by hover. Faint paint lines still remained here and there, echoes of pre-Unification. The entrance was two dark squares angling downward. A formidable-looking collection of concrete barricades had been set up across the entrance, with a single metal gate in place in the middle. Dozens of soldiers manned the entrance, looking bored and nervous, with thousands more within hollering distance, rotated in and out from the caps farther behind the lines. Everything was topped with razor wire, and I could see that once you got through the gate, there was a maze of narrow corridors formed by more barricades that would force anyone approaching to double back fifteen times. Two makeshift towers made from scaffolding jutted up on either end, a lazy-looking soldier up on the platforms on each one, sniper rifle leaning casually against the railing, white cigarette smoke puffing into the air.

The big alarm sirens were mounted up there as well, set to trip if anything crossed the midway point in the tunnels, giving the rest of the force time to assemble.

On the horizon, buildings soared into the air, blue and gray, glass glinting in the dim light. There was no light anywhere, but the sight of so much preserved construction was dizzying. Behind us was a flat wasteland. In front of us, across the water, was fucking civilization.

In my peripheral vision, the Poet nodded. "I agree with you. I would rather swim across." He paused and then looked at me. "I'm afraid of rats."

"She's fuckin' old," Anners bellowed, breath steaming in the cool night air. "Leaks like a sieve, sometimes rumbles like it's your last hour in there. If she fails, hold your breath."

I scowled at Anners. The colonel was bright and alive and cheerful in the twilight, looking like he'd eaten well and had a good shit before coming out to escort us. I wondered, briefly, where the army had found these people. Where did you unearth someone like Colonel Malkem Anners? Did they have them in glass jars for years, plotting the rebellion, freeze-dried and ready for reconstitution? I'd fucking believe it.

I stared at the dark mouth of the tunnel, imagining I could hear the ancient rebar creaking under the weight of the water. It was hard to imagine there had been a time when people had been forced underwater just to get some-place that was so close I could see it. Then I realized with a start: That time was fucking *now*. I was standing in it.

"All right," Anners said, belching. "Let's have a little gatherin' here so I can lay it out for ya." His four hand-picked soldiers had their cowls up, anonymous and grim in their white uniforms, and stepped forward to stand around him. The rest of us didn't move.

I nodded toward the tunnel. "What's in there, Anners?"

"*Now* you're askin'?" Mara groused. "*After* we paid half up front?"

"Push the button or shut up," I snapped. It had become my motto. "Anners?"

The colonel grinned, teeth white and straight. "Bottom-feeders, mostly. Live in there, waiting on anyone tryin' to get in or out of Hong Kong. Like the dark, stay quiet, your throat slit before you even know what happened." He jerked a thumb over his shoulder, vaguely indicating his soldiers. "Stay behind us and let us clear the way. We shoot anything that moves, and we got our night-vision—it ain't hard work dealing with their kind, as long as you go in with your eyes open. You stay outta our way and we'll have you across in a blink."

I turned and looked at Mara and the Poet. I didn't bother with the Monk. Whoever was trapped inside the android body, she'd proven to be uninterested in casual conversation and so far had offered no opinions. Which was fine by me.

I looked back at the colonel. "All right."

He nodded. "No lights in there. Don't light up—cigs, novas, whatever." He smiled. "It attracts 'em. Easiest way to get a blade in your neck is to light up."

"How do we follow?" the Poet asked, his voice betraying an unexpected edge of worry. "If we must stay in the dark, how do we follow?"

Anners glanced at him and shrugged. "Hold fuckin' hands, I don't give a shit. We're here to guide you through. That's it."

The colonel spun. "On me," he barked at the four uniforms. "Remy, you're my back. Stick to me and keep 'em off me."

A short, skinny soldier peeled off from the three others and took up a position behind the colonel. I stared at his white back, heart pounding, my HUD glowing back into life. After a second of hard staring, his text box flared into life again:

EVENS O. REMY, PRIVATE (3), ASSAULT INFANTRY, STF.

Without another word, Anners marched toward the barricades, the squad on guard duty snapping to attention immediately, a wireless signal alerting them to their CO's approach. As they walked off, Remy turned his cowled head to look back at me for a moment.

After a moment, someone grabbed my arm and I spun, taking hold of Mara's wrist and twisting it around in an instinctive reaction. She didn't wince or cry out; she just raised her eyebrows. "You havin' second thoughts, Cates?"

I let her wrist go and ducked my head, launching myself after the colonel, replaying his words in my head. *Remy.* It was too easy to picture Remy inside that cowl, head stuffed full of augments, staying on Anners's ass because he didn't have any other choice.

"Stand down," Anners bellowed to the guards as we approached. "You're all off-line for five minutes. Stand down and step back. Have a smoke."

"Sir," one of the guard duty shouted back, saluting.

We followed Anners through the gate as it swung open at his approach, and began navigating the switchbacks formed by the battered, chipped stone barricades beyond. When we were standing in front of the yawning entrance to the tunnels, I looked back at the Monk, who was still grinning, still silent.

"All right," I said. "Break out the goods and pass it out."

The Monk immediately dropped the green duffel it had been hauling for us since Brussels and pulled it open with a single, vicious tug. The dull metal of the gear I'd gotten straight from the SSF absorbed all of the dim, damp light and tugged at your eyes, as if the duffel was a drain everything was spilling toward. The Monk immediately reached into the bag and produced two gleaming, factory-new shredding rifles with shoulder straps and optional rocket-propelled grenade launchers.

"RPGs?" Anners suddenly barked, stomping back toward us with an unlit cigarette—well-chewed and damp—crushed between his white teeth. "Aw, now, fuck no. You stow that gear. We ain't walking y'all through here *armed*."

The Monk tossed a shredder toward me and I snatched it from the air with augmented reflexes, and then had to work hard to steady myself, a wave of dizziness graying my vision as my heart skipped a few beats, finding its rhythm with a thud. "You gonna...you gonna skip the other half of your paycheck, Colonel? We'll lead *you* if it makes you nervous." Taking a deep breath, I tossed the shredder at the Poet; it almost sailed past him but he lunged and snatched it, making it look natural. My back lit up as if something in it had just torn like paper, immediately settling into a burning throb, but I turned smoothly and caught the second shredder without wincing, and tossed it on to Mara.

Anners stared at me, chewing his cigar, as the Monk tossed me the last shredder. I caught it with my chest, staggering backward a step and managing to hang on to it through magic or luck. I braced myself and stared back at him; I could almost see the wheels turning, the numbers crunching. Finally, he pointed at me.

"All right," he said. "All fucking right."

He turned and marched off, and we gathered around the Monk as it handed up ammunition and grenade clips. While the Poet and Mara checked their weapons, the Monk silently handed up a thumb-sized black box. I put it in my palm and gestured, and a 3-D map of Hong Kong appeared in the air in front of me. I practiced zooming in and out and manipulating the representation for a moment, and then the Monk was holding up a bundle of thick material.

"Body armor," Mara said. "I thought you were old-school, Cates."

I tossed their vests at their feet and held mine up, arms trembling with the weight of it. I thought about having that pulling me down as I tried to move fast through tight spaces. "We're going to be moving through hostile streets under superior fixed positions—people on the god-damn roofs, waiting for us. Old-school don't mean stupid, Mara."

Taking another deep breath, I slowly pulled the vest on. Its weight was immediately suffocating, and a light sweat broke out all over my body. I pictured Michaleen, the little rat, his perpetually cheerful face twisted into a grin. The little bastard was *laughing* at me, and I was going to survive Hong Kong just so I could push a blade into his belly and give it a twist.

When the vest was snug around my middle, the Monk looked at me, that eternal smile on its face.

"Shut up," I muttered. It just kept grinning.

"You okay?" Mara asked, cocking her head and raising one eyebrow. "You look like total shit."

I stared at her face. Something was tugging at me. I'd *seen* her before. I was sure of it. Something in her manner, in her expression, *something* was tickling my memory. "I'm fine," I said slowly. "You light up your brain like a power grid and kill sixteen people in two minutes, see how you feel."

She smirked and turned away, but I kept my eyes on her, her long legs and narrow shoulders. Her perfect skin. She didn't look like someone who'd spent a lifetime doing this work, someone who had Canny Orel's trust and proxy. She didn't look like *anybody*, no one I'd known or ever would know. I forced myself to turn away, full-body shivers making all of my muscles twitch to mysterious music I couldn't hear.

"Let's go, assholes," Anners shouted, fitting his cowl onto his head.

"Any more treats there?" the Poet shouted, grinning, as the Monk pulled the duffel closed and picked it up. "Perhaps a tank or hover? Or midget ninjas?"

"Let's go."

I walked toward the colonel and his troops, not looking back. I felt hot but I was shivering. Sweat was pouring down my back and my heart was pounding in my chest. My vision was blurry. As I neared Anners, he turned without another word and started for the tunnel. I followed, and faster than I thought possible, darkness enveloped me.

Immediately, my vision adjusted, bringing up a version of the world that was tinged green and filled with flare like greasy light clinging to everything. The tunnel was wide, the cracked pavement visible for about twenty or thirty feet, then slowly sliding under the rippling black waves of water.

"How deep?" I called out.

"You won't drown," Anners shouted back. "Now shut up."

We walked. My legs felt rubbery, and when we waded into the water it was so cold my breath was knocked out of me, leaving me gasping as the black water slowly rose up to my belly, encasing my legs in liquid ice. After a minute or two, my legs were numb and I moved forward by magic, by simple mind over matter. The darkness became absolute, and even my night-vision faded to a murky sludge; by the time I realized the Poet was walking next to me, he'd been there for some time.

"You okay, Adrian?" I asked.

"I have been better," he said quietly, his voice tinged with strain. "I do not like the darkness. Talk to me, Cates, please."

I grimaced. I didn't know what to say. You didn't admit weakness—people stomped on weakness when they saw it, exploited it, made a note of it and remembered, forever. Years later, you worked a job against someone and they remembered something you said, something they saw, a moment when you let your guard down, and they hit you on the head with it until you bled.

"Uh—all right, where in hell did 'the Poet' come from?"

He didn't respond right away. I counted six steps before he spoke.

"Did you ever test? I wanted to be IE, to be a damn cop. Can you believe that? But I got FA, fine arts. I wanted a gun. They told me to write stories. So I ran away."

I shook my head in the darkness. Up ahead, there was a sudden burst of gunfire and a few muttered curses. Both the Poet and I dropped to our knees, crouching with our heads just above the frigid water. The floor of the tunnel under my hand was slick and gritty, and I wished very much to not be touching it.

"Clear!" one of the soldiers shouted, and we straightened up, shaking oily water from our hands and sleeves and pushing forward.

"I never tested," I said. I knew, dimly, that any citizen of the System of any standing tested at a young age and got assigned a career, but I'd been out of the mainstream for years by the time I came of age and I'd never even seen one of the Testing Dorms.

"You are lucky, then. To be told what you will *be*—it is terrible. I wanted a gun, and so I went underground and got myself one." I looked at him. His tattoos were monochrome in my enhanced vision, still moving in their silent little scenes, endlessly dying. If I were a superstitious man, I'd think he was making sure they stayed dead, by reminding the universe that he'd killed them. "My father was rich. A big fish in a small pond. I spoke too well, though. My new friends said I was soft, called me the Poet. You can't always choose. You must own what life gives you." He jabbed a finger at his neck. "My *friends* stayed with me."

He did talk pretty. I couldn't put my finger on it—there were no huge words or fancy flourishes, but when Adrian Panić started chatting, I liked it. I didn't even pay attention to what he said half the time.

He suddenly stopped. I splashed ahead a few feet before realizing it, and then waded back, finding him standing stiff and rigid in the water.

"Mr. Cates," he said slowly, his voice cracking, "some fucking *thing* brushed my fucking *leg*."

I studied his face, nodding at him as I hunched down a bit and stared up at his nose. "You gonna move, Adrian?"

He shut his eyes and shook his head. "I will...I will head back. I will...I cannot..." He trailed off and began muttering in his native language again, harsh and growling to my ears. I sighed and straightened up, still shivering, my own legs still feeling treacherous. I took a deep breath and reached up, slapping him hard across the face.

"Get moving," I said with a sigh, "or I will push you under and hold you there while the rats chew out your eyes."

I waited. I knew what it was like to freeze up. I knew fear. After a moment, I leaned forward again and whispered, "The only way out is forward, Adrian."

He nodded as another, longer burst of gunfire ahead of us lit up the tunnel in tiny flashes. "Too bad you've seen this," he whispered, taking a staggering step forward, splashing water everywhere. "Now I will have to kill you. Later. After tunnel."

"That's too bad," I said, concentrating on moving my aching legs. "I'd hate to have to kill you in self-defense. I'm going to need you. You know what this is, right? A smash-and-grab." I looked around to make sure we were isolated from the others, alone in our miserable pocket of darkness. "This thing Londholm has created, this God Augment—everyone wants it. The little shit Michaleen— *he* wants it. Bet your freak ass he does, Adrian. His creature back there, Mara, she's here to make sure he gets it, after we get her in and get her close."

The Poet was still walking like someone was tugging invisible wires embedded in his limbs. "And naturally," he said, "then we're no longer needed." He gestured into the air. "God's Middle Finger."

I nodded. "I'm not going out that way. I've got shit to do." *Like murdering that short little bastard*, I thought.

"I am with you, Cates," he whispered. "First we must get to Londholm. And avoid tunnels."

I nodded. "We're with each other, and fuck the rest of them."

I took two more slow, waterlogged steps and sensed something above me. My HUD lit up with a sudden surge, like it had been dormant and now woke up, and my feeling of heavy pain vanished. I half-ducked, leaning backward in a last momentary flash of energy and speed. Something heavy rolled off me, knocking me down into the thick, greasy water. I was under it for a moment, blind and suffocated, and then a hand was on my neck and someone was pushing at me, holding me under, their skin rough against me, their fingernails long, thick, and sharp.

As my HUD status bars started screaming up and down, I lashed out my arms, grabbing onto a skeletal ankle, slippery and yet rough, like it was covered in scabs. I didn't think about that too hard; I concentrated on not opening my mouth under any circumstances while underwater, no matter how much my lungs burned. I yanked on the ankle hard and the hand disappeared from my neck, allowing me to surge back up, breaking the surface to the sound of gunshots everywhere, a constant screech. Gasping, at first I thought lights were flashing in my vision, but realized it was the flash of the guns.

I tore my Roon from its holster and began putting bullets into the swirling black water in front of me, ticking the gun forward a few inches each time. When I'd emptied the clip, silence crowded in, and Anners's mush-mouthed cursing echoed against the walls.

"Holy fucking *shit*, y'all are damned jumpy. Remy, you take point up front there; Ollie, Hem, and Mullay, sweep back a few feet and make sure we're *clear*—look *up* for fuck's sake. Y'all gonna get a fucking burn tonight for this kind of weak shit, walking right *under* a fucking CHUD." He came into view as a dark shape surfaced a few feet in front of me, facedown and skinny, like a greenish skeleton someone had dumped into the water. Anners glanced at the corpse as he joined the Poet and me. "All right, you got your boots wet," he muttered, giving the body a nudge with his boot. There was a spray of gunfire behind us, and then silence again.

I felt myself deflating, getting heavy again, the all-over ache settling back into my bones. My HUD slowly dimmed. I was in fucking power-save mode.

Anners nodded. "We're clear now," he said, throwing a grin around. He pointed forward, and I squinted, spying a dim square of light up ahead. "All right, motherfuckers, you're in sight o' Hong Kong, eh?" He fell into an easy march next to us. "We won't be walking you out of the tunnel, tho'. Be surprised if there were more than four, five thousand System Pigs holdin' the city, total, but if we poke our noses out there I *ga-run-tee* you all of them will be standing there, grinnin'. You're clear from here on, tho'. We scrubbed it."

I stood dripping, my empty gun still clutched in my hand. I shook uncontrollably, and was glad for the darkness to hide in. I looked at the square of light again and tried to decide if I had the energy to walk it. "You gonna shoot us in the back after we pay up?" I asked as Mara and the Poet joined us.

"Fuck, no," he said immediately, spitting forcefully onto the floor. "You're a fucking gold mine, Mr. Cates. I'm gonna be waiting right here to get your custom on the way *back*."

Mara joined us, her credit dongle already out. "Just fucking transfer your fucking money and get me out of this shithole," she said.

The colonel swiped his thumb across the proffered dongle; Mara gestured and showed the display to him. He nodded crisply. "Pleasure. Most likely you're dead in a few hours, sure, but if y'want an extraction, Mr. Cates can dial up my frequency on the SFNA net." He looked around once and winked. "Good luck."

He spun around. "On *me*," he shouted. "Keep the way fucking clear. I got to pull a trigger, Remy, and I will give you a fucking dose of misery, you hear? And for fuck's sake, watch for the fucking *clingers* on the ceiling."

I watched the soldiers fade into the gloom, and then the Poet's hand was on my shoulder. I spun and stalked after Mara, adjusting the strap of my gun. I felt hot and dizzy, and my feet hurt, sending shots of pain up my legs with every step.

As we edged toward the exit of the tunnel, emerging from the shallow, scummy water, we slowed and got down low, crawling forward. At the edge of the shadows, we paused and studied the scene—almost a mirror image of the other end: barricades, security gates, and a few dozen heavily armed men and women. The only difference was the lack of uniforms. The silence and stillness of the scene was unnerving.

The cops were out in force, and they were all lying on the ground, some squirming and struggling, others just panting. After a moment, I saw him: the old man from my train adventure, dressed in a cheap black suit and sitting on a burly-looking cop who was splayed on the ground, sweat streaming down his blank face. The old man had a face made of beard, gray-white hair wiggling everywhere as he chewed tobacco.

"Come on out, Mr. Cates," he said with a grunt. "Before we pull you out."

XXI

AT LEAST I STILL HAVE MY LOOKS

"Don't fucking move," I whispered. "Tele-K holding them all down. There's no Pusher or we'd already be marching out there with our pants down."

Outside, someone shouted hoarsely: "Avery Fucking *Cates*?" We all paused for an awkward moment, waiting for him to say something more.

"You have a friend here," the Poet said, grinning, his tattoos dancing. "How nice to be welcomed here. You must be famous."

"Fucking hell, I hate these freaks," Mara hissed. "You want to beat someone or kill someone, do it with your bare hands like a fucking human being." Her thin, pretty face was lit up with an ancient sort of rage. "This bullshit gets old."

The Poet was lying on his belly, squinting at the scene. "There's no way to move. The moment we leave shadows, we will be exposed."

"And then we're in the fucking air," Mara spat. "I remember that cocksucking Tele-K."

For a few heartbeats, we lay there in silence, listening to the wind. My body was bonding with the rough pavement, my eyes getting heavy. I wanted to just put my head down and sleep, wake up a thousand years later, when the persistent spiky throb in my head might have faded away. Rolling over onto my back, I took a painful, deep breath, swallowing a spasm of coughs, and stared at the cracked, corroded ceiling, shadow bleeding into the damp, weak light. "Anyone seen the fucking Monk?"

For a second, we were all still, and then they both rolled over, searching the gloom.

"Well, that's fuckin' disturbin'," Mara said after a moment.

"I wished it to go," the Poet said contemplatively. "Now I wish it would come back. A lesson here, yes?"

A tremendous shattering crash made us all jump. Concrete dust rained down just outside the tunnel's exit.

"Mr. Cates," the old man called out. "I know you are cowering in there. Attend to me, please."

"*Attend* to you?!?" I shouted up at the ceiling. "I'm gonna have to ask you to rephrase your request in a language other than *asshole*."

"Maybe we split up," the Poet said. He was completely himself again, all the quaver and strain out of his voice. "Each in his own direction, hell-bent for leather."

I felt peaceful, suddenly, staring up at the ceiling of the tunnel. "That asshole picked up a fucking *train* with his *mind*," I said. "He's squashing, what, fifty, sixty cops to the ground simultaneously. You think he's going to have trouble with three more people?" I rolled over onto my belly and peered out at him. The poor fuck he was sitting on looked like he was waiting for permission for his heart to explode, his face purple, sweat dripping off his nose. A few feet away, in a similar position as if someone had recently been sitting next to the old man, was another cop, his suit a shiny silver job that clashed with his blistered, lobster-red skin, his whole body one big third-degree burn. My HUD was yellow everywhere. I *felt* fucking yellow. I pushed myself up onto my knees and my heart did a crazy little dance in my chest, fluttering.

"We snipe his ass," I said. "Adrian, how're you with a scope?"

He made a face behind his grimy-looking glasses. "I am average," he admitted. "Can kill most things at a distance; can't say kill for sure."

I nodded. He was honest. "You?" I asked Mara.

She gave me a smile that was almost pretty, but I had a creepy shiver, staring into her eyes. The idea of fucking Mara was so distant and alien I wanted to look away, keep my eyes off her.

"I always prefer my kills up close," she said, shaking her head. "And I'm the sort who does everything okay, nothing great, and gets by with gettin' everyone else to do her dirty work."

I nodded. "Okay. Pass me the needle—just keep low and move slow."

The Poet crawled over to our deflated duffel bag and unzipped it without raising his head. Fishing inside, he quickly found the sniper rifle I'd specified back in Brussels and slowly extracted it, inching it from the bag while lying flat beside it. When he had the whole rifle out, he slid it along the damp floor of the tunnel's mouth until I put my hand on it and pulled it in the rest of the way. Carefully flopping back over onto my belly, I squinted out into the light.

This had once been a system of rising roads, concrete, and asphalt, spinning upward in wide loops and then shooting off into different directions. Shacks had been built up on all of the crumbling overpasses, loops within loops of dirty, tiny huts mixed in with a few larger structures. The wood all had a gray, weathered look to it, most of the slats warped, ancient nails being pulled inexorably from their homes. Some shacks were just a few feet wide, some had been built up to dangerous heights—I could see the stories waving in the winds like reeds or branches—but they were all on the verge of turning into dust. A single path wound its way through the crowd, slowly widening until it led directly into the heart of the city. When it had been built, people had used roads to get into Hong Kong, but now people used hovers. Unless they couldn't afford hovers, and who gave a shit about them then?

I reached up and slowly pulled out the built-in barrel supports until they clicked into place, then slowly extended the gun, trusting to instinct for the proper angle and elevation.

The ground suddenly pulled away from me, the rifle dropping as I sailed up, and I was in the middle of an invisible fist being dragged through the air. For a second it was so fast my whole body tensed in preparation for impact, but a second later I stopped cold, hanging a few feet in front of the old man.

And he was *old*. His body was barrel shaped and stretched the cheap fabric of his suit uncomfortably, and his round head had wispy, thin white hair on top of a pink, burned scalp and thick, dirty white whiskers all over the bottom two-thirds of his face. His eyes, round and empty like every other Psionic I'd ever seen, were bright green in a cloudy yellow milk. They were old eyes, and I didn't like looking into them.

"Should've stayed *down*, Mr. Cates," he chided me, chewing his mustache. "That was stupid."

I could hear the gasping breath and moans of the cops around us, floated up by the fierce, damp wind that swirled everywhere. "I've never been very bright," I gasped, the invisible fist tight around me. "Maybe that's why I keep killing all the fucking Spooks I meet. I keep thinking if I eat their brains, I'll get smart."

Someone laughed, one of the cops, a dry, pinched sound.

The Pusher moved his mouth, his bushy mustache like steel wool rippling on his face, a faded caterpillar. "It's men like you, Mr. Cates, with their *technology* that they use without knowing anything, *monkeys* with *buttons*, that have led the world to its present state. Not only are you not going to be allowed to free Londholm's invention and distribute it to the rest of the monkeys out there, Mr. Cates, but it's high time you were put on trial for what you've personally done. Done with guns, with hovers, with circuits and chips and logic gates. With *technology*."

Forcing myself to breathe shallowly, I kept still, my face blank. Something moved in the shadows of the overpass behind him, and instinctively I kept my eyes off it.

"The whole world ruined by technology," he said suddenly, as if in response to something. "Parasites like you— you, who would be sweeping up refuse in the streets, who would have *died young* if not for the prop of machinery. Misguided servants like the SPS think preserving technology is our future—technology is *destroying* us. They will be dealt with." He shifted his weight a little on the poor cop, whose arms and legs were trembling, his whole suit of clothes stained with sweat. "God has appointed us, Mr. Cates, to cleanse this world. We are representatives of his organic power. We do not need machines or electricity or silicone minds. We do not need batteries or wireless uplinks. We were *created* by God, and we will tear down all of this." He raised one hand and waved it about randomly. Then he cocked his head a little, regarding me. "And we will punish men like you who have done so much damage."

Behind him, the Monk stepped out of the shadows. It was still grinning. I kept my eyes moving past it and then shut them, giving in to the excruciating pain that crept up my back and down my legs, beating in time with my fluttering heart. I didn't know if Mara and the Poet could maneuver out of the tunnel without being seen, and I didn't know if either one would chance a rescue attempt. Mara, I was pretty sure, wouldn't shed any tears if I got snapped in half by this freak.

Black spots appeared in my vision, and I felt like my eyes were popping out of my head.

"Perhaps you will tell your people to reveal themselves before I begin to make you *really* suffer."

I couldn't help it. I started to laugh, or tried to, my body shaking painfully. "My people will probably be halfway back to the mainland by now," I managed to squeak out. "You want to talk about tech—I got a head crammed full of the shit, and none of it is doing me any good."

He squinted at me, and suddenly I spun slowly in the air. "I see," he said as I revolved back around. The Monk had crept a few feet closer, its smiling face a frozen, terrible mask that appeared to be staring directly at *me*, like the grinning face of fucking death floating toward me. "This is just your damnation writ large. You're no better than a cyborg. You're no longer even human."

My HUD had faded red; breathing was becoming more and more difficult. "At least ... I still ... have my looks ..."

Next to us, the cop being used as a chair by the old man laughed. "Cates, I'll take up a fucking collection to pay you to kill that hairy motherfucker," he panted. "He's been crushing us for fucking *hours*."

I concentrated, trying to find my calm, quiet sphere, keeping my eyes open through stubborn will. It felt like I'd been fed into a vacuum, like my inner pressure was bulging out, threatening to splatter me everywhere. I put my eyes on the Monk as it stepped gingerly behind the crazy old bastard. I knew that I shouldn't look at it, that I should pretend it wasn't there until it did something useful, but looking away seemed like so much work, so much trouble. I just stared.

"We will not allow you to claim the augment for Mr. Orel's use. I find you *guilty*, Mr. Cates," the old man said as I shut my eyes to rest them as they bulged out of my head. "I sentence you and your kind to death."

Said the mouse to the cur, Dick Marin's voice suddenly whispered lightly in my thoughts. *Such a trial, dear sir, with no jury or judge, would be wasting our breath. I'll be judge, I'll be jury, said cunning old Fury. I'll try the whole case, and condemn you to death.*

Good to hear you, Dick, I thought dreamily, my own thoughts echoing in the sudden dry emptiness of my head. *I thought I'd lost you.*

I opened my eyes again and slowly focused them as the last bit of leeway disappeared around me, locking my diaphragm under tons of invisible pressure. The Monk took one final step, pausing just a few inches behind the old man. For a second, I looked right at it, and it was as if the fucking thing grinned right at me. Then it lunged forward and wrapped its fake arms around the old man's chest. He startled, and I was suddenly tossed into the air, the invisible fist dissolving around me.

And then, the Monk exploded.

XXII

WELCOME TO THE LAND OF THE LIVING

I was hurled backward, suddenly free, and for a second there was a bizarre bloom of joy and relief as I could breathe again. This was immediately replaced with a sudden damp surge of terror, and then the usual vague hope that I wouldn't bite my own tongue off when I hit the ground.

I smacked through a flimsy clapboard wall of one of the shanties built up along the old roads, skidding to a halt on the pitted old asphalt that made up the floors of the place. My HUD blinked off for a second and then flashed back into place, and a dull ache settled into my chest. I'd landed in an awkward sitting position, slumped over myself, and I just sat there for a moment, gasping, feeling like I couldn't take a deep enough breath.

After a moment, I realized that my coat was smoking.

There was a commotion outside, voices shouting, and I forced myself to get onto my knees and straighten up. I felt like wires had been shorted inside me, synapses flickering, sparking, filling me with the smell of ozone. If I'd gone all the way android, if I'd just let the cosmos make me into a fucking robot, I'd be fine right now. Living a dozen lives, all the data spooling onto a server that was the real me while my body could be dispensed with. I wouldn't be sitting here cut up into a dozen pieces with a remote control a few dozen yards away ready to make me dance, make me sing, make me dead.

My HUD suddenly cleared and flashed a quick message to the effect that all military systems were in an acceptable state. My status bars remained a sickly yellow. Thankful that the invasive tech that had been shoved down my throat had survived the explosion, I took a shuddering breath, coughed for thirty seconds or so as the veins in my head turned ropy and purple, and then spat a glob of green phlegm onto the ancient pavement. I let myself fall forward onto my hands and knees and pushed myself up, grabbing onto the splintered wood of my own impact hole to pull myself upright. I leaned out into the damp air and scanned the tunnel plaza, reaching into my coat for my cigarettes, crushed but serviceable.

"Avery Cates!" someone shouted. I peered down through my own exhale and found a short, broad-chested man in a grubby, once-splendid silvery suit. Like him, the suit had been through the ringer. His arms had been torn off a gorilla and sewn onto him, and his head was a puckered mass of reddened, burned flesh, healed now into a plastic layer of scales. I studied him as he walked closer to my perch, just six or seven feet off the ground, and wondered how he'd survived his burns.

"How in fuck are you still alive?" he said. As he got closer, I realized he was stiff, moving with an odd ambling motion, left arm hanging forgotten at his side, the hand encased in a leather glove.

I sucked in smoke. It was making me nauseous, and I considered what would happen to my reputation if I puked all over him. "You a cop?" I said, spitting tobacco from my lips. "You know me?"

The horrible demon's face grinned, revealing a shock of perfect white teeth. "No and fucking no, I guess not," he said. "Welcome to the land of the living. You wanna call out your friends?"

He reached up and extended a hand to me, offering to help me down. A dozen thoughts flashed through my mind, starting with the vague sense that I might *need* a hand down and ending with the suspicion that my *friends* were likely several blocks away. I didn't mind; I knew more than they did about the current situation; I'd catch up with them if Mara didn't move out of range and kill me. I nodded at him. "You in charge of this graveyard?"

He smiled again, nodding. "Welcome to Hong Fucking Kong, population about three thousand these days. What you've got here are probably the last fully human cops left in the SSF." He spread his arms. "We're starting our own country. Or we'll die trying." He looked around. "Gotta thank you for taking out that old bastard. Spooks showed up a couple of days ago and been a wart on my ass ever since. Never seen 'em with that kind of range and strength." He laughed, turning back and eyeing my cigarette. "If there's more on his level, the rest of us are fucked, huh? Did you bring that piece of silicone just to do him?"

I thought of Hense telling me the Monk was *resources*, that she had plans for the old man. I wondered if the smiling Monk had even had a real brain in it, or if it had been fitted with a digital one, programmed to suicide under the right conditions. Fucking cops. If the Spook had been holding me a few feet closer, I'd be the burned cop's twin.

"No," I said, coughing. "No, that was just my luck kicking in."

I took stock of my HUD and decided I wouldn't collapse if I jumped a few feet to the ground. Settling my cigarette in the corner of my mouth, I swung my legs out and dropped. My knees buckled and I had to stumble forward awkwardly, skinning one hand on the rough pavement, but righted myself and struck a relaxed pose while my heart pounded in my chest, my vision swimming. I looked around, noting the defensive positions—the big mounted guns, the hastily poured concrete blinds, the groups of men and women stretching and inspecting themselves. Then I looked back at the burn victim.

"You guys are gonna get fucking creamed," I said, pulling out my most recent pack of cigarettes and shaking one out for him. "You know that, right? The army's got *tanks*."

He plucked the cigarette from my hand and looked at it with wide-eyed, crazy joy. Tucking it behind one sorry, melted ear, he grinned again. "Fuck it. We got some tricks. I should have died already—got blown to fucking hell, burned up and crushed. And what did my brother cops do, the grand old SSF?" He winked. "They jammed needles into my brain and downloaded me into a brick and left me for dead." He shook his head and indicated with an outstretched hand that I should walk with him. "You know there's a standing order for cops like me—in my situation, surviving our own murders—to *report in*? Fuck, that's balls. That's Tricky Dicky for you—balls. That motherfucker has balls the size of *planets*." He sighed, like we were neighborhood pals chatting. "They got a new process, you know? They can make people into avatars without killing them. Good news, right? You know what Dick Marin ordered? He ordered that every fucking person bricked into an avatar *be killed anyway*. He doesn't fucking *want* human beings." He looked at me as we started walking around the plaza. "You're here for the Techie. Londholm. You're here for him and his *gadget*."

I had already shaken out a second cigarette and held it out for him. "Do we have a problem?"

He plucked the smoke from the pack and jammed it between his blistered lips. "Naw, you kidding? Kill the motherfucker. Kill him *now*—*please* kill that bastard. We got fucking *dozens* of freelance talent infesting this island. Got whole neighborhoods, nothin' but Takers and Gunners looking to make their bones on this guy. It's a fucking distraction."

I considered this, looking around as we paused for me to hold my cigarette up for him. "How many are you?"

He shrugged as he leaned into me, puffing at the cigarette until he was rewarded with a thick cloud of smoke. "We're about a thousand." He straightened up, taking a deep drag. "Think about it, man: You got the fucking robots, the cops with digital brains. You got the cyborgs, all the soldiers with tech rammed down them like silicone sausages. And then there's us. Just plain old human beings, and damned few of us left." He looked up. "We got the skies covered—the SSF set this rock up with Droid rocket launchers, so when the grunts try to put asses in the air, we knock 'em down—unless they somehow build about a thousand more hovers in the next few days, we can handle their air force. So it's the tunnel. Numbers don't matter. Y'were in there, man. They're gonna be choked up and we won't need more than fifty meat heads on the mounties to hold 'em back."

I nodded. "The water?"

He shook his head, grinning again. "Mined, and if they find a lane, there ain't more then a hundred boats in the whole fucking *System*—who goes by boat anywhere? They could build, but that'll take time. Their manufacturing system is all fucked up, too. Nope—it's the tunnel. We can hold this piece of shit forever, we need to."

I studied him for a moment. He was like a piece of red rubber shaped into a man. The last fully human cops in the System, maybe, I thought. Eventually, maybe the last fully human folks in the whole goddamn universe, myself and my wired-up brain included. I'd spent a big part of my life hating the cops. All I could remember was cops pushing me this way, threatening me, shaking me down. Arrogant fucks in expensive suits, picking and choosing which laws to enforce. Here I was, now, wishing the last of them luck. At least it had been fellow human beings fucking me over, instead of data bricks with legs.

I fished in my pocket and pulled out my little map of Hong Kong. Placing it in my palm, I held my arm out and twitched my thumb, making the city pop up in a beautiful skein of pink wireframe.

"Any help you wanna give me?" I asked, rolling the cigarette around my lips as I spoke. "You want this shit-head dead, I've been hired to do it."

"Dead?" Pucker said with a cock of his head. "You

sure? Half the assholes here been hired to snatch him, or his little toy."

I shrugged. "I'm here to kill him and make sure that shit gets lost." I knew I might be lying to him, depending on what Mara was going to do once we got there, but I didn't have time for niceties. I looked through the pink city at him. "You see it? In action?"

"The God Augment?" he said, shaking his head. "It's fuckin' vaporware, for all I know."

I considered that, the possibility we were all chasing bullshit. It cheered me up. It felt like the System was back to normal.

"He's here," he said, suddenly jabbing a gnarled finger into my map, making it shimmer briefly. The map automatically telescoped in scale, bringing up a clear wireframe of the tall, skinny building I'd seen in Brussels. "He's got a mercenary team protecting him, and they're professionals. Ex-cops like us, some army deserters, some just hardcases like you picking up a steady credit line. Jap runs the show and he runs a tight ship."

I nodded. "You take a look at their setup?"

"Yeah," he said, all business now, absorbed. "It's tighter than your shit pipe, Cates. No entry at street level anyway, and the building's had all of its legacy infrastructure sealed off, so no way in through old sewer lines or mechanical access lanes from below. They took the top two floors and locked them down, mounted guns, about three, four dozen strong. Good discipline; they've got some portable batteries but you don't see any lights at night, and they must be provisioned pretty well 'cause I guarantee you nothing in or out." He shrugged. "Now"—he gestured expertly and the map zoomed out again, showing the hotel as a tiny rectangle lit up orange—"the area right around it is kind of no-man's land—no one's claimed it. This because the fuckers in the hotel have a tendency to tear shit up with their big guns anytime they see someone creeping around out there. From here"—he gestured again and the map shifted slightly to show our location; I recognized the curling lines of the old streets threading out of the tunnel—"you're gonna have to go through some foreign territory. We got enough manpower to hold the key areas—the hover lot, the tunnel, our own buildings— but the city's divided up right now and to get to Londholm you're going through some sovereign countries. You're gonna have to negotiate your way through."

I nodded. "What about underground? The old transit."

He looked up at me. "I wouldn't. Old tunnels are owned by Triad Federations. When this shit went down, they went underground immediately, setting up a whole shadow city under there. They're protected from air attack and can get anywhere in the city undetected. They're not friendly and they're not trustable, you ask me. They're *thin*"—he shrugged—"so you might slip past 'em in the dark, but that's a chance." He looked back at the map. "On the surface you'll do better, just because no one's got enough materiel to cover their claimed territory, so you can slip through a lot of gaps if you're careful. Your best bet is to go south from here"—he traced a road from our position, lighting it up orange as his finger moved—"through *here*, which is contested by fucking everyone. There's a chance you can even slip through there without seeing anyone, because every time someone tries to set up a stronghold there to claim it, someone else comes by to complain with their guns."

I studied the route. It was a disturbingly straight line from here to there. "You've gotta be kidding me." It was too simple.

He shrugged. "No offense, Cates, but we all think we've got bigger problems than you sneaking in and cutting one asshole's throat. You wanna make it more difficult, I'd be happy to blindfold you and spin you around a few times." Taking the cigarette from his mouth, he pointed with it toward a wide boulevard stretching away from the plaza. "Take that about a mile and turn…" He flicked his hand at my map and it spun dizzying, finally settling back to a long shot of the city. With another curt gesture the boulevard lit up, an orange line stretching away from the knot of old twisted roads off the tunnel. "Here. You can see your way to Londholm from there pretty clearly, and that approach takes you through the least populated territory. Just remember to duck when you get within sight of the building, because they will try to take your head off, trust me."

I nodded, studying the map one more time before gesturing it to save the last settings and snapping my hand shut, making it disappear. "All right. I should thank you…" I looked at him and raised my eyebrows.

"Fuck it," he said, white teeth flashing in his red face. "No need for names, and no need for thanks. We're both likely dead in a day or two." He held out his hand. "Pretty soon none of this shit matters anyway, what we were in the past, right? Everything's fucking changing. We live, this time next week I might be king of fucking Hong Kong and you might be a tax-paying citizen, right?"

I grinned a little, a wave of exhausted dizziness passing through me, and took his hand. His skin was scaly and rough, and I kept my grip gentle. "Taxes are for suckers."

"Suckers, fuck," he said, extracting his hand and turning away. "You stay around after I'm king, you won't have no fucking *choice*."

My grin stayed. Fucking cops. They never changed, no matter what you did to them.

I walked rapidly. My leg ached again, the old familiar pain shooting up my back, my augments maxed out and apparently unable to compensate for it anymore. I was strangely happy to have it back, settling into my familiar limp with a twitchy smile playing across my face.

The cops all stared at me as I passed them, tired-looking men and women far removed from the arrogant bruisers I'd known all my life. These were grubby, their clothing more utilitarian and worse for the wear, sweating and silent. I pulled my auto and made a show of reloading it as I walked, keeping my eyes off them all because they weren't worrying me and I wasn't imagining the shot to my head as I walked away.

When I reached the shadowed edge of the plaza, I tried to make my final drop from the overpass onto the street below smooth and calm instead of suddenly rushed, and I forced myself to walk steadily around the first corner that presented itself, pushing my back against the cracking concrete foundation of an old building. I listened for a moment, the uncanny silence of an empty city pushing down on me. After a few seconds I relaxed and stepped away from the wall.

I was on a wide street, lined on each side by gleaming buildings of glass and metal, each more or less the same height, with many of them achieving that size through several ugly additions bolted on top of them. All along their bases, more grubby wooden shacks had been built, swarming up in loose pyramids like insect nests, spilling crazily and narrowing the cracking pavement, crowding what should have been a dizzyingly wide space. Nothing moved, aside from a few listless pieces of trash being pushed around by a chill breeze finding a way between the towering buildings, the rows of massive skyscrapers and mushroomed shacks stretching east and west as far as I could see. I stood for a moment considering all the space here, all the rooms inside those aging metal boxes, all the air between them. I was the only person in sight, and it made me dizzy for a moment, all that fucking space.

"Cates."

I blinked but didn't turn around. "Hello, Mara."

"About fuckin' time. I thought you were going to trade promise rings with him."

I turned. The Poet stood behind her, glasses on, looking calm. I opened my mouth to tell Mara to go fuck herself when the Poet cocked his head, something in the reflection of his glasses moving. I threw myself at the ground, knocking into Mara and the Poet in the process, and we tumbled into the gutter as the street exploded into gunfire.

XXIII

WE WERE ALL ROBOTS

The pavement at our feet became a fountain of asphalt shooting up into the air as we all pushed ourselves back against the warm wall. My HUD flickered in my vision, giving me a headache on top of the headache I already had and making me blink.

After a second, the droning noise of gas-powered ammunition cut off, leaving my ears throbbing.

I pushed myself up, using the wall for leverage. I kicked Mara savagely.

"Move!"

The Poet surged up to his knees and gave her body a heroic shove, launching himself over her as I turned to run. More gunfire exploded, and I felt a shimmer of concrete dust against my neck as I pounded toward the wooden shacks built up against the nearest skyscraper. With a shout I slammed my shoulder against the plywood door. The simple hinged latch of cheap metal snapped with an unsatisfying ringing surrender, sending me skidding to the floor under my own wasted momentum. My cheek scraped against decades of the world wearing down underfoot: tiny bits of glass, hardened dust, cracks and ridges in the old, melted and refrozen street. As the Poet sailed in, tripping over my legs and falling on top of me, a line of daylight was carved into the wall a foot or so above us, approximately where my chest had been a moment ago. The whole wooden frame shuddered with the dull impact.

"Fucking hell!" I shouted.

Mara followed, doing a nice roll and coming up behind us, flat to the ground. Another booming, loud *rat tat tat* of gunfire, and more fist-sized holes appeared at exactly the same height. The sound ate everything in the tiny stall, which had a hastily abandoned glassed-in counter running along its back.

The gunfire cut off. My ears rang.

"They can't swivel any lower!" I shouted, gesturing at the line of splintered holes punched through the old wood. "We have to keep moving!"

The Poet was on his feet, moving quickly down the rear wall. "We cannot go out!" he shouted. "We'll be sitting ducks out there." He paused at one darkened, charred-looking panel of wood and put his shoulder against it, wrapping his arms around himself. "Let me try something." With a sudden lunge, he took three steps backward and launched himself at the wall, which gave way like paper. In the sudden booming silence, I heard him cursing as he crashed into several breakable things.

I paused to take hold of the duffel bag he'd dropped on the floor and dashed through his ersatz door with it, Mara scrabbling at my heels. We all dropped onto the floor—rough concrete now, instead of asphalt. I looked around; it was a slightly larger plywood cube filled with soft, rotting cardboard boxes. One had split open, spilling dozens of small black discs into the space.

I rolled over onto the duffel and flipped the tiny map of Hong Kong open in one hand, quickly gesturing it down to our present location. My eyes roamed over it, then jumped to the flimsy wall across from me.

"Through it," I said, snapping the map shut and pointing. "Make a hole."

The Poet nodded and sprang to the rear wall, feeling his way from one end to the other.

"Are you fucked?" Mara snarled. "You intend to carve your way through every fucking wall in the city?"

The Poet turned and shook his head; this wall was better built. I nodded, and he dropped down again and crossed back to my side of the tiny space.

"We can't go outside," I hissed, speed-crawling across the gritty stone and flopping up against the far wall. She was still snarling at me, so I gestured at the hole the Poet had made. "Well, *you* are free to go outside." I snapped the map back into life in my palm. "This boulevard is lined with buildings, the old lobbies are behind these shacks, and every fucking one of them, I'll bet your ass, are made of old plate glass." I snapped the map shut again and gestured at the Poet's hole. "Whoever's trying to turn us into a fine mist is getting boots on the fucking ground right *now*, so shut the fuck *up* and let's *make a fucking hole*."

Outside, on cue, the thunderous pounding noise of the big gun erupted again, and the wooden walls of the shanty shook with each impact.

I took a deep breath. My HUD was yellow across the board, but looked pretty steady. Adrenaline had swept away my aches and exhaustion, leaving me jittery and unable to take a deep enough breath. I wondered what the average life expectancy of the common soldier in the SFNA was; my guess was, even assuming no fatal gunshot wounds, about two months, tops. Panting, I pushed up and unslung my shredder, thumbing it into life and checking the status screen. I fished a grenade from my pocket and loaded it into the hideous RPG mounted on top of the barrel, ruining the weight and balance and making the shredder a dancing pig when you squeezed the trigger.

"Brace yourselves," I said, leveling the shredder at the wall.

"Grenades are bad news," the Poet said behind me, sounding out of breath. "Grenades in enclosed spaces," he paused, and I pictured him spreading his hands and waggling his eyebrows, "are even *worse* news."

I pushed the rubber toggle.

The wall dissolved in front of me as I was peppered with splinters and I turned my face away at the last second, catching most of them—propelled fast enough to be projectile weapons—in my neck. Smoke filled the small space and blood poured warmly down my neck, but my HUD flashed into life in the darkness of my closed eyes and assured me nothing was fatal and clotting was proceeding normally. Turning back, I opened my eyes and fished in my pocket for another grenade to feed into the launcher.

"Go!" I yelled. Behind us, I heard shouting—lots of it. I knelt down stiffly and tore open the duffel, extracting a flat black piece of metal with an SFNA serial stamped on one side. The Poet drew two handguns and flicked off the safeties with his thumbs, and Mara slung her shredder around, thumbing it into life, the sour whine familiar and terrifying. I followed them briskly through the hole I'd blown in the makeshift wall, flames still licking the blackened edges, then I stopped and turned around to face the way we'd come, dropping the duffel and slapping the metal brick against the remaining wall.

"What's that?" Mara shouted behind me. Sweat streamed into my eyes, blood was soaking into my shirt.

"Trip mine, motion sensing," I shouted without turning. A small red light blinked into life on the edge of the brick and I stood, stepping back carefully. Turning, I said, "No going back."

We were in a large, dark space. The ceiling soared high above us, lost in shadows, and with my military hearing I could tell a large crowd of something—birds? bats?— was nesting up there, hidden. Which meant a way in, but I ignored that for the moment. The floor was expensive marble, covered in inches of pale dust. In the center of the space was a large, rotting cube of old wood, gaps like missing teeth here and there where banks of equipment had once sat. The walls were all glass, thick and greenish in the dim light, the outer walls looking out onto the cheap wooden walls of the stalls built up against the base of the building. Glass from my grenade blast crunched under my feet as we stood for a moment.

I flipped my little map open again, the wireframe blazing bright in the darkness. "We head west," I said, gesturing to my left. "We keep heading west until we can't anymore. I'm making a bet all these buildings have these plate-glass exteriors and we can just blast our way through."

Wordlessly, the Poet strode off in the direction I'd indicated, Mara following. I picked up the duffel and started to follow, my Roon in one hand.

"Adrian!" I shouted.

He spun and walked backward a few steps.

"If we don't own these buildings, shoot anything that moves."

He nodded curtly, spun back, and stepped quickly toward the large glass wall. When he was about three feet away, he raised both guns and spat six shots in quick succession, shattering the glass in front of him and creating another sudden doorway. He stepped through, followed quickly by Mara, who held her heavy shredder like someone who'd spent time with one before.

No one had used these street-level lobbies in decades. Newer buildings didn't even have street entrances at all; everything was through hover pad on the roof. Kept the riffraff out. Older buildings still had their vestigial lobbies and empty elevator banks, dusty and stale—the elevators usually were capable of hitting the lobby in emergencies, but not during normal operation. Back twenty years or so, a group of heroes in New York had taken over six or seven lobbies in secret, running a hover chop shop and all-purpose pawn business right in the middle of uptown Manhattan, a few blocks away from the Rock, cop central. They were running for weeks before the System Pigs even noticed.

As I stepped through the smashed pane and into the next building, there was an explosion behind me and several of the panes around me shattered as the old concrete floor beneath me shuddered. "Here they come!" I shouted, spinning around and steadying the shredder on my shoulder and walking backward. I found my augments easily kept me on a straight line as I walked, and I kept Mara and the Poet pictured relative to me by the sound of their fast, scraping footsteps. After three backward steps I heard the quick spit of the Poet's guns again and more shattered glass.

Movement in the gloom behind us, and before I even thought of it consciously, my finger twitched, sending a contact grenade through our new doorway, filling the lobby with an instant of fire and noise. As I spun away to jog a little, I had a momentary sight of several figures on fire, dancing.

I caught up with Mara just as she stepped through the next hole created by the Poet. The third lobby along the block was in bad shape; some sort of disaster had happened in the building at one point that had burned it up pretty good, the ceiling tiles littering the floor, along with charred hunks of piping and wires. The whole place smelled like smoke and rot. Up above us, the ceiling had been repaired, sealing off the lobby from the rest of the building, but they hadn't bothered cleaning up the ground floor. All the glass encasing it was cloudy and warped in its frame, frozen bubbles and waves that let in the light as a silvery cloud. My eyesight immediately sharpened, taking on a green tint that made me nauseous.

"Mara!"

She spun, shredder up. She wasn't sweating. She looked ready to do some sit-ups and then call me names.

I motioned her over and then turned to face the entryway, bending stiffly and awkwardly onto one knee. I let my augments kick in and hold the gun steady. "Let's make 'em think twice about following. I'd rather have them in front of us, if it comes to that."

I was running on invisible fumes, but I felt steady. Not like I was eighteen again, like I had before, but pretty good.

"Sure, the two o' us will just kill every fucking asshole in Hong Kong," she muttered darkly, but put herself in position next to me, angled slightly to get a good crossfire going. I studied her again for a second, that strange, uncanny feeling hitting me. And then, suddenly, I felt like an idiot. Her calm, greaseless expression, her dry, easy energy—Mara was a fucking avatar, and I should have known it from the very first time the tiny little bastard had introduced us.

I was frozen for a moment. *I am the stupidest bastard in the fucking world*, I thought, wonderingly. I expected one of my ghosts to confirm this, but they were silent.

She turned her head and stared back at me. "You fallin' in love, Mr. Cates?"

I blinked and forced a smile, shaking my head. We both strained to see some movement. So fucking what. Half the fucking people you met these days were made of silicone and circuits, their brains backed up via shortwave and defragged every week. So what if Mara had been sucked into a brick? I had my brain wired up. We were all robots, these days. Everything else was just semantics.

Movement in my peripheral vision made me jerk my head back. Mara sent a whining stream of metal into the next building, two seconds of noise and shattering glass. When she relaxed, I squeezed my trigger and followed it immediately with another burst, moving the humming rifle in a tight sweep, clearing the air.

Silently, we both displaced, rolling in opposite directions and climbing to our feet to run at an angle toward the new hole the Poet had created.

"Now what's t'stop 'em," Mara shouted as we ran, my HUD levels bouncing up and down as if affected by my gait, "from creepin' up ahead o'us or maybe even—"

There was a sudden explosion up ahead of us and way up above, followed by the tearing roar of bending metal. The whole empty lobby around us shivered.

"—from above," she finished.

The Poet was suddenly running back toward us, guns holstered. I slung my shredder over my shoulder and popped the map up in my hand again, gesturing down until I had the building plans spreading out in the air around us.

"It's no-go that way," the Poet panted as he joined us, smoothly extracting his guns again and keeping his eyes moving. "Party crashers on the way. Want to be elsewhere."

Mara checked her rifle over. "Well, perfesser, where do we go?"

I kept my eyes on the tiny building in my palm, searching the plans, and then looked up, squinting into the bluish gloom. My augments adjusted and the ancient lobby slowly glowed into life, and I saw the old stairs sinking into the old transit system in the back, past the old, empty elevator shafts.

I sighed, snapping the map shut. "Down," I said into the freshening darkness. "We go down."

XXIV

YOU SURE DO MAKE FRIENDS EVERYWHERE YOU GO

"This," Mara said beside me, her voice swallowed up and muted by the still, hot air, "is the cleanest fucking subway I've ever seen. And I've been in some fucking *subways*."

I finished placing the last of three trip mines and slowly backed away from the dusty stairs leading down from the lobby. When I was five or six feet past their specced range, I spun and swung my shredder around into my hands.

"Give me your thoughts and impressions on the move, Mara," I said, pushing myself to trot into the gloom. "If we're standing here hand-jobbing each other when the welcome wagon gets down here, we're all going to be *part* of the fucking subway."

"Don't fucking tell *me*," she huffed behind me, her voice bouncing off the tiled walls around us and pinging back and forth. "Been at this longer than y'been *alive*, kiddo."

I ignored her. We had to keep moving, to distance

ourselves from the blast if our pursuers fell for the same damn trick twice—and shame on them if they did—and because I didn't know what we were going to find down here and wanted to cover as much ground as I could before the cosmos caught up with me with a new dance in mind. We were on a short, dusty platform, the tracks running alongside and stretching off forward and back into darkness. A few scraps of furniture were still rotting away, and a few square tiles still clung to the walls. I made for the edge and dropped over into the rut.

The Poet fell in beside me, pistols still in his hands, sunglasses still on. They were certainly made to adjust to all lighting conditions, but I found myself irritated that he'd leave them on like some punk interested in looking like a fucking Gunner instead of actually doing the job right. I didn't say anything. There was no time. I felt like the cosmos had put me back on the rail a few weeks ago, but that I'd jumped the track, that I wasn't *supposed* to kill Londholm, wasn't *supposed* to take the God Augment and turn it on Michaleen. I couldn't explain it. It was just a feeling. I thought if I kept moving, kept my head down, I might tell the fucking cosmos to go fuck itself for a change.

"Something on your mind, Adrian?"

The tunnel was slowly grinding down to pitch-black; my augments were struggling to make it visible. My HUD showed my climbing respiration as I jogged with the duffel and shredder hanging off me, some of my stats edging down into the red—I was pretty much staying upright with augment power at this point: If someone had been able to dissolve them out of me by magic, I'd probably drop dead. I hoped the fact that the subway entrance had been completely unmonitored or defended indicated that the Triads, or whoever owned the tunnels, had forgotten about lobby entrances, buying us some time. If we were quiet enough, we might make it through without having to pay a toll.

I didn't think we could afford any tolls.

"You're improvising," he said, his voice picking up the strained pitch I'd heard before, in the tunnel. "This makes me very nervous. Bag of secrets, too."

"Noted, and who gives a fuck. You got a better idea, let's hear it."

He didn't say anything for a few steps. "That disturbs me, too." He looked over his shoulder for a second. "We are not out from under. Push button."

"I'm right here, assholes," she whispered. "I can fuck-ing *hear* you."

"You surprised we'd gladly twist your head off? That hurts your feelings?" I whispered into the air without turning. I glanced at the Poet. "You see any opportunity to get out from under, Adrian, and I am listening. Until then—the only way out is forward."

We walked a few steps, the darkness tightening up around us. With a silent stutter, my vision suddenly turned murky green, lighting the place up a little better.

"Also disturbing," he said suddenly, his voice pitched lower, "someone is following us. Stealthy but clumsy."

I kept moving, but strained my augmented ears. After a moment I heard it, the creeping scrape of someone being careful with their foot placement but sloppy with their advance. "One person," I whispered after a moment.

The Poet nodded.

I considered: They'd either already been down here,

or they'd somehow bypassed my trip mines. Nothing was impossible, I knew that—you put down trip mines, someone walked right through them; it could be done. If they were already down here, they were possibly Triad, a guard, or just some poor shit wandering around. Either way, noise would be a mistake.

Wordlessly, the Poet faded back, and I hoped he didn't freak out again. I kept my eyes forward, struggling to pick out details. The tracks snaked under us clearly enough, and the rough concrete walls slipped past us in a steady scroll. The air was getting thick. I couldn't imagine a train barreling through these narrow tunnels, pushing through this fog—I couldn't imagine anyone voluntarily rushing through the darkness in a fucking tube, clinging to each other for dear life. If I'd been in charge during Unification thirty years ago, I would have poured concrete down each of these holes and not looked back.

Walking along, knowing that someone was shadowing us, was stress. My hands were tight on the body of the shredder, still warm. I wanted to spin and just send fire everywhere, taking down everyone, taking down Mara, too, and feeling my head explode as a result of the frag. It was tempting.

The only way out is forward, Dennis Squalor whispered, the sound of a ghost, a man long dead even before I pulled his plug.

Something sizzled through the air to my right, and I stopped, shredder coming up and trying to track it as it landed with a hard-sounding skittle across the tracks. Something small and dense. For a second, there was no sound.

"That's an RD mine," a voice called out from behind. "If I toggle it, we're all dead. No one move."

My eyes strained to pick it out, though I wasn't sure what I planned to do if I found it. "You blow it, you're dead too."

"That's what 'we're all dead' means, Mr. Cates."

I closed my eyes. *Mr. Cates.* I suddenly recognized the voice. "How'd you get down here, Remy?"

"I've been trained in live explosive decommission," he said, sounding older and colder than I remembered. "Those are military-issue trips; I know 'em well. Don't worry, I set them again when I was through."

I nodded. Remy had always been a smart kid. "How'd you get away from Anners?"

He didn't answer for a second or two. "I just walked away. It'll be a few hours before he realizes I'm gone, and then he'll probably pop me. Or maybe he'll wander out of range and I'll get popped automatically. I don't know. I don't care."

I opened my eyes again, HUD automatically fading to a transparent film on my vision. For a heartbeat or two, we were all silent again, and then I took a breath. "I tried—"

"Yeah, you tried real fucking hard, Mr. Cates," he said coldly. "You paid that asshole a fucking fortune to get you escorted into Hong Kong, but I guess I wasn't worth that much."

"Who the fuck is this pip, Cates?" Mara snapped. "One o' your bastards come to pay his respects?"

Just someone on my list, I thought. "What do you want, Remy?"

"What do I *want*? You're a fucking piece of shit, Mr. Cates. If they hadn't pressed you, you'd have just run for it back in Englewood. You didn't give a fuck about us then, and you didn't give a fuck about *me* here. So what do I want? What do you think I want? My head hurts, Mr. Cates. I got a blinding headache every fucking day from these augments. I can't sleep. I can't eat. They push tabs down my throat to keep me alive. Whatever they want me to do, I do. I can't not do it; I'm fucking plugged in. They push a button, I'm on the floor, screaming. They push a button, I'm comatose. They push a button, I'm killing people with my bare hands. Some of the officers…" He paused, his words bouncing around us. "Some of the officers like to *have their fun* with us. Make us dance, like puppets. So dying, I'm okay with. I've been thinking of just wandering off, seeing how long I got before Anners pops me. And then you showed up and sailed on past and I thought, 'Fuck it, I'm going to kill him first. If I can.'"

"Hell, Cates," Mara said cheerily, "you sure do make friends everywhere you go, huh? Kid, am I to understand that you're only concerned with Cates and his less-than-noble past?"

"Stop talking."

"Sure, sure, but let me be more blunt: Are you sayin' if we give ya Cates, we can just walk on off?"

I froze.

"You cannot do this," the Poet hissed. "You cannot just leave him here. We will *need* the man."

"Mr. Panić, you'll do best to shut the fuck up before I pop you, right? Now, kid, what's the word?"

Another few seconds of quiet passed us by. "I don't give a shit what you two do. I want Mr. Cates to stay right here."

"Done," Mara said immediately. "He's all yours."

"You—"

"Mr. *Panić*," Mara snarled. "Say one more word and your brain'll be mush. We're going."

"Go ahead, Adrian," I said, surprising myself. "No sense in both of us getting killed."

"If you come back, I'll just blow the mine," Remy said flatly.

I heard the scrape of Mara and the Poet getting to their feet and walking toward me. I felt someone looming up behind me, and then there was a hand on my shoulder. "We ain't comin' back," Mara said cheerfully.

"I am sorry, friend," Adrian said, his voice tight and shaky. "This is not how I want it. I would—"

"Just fucking go," I said, not moving. "This isn't your fuckup."

His hand stayed on my shoulder for a moment, and then slipped away, and the two of them crept into the gloom, dissolving slowly into particles of light too diffuse to be coherent. I thought the Poet looked back at me as he was swallowed by the darkness, but I couldn't be sure. At least Adrian wasn't on *my* list, I thought. On someone's list, sure, but not mine.

"Remy," I said slowly, still not turning. I was curiously calm, my HUD still pus yellow and pulsing in alarm here and there, but I felt nothing aside from vague aching in my leg and a general weariness. The bold exclamation point in the corner of my HUD was still blinking, and it expanded slightly as I focused on it. I could go that route, I thought. Go into Berserker Mode again and go for Remy, if I didn't stroke out, if I didn't just kill myself in the attempt.

The exclamation point shrank down, slowly, as my thoughts slid off of it. I could hear the kid approaching, stuffed full of augments, but still dumb enough to think that just having me with my back turned made me defenseless. Made me easy.

"Don't talk, Mr. Cates," he said, closer.

I decided to irritate him, on the premise that it couldn't make my situation any *worse*. "Fuck you, don't talk. A fucking *brigade* snatches you out from under me and I'm to blame? You assholes begged me to stay. I told you all to get the fuck away, to *run*, but you all stood there with your sad little faces kicking the dirt, fucking useless pricks who can't handle shit for *themselves*, and suddenly I'm supposed to be your big fucking brother? Fuck that noise. I did what I could for you."

"You were supposed to take care of *me*," he said, voice rising and suddenly sounding young, like the little kid I'd known. "You *ran away.*"

He was right behind me. I thought of the mine up ahead, near enough to turn me into a fine mist. I thought of the gun he must have behind me. Would it be the shredder, like an inexperienced asshole, a gun that bucked like a horse, entirely wrong for an up-close attack, or a handgun? Would he just put the barrel against my skull and pull the trigger, or would there be drama, speeches, tears? I didn't like to think of Remy as an asshole, but I hoped he was.

Then he was right behind me, and I cleared my mind, imagining the old glass sphere I used to hide in when my mind had been filled with ghosts, right after my half-processing into an avatar. I pushed all thoughts outside and closed my eyes, ready, listening. Remy was on my list, but I wasn't going to die in this shithole tunnel. I wasn't going to die with Michaleen Garda still out there, laughing at me.

Remy was right behind me. "On your knees, then."

XXV

THEY RESTED, THEY PLANNED, AND THEY CAME BACK

"I said, on your knees."

I didn't move. "Remy, if you're going to kill me, just fucking *do* it."

I listened. My augmented hearing brought me every tiny scrape and every hitch in his breathing, which was short and labored like he had a cough he was suppressing. I knew what kind of training the military gave its pressers—assuming augments surgeried in counted as training—and was ready for him when he put the barrel of the shredder against the back of my head, like somehow its presence there would hold me in place. My HUD clarified as a surge of calm and energy swept through me like cool fire, briefly masking my exhaustion and pain, slowing things down and steadying me.

I took a deep breath, flopped down onto my belly in one sudden swoon, scissored my legs around his, and rolled, jerking the lower half of my body with as much force as I could. He lost his balance and fell backward onto his ass, sending a quick burst of shredder fire up into the air, a rain of broken tile and concrete drifting down onto us.

I leaped up and dived, letting gravity pull me down onto him hard enough to crack a few ribs, the shredder pinned between us. He still had his cowl on, his face a blank swatch of hardened plastic. I raised up a little to get some leverage and he jerked his knee up into my balls about as hard as I'd ever had it done to me, and stars burst into my sight, everything going fuzzy and loose. The kid brought the shredder up and smacked me in the chin with it, snapping my head back and cracking my teeth against each other. I lashed out one hand and took hold of the hot barrel of his gun and held on for all I was worth, hanging from it and letting my weight make control of it impossible.

"Let *go*!" he snarled, his voice going pitchy.

The low, nauseous ball in my belly faded as my strained augments kicked in, smothering it, and I yanked hard on the shredder, using my dead weight to overbalance him— he was still thin, barely there, and in a second he had a choice to make—either let go of the gun or let me pull him back down on top of me.

He didn't let go, and he crashed down on me with a growl of pure frustration. I was ready and rolled immediately, pushing him over before he could settle in and get his weight spread. Slamming him onto his back again, I pushed the shredder down onto his neck, making sure to lock his legs under me to stop him from kneeing me again. I gave it what I had, leaning down and pushing the gun onto his throat, my sweat dripping down onto his cowl in a steady stream of fat drops.

In the distance back the way I'd come, three quick explosions shook the tunnel around us. I looked up; I could feel the vibration in the tracks beneath us; my other friends tripping the mines. With any luck, they'd caved in the stairwell, but I wasn't sure I was that blessed. If not, it wouldn't be long before their next wave crept down. My HUD was creeping into red, all my status bars getting a bleary, dangerous look to them, and I wondered, for a second, if this is what it looked like to die. If these were the visuals.

"I fucking *hate* you!"

Remy surged beneath me and with surprising strength flung me off to the right; I kept my death-clutch on the shredder and tore it from his hands as I sailed a few feet, landing on my back on the tracks, the wide rail trying its best to snap me in two. My HUD flashed again, and then normalized. I didn't wait to interpret it; I got my hands and feet under me and scrabbled backward as fast as I could manage, then rolled myself to the left, tucking my legs under and pushing myself up into a stumbling run that smoothed out after the first few steps. I sprinted, marveling at the effortlessness of it, the way my wired-up body just pulled the necessary resources, dumped the necessary chemicals, and pushed my limbs into motion. On one level, I *knew* I was exhausted, too tired to stay alive, but on another, I was removed from it, cushioned, and I knew I could run full tilt until I dropped dead, with no warning in between, aside from the light show in my head.

As I ran, a new icon faded in on my HUD, blinking a dull orange: four military pips surrounding a distance meter. Mara, my nominal commanding officer, was closing in on the range that would define me as a deserter. When she crossed that invisible barrier, I'd be dead.

Just as this new anxiety splashed itself across my thoughts, Remy slammed into me from behind, like a bag of wet cement, knocking me down and slamming me back onto the gritty tracks. I held onto his shredder, letting my nose take one track straight on and crunching into mulch with the ease of the frequently broken. Remy was younger, in better condition, and wired up just like me. I wasn't going to get past him one on one.

He didn't weigh anything, though, and I rolled us over halfway, shifted my hands on the rifle, and pushed the firing toggle for all it was worth. The high-pitched whine of the shredder sent my audio status into the dark angry red for fifteen seconds as thousands of rounds spat up into the air as I waved the rifle around, aiming at nothing. Remy scrabbled back, startled, moving awkwardly on his hands behind him, and I swung myself up onto my knees and took hold of the shredder's sizzling barrel again, ignoring the searing pain as my hands burned, and swung it down at him like a club.

He dodged with sudden speed and shot up, taking hold of the shredder and yanking it toward him violently; I angled one arm down and sent the stock into his face using his own force, giving him a good crack against the side of his head that splintered his visor and sent him staggering backward. I didn't hesitate. I'd had enough people want to kill me to know the one lesson they taught you: They never gave up. Even if you half killed them, they rested, they planned, and they came back.

I lunged forward and used the rifle as a lance, driving it into his belly and knocking him backward. There was no time for anything fancy; our new friends from up above might already be picking their way down into the murk. I ran him down until he finally overbalanced and I knocked him back onto his ass. Raising the shredder over my head, I steadied myself for a second and brought it down on his skull with every bit of strength I had. He twitched once and went limp.

I stood over him for a moment, panting. I was swimming in my own sweat. I struggled to stay alert and ready, watching the kid closely for signs of playing possum, and when I was certain he was down I dropped the shredder, fell to my knees, and reached for his cowl as I pulled my Roon. With a jerk, I tore it off of him, ready to put two in his face, something I'd done a hundred times before with no hesitation.

He stared back at me, conscious, eyes bloodshot a deep red, like a vessel had exploded in his head, filling him with his own blood like pus, looking confused and demanding. He was a fucking *kid*. No older than I'd left him, fifteen, maybe, and a soft fifteen. He was *crying*, silent tears just streaming down the sides of his shaved head.

"You *left* me," he said. "You fucking *left* me."

I flinched, and racked a shell into the chamber.

"I told everyone you were coming back for me." He coughed. "You never came back."

I pinned his arms with my knees and put the gun against his forehead. He shut his eyes and just lay there, breathing, his flushed face twisting and untwisting as he waited. I'd had this kid following me around for months, fetching me things, cleaning my boots at night, king of all his friends because he was with me. Slept on the floor of my room above Bixon's half the time, scrambling up

when I woke to get me whatever warm shit they were calling coffee that day. And here he was, wired up and ten
minutes from a summary execution delivered via sub-
routine and wireless link, with no judge or jury.

I eased the Roon off his forehead and leaned back,
keeping my weight on his arms.

"You know who protected me when I was your age?" I
hissed. "When I was fucking *younger* than you? No one.
Not a fucking soul."

He just stared back at me, chest heaving.

I couldn't hear anything. The new symbol in my HUD
had swollen up to a size impossible to ignore, the count-
down within it small and shrinking. I was going to be
buzzed by God's Middle Finger soon enough myself. I
jumped back and let my augments steady me, then quickly
retrieved both shredders and the duffel from the ground,
along with Remy's handgun. I didn't doubt he had other
weapons hidden away, but he was content to just lie on his
back and say nothing while I huffed around. I didn't know
if I'd broken something, or if he'd just expended his hate
for me for the moment.

"Don't follow me," I said, turning away.

"Mr. Cates."

I stopped and shut my eyes. I was always telling myself
about my fucking list, what I owed, and I should have
known the cosmos would wait until the worst possible
fucking moment to make me eat my words.

"I can't go back," he said quietly, a kid again. "I want
to come with you. I can't go *back*."

I swallowed hard. "You don't have a choice. I can't
save you—even if you could come with me, you'd just get
killed. Trust me on that. Everyone who comes with me

dies." I shook my head, keeping my eyes closed. "Go back to your unit. Survive. That's what your skill set should be. Don't follow me."

I jogged away. After the first turn I couldn't hear the kid snuffling anymore. The silence was disturbing; I knew they'd blown my mines at the entrance and I didn't doubt they'd be after me, but I should have heard *something*. But the subway was big and dark. A fucking army could have wandered around in the tunnels and not be noticed.

I moved easily down the tunnel, the blinking icon showing how dangerously far away Mara had gotten from the tiny bomb in my head slowly shrinking as I moved. She stood still, at least, for the time being. For several minutes I jogged in silence, the flashing number in the corner of my HUD shrinking and then suddenly fading out completely, the darkness and density of the atmosphere almost total. As I ran, I pulled the tiny disc from my pocket and snapped it open in my palm again, the glowing red map of Hong Kong blooming. With a twitch of my hand, I tunneled down into the subways and scoped to my present location; I was just a few minutes' jog away from the Shannara Hotel.

Something pinged my senses from the darkness up above. Crouching low, I holstered the auto and unslung one of the shredders, slowing to a walk. A haze of slightly brighter tunnel was swelling up in front of me, the wall to my right ending as another platform rose up on my right. It was in slightly better shape and still had most of its wall tiles, and a single poster still clung to the wall, tattered and rusted. The stairs were wider and steeper, rising into a vague haze of twilight above me, its concrete steps chipped and crumbling. I pulled myself up onto the platform and crept toward the stairs, shredder ready, duckwalking my way to the very bottom.

The Poet was standing at the top, smoking a cigarette. He waved.

"We did not get far," he said, giving me a humorless smile. "You might as well come on up. We have been delayed."

XXVI

SHOOTING HEAT BEAMS FROM HER EYES

I squinted up at the Poet, studying his body language. It was in between alarmed and batshit agitated, so I tightened my grip on the shredder and stayed right where I was.

"Too bright up there," I said, loud. "Rats like me like the dark."

He smiled. "Everyone likes dark—"

The Poet broke off. I sensed them behind me.

"Don't move," said a civil, calm, male voice. "Please relax. We are under parley, and you will not be hurt. We are going to let you keep your weapons, because you are a reasonable man. Please walk up the stairs."

I didn't move. My hands were on the shredder and my eyes were on the Poet. I cursed myself for letting someone sneak up behind me, but I was exhausted and my augments weren't running at full capacity. I was in a strange tunnel and I was, I was increasingly aware, a fucking idiot.

Keeping my eyes on the Poet, I shrugged my eyebrows

at him. He shook his head slightly, a bare tick of his head, and I loosened my grip on the gun.

"I'm gonna assume you've got guns back there," I said, pushing a smile onto my face. "So when people ask you about this, make sure they understand I didn't roll over and show you my belly because you called me 'reasonable.'"

There was a deep peal of laughter disturbingly close to my ear. "We will tell the Vids that it took dozens to make you see reason. Now, ascend, please."

I slung the shredder back onto my shoulder to join Remy's and climbed the crumbling stairs, keeping my eyes on the Poet's face for any signs or hints. He just stared back, smoking. I emerged into another stuffy, shuttered-in lobby, dark and dusty. This one had once been something—we'd moved up in the world of old Hong Kong. The floor was smooth marble polished by a billion long-dead feet, with thick columns soaring up to an impossibly high ceiling. The columns were sheathed in marble too, white and veiny, but some of the huge slabs had lost their grip and smashed onto the floor.

In the center of the lobby was a big hunk of metal, a sculpture of some sort, vaguely cube shaped, made from thick strands of twisted metal. It had fallen off its squat stone base and lay on the cracked floor oddly balanced, as if it had been frozen in the act of rolling over. Whatever it had meant was lost, and I had the immediate impression that if you made any sudden movements, it would animate and finish its endless fall.

Mara, looking like she might start shooting heat beams from her eyes, sat up against it, her hands bound behind her in a pair of bright metal bracelets. Standing at ease around me were four people, a woman in a bright yellow suit that was cut to drape elegantly from her thin, wide shoulders, and three heavily armed, broad-shouldered men, young and well fed, wearing a ragged collection of military clothing that looked old, nothing like the gear the SFNA wore. The men were dark skinned, and they all wore big, pitch-black sunglasses. Each of them had an almost comical amount of hardware: old-fashioned semiauto rifles in their hands and two more crisscrossed on their backs, two pistols on their hips and one or two crowding their shoulders, ammo belts looped across their chests, and bizarre fruit-shaped grenades clipped to their pants.

I'd seen the woman in yellow before, back at the SFNA Press Camp. Her hair had been green then, to match her suit. Today it was yellow, too. Her eyes still glowed blue, sucking data from the air.

I glanced at the Poet. He nodded at Mara. "They asked us to wait. They were quite calm and polite." He shrugged. "Mara told them no."

"Fuckers got hidey-holes everywhere," she shouted suddenly. "Don't be fooled, Mr. Cates—looks like three, but there's a fucking roach motel of 'em hidden away."

"If you got any hand on this one, Mr. Cates," the woman said, her accent the same as my memory with its round vowels, "make her shut the fuck up, okay?"

I turned and found three more men coming up the stairs, more big bruisers, massive piles of flesh that gleamed in the low light, skin about as dark as I'd ever seen it, weighed down with the same ridiculous amount of old hardware.

"I'll put a fucking hand on *you*, you goddamn piece o' shit," Mara said in a calm, steady voice. "I don't forget a face."

The woman grinned and winked at me. "I don't doubt she's got my face, and she'll run it on the nets—whatever fucking nets are still around—as soon as she can." She shrugged. "You know what she'll find, Mr. Cates?"

I gave myself a second or two to study her. She was relaxed and amused, a woman who felt like she was in charge. I pictured Mara, miserable on the floor, and thought, shit, she pretty much was. So I smiled at her. "You mean you're not famous, like me?"

She laughed, mouth splitting to reveal two rows of yellow teeth.

"Enough horseshit. Mr. Cates, I have an offer for you. My name is Mardea, and I represent Dai Takahashi. You know the name?"

I nodded. "Sure." I forced myself to affect a relaxed, easy mood, and gestured at my pocket. "Mind if I reach for my cigarettes? I have a feeling you're the chatty type."

She cocked her head, her flat, curly hair glistening in the twilight like it was perpetually damp; it looked like spun gold on her head. "Of course. Make yourself comfortable. We are under parley."

I fumbled in my pockets for a pack of the cop smokes Hense had gifted me with when she'd fooled me into taking her fucking bomb into Hong Kong with me. "You keep saying that word, *par-lay*," I said, putting a stick into my mouth and patting myself for my lighter. "I thought I knew what it meant. You sure you do? 'Cause this looks like I just got fucking kidnapped."

She shook her head, her glowing blue eyes locked on me. She never blinked, and it was starting to freak me out. I wondered if she'd flinch if I went up to her and snapped my fingers in her face. "It means we are negotiating in good faith, and are not combatants. We pledge not to attack you, and you do likewise."

I nodded, lighting up and sending a plume of smoke into the air. "Uh-huh. My understanding is that that's supposed to be a *mutual* agreement. I didn't get a memo from your office."

She nodded, not smiling anymore, and spread her hands. "Consider this a fucking *memo*, Mr. Cates. Mr. Takahashi is a man of honor. This is why we choose to deal with you instead of"—she glanced at Mara for a second—"others. He has an offer for you. You may consider it and then accept or reject it; either way, I and my retinue will withdraw and you can continue your business here unmolested—by us—until you come into direct opposition to our interests."

I nodded, puckering my face around my cigarette. "Uh-huh. You talk like a fucking Techie, you know that?"

She smiled again. "Which means I talk like a *bitch*, yes, Mr. Cates? I assure you, I am of sterner stuff. Will you hear our proposal?"

I shrugged. "You might want to hurry it up. I seem to have offended some of the locals on my way here." I pushed more grin into my face. "That happens a lot with me."

"Do not worry. They will not bother us while we are meeting," she said with complete, bland confidence. From what I'd heard of Takahashi's outfit, she was probably justified—in small-scale territorial beefs, his group could probably hold down any building or block against anything smaller than an army brigade without too much trouble. That's what he got paid for.

I nodded. "All right then. I could use the breather. Go on and talk."

My HUD was red across the board. Although I felt

fine, a glance at my vitals on the readout was depressing: If I were a doctor assessing me from data points, I'd start making room in the morgue.

She began to stroll lazily around an invisible box, a few short steps one way, a spin, a few short steps back. "Mr. Takahashi would like to offer you the . . . person of interest in return for a fair settlement in yen." She glanced at me, eyes shining. "We have determined that you have *access* to sufficient funds."

I gave her my screwed-up, serious expression. "What's to say you won't take our yen and then remove us from the equation?"

"We are under *parley*, Mr. Cates," she said with a raised eyebrow. "The sanctity of parley cannot be violated. Mr. Takahashi has a reputation to preserve. If he engages in good-faith negotiations, the safety of the interested parties is guaranteed."

I snorted, waving a hand in the air. "Who's to know? We pay your fee, you slit our throats—this city is fucking *deserted*."

She tapped her own temple with one short, dark finger. "This is the System, Mr. Cates. There's no such thing as privacy. Mr. Takahashi knows this—there are *no* secrets. Not anymore. A man's actions always come back to haunt him." She rasied her bright yellow eyebrows. "The reason Mr. Takahashi has decided to deal with *you* is because your past behavior inspires confidence in any deal we might make with you."

"This ain't the fucking *System* anymore," Mara growled like a beat dog from the floor. "In case you ain't fucking *noticed*."

I considered this. I wanted to look at Adrian, get a

sense of his opinion, but I didn't want to turn around. If
Takahashi—or his girl here—thought I was in charge,
I didn't want to disturb that impression. So I glanced at
Mara, who was staring at me like she'd read my mind
about heat beams and was trying to evolve them right
then and there. I considered, for a second, the fact that
she was an avatar, and rummaged my brain again trying to place her—she seemed so familiar. I drew a blank
again, and looked back at Takahashi's girl. She was tiny,
and could have passed for about ten if she wanted, but her
expensive suit and complex augments argued against that.
Brain augments usually didn't go over well in kids under
fourteen or so. Too much growth, too much development,
and the augments went sour fast.

I dialed my smile to sweet. "So, let me get this straight:
Your boss was hired to protect Londholm. And he's so
fucking concerned about his honor, he's willing to *sell* his
client to me."

Her own face went blank, her glowing eyes locked on
me. She hesitated, stock still, and I imagined her radio-
ing home for instructions and getting them beamed back
at her. "Mr. Londholm has broken his contract with Mr.
Takahashi. Mr. Takahashi considers all obligations to
Mr. Londholm as severed, and he is comfortable that his
peers and associates will agree with his assessment of the
situation."

Broken his contract, I thought. Meaning his funds were
exhausted and he couldn't pay his own security anymore.
Takahashi was trying to wring every last bit of profit from
this adventure before the army came busting down the
door. Takahashi couldn't handle an entire fucking army,
much less the three or four that Anners was bringing with

him, so the mercenary wanted out. It made sense: Every one of us could just walk away clean, a simple, easy deal instead of a protracted battle with the army breathing down our necks.

I looked back at Mara. She stared at me with her perfect, fake eyes, and then nodded, once. I turned and looked at the Poet, who tossed the stub of his cigarette onto the floor and ground it out with his boot.

"We are all but flesh," he said with a burst of smoke. "The road has been a long one, and I am tired."

I stared at him a moment longer, and then looked back at the girl. "All right," I said. "Let's come to terms."

She smiled again. "Excellent. Mr. Cates, you are a reasonable man and I salute your pragmatism." She paused and stood for a moment, blinking. "Excuse me, I am receiving..." She trailed off and half spun away from me, one hand flying to her temple as she bent over slightly. "Excuse me," she repeated, and then suddenly went down on one knee.

Around us, her bodyguard stiffened as one, and I felt my augments kicking in with yet another shivery adrenaline dump. Her body language and posture suddenly screamed *not right*.

"Excuse..."

She went still, then slowly stood, smoothing her suit and pushing a hand through her golden hair. Then she turned back to me, her smile exactly as it had been. Her glowing eyes had gone from blue to a bloody, rusty red.

"Excuse me," she said conversationally. "I have been... hacked."

XXVII

OPERATING UNDER THREAT OF THE MIDDLE FINGER OF GOD

"Sweet fucking hell," Mara hissed, kicking her way awkwardly to her feet. "What kind of fucking rinky-dink bullshit is *this*?"

I didn't move. I looked around at her Gunners, all of whom stood uncertainly on the balls of their feet and sensing that something was wrong, but not sure how to approach it. She was still standing there, looking more or less the same. I knew what was running through their minds: If they moved, and this was just her having a bad day, they'd be screwed. If they stood there like recently erected statues of themselves and this was a bad thing, they'd be screwed.

Suddenly, they all relaxed at once.

"Please relax," Mardea said in a calm voice, holding up one hand after a second's delay. "These are military drafts and we are in possession of their controls as their nominal commanding officer." She suddenly looked up at me, her glowing red eyes two small circles in the air, and then was still for a moment. "It's good to see you still alive, Avery."

I blinked. "What?"

She stared, and then said, "We are SPS. We cannot allow the augment to leave the city."

I rolled my shoulders to feel the shredders on my back, and squinted at her. "Who the fuck are *you*?"

Mardea grinned as if someone had just figured out the controls of her face. "We are SPS."

Hacked. Someone like Mardea, with her wired-up brain, had enough tech buried under her skin—fuck, so did *I*—to almost count as a Droid. We were all turning into cyborgs, and crazy Techies like SPS could dive in over the air and crack us open. I studied her calm, flat face.

"Yeah," I asked unnecessarily, "but who is SPS?"

Again, a heartbeat went by before she tilted her head slightly. "There are many. We are committed to salvaging what we can of knowledge and technology through the coming Dark Age. The whole System is falling apart. Warfare, revolution, coming on the end of decades of stagnation and rot—if something is not done, if steps are not taken, civilization will fade and regress. SPS intends to shelter technology and the knowledge necessary to create and use it until things stabilize."

The delay was short but significant. Whoever had seized control of Mardea was over the air and had some lag on their connection—a second, two sometimes. Maybe enough to take advantage of, if I timed it right.

"But you don't want this particular piece of tech protected, huh?" I asked, taking a step to the left, casually, slowly, just shifting my weight. The Poet came into my peripheral vision, and I felt his eyes on me. Good man, waiting for a signal. "You don't want the God Augment preserved."

I counted to two before Mardea shifted her focus to match me. "That augment will be the end of everything. That augment will be the end of the world. We protected Londholm at first, as one of us. We do not protect him any longer. You cannot be allowed to remove the augment from Hong Kong."

I nodded. "We're not here to remove it. We're here to blow his brains out."

After a moment she turned to look back at Mara. "Yes? Indeed?"

This was our moment. Trusting that Adrian would follow my lead, I spun, pushing my hips out a little and letting the shredders swivel on their straps around my torso, sending one into my hands. Without waiting to see what anyone else was doing, I toggled off the safety and fired as I spun, cutting down one of the three behind me before the rifle barked out a flat empty-clip warning, going numb in my hands. Sliding my hands down to the stock, I pushed it out straight in front of me as a ram and launched myself forward at the next man in front of the stairwell, jamming the gun into his belly and knocking him over. As he dropped away in front of me, I couldn't stop my forward momentum, and with shots blasting out behind me, the floor slid away and I went bouncing down the stairs on my ass, teeth clicking painfully with each impact.

I hit the tiled floor of the platform below with a grunt, a gun in my face; still sliding with forward momentum, I grabbed the thick black wrist and pushed, the gun redlining my audio status as it exploded right next to my ear. I went for his balls, a savage punch into his groin as I used his own arm as leverage to pull myself up on top of him, digging my fingers into the thin flesh of his wrist and twisting the delicate tendons within. He was big, but he panted with a cracked-rib wheeze and looked dopey, like the lag on his CO's feed was confusing him. Some officers, I knew, kept their units on short, short leashes. Anners let his troops have a little illusion of free will. Looked like Mardea had kept this bunch locked down on her signal, and when she wasn't issuing orders they got slow.

I punched the motherfucker again, and this time he howled and the gun dropped from his hand.

I scrambled up onto his chest, trying to pin his arms with my legs like I'd done to Remy just—fuck, just a few minutes ago. I threw myself down onto the mercenary and then had to hang on for dear life as the fucking giant surged beneath me, suddenly getting his shit together and putting his back into it. I was almost flipped right off of him but managed to hang on, clenching my thighs tight on his waist. With my free hand, I reached across myself and pulled my Roon, whipping it down to put two in his face, but as I brought it in line, he suddenly surged forward using nothing but his stomach muscles and smacked his own head into my hand, knocking the Roon off into the air.

"Mother—" I managed to hiss before he did it again, slamming his forehead into my already broken nose.

My HUD sizzled into static for a moment and I went rolling backward, my whole body going limp. I skidded along the dusty tile of the platform for a second or two, coming slowly to a stop, and then just lay there, suddenly

peaceful. There was a dull ringing in my ears and my arms
and legs felt incredibly heavy, so I opted to just lie there
and rest for a moment. I lifted my head to look down the
length of my body, curious, and saw the big motherfucker
lumbering to his feet. He was slow. So fucking slow, my
augments stretching things out for me. I watched him
getting up and thought I could have fucking built Hong
Kong by the time he managed to rise. He had a gash on
his forehead that was pouring blood into his eyes, and he
staggered a little when he was up.

I thought about him. He'd been pressed, maybe, or
maybe he'd joined. Did people join the army? I didn't
fucking know. And then he'd gotten his ass sold to Takahashi and here he was. I had nothing against him.

As he spun, wobbling, peering through the gloom, I
thought about maybe opening that conversation with
him. Comparing augments. We were both owned by the
augments in our heads, why not sit down and figure this
shit out?

Then he turned and saw me, and our eyes met. He
started for me, the ground shaking as this fucking levia-
than leaped, and it seemed like I had all the time in the
world as he hung there. I reached across my other side and
pulled my second Roon, lifted it up, and shot the levia-
than in the face just before he crashed into me, all dead
weight and warm brains and blood. His hardware jammed
into my abdomen as gravity grabbed him, sending a jolt
of pain searing through me. I snapped back into clarity,
head pounding, suffocating under him as his blood seeped
between us, soaking me and filling my nostrils with cop-
per and rot.

Every limb aching, I rolled from under him, picking up

a fine coating of dust and grit. I pushed up onto my knees and leaned on my hands, my whole body shaking for a moment, the Roon still in hand. The air seemed thick and unbreathable, an oxygenated syrup, and above me, distant and vague, there was gunfire; I took a deep, painful breath and got on my feet and stumbled for the stairs. Halfway there, I realized I still had a shredder looped around me, and I pushed the Roon into my coat pocket, swinging the rifle around into my hands.

In the shadows, I ducked low and pushed myself up against the bottom step, peering up. I couldn't see anything, but the noise suddenly swelled to deafening levels. I took another deep breath, feeling like fishhooks had been pushed into my lungs, and took the next few steps in a rush, staying low and moving diagonally across them to stay in the shadows as long as possible. As I rose, the silence firmed up around me, the peculiar vacuum that snapped into place after violence. Standing up with a wince at my stiffening back, I found the Poet on the other end of the lobby, strangling one of the beefy mercenaries with his bare hands, powerful arms vibrating with the effort. He glanced up at me as I emerged from the shadows.

"So many tendons," he shouted breathlessly, grinning. "These bastards are dumb, but big." He sat back on his haunches, breathing hard. The Gunner twitched and gurgled beneath him. "Have fun in the dark?"

I glanced over at Mara, who had her skinny arm locked around Mardea's neck, a small shiv pressed against the black woman's throat hard enough to draw a steady stream of blood. Mara's hands were still bound, and I elected to not puzzle out how she'd overpowered the woman. Mara grinned at me, too.

"We was just takin' the vote whether t'kill this or not," she said jovially. "We're tied."

I knew how Mara had voted—a more bloodthirsty bitch I'd never encountered. Fighting the urge to sit down and take a little nap, I scanned my own HUD—which was a grim snapshot of failing systems—and shrugged. "Just knock her out and leave her here. We can't take her; she's compromised. But there's no need to kill her. Besides," I said, gummily struggling for an argument that would resonate with Mara, "she's here under a white flag. You can't just kill her."

Mara's grin was mischievous. "You're a soft one, Mr. Cates. You had New York in your pocket? You killed System Pigs for a hobby? I don't fucking believe it. You're a weeper."

Mara stared at me a moment more, and then dragged the knife across Mardea's throat. The black woman's eyes widened in shock for a second and then shut tightly as blood spurted from the wound. I stared back at Mara and we watched each other while Mardea died, and I felt nothing. No regret. No blame. I just shrugged and turned away, walking slowly toward the duffel bag, sitting exactly where I'd left it moments before.

"Let's go, then," I said. "You can fucking figure out how to get your cuffs off yourself."

XXVIII

A REALLY POOR QUALITY OF HARDASS

"You are not happy," the Poet said, falling in next to me. "You would have preferred she live? Last rung of ladder."

I shifted the duffel bag's weight on my shoulder. "Adrian, by most recent fucking calculation, the last time I was *happy* was several goddamn decades ago. It had something to do with a dead basehead in an alley and a plump credit dongle I found in his pockets. I just think that slitting throats for no good fucking reason is bad business."

We were walking rapidly through the lobby toward the nearest plate glass. I reached into a pocket and pulled out a grenade to feed into the launcher. I wanted to look over my shoulder and keep Mara in sight, but didn't want to look like I was worried about her. I was. I was suddenly concerned as fucking hell that she was not only behind me, but in fucking *charge* of me. I wanted her as nearby as possible so I could keep a boot on her neck and I wanted her as far away as I could; she made my skin crawl. Fucking avatars. White coolant and who knew what else pulsating under that synthetic skin, complete with a layer of skin and tiny blood vessels ready to seep blood on demand.

When we were fifteen feet away from the glass, I toggled the rifle and it disintegrated with a loud boom, sucking the stale air out of the building in a breeze that pushed past us roughly.

"She was compromised," the Poet said. "Even restrained, dangerous. Killing her was best."

At the edge of the lobby we both stopped and I knelt down in the spray of broken glass, and he did the same. I leaned out the hole carefully, ears wide open, and squinted around: We were at a high point, the old roads sliding down a gentle grade from here, the roads spinning off like thick threads into overpasses. Across the road was a grubby-looking retaining wall, dirt brown and much abused. Right next to it was a squat, ugly structure made up of shadowed open-air levels. I paused. Sitting like a hidden jewel on one of the floors of the building was, unmistakably, a hover. It looked new, too, though at distance I couldn't tell what shape it was really in. I filed the image away and spat on the floor, flipping open my wireframe map, which bloomed like a bright flower in my hand, scoping out to small scale and slowly rotating. As Mara joined us, I gestured at the map and it zoomed out, giving us a bird's-eye view.

"You ain't fucking serious about these," Mara said, thrusting her hands into my face, holding the loose metal straps in one. She dropped them at my feet. "I don't care how fucking stupid you are, Cates—and I'm beginning to think maybe you're brain damaged in some *subtle* way—but even you don't wanta head out into those streets again with one gun down, huh?"

I glanced at her wrists, then looked back at the map. "We're headed here," I said, gesturing and making the Shannara Hotel light up orange. I looked up through the gash we'd just blown in the building and pointed. "Right there." It was a needle of a building rising up about half a mile away, silver and impossible looking. It looked like someone had spun an entire vein of metal into a thin, smooth thread and pushed it up into the air. It looked like it ought to be swaying back and forth, slowly falling to the ground.

"It's a straight shot," Mara said, gesturing at the map. The boulevard lit up, showing our position. On the map's scale, it looked like we were about an inch away.

I nodded, snapping the map shut and taking my shredder in both hands. Dropping my ammo clip, I fished in my pocket for another. "The minute we step outside, it's gonna be harsh," I pointed out. "Whoever tried to perforate us back there is still on the high ground. So be ready to *move* once you hit the air. There won't be much time for consultation." I looked back out into the street, which once again appeared abandoned and peaceful. Squinting, I cocked my head for a better angle.

"The overpass," I said, pointing at a spot where the road we'd been following suddenly lifted up for a few hundred feet to allow a smaller road to wriggle below. "Stop there. We take this in quick stages, dashing from spot to spot. You stay out in the open too long and they'll nail you, no doubt. Make for the overpass and *stop*. We'll regroup and plan the next dash from there."

I looked at Adrian, who nodded, smiling. "It is like a game: Kill me if you can catch me. We must keep moving."

"What about goin' back underground? Now that your fanboy has been put down, that seemed fucking *idyllic* compared to this."

I shook my head. "No tunnels that way. Wherever we come up, we'll regret it."

For a moment we all just peered out into the open air, the wide street, the canyon walls of buildings on either side, crawling with death.

"Well, what's not to love about a plan cooked up in five minutes after you've been beaten half to death twice in an hour?" Mara suddenly said, grinning, guns magically in both hands. "I sure ain't got anything better."

I slapped the fresh clip into the shredder while the Poet produced his own autos. "Remember, you can't hit anything up high, so don't waste ammo."

"Fuck you," Mara said cheerfully. "I done this before, follow?"

I gave her a tired grin. "Fuck, I hope your head gets blown off out there."

To my surprise, she grinned back. "Welcome to Hong Kong, Mr. Cates," she said. "You'll do well."

A moment of quiet slipped past us, and then I pushed off. "Go!"

The second I hit the dim twilight, gunfire. The asphalt and concrete erupted around me, a sudden spontaneous fountain of material pinging my face and hands with shards and pebbles. The noise was deafening; I couldn't hear my breath or the scraping of my boots as I sprinted with everything I had for the overpass—I could *feel* myself breathing, I could sense my feet hitting the pavement, but all I heard was the crunching roar of high-caliber bullets being spat at me, a half second behind my pace.

Whoever was manning the guns was absolute shit as far as gunning went, but I knew if I slowed down for a second, I'd be turned into a satisfying red mist.

The overpass tilted and swung in front of me as I ran; I couldn't tell if Mara and Adrian were keeping up. I judged I was about halfway there, and without thinking any harder, I veered sharply to my left, toward the road, angling smoothly.

For a brief second the firing stopped, and there were three pounding steps where I could hear myself breathing. It wasn't a pretty sound. I counted three in my head and veered back to my right, the ground behind me exploding in a spray of chewed-up pavement just as I changed direction. With the overpass jiggling up and down as I ran, a second gun suddenly bloomed into life from above and behind me. He was too eager and carved the ground up in front of me, allowing me to change directions again, zigging suddenly left and then immediately right. I summoned every bit of strength and pushed myself across the last ten feet as both guns blended together into a single chest-rattling rhythm. The duffel and shredder on my back seemed to get heavier as I ran, sweat pouring into my eyes, and the thick air smelled like burning metal and I hated sucking it into myself—it clawed at my throat and made me nauseous.

My HUD started blinking on and off. Head pounding, I felt my legs giving out and I leaped for it, slapping down onto the pavement and skidding into the shadows—followed immediately by the invisible scalpel of the guns—tearing up my stomach as I scraped up against the wall of the underpass.

Suddenly, the noise stopped.

Someone was laughing—the Poet, I realized—a deep, sawing laugh. In the sudden silence my ears rang, and his laughter seemed to come from far away, from inside something insulated and thick.

"That was less than fun," he said, chuckling. "Now we have, what, five more runs? No, I surrender."

As I flopped over onto my back, chest heaving, Mara came skidding in from the light, sliding in feet first, graceful and annoying. Only her last dozen feet or so had been tracked by the guns; she'd held back until their attention was focused on Adrian and me, and then scampered in our wake.

Smart. I wanted to fucking strangle her, but I was too busy drowning in my own phlegm.

The sudden quiet boomed in my ears. Distant, someone started to shout. It was a language I didn't understand. We all sat listening for a moment.

"What he is saying," the Poet suddenly said, "is, he doesn't wish to kill, he just wants to talk."

"He must get a really poor quality of hardass through this town," I gasped, and then lifted my head and peered through my faded HUD at him. "You fucking speak... whatever the fuck that is?"

The Poet grinned. "I've been here—" He stopped suddenly, as a small red disc sailed on a steep arc from the light, skidding along the gravel under the road to come to a rest in the midst of us. A small red light blinked rapidly on top of it.

The disc blinked twice more before we all moved. My heart thudded, stopped, and then burst into a staccato rhythm against my ribs as I rolled onto my feet, hands scrabbling against the gravel to get some forward momentum. The Poet shot forward, pebbles flying as he kicked them up, and he plucked the grenade from the ground without even a second of visible hesitation, flinging it sidearm back out into the open air. It detonated a second later, a burst of smoke and flame. The bounce from it knocked me back onto my ass.

With effort I forced myself back onto my feet. I was shaking, my heart rattling off-rhythm in my chest, skipping a few beats with a twitchy restlessness, then thudding back into time for a few seconds. I limped quickly to the blurry edge that divided our shadowed shelter from the killing field and knelt down, scanning the street again. I looked over a dirt-brown retaining wall snaking its way along the left-hand side of the road, about ten feet high. It looked older than everything else, older even than the unused roads that were already crumbling years before we had gotten here.

"Adrian," I panted as a wave of dizziness passed through me. "Any fire coming from our right?"

He and Mara crept up beside me and knelt down, forming a hot, unhappy circle of distrust and murder in the shadows. "I do not think so," he whispered.

"Why are you fucking *whisperin'*?" Mara hissed. "You think they forgot we're *here*?"

He stared at her for a second or two, steady and expressionless, then glanced at me with a slight smile. "I was not taking good notes, but the left only."

I nodded, gesturing up at the jagged row of shining skyscrapers across from us. "They own the treetops, right? They've got a great view of this whole fucking boulevard. But they don't own the *other side*, or they'd have carved us into pieces with crossfire." I pointed. "Make for the wall. They've got fixed-position heavy-cal guns with a wide horizontal and vertical scope, but they won't be able to shoot steep enough if we press up against it. Single file, we can follow it practically all the way to the hotel."

Mara shouldered her way closer to the edge. "The road curves...there," she said, pointing one slender finger. "It'll open up their field and eventually they'll have us."

I shrugged. "Sure. That's twenty minutes from now. You can either sit here and pitch grenades until someone dials back their timers and you get blown to shit, or you can go back to sprinting endlessly with murder on your heels."

She stared out at the scene around us, and finally nodded. "All right, may—"

Something hit the ground behind us, followed immediately by three more tiny impacts.

"Move!" I shouted, shut my eyes, and stumbled into motion.

XXIX

A LONG HISTORY OF POKING ME
WITH A SHARP STICK

The moment I hit the watery light that infused Hong Kong like a liquid version of the dull metal every building seemed to have been carved out of, like glassy, smooth stalagmites, the churning roar of the guns started. They took two, three seconds to warm up and start spitting metal, and I pushed myself into a redlining sprint, duffel and rifle slapping into my thighs painfully as I forced my leaden legs to pump up and down.

The monolithic buildings on either side were disorienting—all this empty space, these yards and yards of old pavement, old yellowed weeds cracking through and creating a crazy pattern that kept trying to catch a toe and ruin me, and then on either side these faceless buildings, taller than anything I'd ever seen, taller than anything New York had offered. The feeling of all that steel and glass and concrete sailing down onto me was crushing.

All along the bases of them were the scabby little huts, but even these were too precise, too neat. In New York, people had clogged the old streets with hovels like these, but it had been chaos, huts built on huts, huts built on top of other huts, slowly creeping upward along the cracked and crumbling facades of the old buildings. Here, they were orderly, just a line of them snaking along the walkways, no more than two levels high, like wooden barnacles. Some had been secured with chains and locks, as if the evacuation of Hong Kong had been orderly and expected.

Thinking, *Three seconds*, I closed my eyes and veered sharply to my left. The sound of asphalt being chewed into oatmeal accompanied a drumming, heavy vibration under my feet and I was sprayed with hot chunks of the road.

Keep moving, I thought. *Keep moving.*

I opened my eyes again and the wall was weaving and wobbling toward me, the ground still rumbling under my feet. For two steps, the single line of fire continued to chew up the road to my right, and then with a coughing whine, the second gun began to warm up. If they crisscrossed me, I knew I'd be cut in half and be dead before I felt a goddamn thing. I thought of Michaleen. I thought of that short little murderous bastard and what he'd done to me—first in Chengara, using me, lying to me and then leaving me for fucking dead, and then buying me out of the army and setting my boots on this road. It was suddenly very clear to me that Mickey had found me first and somehow arranged for the Press Unit. Somehow. I didn't know how, but I knew Michaleen had connections. His SSF file we'd found was open only to Director Marin—and *that* devious motherfucker had a long history of poking me with a sharp stick.

As I ran, I made fists.

Just as the second gun came online, I tried to veer right, but my left foot jammed into a deep pothole and I went down, managing to cross my arms in front of my face before giving my nose its third smashing in an hour. My HUD flickered again as the wind was knocked out of me, but the twin trails of piano wire dicing up the street and trying to carve me up crisscrossed three feet ahead of me, approximately where I would have been, and as I swallowed something thick and hot that tasted suspiciously like my own polluted blood, I pushed myself up and yanked my foot free, the ankle barking. I ran right for the spot, figuring the geniuses running the guns would assume I'd be taking the angle again. My ankle didn't like taking my weight and I almost went down again, windmilling my arms as I crashed forward, finally getting my balance back as my overworked augments dumbed down the pain.

Both guns were hot now, and the phlegmy rumble filled the air, the road humming with it, this twitchy zombie energy that just wanted to eat everything in its path. I imagined the gun operators up there, fucking pinheads most probably, wastes who had been standing on street corners jonesing for a hit two months ago now suddenly warned on pain of death to read a very long and unillustrated user manual and put in charge of a mounted gun the size of a fucking hover. All controlled via dermal pickup—your fucking *thoughts*. These assholes hadn't had a thought that didn't involve slitting a throat or getting high in decades. And the guns were twitchy, overreacting, spinning like they were greased one moment and fighting you for every inch the next.

I kept my steaming eyes on the shit-brown retaining wall and thought, *These cocksuckers are gonna nail me by fucking* accident.

The wall suddenly rushed up toward me, and before I could get out of its way I smashed into it. I let myself go limp and just leaned into it, dragging the thick air in through my open mouth in spastic, painful gasps that never felt deep enough, long enough.

The wet roar and underground rumble continued for a few seconds, and then suddenly stopped.

"Stop runnin', Cates!" Mara shouted, closer than I'd expected, to my right. "You made it!"

"And you were correct," the Poet shouted from farther away in the same direction. "They can't adjust the angle. We are quite sheltered."

I struggled to suck in enough air and turned my head toward them, scraping my forehead against the old brick. Mara and the Poet were close together a few feet away. "Move," I said. "We'll have a few minutes before the curve exposes us."

Mara did a good job of nodding tiredly, as if she wasn't nuclear powered and shock absorbing, and they both turned and began walking, keeping as close to the wall as possible. I watched them for a few unsteady heartbeats, my breathing starting to slow down to mere desperate gulps, and then I shifted the weight of the duffel and the shredder on my back and stumbled after them.

It was peaceful, suddenly. In the guns' blind spot, we were all in a holding pattern: They couldn't get a shot at us, and we had just a few hundred feet of peace before we had to make another dash into hell.

I walked blankly, not thinking about anything but how my breathing got a little easier every step. I thought about the last real dinner I'd had—the last dinner that hadn't come in a pill or been pumped into my veins while I slept. Englewood: boiled rabbit, fucking disgusting, a hunk of greasy flesh with a pile of stringy green shit on the side so you could sandblast one horrible taste from your mouth with another horrible taste. I could still taste it, now that I brought it to mind.

I looked up and squinted at the city through my own greasy layer of sweat. Rain had started falling again, a quiet hum of background noise. In the moment of calm, Hong Kong was beautiful. Everything gleamed—it was all glass and steel, and the steel swooped and bent in ways that I'd never seen before. Everything tore your eye up until your neck hurt and you were squinting into a thousand tiny flares. Some of the buildings were so weird, with their odd angles and curved edges, I didn't understand how they stayed up. As you dragged your eyes down, though, everything got crowded and muddy, swelling out from the elegant metal needles like rotting roots, bursting up through the ground—the scabby wood huts, the old stone walls with deep cracks and layers of grimy graffiti in characters I didn't recognize.

I kept my eyes up as I walked, one hand trailing the rough surface of the retaining wall. I liked the skyscrapers. I imagined it was quiet and open up there.

"Cates," Mara shouted back at me, "I think—"

She was interrupted by the twin whine of the two big guns warming up.

"Take a step back!" I shouted, snapping my eyes down to ground level and trotting forward to catch up with them. We were under the shadows of the ugly, squat structure I'd spied earlier on the other side of the wall, a series of shallow levels, all concrete, open to the air. I remembered the hover I'd seen. It was amazing that someone had piloted it through the narrow bands of the structure to land it, although it was possible it had just somehow crashed that way; the building was cracked and shabby looking, with some of its facade fallen away to reveal the rusting girders beneath, so any crash damage would have been easy to miss. I was still covered in a layer of chilled sweat, my hair plastered against my skull, and I could feel myself shivering, my hands shaking, as I trotted.

As I caught up to Mara and the Poet, the guns vomited back into life. Right in front of us was a blurry line of shadow made by the wall, and a few feet beyond that, the pavement fountained up again.

Mara turned to me, raising a smug eyebrow like she wouldn't be cut to fucking chum just like me if we made a wrong move. "You're a fucking sherpa of rare talent, Cates. We're hiding in the shadow of a fucking wall in the middle of fucking Hong Kong, and I doubt any other living person coulda brought us here so skillfully."

"I didn't hear any ideas oozing out of you," I snarled. I planned to reserve my last half hour of augmented existence for finding some way to make an avatar suffer. Shoving past her to toe the invisible line that marked the end of our protected space, I paused to push a finger into her face. She flinched, which made me feel better.

"You're closer to Londholm than you'd be without me, yes?" I hissed. "You want to carp on fucking *details*, carp away, but keep it up and soon enough we're going to quality test that piece of tech in your pocket, *capisce*?"

I liked that word. I'd heard a cop say it once.

She smirked and flourished a little bow, indicating I should proceed. It felt a little forced, and I was satisfied I'd made her hesitate, at least. I felt happy, and I knelt down to have a look at our options.

The big, wide road merged with the ground again, snaking away a few dozen feet to our right, with the wall snaking right along with it, pushing us unavoidably out into the guns' range again. The road also rose up, taking away even the illusion of cover. The rain felt like it was weighing me down, soaking into me and making me swell up. I reached down and picked up a handful of muddy dust, rubbing it between my fingers and craning my neck to look around. After a moment, I twisted around to stare past Mara and the Poet at the retaining wall and the crumbling building just beyond it. A few feet, maybe ten. Jumpable, maybe. I'd seen it on the map, a square layered building that went a few stories below us and a few above.

I looked at Mara. "You ever steal a hover?"

XXX

THE HAPPIEST MOMENT OF
MY RECENT LIFE

"Are you fuckin' out of your mind, boy?" Mara half shouted. "Have y'gone fucking daft?"

She followed me back the way we'd come as I traced my hand along the wall, examining it.

"Y'want us to climb up on top of this wall, in clear fucking view, and *jump* to that fucking building, where a dead hover sits like god's fucking turd and we're gonna just hope and pray it'll grab air? Holy fucking *shit*, Cates, I think you've finally fried your brain."

I forced myself to stay calm. I glanced at her and saw the Poet trailing behind us slowly, thoughtful, examining the wall, too.

"We're still out of range of the big guns if we climb," I said. "It's not an issue of vertical height."

She spat on the ground, growling. "And what's t'stop them from just grabbin' some unsexy needle guns and just snipin' us the old-fashioned way?"

I shrugged. "What's to stop them from doing that right *now*?" I said. "Aside from the general quality of thug you leave sitting on a gun installation for weeks on end, bored out of their mind. Fuck, Mara, if we hit the ground again, we're not gonna outrun those guns forever, and if we stand here having a fucking conversation about it we'll end up sniped eventually." I reached back and slapped my duffel. "If it's in decent condition, I think I can get it up in the air. I've worked with some talented fucking thieves in my time, and I learned a thing or two."

She didn't say anything. The Poet stood next to her. "Famous though you are, you're no Milton and Tanner, please do not forget." He nodded. "But, I like this plan," he said, stepping past her. "Better than sitting on thumbs, play target practice."

I wondered where he'd heard those names, but there was no time for comparing careers. "If the hover's a dud," I said, "at least we're on the far side of those guns."

She threw her hands up in the air. "Fuck, every block of this city's owned by someone else. They've all got these installations, dammit. Hoppin' the fuckin' wall ain't going to solve *that*."

I nodded. "Then hope the hover lifts."

The Poet slapped a hand against the wall. "Here is a good spot," he said, eyes moving appraisingly up and down the old, corrupt stone. "Good handholds and the wall slopes." He looked at me, the tiny images of murder on his skin flickering, endlessly killing each other. "I should go first, then."

The urge to argue with him was weak. We were all professionals here and if Adrian thought he had the best shot, I wasn't going to volunteer. "We'll try to distract them," I offered. "Move fast, in case there *is* a bright boy up there with a sniper rifle and half a brain."

He smiled, white teeth breaking through his beard like the sun through clouds. "Always teaching, you. I'm able to climb a wall." He gave me an obvious look of appraisal. "Will *you* be able?"

I grimaced. "I got twenty years and a couple of fucking major surgeries on you," I growled, trying to sound mean. I liked Adrian, but even folks you liked you had to keep in line. "You want me to carry you up and over?"

He laughed, waving a hand. "When was the last time," he said, backing away, "that you took a bath, Avery? No, I'll go alone."

I couldn't help but smile. I thought, maybe, if we both survived this, I might see where the Poet ended up and see what we might do together. See if he was pissed off at Mickey enough to take a hand in my business there, see what we might do working our own line, without augments in our heads forcing us into someone else's.

He spun away and without hesitation leaped up onto the wall, his hands finding decent holds. For a moment he just hung there, arms and legs splayed, suspended on the wall as if stuck there. Then he reached out his right hand and found another hold.

"A little faster, eh?" Mara shouted. "Or they'll be able to walk over here with pistolas and beat us to death before we're over."

The Poet took a moment to wave a hand at us, and I shrugged the duffel onto my back. I took the wall on a short run, launching myself up and grabbing some shallow holds with my fingernails and the narrow tips of my boots. One foot slipped and I had to scrabble a little, determined not to punk in front of Mara, finally catching hold and pushing myself up. I began sweating again immediately, my legs getting shaky. After three or four pulls I paused, hanging there and blowing like a fat man at dinner again.

Mara was suddenly at my side, clinging to the wall like she was glued to it.

"Don't say a fucking word," I managed to wheeze. "Or I'll—" I stopped myself, shutting my mouth and grunting. If she didn't know I'd figured her for an avatar, there was no margin in letting her in on it. As far as advantages went, letting her think I was stupid was about the best I could do for one. I allowed myself to start coughing, and she smirked and pulled on past me.

When I was halfway up, the Poet's feet disappearing over the edge above me, the hum of the big guns suddenly cut off, leaving me clinging to the irregular wall in almost total silence. I closed my eyes and settled into a rhythm for a few minutes, just concentrating on pulling myself up a few inches at a time. When I opened my eyes, I was a foot from the top, and the Poet was lying flat, holding out his hand.

"Come on up, old man," he said. "All you have to do is jump. I think we'll make it."

I took his hand and with one last push I was on top of the surprisingly wide wall; it was about two feet thick and we could crouch on it easily enough. The crumbling structure across the way from us loomed higher, but since every floor was open to the air, it would be possible, I thought, to leap the fifteen or so feet and angle down through one of the gaps. It would be a hard landing, but with any luck my augments had enough juice left in them to give me a decent tuck and roll I'd never have pulled off in my previous incarnation as a fucking human being.

Mara and the Poet I had no doubt about. They'd make it without breaking a sweat.

"All right." I twisted my head until I got a satisfying crack from my neck. "I go first. If I eat it, go for the duffel. You'll need it."

I let them ponder that for a moment, and then stood up. I felt immediately exposed and had to resist the urge to rush, to get out of sight. The wind blew the rain into my face, a gentle mist that kept me blinking, as I stood for a moment judging the load on my back and shifting the straps of the rifle and the bag slightly. The Poet and Mara just stared at me. I put my eyes on the spot I wanted, about five floors down, and fixed the black rectangle of empty space in my head. Then I took one step backward, found the edge of the wall with my heel, rocked back, took one bounding step forward, and threw myself off the wall, feet first.

Slapping my arms down at my sides, I tried to be aerodynamic. My HUD lit up again, a tiny number popping up on a transparent overlay announcing how many feet from the ground I'd just become. For one second it was serene, the happiest moment of my recent life, and I thought, *This is what suicide is like. The happiest you've felt in fucking* years.

The gap screamed up at me and just before I hit it, I knew I was going to make it; the opening was pretty wide and I sailed through without hitting my head and decapitating myself, which would have been my vote for most likely end to this little experiment. When my HUD counter was just about to turn zero, I balled myself up, knees in my chest, and hit the concrete floor hard enough to bounce, then managed a decent roll, ass over tits, until I smacked into the far wall.

I lay for a moment and felt myself vibrating. A few seconds later I sat up as the Poet sailed through the opening, landing bad and scraping himself, squawking, along the rough floor for several feet before the friction of his own body managed to stop him. He flipped around and sat up and we stared at each other.

I heard Mara a moment before we saw her, her words unintelligible as she came flying toward us. She misjudged it and smacked into the floor at about waist height, immediately dropping out of sight.

The Poet and I looked back at each other.

"If she falls, we die," he said in a flat voice, a slight lisp his gift from Hong Kong. "Beginning to think, Why not? A moment of peace."

I grunted, hauling myself up. "If she's going to crap out and take us with her, I'm going to at least enjoy the fucking moment and kill her myself." My leg sent a sharp lance of pain up my side as I limped over to the edge. I leaned out and looked down; Mara was dangling from a piece of rebar that jutted from the concrete just a few feet below us. She glared up at me and we said nothing.

I turned and walked back toward the Poet. "You reel her in. I'm going to see if there's any hope of getting that hover up. I'm tired of running from lines of fire."

"Much better to crash," he said as he got to his feet, looking steady despite the ugly landing. "I have always maintained this. The best way to die."

The hover was an amazing sight: With just a few feet of clearance, it sat in the rough center of the empty slab of floor and looked to be in pretty good shape, at least on the outside. Whoever had piloted it into this space had been a master, and getting it out was going to be impossible. But I wasn't going to make it to the Shannara if I had to run the whole way, and if we could avoid for about thirty seconds the antiair munitions Pucker the Pig had mentioned, we'd be home free.

It was a military-issue craft; I recognized the sleek silver design and the SFNA logo—a globe surrounded by arrowheads—was painted up near the front. It was shaped like a cigar and looked to seat about five people at most, maybe six if you didn't need to actually sit down in flight. The hatch was up, a yawning rectangular wound in the hover's silver skin. Swinging the duffel off my back, I dropped it on the floor and drew my Roon, keeping my finger off the trigger as I stepped up to the hatch and leaned in.

It smelled like damp and dust, but the interior of the hover was empty, just a wad of safety netting and nothing else. I hopped in, feeling the whole thing rock and settle under me, and took two steps to the cockpit hatch. Gently pushing it open, I found the controls abandoned as well. Stuffing the gun back into my pocket, I limped to the pilot's seat and sat down, instantly feeling tired.

I studied the controls. I was no expert; in the past, I'd always had someone to do the flying, but I knew the basics, and at a glance I could see that the military had just adjusted the standard old SSF hover designs for its own use. The control panel was almost identical to the ones I'd seen in plenty of SSF hovs, and I had a list of standard gestures that usually worked to get things unlocked.

I raised my hand and then hesitated, thinking that it might be trapped, rigged to blow.

Did I care? I wasn't sure. As I sat there, I noticed my HUD had a new icon just above the blinking exclamation mark my mind's eye still shied away from. It was a tiny representation of a hover; my military augments recognizing I was in a military vehicle. I wondered if that was good or bad.

Closing my eyes, I tried a gesture. Nothing happened.

I ran through the ones I could remember, ones that had worked at one time or another for waking up hovers. None of them worked. With a sigh, I stood up and retrieved the duffel from outside, dropping it in the belly of the hover as the Poet and Mara, both looking scratched up and bruised, joined me.

"This is fuckin' unbelievable," Mara said, touching the silvery skin of the vessel with one bloodied hand. "I need to find this pilot and hire 'im." She looked at me as I reached into the duffel and extracted one of the gifts Hense had given me back in Brussels. It was a large black disc, its surface rough and nonreflective, swallowing all the light and looking like a piece of the night sky in my hands. It vibrated slightly, a barely there ripple from inside it, and it was hot and heavy.

"Why, Avery," she said, "you've bin keepin' secrets. What t'fuck is *that*?"

I stood up by increments, holding the disc carefully in my hands. "This is how we're getting this tub in the air, and this is how we're getting into the hotel to pay Londholm a visit," I said, turning slowly toward the cockpit. "This is a multiuse, SSF-property uranium hydride portable reactor, capable of generating sustained two hundred and fifty megawatts over the air."

"I confess I'm slow," the Poet said. "Too old for the latest tech, but what does that *mean*?"

I could picture Mara grinning behind me—I *knew* her, somehow. "Old friend," she said, "it means, don't fucking drop it."

XXXI

THE PERFECT PLAN, A CLOSED CIRCUIT
WITH THE CADENCE BEING DEATH

"You know how to pilot one o' these bastards, right?"
Mara said from where she'd perched on the copilot's seat,
sitting with her legs splayed, leaning forward.

"I've crashed several times," I said. "And once jumped
out of one that *wasn't* crashing."

Behind us, the Poet, hanging from his beefy arms in
the hatchway, barked a short, compact laugh. After a few
hours of dodging bullets, we were all enjoying that weird
euphoria that came during lulls. I'd seen it get folks killed,
but it was hard to resist.

I'd set the disc on the floor of the cockpit and gestured
it online; it had started to hum loudly, and the temperature
in the cabin had risen immediately, making me sweat. In
my head, I ran over everything Hense had told me back in
Brussels, trying to remember every detail.

"It all depends on whether the hover was locked down,"
I said, reaching out and pulling the console's plastic cover

off; it came easy, popping off like it was supposed to and revealing a mass of thin, threadlike wires. "If the pilot encrypted it before leaving the cabin, there's no way I can do anything without a Tech Associate." I looked at Mara while leaning forward and reaching into the mass of wires up to my shoulder. "You got any Techies in your pocket?"

She shook her head, looking for a moment just like a real seventeen-year-old girl. "I never had any way with tech," she said. "I'm old-school. Anything more complex than a gun is too much for me."

"Me too," I grunted, finding the diamond-shaped short-term battery the hover used when main power was off-line. It was cold, which told me the craft had been completely without power for some time. "Okay," I said, retrieving my arm, "let's put some juice into her and see what happens."

I gestured at the disc, and the humming revved up, pulsing through my chest. I glanced up at the Poet, who raised his thick eyebrows at me.

"You're sure we are safe?" he said. "It's like *I'm* drawing power. Hairs on arm stand up."

I shrugged. "Does it look like I read the fucking manual? You've got wires in your *brain*. I wouldn't worry about this shit. The battery's dead, so the hover won't have any history in its databanks. Without a history, it will assume a crash or other emergency situation. When we power this up, we should be dropped into an emergency shell, which will accept a small number of generic commands. It won't be fancy and weapons will be off-line, but it'll get us into the air. Any last words?"

No one said anything. I glanced back at the exploded console and gestured at the disc again.

Immediately, the cabin's lights flickered on, and various readout screens mounted on the interior windshield burped into life and started throwing numbers my way. The hover's climate control kicked into whining overdrive, and a Klaxon, the loudest sound I'd ever heard in my life, immediately began to wail. I had no idea what it meant, but if I were forced to come up with a sound that meant imminent explosion, it would be pretty close.

"Fucking hell! Shut that noise off!"

I shook my head. "I know exactly fifteen standard HOV protocol gestures! Shutting off the alarm ain't one of them!"

"Then get this fucking brick off the fucking ground!"

I gestured at the console and with a squeal of sudden metal fatigue the hover jerked upward, smashing into the concrete above us. Several ceiling panels fell from above and something sparked inside the console, sending a thin acrid plume of smoke into the crank air. Outside, several large chunks of concrete fell to the floor around us.

The Klaxon continued to wail, now joined by another, subtly different alarm.

"Cates!" Mara screeched. I wanted to reach over and clamp her mouth shut. I gestured at the console again and the hover began to inch forward, slowly, scraping along the ceiling, the dry, high-pitched squeal of metal on rock adding to the noise. I found myself making fists and grinding my teeth as we slowly drifted toward the gap in the wall.

"There is no clearance!" The Poet was suddenly in my ear, his body crouched down between Mara and me, almost on top of the humming disc. "You must adjust vertical! The lip, Mr. Cates!"

The view screen showed the approach interior wall; there was a stone and rebar lip that came down from the ceiling about a foot. From the floor, a taller railing rose up, three or four feet high, leaving just enough room between them for the hover to squeak through. I shook my head.

"I don't have a fine touch here! It's either scrape the top or scrape the bottom! Top's shallower!"

"Well give it some fucking *speed* then, or we're go—"

I reached over and clamped my thumb and forefinger onto Mara's lips. They felt real enough: warm and damp, elastic. The avatar business had gone luxe. I looked across the Poet's body and met Mara's eyes, then winked and let go.

"Hang on!"

I gestured again, and the hover shot forward, the scraping from above becoming a keening, shuddering noise that even drowned out the alarms. The whole hover began to shake as we tore through the empty space, the gap approaching so fast I didn't even have time to shut my eyes before we hit the lip.

There was a noise just like an explosion, a bomb going off above us, and we rocketed out of the building on an angle, the hover fishtailing spastically and immediately dropping fifteen feet before recovering some of its vertical thrust. It continued to waggle crazily, yawing this way and that as I frantically gestured at it, running through every command I knew and trying to shake it back into something I could control.

Instantly, a third alarm began squawking, and on the heels of that, a fourth one, this one heralded by the cabin lights turning a light red, bathing us in urgency.

Mara leaned as far over toward me as she could from her chair. "What! The! Fuck! Is! That!"

THE TERMINAL STATE 301

I smiled. "Defensive scan! We've been targeted by the city's antiaircraft weaponry!" I pointed at one of the smaller Vidscreens. "I don't know what kind of system those assholes have in place, but we're gonna find out real soon!"

We only needed thirty seconds in the air. Thirty seconds at good speed would put us right over the hotel, and then we could land the brick and the last human cops in the world could blow the hover to pieces for all I cared. I kept repeating the same gesture to turn on the small stabilizing thrusts on the sides of the tail, and the hover kept ignoring me as we spun in a crazy circle.

"You think about it!" the Poet shouted directly in my ear. "There is a metaphor here!" He yelled something else I didn't catch, and when I looked at him, he was grinning. I grinned back. I was pretty sure I knew what *metaphor* meant, and he was so fucking right that I almost gave up on the spot and let us crash into the fucking ground, maybe the best idea I'd had in a long time. Just seeing the look of horror on Mara's face would have made it worth it.

If we stayed hanging in the air, we were going to die.

I closed my eyes and imagined the sphere of glass I'd used to hold the voices at bay while they persisted. I hadn't heard much from them in recent months, but I still had the knack with the imaginary wall, and put it in place without much effort. Inside, it was quiet and serene.

I combined a couple of gestures and the hover dropped another ten feet in one sudden lurch before stabilizing back into its crazy swinging in place.

I started to think maybe letting the fucking thing crash *was* our best bet. If it dropped to the ground, the city's antiaircraft system might shut down, and since we were only a few dozen feet up, we'd survive. Unless I was wrong and the AA system pounded the crash site anyway, which would take us right on back to being dead anyway. It looked like the perfect plan, a closed circuit with the cadence being death.

"Cates!" Mara shouted, jabbing a long finger at the bank of screens. "One of the displacers is crapped out! Shut it down!"

I followed her finger and nodded—she was right. I gestured my way through the clunky generic commands and managed to kill it, and the hover immediately steadied. The Klaxons kept ringing away, though, jamming into our ears mercilessly. We were slow and wouldn't be able to manage much altitude, but I suddenly had some coherent control of the brick. Carefully, I pushed us forward. The Shannara, a thin needle of a building, stood out on the view screen clearly enough, and I steered toward it, the hover swinging around like we were filled with fucking gas and floating our way over on the wind.

"Hell, at least we're not in a fucking *rush*!" Mara shouted. "I'm gonna take a goddamn nap while you *drift* over there!"

I ran through my slim repertoire of commands but couldn't find any way of coaxing more power out of the hover. The generator was rated high enough to power a fucking building for an hour—I knew that well enough— but the hover maybe wasn't pulling enough juice from it, or the displacer was damaged, or the emergency status kept it in a crippled state—whatever the reason, we were drifting at a speed only slightly faster than me running across the empty pavement of Hong Kong below us. Which was better than doing the actual *running*, but I decided not to argue the point with Mara. A hot red light bloomed on the console, and suddenly all of the alarms cut off, leaving us in relative silence, the only sound the familiar, though muted, roar of the displacers.

"Well, fucking *finally*," Mara snarled.

"Yeah, fucking hurrah for us," I said back. "We've been targeted. Better get back into the bay and wrap up in the netting, 'cause I can't make this thing fast via sheer will-power, so we're going down in about twenty seconds."

She stared at me. "Well, this has turned out to be a huge fuckin' success for you, eh?"

I ignored her and tried my best to push the hover as fast as it would go, which remained a stodgy and stubborn twenty miles per hour, putting along. Hong Kong was the biggest collection of huge I'd ever seen—the buildings were packed in tight, of all sizes and shapes, glittering empty tombs in the dim rainy twilight. Steering down the canyons created by them at our gentle speed was easy, and I urged the brick on as the collision detection started to beep. On the view screen, the rear field showed a tiny black dot in the sky behind us.

The alarms cut in again. They made me want to crash the fucking brick just to shut them down.

"Okay!" I yelled. "We're hooked."

"Ditch it!" Mara shouted.

I shook my head. "Ten more seconds!" Every moment we were in the air gained us ground we wouldn't have to run a gauntlet through.

She slapped me lightly on the side of the head. I twisted around in the pilot's seat to look at her; she held up the tiny black remote. "Ditch it!"

I forced a smile to my face and put my hands up. "All

right!" I shouted. I turned back to the controls and gestured the flaps down so nothing would slow us, and with a
curt movement of my hand the hover went dead, coasting
on inertia for a second. The sudden silence popped into
place as if it had always been there, like air. "I hope we
don't get blown to hell on the ground!"

"You're always inspirin', Cates!" Mara bellowed,
strapping herself into the copilot's chair. "That's what I
like about—"

XXXII

I'M MAKING A BET HERE

Someone was laughing.

Behind it there was another noise, a damp hissing sound that was puzzling for a moment.

I opened my eyes. The ceiling of the hover was sliding away behind a thin haze of smoke. It was rippled and bent but gliding along like a river glimpsed from high altitude. At first I thought my HUD was smoke in my eyes and I blinked furiously trying to dislodge it.

Lifting my head, I stared down at myself. The Poet had my feet and was dragging me from the cockpit into the bay. His sunglasses had lost one arm and one lens was shattered, and they almost fell off his face when he grinned at me and dropped my feet with a thud.

"Good to see you well," he said. I turned my head and found Mara sitting on a loose pile of safety netting. "You pilot like you're angry. At the universe."

"A necessary procedure," Mara chuckled, standing up. She looked fresh and rested, like she'd been napping through the whole flight. "The only way to fucking kill those goddamn alarms, I think. You up, Cates? You can walk?"

I nodded, wondering if she'd just shoot me in the head if I'd turned up lame. I sat up and got my legs under me, my back complaining and my stiff leg making me wince. I'd managed to hit the street more or less level and we'd skidded a fair ways, plowing up some concrete and asphalt. The hover was never going to rise again, but we hadn't broken apart and we'd covered a mile in just a few minutes.

"Any guns out there?"

The Poet shrugged, swinging his shredder around and checking it over.

I pushed up onto my legs and tested them; I didn't collapse immediately and piss myself, so I figured I still had some fuel left in the engine. I nodded at Adrian and he shrugged back, turning and popping the hatch with the manual lever, letting the damp blue light in. None of us moved. After a few heartbeats, I took a deep breath and stepped forward, trying to rally what was left of my energy to start running if I heard that terrible click and hum of a big gun warming up.

We'd landed pretty much dead center on the big wide boulevard we'd been creeping up earlier. Right in front of me, to the right of the hover, the lobby of a squat, rust-covered building was burning cheerfully, glass and concrete splashed liberally around—whatever had been tracking the hover had smacked into the building instead, and with any luck, that had put the antiaircraft systems on standby again. The building looked like it was going to melt, the way the orange-brown rust had taken over, and I decided that we'd done it a favor by destroying it.

I looked to my left, and there it was: the Shannara. From street level, it looked like every other building we'd passed. Its ground floor was scabbed with the wooden hovels, although these went up to three levels high in a ragged pyramid structure, complete with rusting metal ladders leading upward. Then it was a greenish-blue metal and reflective glass, blind eyes glaring at us. There was no sign of life. It was as if the city had been carved out of something solid, with no interior, no pathways for people to crawl through, just an island of sculptures. I felt like we were alone in the city.

Hense had told me it had been one of the best hotels in Hong Kong. Big shots had paid through the nose to stay there and it had offered the best of everything: real organic food, real human service staff—Droids only in the unseen areas. Exclusive rooftop access and complete security teams assigned to every guest, absolute discretion guaranteed and pretty much the entire local squad of System Pigs on its payroll, back before the civil war, before everything had gone to hell.

I'd been staring for thirty seconds before I came back to myself wearily, pulling my consciousness back with tired spasms of effort. No one had shot me, and I didn't hear anything aside from the sizzling death throes of the hover, the wind, and the rain.

"Come on out," I said.

A giddy sort of energy swelled up inside me. I knew it was just exhaustion and unstable augments compensating by opening the floodgates on adrenaline and endorphins, but it swamped me, making me shaky and excited. I grinned at nothing. The fucking city was terrified of us. Of *me*. We were standing in the middle of the street after crash-landing a military hover, and the three of us with two shredders and a couple of handguns had the whole city on the run. It made no fucking sense, but it was the goddamn truth. Avery Cates, the Gweat and Tewwible.

A voice from a long time ago echoed in my head. "Hello, rats," I whispered to Hong Kong. "Time to run."

"What?"

I glanced at Mara, who looked gorgeous for once: hair disheveled, hands on her hips, her fake skin and tiny servo-controlled expression glowing. Or maybe that was my imagination, my overheated brain swimming in juice and giving everything an extra shimmer. I wondered, suddenly, what Mara looked like naked. How deep those avatars *went*.

The smile that landed on my face was a fucking nightmare, but I couldn't swat it away. It stayed there, twitching. I shrugged the duffel, the generator stuffed back into it, onto my shoulders and checked the RPG on the shredder. I felt good again, suddenly. Like my augments had just burned out my pain receptors and turned my endorphins on to max and walked out of the room. "Come on," I said, my voice cracking a little.

I walked slowly toward the hotel. It dominated the street, a mountain of metal and glass rising up. I felt like I could take the whole building down by myself. This was what massive cell death felt like; this was burning yourself for fuel, your body dismantling itself. It would hurt like hell, eventually, but for the moment it was just getting lighter, faster, sleeker. I didn't care if they followed, didn't care if Mara decided I'd gotten her close enough and just toggled me dead. I hefted the shredder and braced it against my

belly and walked toward the Shannara Hotel, where our
week-old intel said Londholm, the unluckiest bastard in
the world, was living behind Takahashi's security team.
Somewhere behind me, around me, in front of me, there
were plenty of people who didn't want me here—Spooks
who wanted to put me on trial, Techies who didn't want
the God Augment out in the wild, the usual assortment of
assholes who just didn't like me. I didn't care.

Mara spoke up behind me. "How are we gonna—"

My finger jerked and I launched a grenade at the hotel.
For a jittery second I imagined the whole thing just crashing down, the foundation shattering and miles and miles
of steel and glass raining down on us, chunks the size of
planets burying us deeper and deeper. Instead, a big section of the wooden stalls exploded, a fireball of impressive size blooming in the shadows of their interior and
then pluming out, fading into black, choking smoke that
suddenly filled the air. A few hunks of burning wood
slammed down around me, but I didn't stop walking.
There was no opposition. Pucker had told me that Takahashi punished anyone who approached—but Takahashi
had tried to sell his share to me just an hour ago, and I
figured he maybe didn't have the necessary inspiration to
keep people like me away.

"Okay," Mara said softly. "We walk in. Got it."

"There won't be any security on the ground floor, anyway," I said. "Even someone like Takahashi, with a permanent, trained crew, can't have assholes loitering in the
lobby, especially with power down throughout the city."

"Yeah, sure," Mara said, catching up to me and match-
ing my stride. "That's because y'canna get *up* from the
lobbies. Most of 'em are sealed."

I nodded, still grinning as we approached the flaming hole I'd blown into the building. "The Shannara is pre-Unification, with a retrofitted building shell made by the MiSun corporation. The elevators, when operational, still go to the lobby level when an emergency shell response is triggered, because if the zoning codes had been enforced and the little folks hadn't been allowed to build their shitty little shacks up against every building, there would have been a street exit on the lobby level." I paused right outside the hot lip of the hole I'd created and glanced at her. "So, no, it's not sealed."

I turned and stepped through the fire and smoke, picking my way into the lobby. Stepping inside was like moving through a portal: Suddenly it was dark and the air was clear, cool, and moving softly against me as it was sucked out of the space.

The old lobby was as dusty and ignored as the others we'd smashed our way through, remnants of an old way of doing things, but they'd never bothered tearing out the old infrastructure—the old pipes and wires, the old access panels and ducts. They just left that shit in there, online in some cases. Cheaper to just leave it, especially if you could think of a use for it. I squinted around and spotted the ancient desk in the middle of the huge space. Once, this had been carpeted, filled with light and decorations and people and chumps in shit suits had sat behind that desk.

I started walking toward it.

"The MiSun Autonomous Building Shell version 11.1," I recited as they followed me, "was a service release designed to solve a few minor problems with climate control that plagued the production release. It was installed in the Shannara six years ago. It has been off-line since Hong Kong's power went, which means its backup batteries are all drained and the shell is sitting on cold iron and, as far as it knows, when the power returns it will boot as if it was just installed and run one-time-only protocols."

"Bullshit," Mara snapped. "It'll have security backups in quantum states."

I spun and walked backward. She was right on my heels, and flinched a little, which made me happy. Happier. I bubbled along on a high that felt dangerous and wonderful, ants under my skin but it was okay, more than okay, I *liked* it.

My HUD, I noticed, was throbbing in permanent alarm.

"You'd think," I said. "Assuming the owners follow protocols. Assuming they're not idiots and have those backups off-site where they won't be affected by local conditions." I winked. "I'm making a bet here."

I'd been told, point-blank, by Hense that there were no backups. I'd been told just about all of this by Hense, as I'd neglected my reading on building shell programming and protocols these past few years. As I spun back toward the sagging desk—which was made of fake wood, particles pasted together and now exploding outward in a rainbow of mold that appeared to be eating the entire building at the rate of an inch a year—I decided there was no margin in offering that up. Why not be mysterious, inexplicably informed, Avery Cates, Destroyer of Fucking Worlds?

I dropped the duffel, still buzzing with my jittery, death-wish energy, and knelt down to extract the heavy, warm disc again, sliding it onto the floor and standing up. The exploded desk still encased an ancient Vidscreen and a weird device with a chunky handset and several buttons, which I ignored as a vestige of old tech. I glanced at Mara, who shrugged an eyebrow at me, and then at the Poet who grinned again, his broken glasses making him look crazy, his dancing ink just blurs in the blue light.

"Little less flair, yes?" he said. "Our friends on rooftops coming. Won't just let us be."

I shrugged. "They won't matter in a moment." I knelt down again and gestured the generator on, and the same invisible sizzle slapped over me, making my skin crawl. Anything within fifty feet or so designed to take on power over the air would automatically link to it, and—

A single bright LED flickered into life on the desk, and the screen blinked a few times and then displayed a nifty-looking pair of stylized letters: MS.

"Shannara Custom ABS cold boot protocol," a neutral, pleasant woman's voice whispered from somewhere. I stood up and winked at Mara again. "Searching: relevant flags. No flags found. Searching: relevant log files. No log files found. Searching: emergency limited shell login. No account found. Administrator token?"

I was ready, and I spoke before anyone else could get a bright idea. As I spoke, I heard Hense's voice in that makeshift office, the Monk grinning at me—dreaming of blowing me up, no doubt—echoing me. "DNA bypass, voiceprint on my mark. Mark."

"Confirmed and stored. Please supply reference."

"Cates, Avery."

"Cates, Avery." There was a pause, and suddenly the lobby flickered into a dim yellow lighting scheme. "Welcome to the Shannara Hotel, Hong Kong, System of Federated Nations, Mr. Cates," the voice said more cheerfully. "Bringing systems online."

I was ready for this, too. "Put building into lockdown mode, level four," I said. "Elevators to my location, no overrides. Terminate climate control, housekeeping, maintenance Droids, kitchen and lavatory systems." We couldn't afford the power. "Security systems on standby, low-power mode."

"Acknowledged. Elevator en route. I am sorry to report only one elevator appears to be in working condition, Mr. Cates. I am unable to raise customer service on local network. I will make a note of it and will request service as soon as local network connection is restored. Elevator will arrive subground floor in twelve seconds."

I nodded. "Thank you. Brief mode, please."

"Brief mode."

I stepped away from the desk. "Well, it'll only last forty-five minutes or so," I said, hands shaking, my smile horrible on my face. "But I own this building."

XXXIII

AGAINST ALL MY BEST INSTINCTS.
GO ON, KILL US ALL

"You're almost a Techie yerself, Cates," Mara said quietly as she followed me toward the elevator banks. "Maybe all that tech buried in your brain is leaching into your thoughts."

I think maybe having Dennis Squalor in your head has sucked some knowledge into you, Dick Marin suddenly whispered.

I shook my head, trying to shake him loose, the tingly, electric feeling all over my body still buzzing, still making me grin and urging me forward, faster, faster. We were kicking up a storm of dust as we walked, soft clouds of it shimmering around us. Whatever was making the dust glow and twinkle was probably not good for me, but I was beyond caring and I sucked it in with relish, letting my increasingly feeble, overworked augments suppress my gag reflex and keep me breathing in order to keep oxygen levels high. I could die later; right now I had to fight.

The lobby narrowed down rapidly toward the back, ending in a small elevator bank. There were six on each side. On our left, all three were derelict, toothless yawning squares of blackness; in the center of the wall, several wires protruded and hung, limp and defeated. On the right, two of the elevators seemed to still be in working condition, doors demurely closed and expectant, with the last one on the far end sagging open. As we all settled to a stop, there was a low, sour-sounding noise and the doors closest to the end snapped open an inch, then shut, then slowly opened all the way, the doors drifting apart lazily.

"Three words: do not want," the Poet whispered. "I doubt these have been *maintained*. That is a long fall."

I stepped into the cab, which smelled like damp and mold. It swayed under my weight, but held, and the softly glowing level indicators were a steady light blue. I turned and smiled at Mara and the Poet.

"You want, I'll go kill this motherfucker myself," I said. The jumpy nervous energy bubbling under my skin was hard to control, and as I stood there I shifted from foot to foot and tightened my grip on the shredder. Mara spat on the floor and followed me into the elevator, followed closely by the Poet, who was still wearing his broken glasses. The strong urge to smack them off his face rippled through me, and my arm came up halfway before I mastered myself.

The doors rolled shut as slowly as they'd opened, and from inside, a raw scraping noise was audible as they slowly clenched.

"Floor, please," the feminine voice spoke, sounding flatter and more artificial in the close-up confines of the elevator.

"Twenty-three," I said.

The elevator lights rippled off and on, and I felt the distinct tug of gravity as we rose into the air. After a few seconds of claustrophobic motion, the light changed, and I turned in surprise to find that one side of the elevator was actually transparent. As we cleared the third floor, we had an unobstructed view of Hong Kong, damp and dim, buildings thrusting up like they were trying to escape. Behind the skyline were soft, green hills, hazy and distant. It was beautiful. I thought of all that space, empty, wasted.

"Ah, shit," Mara said, pointing. "We better get a move on."

I squinted along the line of her arm and saw dots in the sky, hundreds, thousands of them, a swarm of insects descending on Hong Kong.

"The army, I guess," the Poet said quietly. "Come to reduce the city. Soon, no cities left."

"Doesn't fucking matter to us," I said. "We're on the clock. We're after Londholm."

"It'll fucking *matter* if the whole fucking building goes down on top of us," Mara said, checking her gun over. I smiled at her until she looked up at me.

"Yeah? It'll matter to *you*? You fucking *sure*?"

We stared at each other. I tried to get the fucking smile off my face, but it was impossible. I was so fucking happy I wanted to just shoot the two of them right there in the elevator.

There was another of those sour off-notes, and the elevator stopped. The Poet crouched down with his shredder held out in front of him, and Mara pasted herself to the side of the cab. I just stood there, too fucking elated to give a shit. I was in my element. I was working a job, and everything felt natural again.

The doors slowly rolled open to reveal a wide elevator lobby, lit by pale yellow emergency lights. The floor was a highly polished white stone, and the walls were half some sort of wood paneling and half some sort of fabric with a hideous imprint of plants and flowers snaking up and down. A large mirror was directly opposite us, bouncing our muddy, unwashed selves back at us like the cosmos was smirking in derision.

It was perfectly silent.

"Wonder we didn't get torn up just standing here in the fucking elevator like a bunch of assholes," Mara hissed.

I stepped out into the lobby. "Londholm's on twenty-five, last I heard," I whispered, struggling to stop myself from laughing. "We take the fucking stairs from here."

She cursed lightly as I turned and walked away. Ten feet from the elevators, the hallway, carpeted and smelling of mold, stretched off to the left and right, lit by the same tiny, weak lights. A sign bolted to the wall indicated stairs to our left, and I turned that way immediately, the carpet swallowing my feet and insulating us from every noise. For a few seconds, we glided down the seemingly endless hallway, passing the closed doors of the rooms and the occasional useless, ornate table decorated with dead flowers.

"You have, of course, thought," the Poet whispered from behind me, "that this is far too quiet. There should be *someone*."

I nodded. He was right—even with the hotel suddenly locked down, Takahashi should have had people all over the place, and I would have covered the floors above and below where I had Londholm holed up, to guard against just this eventuality. I'd hoped to trap most of the security behind locked doors and sow some confusion—but there was *no one*, and no noise. No sound of spooked mercenaries relaying information, no noise of people on the move. Nothing.

"We're either in the wrong place," I whispered back, voicing the nightmare scenario of Londholm having been displaced from the Shannara before we got there, "or Takahashi's better at his job than we thought and we're about to get a face full of fuck you."

"I vote for the last one. Idea of going crosstown, I would want to cry."

"Baby," I said, fishing for an appropriate insult and then pausing. The hallway suddenly deteriorated into a grisly battle scar: The carpet was scorched and stained brown with dried blood, the walls had been battered and dented, the tiny useless table smashed to pieces. The room door directly opposite was still shut, but it had been battered inward at the center, bowing into a convex shape. The carnage lasted for three or four feet and then the hallway resumed its pristine, insulated appearance, like the combatants had teleported in and out, leaving the rest of the place alone.

The stairs were just a few steps beyond, behind a metal fire door. I gestured Mara and Adrian to each side and crouched down, pushing myself up against the door carefully while Mara turned to cover our rear and the Poet stood over me, autos in hand. I listened for a moment, then reached up and pushed the door suddenly inward, finger along the side of the trigger of my rifle.

Nothing. I stayed on alert for a moment, staring into

the dim, tight stairwell. Hot, thick air that smelled worse than the perma-mold we'd been breathing flowed against us, gently pushing, like a thick syrup that had been stored in the stairwells too long and had gone sour. The stairs themselves were old and rudimentary: rusting metal, wide enough for maybe two people to walk side by side if they weren't too excited. No windows, no real lights aside from widely spaced emergency LEDs. They stretched up and down with narrow, dusty landings that would constrict and bottleneck us.

"It would be easy," the Poet said thoughtfully, "to bury someone in there. Completely crush us."

I nodded, standing up. "Yup."

I stepped into the murk and spun around, exposing myself to the upper landing. Stupid, but I felt so fucking good it didn't matter. Why be careful? What was I surviving *for*?

There was nothing there. I relaxed and straightened up, and we mounted the stairs. Dust came up in clouds again, choking us, and despite our care, our feet scraped and pinged the metal stairs as we ascended, making more noise than I would have advised in better days. My heart was pounding irregularly, and my blood was right under my skin, hot and eager, and I took the last three steps in bounds, coming up against the fire door on the twenty-fifth floor with a crash.

"Fucking *hell*, Cates!" Mara hissed.

"Push the button or *shut the fuck up*, Mara." Glancing at the Poet, I put my hand on the fire door's latch and raised an eyebrow, and to my surprise he smiled and nodded.

"I've always liked you," he said. "Against all my best instincts. Go on, kill us all."

I pushed the door open. It squealed like a living thing whose tail had been stepped on, slowly revealing another hallway like the one we'd just left. It was just as dim and just as carpeted, and it stretched off into shadow, the same doors on either side.

There was a muffled, distant explosion, and after a moment the floor vibrated under my feet as dust and grit rained down on us. I paused, looking around like an idiot, and then stepped into the hall. I'd walked only a few steps before another explosion made the hotel shake, and then another, and then a constant cluster of them, dust sifting down on me. I didn't slow down. If the army was coming in heavy, if the army knocked the hotel down around me, that would be fine. At least Michaleen wouldn't get his toy out of it.

I reminded myself to be ready when Mara made her move—the most likely moment was the second we found Londholm, I guessed, as she wouldn't need me to put a bullet in him. I wondered how Adrian would handle it, if we'd have time to team up or if it would just be every man for himself.

The hall was just as deserted as the last, though in worse shape. The carpet was torn up and charred, looking like the whole length of the hall had burned at some point. The walls were pocked with holes and dents, the wallpaper torn down on most of them, the floor damp and squishy as we walked. The only things that were preserved and untouched were the fucking doors, each of which crept past me without blemish or any sign that anyone had ever touched them, ever.

"Don't y'fucking *say* we're gonna try each one," Mara hissed.

I ignored her, puzzling over the emptiness. My good mood soured into sudden anxiety—we were fucked, we were crawling into a trap, the whole fucking hallway was about to explode into mercenaries up our asses and we were never going to walk straight again.

And then I stopped, staring at the black square of a doorway without a door. The wall had buckled around the edges, indicating that something powerful had kicked the door in, tearing it out of its pocket.

I slid over to the wall, letting Adrian dash past the open door and paste himself against the wall on the other side of the doorway. I put my arm out to hold Mara back, glancing at her until she nodded, stiffly, and then I reached into my coat pocket and pulled out a smoke grenade: tiny, harmless, and light. I held it up for her and she nodded again, a little more friendly. I shook it once, forcefully, and leaned forward to lob it into the room. I counted to three, heart skipping all over itself, finding it impossible to take a deep enough breath, and with a glance at Adrian, I rolled myself into the doorway, shredder first, just as the grenade popped and white smoke exploded into the room.

I crouched and duckwalked my way in, augments struggling to sift through the smoke. The room had been broken up, the rich furniture and decorations smashed and burned and torn to pieces, left in big piles everywhere. I passed a small open space filled with debris—once a closet, I guessed—and a closed door on my left that I crept past and left for Adrian and Mara. The rest of the room was just a large box with one wall of windows looking out onto Hong Kong. There was a single chair left in one piece right in front of the windows.

Outside, the sky bloomed with fireworks: field-contained armaments exploding in the sky, the dark shadows of hovers flitting here and there. Tracers streaked from the ground and as I straightened up, one of the hovers was hit and bloomed into a bright orange fireball. The floor shook under me again, but the soundproofing was so good I only heard a dim rumble. It might as well have been a Vid, or a portal into the future for all I could hear.

The chair had been set in front of the windows as if for an audience of one to watch the festivities. A figure sat slumped in the chair, its hands bound behind it with a pair of standard-issue SSF bracelets. I lowered the shredder as Mara and Adrian kicked in the shut door, and I stepped around between the chair and the windows.

"Oh, *fuck*, I wish I hadn't opened that door," Mara said.

I stared. Based on the photos I'd seen, the figure in the chair was Alf Londholm. Based on the smell and the condition of his skin, he'd been dead about two days.

XXXIV

RIDING HERD ON MR. CATES AND HIS CHARMING ARRAY OF PERSONAL TICS

A new icon bloomed on my HUD, a red, angry star that pulsed. Under it, in the dull font the military favored, it read SEEK MEDICAL ASSISTANCE.

"This place is fucking deserted," Mara said as she approached the chair, shaking her head, "so those fucks back there were tryin' to sell us bullshit—"

She stopped, blinking, staring at the jellied, torn-up skull of Londholm. Someone hadn't been gentle. His skull had been cracked open and the topmost part of the dome sawed off with what looked like an extremely dull blade. Old blood was dried in streams down his torso, coating his hands as they clawed into the armrests they were tied to. His eyes were open, yellowed, and dry looking, and his face was sagged in a mask of suffering. Whoever had collected the God Augment from Mr. Londholm had done it while he was *alive*. Which begged the question: If the

God Augment made you a fucking *god*, how did mere mortals sneak up on you and tear your brains apart?

"He's been dead some time," I said, wondering if Mara was just going to pop me now. This was it, mission failed, nothing more for old Avery to do for the Little Man. Unless he was going to keep me on a leash and pull me out of the box whenever he needed some dirty work that was beneath him done. For a second, I saw my brief, unhappy future cleaning up Michaleen's details. I clenched my fists. This was fucking unfair. This was not *fucking fair*.

It took me a moment to realize Mara was laughing.

"Oh, you're a piece o' work," she stuttered, shaking her head and grinning. "You let me spin my fuckin' wheels in this bullshit for days!"

I frowned. I could feel every crazy heartbeat in my head, a tide breaking against my skull.

She turned to face the Poet. "How long you think you beat us by?"

Adrian shrugged, grinning, and stepped past her, circling around Londholm to stand next to me. He put his hand up to his chin, considering. "By the look of it, I guess a few days. Two, three. Maybe two."

Mara produced a pack of cigarettes from somewhere on her and shook two out. "We can't feel 'em, sure, but habits die hard, eh?" she said, holding one out to Adrian. He took it with a smirk, finally reaching up and tossing his sunglasses away.

"A celebration," he said.

I looked from the Poet to Mara and back again. "What?" I said. I'd had a lot more words in my head, but that was all that came out.

They both glanced at me. "Och, poor, poor Avery," Mara said, sticking the cigarette in her mouth. "You *are* pretty good dealing the cards, eh? Sure, sure. But not so good at thinkin' things through."

Dealing the cards. I had a sudden flashback to the yard, Chengara, dead Stormers around me, and the hover just sitting there, ours for the taking. And the Little Man, Michaleen.

I brought the shredder up, but before I could get my hands right, I felt the cold kiss of a Hamada custom automatic against my temple.

"Don't be tiresome, Avery," the Poet said. "You're always making dramatic gestures. It's not very professional. Besides, it's an *avatar*. Kill it twice, makes you feel better."

"Michaleen," I said. Nothing else would come out. The words were clogged in my throat like clotted blood.

Mara did a little curtsy, lifting the hem of an imaginary dress. "At your service, you fucking moron." She smiled again, lighting her cigarette. "Wallace, you're a national treasure."

I shut my eyes.

"You're like some sort of idiot savant," the Poet's voice said into my ear. "I *swear* I don't know how you've lived this long. Put you in a room with a gun and ten men trying to kill you and you're genius. But you can spend weeks with the two of us and not have a clue as to what's going on."

"Hello, Wa," I said.

"That's why I like 'im," Mara—Michaleen—said, sounding cheerful in a way that voice had never sounded before. "He's fuckin' *useful*, Wallace. Y'wind 'im up and point 'im at somethin', and he waddles on over and *does* it. Avery, Wallace has a theatrical bend, don't he—he got all into it, didn't he just, cookin' up your new best friend, backstory, everything. You was havin' *fun*, eh, Wallace?"

Belling grunted in my ear. The gun in my cheek didn't move. I heard Mara moving and opened my eyes as she came close to me, dragging on her cigarette like she could actually taste it, feel it. I opened my eyes. She smiled at me. "I've run cons longer than this, boyo. Your problem has always been, you got tunnel vision. You only see what's in front of you. And you're fucking impatient. Did you really think I'd hang this on *one* vector?" She shook her head, her red hair swimming in the air. "I don't take chances, Av'ry. I had Mr. Belling working his own line." She turned and threw her arms out. "And *damn* if that old bastard didn't come through."

She paused, studying the Poet.

Belling moved the Poet's face, frowning. "What?"

I marveled. Adrian was right there, ridiculous tats, ridiculous nickname. So fucking ridiculous I'd bought him completely. Wa Belling—I'd known Belling for *years*. I'd worked with him. And I'd been absolutely convinced he was a young kid from Belgrade, his kills animated on his skin, someone I could rely on.

I remembered Belling in London, pretending to be Cainnic Orel.

"How did you survive the process?" I managed to grind out. "Getting shoved into an avatar—"

"Used to kill you, sure, sure," Michaleen said, his almost-pretty eyes still locked on Belling. "Time marches on, Avery, technology advances. The refined process has reduced fatalities to about one percent. We rolled the bones." He cocked Mara's head and squinted at Belling. "Where are you?"

I put Belling in my peripheral vision, his gun and hand impossibly huge, his face far away. The tats still danced, a blur of red and black, up and down.

"You pursued your own track," Michaleen said, taking a step back and pulling his gun so quickly it was just a blur. "That was *your* fucking suggestion, Wallace. You're supposed to be *here* waitin' on me if you got through. So where the fuck are you, Wallace?"

"I am sure that I don't know," Belling said in the Poet's voice, without the Poet's inflections or rhythms. "Because I'm a separate entity, you see."

Michaleen nodded, pursing Mara's lips, ticked his arm up an inch and put two shells into the wall behind Belling, missing him by precise centimeters. Belling didn't flinch or move the gun from my cheek. Sweat streamed down my face. I felt like the gun attached to me was all that was holding me up, like I was hanging off of it.

"*Don't* get fucking smart with *me*, Wallace," Michaleen snapped. "Dying ain't pleasant whether you're flesh and blood or silicone and coolant, I'm thinking. At least when there's a professional involved. And if you die *here*, Wa, die knowin' I'm gonna kill each and every one of you out and about, yeah? So you got any theories on where you are right now, with my fucking property? And keep the fucking vocabulary small, eh, 'cause you know I'm just a rat from the streets, lackin' your education."

"Cainnic," Belling said slowly, "I do not *know* where my physical body is. I have been with you, riding herd on Mr. Cates and his charming array of personal tics.

We are, in fact, *assuming* that this is my doing. Perhaps I failed in my mission."

Mickey grinned, shaking Mara's head again. "Nope, this is classic Wallace Belling, ain't it? You probably spent days loitering about, sneaking in and out just to show you could, and when you finally got tired of fuckin' with them, you came in here and made the biggest fuckin' mess you could. That's you all over, Wallace. Nice suits and pretty words but you're still that fucked-up kid I took under my wing, performing surgeries on dogs without anesthesia."

Belling's avatar shrugged as I went over the preceding weeks in my mind, searching for clues. It was uncanny how well Belling had played his role. I'd figured Mara for an avatar, and on some inner level I'd suspected much longer, but Belling had completely fooled me, and it made me want to reach out and strangle him. But there was no fucking point. Michaleen had his toy, and if it actually worked, he was going to be the most dangerous man in the System—what was left of it—and I'd lost my chance to make him regret ever fucking with me.

"If it *was* me, Cainnic, I still don't know where *me* is, okay? Stop living down to my expectations. We need to—"

"Ah, the hell," Michaleen muttered, jerked his arm up precisely, and shot him three times in the chest.

Belling dropped to the floor and Michaleen was in the air, launching his avatar toward us. Belling rolled into my legs, knocking me over and taking me out of the equation for a second—which seemed unnecessary; I was filled with lead and acid. It felt like I was dying, a little faster than usual.

Before I hit the floor, Belling's avatar was up, a pinkish

mixture of fake blood and white coolant spraying out of his belly and coating me. Michaleen landed where he'd been a moment earlier and slid an extra foot, losing his balance in Mara's slim, flexible form, his feet shooting out from under him. I pulled on every remaining bit of energy left to me and scissored my legs underneath myself, pushing me up into a wild stagger. I crashed back into Londholm, knocking the chair and its grisly occupant over and landing on top of him. He burst open under my weight, the smell hitting me in the face as I flipped backward over him, avoiding clubbing my head on the windows by an inch or so.

I dragged my Roon from its pocket; it felt heavy and impossible in my hand, and as I tried to get a bead on either one of the fucking robots, it was like I'd slowed down my own personal time; the gun trailed behind them, waving this way and that, fucking useless. The tiny exclamation point representing Berserker Mode blinked in the corner of my eye, the only part of my HUD that hadn't wilted into a dark, angry red or yellow, every single system monitored by my augments warning me of impending shutdown.

Michaleen sprang up, whipping his gun around, but Belling ducked low and barreled into the smaller avatar, slamming him back against the wall hard enough to crack the drywall. The old man—in his shiny young avatar—sprang back immediately and dived down, taking hold of Michaleen's thin, girlish legs and jerking backward, straightening up and letting him slap down hard on the floor again.

I caught sight of Belling's face—the motherfucker was grinning.

He stepped halfway backward and swung Michaleen around once, halfway again, and let go, sending him sailing into the wall that separated the bathroom from the rest of the space. Mara's taut body slammed into it and formed a deep impression, then fell on her ass into a perfect sitting position. Without even a second of hesitation, she raised her gun and fired six times at Belling as he danced to the side and retreated toward the entrance of the room. Three of the shots shattered the glass behind me, letting in a sudden maelstrom of damp wind and noise.

Michaleen leaped, tucked and rolled, and came up gun in hand in the hallway, but Belling had disappeared. He dropped a clip and reloaded as Belling shouted from beyond the walls, the Poet's voice still sounding crazy in my ears without the weird beats he'd always had.

"C'mon, you ancient cunt! You still think you have a step on me? I'm not twelve any more, Cainnic, and I am sick to fucking death of your mush-mouthed bullshit!"

Mara's body sprinted into the darkness of the outside hall. I put my gun on her back and held it there, shaking, until she was swallowed up. Then I let my arm drop and turned to look over my shoulder.

Hong Kong was being burned to the ground.

There was fire everywhere. Darkness had crept up on us and the sky was near black, the military hovers outlined in dim lights like tiny stars cutting through a haze. Directly across from me, a tall building that was like increasingly smaller blocks set one on top of each other was burning, fire licking out of all its windows above the fifth floor or so, and it wasn't the only building on fire. New blooms of flame erupted on the ground every few seconds, and in between the roar of them was a constant noise, without shape or definition, just an undercurrent of sound I felt more than heard.

As I stared, something streaked through the air, almost invisible, and seemed to be coming right at me for a moment, disappearing overhead for a second and then smacking into the Shannara, making the room roil around me for a second like it was made of rubber, undulating in a way that rooms normally don't. All of the remaining glass in the window shattered and fell away, and my audio augments flatlined as the explosion pushed all the air out of the whole fucking building. Huge flaming chunks of building sailed dreamily down, like giant misshapen birds set on fire.

The building began to groan, a steady, unchanging note of severe distress.

"Might be time to get out."

I turned, slowly, and found Michaleen standing just beyond the bathroom. Mara's avatar had been torn up; one arm hung limp and bent at her side, and she was stained with coolant and fake blood. One of her cheeks had been sliced and torn and hung like a flap on the side of her face, something unnaturally white poking through the layer of artificial gore.

I raised the gun and held it up again. *If I had unlimited bullets*, I thought, *I might manage to hit a wall*. Before I could do anything else, the voice of the building's shell boomed through the air.

"Attention: This structure has suffered damage. Insufficient power to engage safety systems. Structural integrity is threatened. Please evacuate immediately."

I looked at Michaleen; our eyes met, and he put the gun right on my face from across the room and squeezed the trigger, getting the dry click of an empty chamber in return. I couldn't focus and hold my own gun up at the same time, so I let my arm drop and got my legs under me, forcing them to move. "Seal all exits," I said into the air. "Invoke special provision for public safety. Elevators to lobby and locked."

There was a beat. "Token confirmed."

"Fuckin' *pain in the ass*," Michaleen snarled, stuffing the gun into Mara's coat pocket and coming up with the tiny black square of my remote. "One thing I'll give ya, Cates," he said in Mara's soft, almost pretty voice, "you never know when to—"

I launched myself forward as he extended the remote toward me. As his finger came down, toggling me to *dead*, I jabbed the exclamation point in the bottom corner of my HUD and everything turned red.

XXXV

I'LL DO IT

I crashed into Mara's body in slow motion, a sharp pain like an ice pick jabbing into my head—but that just dissolved into the general feeling of being on fire, my skin burning, every muscle feeling torn. We hit the floor and skidded into the already smashed-up wall outside the bathroom, and I felt nothing—well, I felt *everything*, but the new pain was lost in the ocean of acid I was suddenly floating in.

Like on the train, I felt like I was just faster than everything. Beneath me, Michaleen was squirming, trying to break out from under my weight, and I knew that as an avatar he would be able to just toss me off, but he was so *slow*. I marveled at being able to feel him writhing beneath me, being able to anticipate his movements. He twisted left, digging his hands into the carpet to give himself some leverage, and tried to buck me off, so I reached around the slim waist of the avatar and hugged it to me, squeezing with everything my shredded, crystallized muscles had in them, and jabbed the Roon into Michaleen's chest, firing twice.

Dying ain't pleasant whether you're flesh and blood or silicone and coolant, I'm thinkin', he'd said, and I hoped he was right.

The back of the avatar exploded, inches from my face, showering me with the same pinkish mix of fake blood and coolant I'd seen erupting from Belling—I wondered how much longer they'd bother putting in the fake gore, the layer of blood and tissue designed to fool assholes like me into buying the Droids as real people; one of these days, probably tomorrow, everyone in the fucking System was going to be an avatar, and what would be the point?

He flopped once under me and then went still, a thick, warm pool of white coolant spilling out beneath us. Something like an ice pick traveled through my head, making me flinch and twitch, the pain rising until I couldn't bear it anymore. I tried to put my hands on my head to contain the swelling, but my left arm refused to move, just hanging limp and suddenly numb by my side. Then Michaleen started to laugh, and it was strange, because everything seemed to be moving in slow motion, taking decades to get to me while I hummed along, but when he started to speak in Mara's hoarse, high-pitched voice, I had no trouble understanding him.

"Shit, this is unpleasant," he spluttered, gouts of coolant drooling from his mouth. Then he focused on me. "You're not dead. Ain't that fucking bullshit, huh? Damn military tech's as bad as the Pigs. Half the shit don't work."

I tried to say something back at him, but my mouth just moved in an odd way I didn't understand. My face felt heavy and numb.

"You gonna shoot me again? Funny thing is, Avery, tomorrow I'm gonna wake up *somewhere*, y'know? And you're not."

The whole room suddenly twisted under us, the floor moving like rubber before settling again. The persistent groan of the building got louder.

I was shaking, heart pounding. Everything still seemed to be happening slowly, and my ruined hand didn't bother me at all. I pushed myself up onto my knees and then tried to get up onto my feet. My left leg didn't want to take my weight, and I staggered backward a few steps before finding the right distribution and getting stable. I dragged myself back toward the avatar, beat to hell and still grinning at me, Michaleen's ancient mind inside the girl's head.

"Ah, shit, I've pissed him off now," Michaleen cackled as I limped toward him. "You ain't looking so good, Avery. Maybe the revenge business isn't good for you, eh? You should stick to doing my dirty work for me. It suits ya."

I leaned down and with my good hand I took hold of the avatar's coat. Blood pounding in my temples and static electricity sizzling under my skin, lifting the avatar was easy, my back popping and a searing line of distant pain shooting down into my legs as I jerked it up off the floor. Turning, I started walking toward the smashed-in windows, dragging Michaleen's avatar behind me.

Outside, more of the city was burning, and the sky was filled with the shimmering lights of hovers. Tracers still seared up from the ground into the sky, and off in the distance a hover was crashing slowly, flames outlining it against the night. It looked like a cloud of fire just drifting lazily toward the ground. The floor shook again as I arrived at the edge of the window frame, shattered glass crunching under my feet. Wind, damp and heavy, pushed in at me, dark gray smoke trailing in behind it and slithering to the floor.

With a jerk, I tossed the avatar at the floor, where it landed awkwardly and slid a few inches to rest up against the lip of the window frame right above the floor. Mara's face grinned at me, the flap of torn skin making it look like it had two mouths beaming at me.

"Sure you don't wanna stuff me in a bag and carry me around?" Michaleen squawked as I leaned down and took hold of one thin leg with my working hand. "For company? You're a lonely guy, Avery."

I wanted to say something back, to say, *I got enough fucking demons whispering in my ear.* I wanted to promise him that I was going to find him, the *real* him, and then we could have a little chat. I moved my mouth, but it was like the muscles had been disconnected, and nothing manifested. So I just took hold of the avatar's leg and lurched forward, Michaleen's laughter—Mara's laughter—bubbling up from below as I flipped the avatar over and rolled it out of the window.

Glancing down, Mara's upturned face was swallowed by the darkness immediately, the sound of her digital laughter cut off as if the dark were a solid barrier between us.

I stood there for a moment, panting. I couldn't take a deep enough breath, and my head hurt with every heartbeat, a lance of sharp pain that skipped and lurched like my pulse, random and ragged. The building roiled beneath me again, almost knocking me off balance and into the dark, damp air, so I limped backward, scanning the floor until I found my handgun. Leaving the duffel and the shredder, I staggered for the doorway and back out into the hallway, where some ceiling tiles had shaken loose and smashed onto the floor.

"There is approximately five minutes of operational power," the hotel's shell announced suddenly. The PA system was exceptional and it sounded muted and local, like someone invisible was standing next to you. "Please proceed with evacuation."

To my left, splayed on the carpet in a thickening pool of pink-tinged coolant, was the Poet's body, the avatar's fake skin still flickering with the silent movement of its animated tattoos. It lay chest down, the head missing, one arm bent back at an unnatural angle, the Hamada still clutched in its hand. Michaleen, in whatever body, was a pro. So was Belling. And not a fucking ounce of mercy between them. I stared at the body and realized I felt like I'd lost a friend, even though I'd never actually had one.

"Cates."

I startled, whirling on the last fumes of Berserker Mode and almost pitching forward when my delicate balance on my bad leg was upset. I didn't see anyone, swinging the Roon around in a sloppy arc, and then glanced down to see the Poet's head, pristine except for the ragged line of fake flesh just below the chin, looking at me.

It blinked.

"Cates," it said, sounding normal. "Battery backup. Only a few minutes. Supposed to give you a chance to upload your recent experiences if you get caught out." It blinked again. "You look *terrible*, Mr. Cates. If I had to guess, I'd say you look like you've had a small stroke."

I just stared. I thought that if Belling asked me to carry his head around for company, I might just sit down and wait for the fucking building to collapse.

"You're like a roach, you know? Every time I think you *must* be dead, you crawl out from under it and strut about. You're a miracle of science. I have always thought you were a mediocre Gunner, Mr. Cates, not in my league, but I think I have overlooked your true talent: survival."

I wondered if I could get away with kicking him like a ball, or if that would topple me to the floor. I started to walk toward the stairs, wondering how I'd summon the elevator if my tongue continued to elude me.

"Cates," Belling hissed after me. "You and I have one thing in common now: Cainnic is coming after us both. You might want to find me. We could be useful to each other."

I closed my eyes. *Translation*, I thought: *You can't trade body blows with Canny Orel either—even with the fucking God Augment, if it actually works, so you'd like to stand behind me while I absorb bullets for you.*

"That crazy old man has a modified Monk chassis waiting for him. He figures he can live forever, and with that augment he can be a god," Belling said behind me, sounding suddenly weak and tired. "You think I took this on out of greed? Mr. Cates, I am a fucking *hero*."

I nodded, opening my eyes and limping away. *You sure are, Wa,* I thought.

As I reached the door leading to the stairwell, the hotel's shell spoke around me again. "Emergency Shutdown Protocols engaged. Thank you for choosing the Shannara. Good-bye."

The lights faded out, leaving me in darkness. I heard Belling whisper, "Ah, fuck, not in the *dark*, please."

After a moment, my visual augment managed to scrape up a pale green image that somewhat resembled the stairs, and I made for them, swinging my bum leg down and tottering on the verge of falling over with each step. When I'd made it down the first flight, the whole building shook again in response to a dull explosion, the metal steps vibrating under me, the handrail humming in my hand. I was pouring sweat and trembling, and I estimated that it would take about an hour to climb down the whole way, and if I sat down I'd never get up again.

I stopped thinking. I just swung my leg, tottered left, grabbed the handrail, stepped down. I breathed in short, painful gasps. Every now and then, everything bucked and rumbled and I clung to the handrail desperately, wondering if the whole place was going to come down on top of me. When the sickly green glowing EXIT sign loomed up in front of me, the dust of the bottom landing making me gag and cough so hard flares lit up in my vision, I just stared for a moment, unsure of what the next step was supposed to be. Slowly, I limped toward it, crashing through and out into a greasy-looking alley just off the boulevard.

The noise immediately surrounded me: hover displacement multiplied by a thousand and poured down onto the street steadily, explosions, and the sharp, quick punch of small-arms fire. The air smelled like smoke, charred wood, and something darker and more rotten, and my lungs tried to kick it back up for a better sample, sending me down on my hands and knees, shivering and coughing, every part of my body burning. I wasn't sure what I'd accomplished when I'd triggered my Berserker Mode, but it had maybe saved my life when Michaleen had triggered my remote.

The sound of boots thumping along closer and closer didn't really register until it had stopped, and I slowly raised my head to find about a dozen soldiers in soiled whites, cowls up and face masks on, standing in a loose semicircle around me. A tall officer with shiny pips on his shoulder had one hand up in the air, signaling a halt, and he looked down at me with his head cocked for a long moment, silent. Then he slowly lowered his arm and peeled back his face mask, grinning, just as faded text boxes bloomed everywhere, giving me the names and ranks of a bunch of assholes I didn't give a shit about.

"Well, *sheeyit*," Colonel Anners said, sounding breathless but pleased. "It's Mr. Moneybags Cates. Motherfucked, Cates, you look like nine hundred types of crap rolled together."

For some reason I couldn't identify, I smiled, sinking back onto my haunches. Without seeing it, I knew that the smile was a travesty, but once it had leaked out onto my face, I found it impossible to recall.

Anners looked around as if we'd met in some bar somewhere, old friends. "We got ourselves a beachhead, here," he said as the ground rumbled beneath us. "But these Hong Kong cops ain't givin' in *easy*, and I got shit to do." He looked back at me. "I got bitches out there ain't got no *idea* what to do with a bridgehead once you got one, and I got fucking *superiors* who seem like they're afraid to get some kids shot to hell." He spat on the ground. "I've only been at this war shit for a few years, Mr. Cates, but I got a *belly* for it, as some don't. But I'm stretched mighty fuckin' thin here trying to keep up. On top of it all, we got malfunctions on the unit implant settings and I had six decent grunts keel over from false frag alerts this past hour. It's fuckin' *chaos*, and I love it."

Somewhere nearby, something approximately the size of New York exploded, and the night air got brighter for a moment. The next few things Anners said were lost to the roar, but the colonel just stood there yapping like nothing bothered him much.

"So, you got anything to offer me, Mr. Cates? 'Cause I got a fucking bevy of generals up my *ass* and I can't have you just wandering around behind the lines knowing my name. But it might be worth it, if you still got your wallet."

I stared up at him. Even smudged with dirt and sweat, he was so fucking happy and healthy I was overpowered by the bright light that was Colonel Malkem Anners, so I smiled and spread my hands in front of me, trying to say, *Sorry, I threw my wallet out the fucking window.*

He nodded once, crisply, and turned to his squad. "All right, we got ourselves a drum trial, and as presiding officer, I waive the fucking drum and the fucking trial. Who wants to walk Mr. Cates around the corner and pronounce him dead in the name of the constitutionally legitimized Joint Council and its undersecretaries? Nothing in it but extra credit."

After a moment of quiet, one of the soldiers stepped forward and peeled back his face mask, his beaten-up face impassive, his eyes locked on me. I imagined there was something in them aside from hatred, but it might have been my imagination or my downward-spiraling brain.

"I'll do it," Remy said.

APPENDIX

Field dump of flash storage unit retrieved from Sector 97, Hong Kong Offensive, during routine investigation and benefits analysis. Retrieving Officer Hayes, 657483-560.

Transcript of field statement recorded with Ts. Sarangerel, Private (2), Small Infantry, 3356411-562 prior to termination and internal unit recycling. Per standing JC order 900-c regarding in-field AWOL officers, all FS Unit Dumps connected to the Anners incident will be kept perpetually in-system for access.

Note (D. Hayes): Although Private Sarangerel's statement does not touch on Colonel Anners specifically and her contact with her CO was brief and uniformly appropriate, her perspective on the operations and health of Anners's unit is enlightening and is included in this report as depth-of-field material.

It began after Nickles took it, the fucking moron. We'd been ordered to take the fucking building—who knew what the hell it was, it was just a building, gray and square and all the glass shattered out of it like someone had picked it up and shaken it a little. Why those fucking cops wouldn't just fall back and give it up was beyond me; why Crazy Anners wanted it so bad was beyond me, but six times he'd formed up an assault team from the stragglers streaming back from the bridgeheads and tossed them at it. Building 159. One-fiver-nine. On the map. Nickles had been acting sub-louie since Barnes ate it in the tunnel, and somehow he'd survived all six assaults, limping back from one-fiver-nine with two or three survivors, and Crazy Anners would scrape up another fifty assholes and hand them to Nick and say, "Take the fucking building."

One-fiver-nine. I thought, fuck, it must be filled with Dry Compressed Rations or booze, he wants it so bad. But what did we know. Crazy Anners says, take that building or I'll fry you, you had better odds taking the building.

Me and Nickles and the kid, Remy, we were in all the waves. Six fucking times we jazzed up and tore ass across the little square right in front, fire raking down on us from their superior position. Six times we were fifty percent down just getting to the building. Nickles screaming orders—this many left, this many right, door pounders out and loaded, goddammit. Nicks kept me and the kid close as his aides, and we weren't arguing. Nickles was a lucky charm.

Stair fighting. The first three times, we waited for the promised bombardment like suckers. After that, we just went for the stairs, small squads, backups stepping forward as people fell, fighting for every fucking step up. Crazy Anners thought we could take the building that way, but he was fucking wrong and we all knew it. We were never going to take one-fiver-nine.

On the third wave, we made it to the third floor, somehow. Maybe it was the big guy, Mendoza, we picked up when

forming up for the third try. He was fucking *huge*. When he
was on the stairs, he blocked out the light, and he screamed
like a lion the whole way, just pouring shredder fire—
reloaded his rifle like a natural, like he'd been born passing
clips every eight seconds into the beast. We all hid behind
him, figuring if he got nailed, his bulk would be a shield and
if we could outrun his falling corpse we'd probably live to
wave four, which was the best we could hope for. We were
massed behind him on the landing when his head exploded,
and then it all turned to shit and chaos and we went tearing
ass back into the open air for a re-form and replacements.

That's what Anners and his crazy pals didn't understand: They could stick a knife up our ass and make us go
into one-fiver-nine, sure. But we were just waiting for an
excuse to turn around and get the fuck *out*. A successful
assault was just one where we never got an excuse.

After the sixth wave, I thought, hell, they can't make us
go again. Not until we'd scraped up a full assault-strength
unit, not until they got the big guns set up and the hover
drones in the air, not until special-ops had taken out the
air defense grid. No fucking way. I told Nickles, no fucking way, as I lit a butt, panting in the shelter of a crumbling
concrete wall. And then Anners hit us all with a broadcast
flag: *form up*. Form fucking up. The words imprinted on
my vision, blood red. I looked at Nicks and he shook his
head and I'll never forget the expression on his face. It
was fucking defeat, fucking doom. Surviving six times
into one-fiver-nine was impossible. A seventh sortie was
kicking us over into bullshit.

One of the noncoms started shouting behind us, and I
looked over. A trio of privates were lying on the ground,
gasping like fish behind a scrap of old wall, and the NC

was trying to lift them back onto their feet with the power of his voice. It wasn't working, and one of the privates had a moment of fucking awesome when she lifted one arm weakly and gave the NC the finger, just jabbing it right up into his face.

"Fucking-A," Nickles muttered behind me.

The NC didn't find that humorous, and in a flash the private's blackjack was in the NC's hand. "You wanta get gimped, private?" the NC shouted. "You form the fuck up or I'm gonna light you up until your eyes boil outta your skull."

The private did it again—arm up, hand out, finger extended. She couldn't even talk, she was so winded. A ripple of laughter went up and I looked around, startled. Half the fucking party was watching.

The NC knew it, too, and without another word he jabbed the remote at her and the laughter stopped like it had been edited out. The NC was gonna pop her. For field insubordination. That was fucking *unfair*, and I could feel the whole unit tensing, outraged.

But nothing happened. The private just lay there gasping, and the NC cursed and worked the remote again and again. Finally, he thrust the blackjack into his pocket again and settled for a series of savage kicks to the private's chest.

I looked away. The NC was just beating on her now, and it was boring. She'd get up eventually and stagger into line just like the rest of us, and she'd run into one-fiver-nine again, just like the rest of us.

"What happens," Remy suddenly said, slow and steady, "if we don't go in? They can't execute all of us."

I stared at the kid. I'd never heard him speak before. His words were round and distinct. The boy had education.

"Can and would," Nickles grunted, standing up. "I was in Dresden two months ago, the CO popped an entire fucking battalion. They were fucking starving to death, hunting fucking squirrels in the woods and eatin' 'em raw, so they sat on their guns. Every one of them, dropped dead, left to rot." He spat on the ground. "C'mon. Die sitting out here or die fighting, your choice."

I didn't stand up right away. I'd fucked Nicks a couple of times. I liked him, and he was a good sublieutenant, a good field unit commander. But I sat there for a moment with the kid, and I knew what we were both thinking: More and more the blackjacks were shitting the bed, for whatever reason. This was the third time I'd seen an NC or an officer try to pop someone and nothing happen. I'd also seen dozens of successful executions, but all I could think of were those three.

"Maybe I just stand up and walk away," Remy said. "No one's watching. I could be a mile away in a few minutes."

Nicks nodded. He understood. He wasn't going to try and stop the kid. "Sure. Anners has his proximities set wide. But eventually you'll pass outside his field and then you autopop."

Remy nodded back, shrugging. "An hour of not running up those stairs? An hour of not getting yelled at and kicked and pushed into that *fucking* building?" He said the word *fucking* like he'd learned it recently. "Sounds like a deal to me."

Nicks nodded again, checking his semiauto rifle. "Go for it. I ain't gonna see anything. Me, I'm going back in." He suddenly smiled, yellow cracked teeth, one side of his face kinking up into leathery wrinkles. "Seven's my fucking lucky number."

Nicks was ancient, thirty if he was a day, and he looked it. Old. Old as the fucking hills, and covered in scars. Remy was a kid. I guessed he was sixteen, seventeen. Maybe younger. Me, I was twenty-four and I'd lived a good life up until the last six months, getting pressed outside Des Moines, getting shipped to Brussels for the assault there, getting shipped here. The idea of leaving Nickles to try one-fiver-nine again by himself was unthinkable. If Nicks had said, "fuck it, let's take a walk," I would have. But if he was going back in, so was I. I stood up.

"Let's form up."

Nickles nodded without looking at me. "Form up!" he shouted. "Come on, you shit sacks, let me see some fucking discipline. Tight squads—Monserret, where the fuck is your demo pack? If I order you to blow a door in there, what're you gonna do, fart it down? Sweet fucking hell— there's a pile of dead cunts over there, go sift for a demo pack. We'll just *wait* here for you."

I was next to Nickles when he took it in the face. In the *face*. His cowl just imploded like someone invisible had smashed him with a hammer, and for a moment he kept standing like it was just a flesh wound, something to shrug off. Then he crumpled to the stairs and became just another white suit on the floor, something to step over. Me and Remy, we both just turned and walked out. We were only a few seconds ahead of the general fallback, so no one noticed, and we both just sat down and pulled our cowls off, protected from fire by a pile of bricks that had once been a building.

That's when Remy began his quiet mutiny.

He just quit fighting. We both got ordered into the eighth wave, and he formed up without a word. But when

we were inside one-fiver-nine again, Remy just hung back.
He didn't make for the stairs. He stood his ground and let
the rest of the unit move past him. I got swept past him,
carried up by the squirming wave. Wave eight was just
a blur. I don't know how I made it back out alive. I was
setting records. When I stumbled out, soaking in my own
sweat and jittery from adrenaline, we still hadn't taken
the fucking building, and Remy was sitting outside, calm
and relaxed.

He kept doing it. I was amazed, because we'd all seen
enough idiots getting popped for insufficient enthusiasm.
The idea that you could just fucking ignore orders and
sit in that gray area between running away and throwing yourself at bullets—it was an amazing idea. We got
formed up for two more waves before Anners finally
decided his tactics needed some massage, and both times
Remy just...stepped aside, let the wave move past him,
and waited it out.

We rotated out of one-fiver-nine, but Anners had a
lot of asshole projects he was burning people for, and
all we got was three hours down for wound remediation
and R&R. Three hours wasn't the most I'd ever gotten
between assaults, but it was close. It was nice to let my
levels drop a little; some even got green.

I asked Remy what the fuck he thought he was doing.
Sooner or later he was gonna get nailed by some officer
looking to bust balls. He just shrugged. He didn't blink. I
watched him for a while and he didn't blink once.

"I'm going to die either way. At least this way, I'm not
running up and down the stairs all day."

The idea got into my head: We were going to fucking
die anyway, why not relax on the way? I thought about

it. Getting a vessel blown in your head by some screaming asshole with a pip on his collar versus getting shot in
the face in a dusty stairwell, sweating your ass off, and
staring at someone's grass-stained ass? It made this crazy
kind of sense.

Some other unit took one-fiver-nine three days later,
but we were already heading south, the blooms bright
orange and yellow on the horizon as we humped. None of
us had seen a hover or even a truck in weeks. It was just
walking and walking, two hours down and eight up, two
hours down and eight up, until you forgot there was anything but ground and your boots, the lights in the sky—
the hell we were walking toward—and N-tabs, dry and
dusty, swallowed hard and held down with discipline.

I studied Remy. He obeyed orders. Anners took a liking to him—the cunt liked to slip into the line for an hour
here and there, acting like he was one of the grunts, salt of
the fucking earth. Remy didn't talk back, didn't hesitate.
You wouldn't know the kid had decided to just sit it all
out. Just outside Shenzhen, Anners attached him to his
staff.

"Maybe I can slit that motherfucker's throat," he said
that night while we were down. I'd thought about fucking
him, see if he was cherry or not, but he was creeping me
out with the staring. "Now I'm on *staff.*"

Man's got to have a purpose.

I told him he'd be dead a second later, if he did that,
and the kid shrugged again.

Shenzhen was gone by the time we arrived. The ground
was hot, sour steam rising everywhere, the city just a collection of rubble. The cops had beat their way out of it
before we shelled, so it was just a few days of securing

whatever was left standing and organizing sorties out into
the brush to see where they were hiding out, massing for a
counterpush. Eight up, two down, walking the perimeter
and reporting contacts, sometimes we even got our blood
pressure up if we flushed a dozen Stormers out of some
sagging old building and had to mop 'em up. Remy was
on Anners's staff, and so I didn't see him too much. He
started going for walks.

We hit him on a patrol, way out in the fucking suburbs,
all of a sudden his name and number floating up. He was
just tramping it, didn't even have his rifle, just his sidearm
strapped to his side. We all relaxed and a couple of the
guys gave Remy some shit for making us tense up, but
Remy just floated by as if he didn't hear. I called his name
a couple of times, but he didn't look at me, just kept walking. Normally, he would've been SOL, getting caught outside his unit, but he was staff, and no one wanted to take
a risk by questioning Anners's boy. Thing was, he was far,
far away from his CO. Anners had a rep for being careless
with his staff, setting his proximities tight and then forgetting, so wandering away from him—especially without
permission—was fucking suicide. But that was Remy's
gig. Suicide. He knew none of us was getting out alive; he
just didn't want to do the work before his card got pulled.

After that, I started finding him all the fucking time.
He just wandered. He *tried* to get popped. He still did his
job; he still humped after Anners everywhere the crazy
fuck went; he still jumped to it whenever he was given
an order. But whenever Anners forgot about him, the kid
wandered off and really pushed it, really took his time.
It was coward's suicide, sure, hoping the universe would
deal him out, but it was still fucking balls.

And then we moved into Hong Kong. The tunnel, shit, I don't want to talk about that.

On the other side, I saw Anners. There was this five-minute window when my sub-louie had eaten some bullets and I had no intermediary CO, which technically put me under Crazy Anners's command, and he had so much shit going on, he couldn't pay any attention to a detail like me, so I got a breather. I was hunkered down in a pit with my cowl off, gasping for air and trying to let my trembling muscles relax, but Anners was like a sun shining there, all the crazy just beaming off him, and I watched him at his mobile command, swishing holomaps through the air, shouting and hollering. And Remy wasn't there. His whole staff was hopping to, either running his errands or at least standing there and looking busy, but Remy was nowhere. I didn't know at the time if he'd gotten clipped or if he was on another of his walkabouts.

After that, I got transferred to a new sublieutenant, Second Lieutenant Mortenson of the Asshole Division, who didn't like me on sight and gave me a zap just for the hell of it. Mortenson liked to goose you. He had his fucking blackjack in his hands all the time, just making you hurt constantly. Too slow, sloppy aim, forgetting to say "sir" after every sentence—the motherfucker was the worst sub-louie I ever had. We all would have taken a chance and fragged him if we'd had a moment to think, but the next couple of hours was just one-fiver-nine all over again, just squirming our way up stairwells, taking buildings one fucking block at a time.

Later in the day, though, Anners decided to form up a unit under his personal command. Most of the COs didn't do shit like that, because they had a fucking war to run, you know, but Anners did shit like that all the fucking time. An honor guard or something, I dunno; he liked getting up a couple dozen grunts and double-timing it around the field with 'em. When I linked up with him, Remy was there. The kid didn't say a word, just humped after Anners with his cowl down.

Anners had gone fucking batshit. Hong Kong wasn't *subdued* yet. Those cops were hanging onto every block with their fingernails, and we were getting bogged down because we didn't have the manpower to occupy every slab of concrete we took, so the cops kept sneaking three or four people behind us. Just three or four—sometimes two. Or one. One guy with a gas-powered gun bolted to the floor on an elevated angle could fuck us up, and it happened again and again. I began to wonder if our intel on the manpower stationed in Hong Kong was wrong. Anners should have been hunkered down in a stable command center running the show. Instead, he was on the move, and no one knew where the fuck he was one minute to the next and it was causing chaos. But he didn't give a shit. He didn't seem to even be aware of it. He just kept charging this way and that—shit, members of his staff were getting nailed by sniper fire as he trotted around, and he didn't seem worried.

You wanna know why we didn't take Hong Kong despite an overwhelming advantage in metal, look at Colonel Malkem Fucking Anners.

Some of us, though, they *loved* Anners. They loved the way he couldn't be sniped, the way he was fearless.

Remy deserted about an hour after I linked up. It was amazing—I think I was the only one who noticed, although Anners must have gotten a red flag in his HUD when the kid slipped out of range. But Anners never flinched. We'd come across some shitbag crawling out of a burning building. Anners talked to him like they knew each other, so he was a cop, maybe, but Anners asked for a volunteer to put one in the shitbag's head. And Remy volunteered. Last time I ever saw the kid, or heard him. He took the shitbag around a corner to put a bullet in his head, and he must have just gone on one of his walks. Anners had us humping away immediately, expecting Remy to catch up. He never did.

It didn't matter. I pictured him sitting with his back to a wall, just watching the smoke and fire go by. It didn't make any difference. Either way, we were dead. The only difference was, I was breaking a sweat doing it.

ACKNOWLEDGMENTS

As I continue to work off my gambling debts and bar tabs by writing and publishing books, more and more people are involved every year in helping me create these stories and get them into your hands. I am of course speaking of the various bartenders of Hoboken, New Jersey, who serve me heroic amounts of inspiration while tolerating my tendency to ramble on about baseball statistics and alternate universes. Of course, they do not labor alone.

If the fabulous Lili Saintcrow had not rescued me from that well all those years ago, none of these books could have been written. I can't say why I was in that well, due to the blood oath we swore, but the story will come out someday. Someday.

The fearsome Devi Pillai has improved everything I've written since 2007—books, e-mails, grocery lists, insane scribblings on the backs of cocktail napkins. This book is no exception.

Everyone else at Orbit Books US—Alex, Jennifer, Lauren, DongWon, Jack, and, of course, their fearless leader, Tim Holman—has either improved my books, improved my chances of anyone ever reading those books, or simply improved my mood, and for that they all deserve thanks.

My agent, Janet, has not kicked me to the curb despite overwhelming evidence that she should do so immediately. She also saved my bacon at the New York marathon this year, where her miraculous presence probably saved my marriage.

My parents always loved me, always encouraged me, and were not at all dismayed (that I know of) the first time I handed them a thirty-page fantasy novel and suggested I might want to do that for a living. Considering the odds, this was either tremendously great parenting or foolishly terrible parenting, but I love them for it!

My lovely wife, Danette, was the first one to see these books as something special and has never lost faith in me once, despite my rather obvious failings (mostly fashion related). Without her, I would be doomed.

extras

orbit

meet the author

JEFF SOMERS was born in Jersey City, New Jersey. After graduating from college, he wandered aimlessly for a while, but the peculiar siren call of New Jersey brought him back to his homeland. In 1995, Jeff began publishing his own magazine, *The Inner Swine* (www.innerswine.com). Find out more about the author at www.jeffreysomers.com.

introducing

If you enjoyed THE TERMINAL STATE,
look out for

THE FINAL EVOLUTION

by Jeff Somers

"Tell me something," I said, easing the barrel into the soft
spot on the back of his neck just below the skull. "How's
someone as stupid as you get a job like this?"

He tensed for a moment, then slumped a little. "I used
to be smarter."

I smiled, pressing the gun down hard while I hugged
him with my free arm, feeling him up for surprises. "We
all used to," I said. "Me, I used to be a fucking *genius*."

I found a gun shoved down into his crotch, a battered
old alloy auto with the safety chiseled off, ready to blow his
balls off if he zipped up wrong. I weighed it in my hand.

"It'll go easier on you if you tell me what else you've
got."

He chewed on this for a second or two. It was dark and cold as hell, the wind whipping up over the ruined outer wall of the old church and smacking into us. I stared over his shoulder at the glowing whitewashed walls, twin bell towers sticking up into the blue-black sky like broken bones. The church proper was ringed by the remnants of the old wall, a tiny, squat cottage connected to my right, the roof a vague memory. The whole world was being worn down, erased, one inch at a time. In twenty years, the cottage would be gone down to the foundation. So would I.

"Nothing," he said, giving me a little shrug. "I'm just supposed to yell the alarm, give 'em some warning, anybody gets past me."

"Yell if you want to find out what your brain feels like flying through the air," I said. "Besides, it doesn't matter. We're inside already anyway. Walk me in."

If he was in the mood to be reasonable, I was in the mood to let him live. I'd killed enough assholes already. Why be greedy?

"All right," he said after another moment.

I pocketed his gun and let him put an inch or two between us, then followed him toward the church. We scraped along the frozen dirt for a few seconds in silence.

"Listen," he said quietly. "There's two guys on the first floor, right inside the doors."

I nodded. "We know."

"Let me take the slip," he said. He didn't say it pleading, he just asked, like he was asking for a cigarette. "I'll catch hell if I walk in there with you pushing me along."

I studied the back of his head. He was younger than me, but so was everyone. His head was shaved and a delicate tattoo of a spiderweb had been penned onto his skull, a blurry blue design done in a shaky hand. It glinted slightly in the cold moonlight. For a moment, I considered just letting him run. My gut told me that he would just melt away and never bother me again, but I hadn't lived this long by taking stupid chances, so I sighed as if thinking about it and then I brought my Roon down on top of his head as hard as I could.

He dropped to the ground silently, and I stepped over him, glancing up at the hill that framed the church against the sky, a dome of green and brown. There was no noise, aside from the crunch of my boots on the frost.

I crept forward; when I was a few feet from the big wooden double doors, they swung outward on silent, greased hinges.

"You stupid fuck," I hissed. "What are you thinking? You check your field, or you'll get punished."

"Yes," Remy said, leaning against the doorway with one of his ersatz brown cigarettes hanging from one lip. "The day you can't handle one guard who doesn't know you're coming, Avery, I'm dead anyway."

I looked him over. He'd grown like a weed the last three years, getting broad and tall, every movement taut and powerful. He'd let his black hair grow out, hanging over his face, and he'd started a beard, a thick scum of hair that enveloped his cheeks and neck, making him look even skinnier, strangely. He dressed in black, like an asshole, but I pardoned him; he was still just a kid.

"All right," I said, giving him a little slap on his cheek as I pushed past him. "Then today's lesson is, don't rely on someone else doing *their* job to keep you alive, you stupid fuck."

"Stupid fuck" had become my term of endearment for Remy.

Just inside the doors were two bodies, big guys sprawled in the sawdust poured all over the floor, a bloody mess. They were both locals, tall beefy guys, tan skin and long, dark hair tied back into tails, guns in their slack hands. Both had tiny, small-caliber holes in their heads. I stood there studying them for a moment while the kid closed the doors behind us.

"You didn't have to kill them," I said, carefully. I didn't want to prompt another speech about the military augments in his head that might explode at any moment—from decay, or stray microwaves, or an old SFNA officer with a spare remote in his pocket. I'd heard it too often. I had the same augments, forced on me by the Press Squad, but mine had been damaged. The one time someone tried to pop me with a military remote—a blackjack, the old soldiers called it—it hadn't killed me, though I wished it had, for a while. When Remy didn't respond, I sighed. "Quiet work, though," I said, looking back at him. His face was impassive, as always. He hadn't spoken for the first six months after we got out of Hong Kong, him a deserter and me just an idiot, and even now he wasn't one for speeches.

"I think that was lesson three," he said, crossing his arms in front of himself. "Noise gets you killed."

The church had been gutted and was just a cold shell of old wooden beams and empty windows. Up front, there was a twisting set of stairs, apparently held together with wishes and good intentions, leading up to a sagging balcony that wrapped around three of the walls. I could see a door at the top of the stairs, a gleaming steel number that sported a nifty DNA-swipe magnetic lock. It didn't work anymore, of course; electricity was hard to come by in Bolivia. *Everything* was hard to come by, everywhere, since the System had fallen into a million little pieces.

"No one at that door?" I wondered aloud, walking forward and turning my head this way and that, trying to see everything, get the place fixed in my head.

"Assholes," Remy said by way of explanation. "Garces is nobody. A local strongman. I'm amazed he has a steel door instead of some glass beads on string."

I clucked my tongue. "Don't be fucking cynical, Remy. Yeah, Garces doesn't run anything half a mile away from this fucking building, but Morales is paying us a lot of worthless yen to kill him. And my intel says there should be two assholes at the front door and one asshole at the back door." I gestured up at it. "That bothers me. This lack of assholes."

"Well, there's *us*," he said with his usual flat tone.

I checked my Roon, scorched and battered but still smooth as silk—no one made guns like the old Roon corporation, rest in peace—then I took out the first guard's iron and looked it over. It was no Roon, but it looked like it wouldn't blow up in my hand, at least, so I slipped it back into my coat pocket.

"Well, let's find out what's up there."

I walked toward the stairs, thinking. Remy was right— Garces was a local boss, one of a million who'd sprung up when the army and the cops had dissolved, scattering, the System of Federated Nations getting unfederated over the course of a few chaotic months. The fact that the best people he could hire were low-quality wasn't surprising. It still felt wrong. I'd learned that when unexpected things happened, it usually went badly for you. We'd been working so much lately, I was in practice and in shape—my augments, my gift from Colonel Malkem Anners and Michaleen Garda, were damaged but still partially functional. I still had a flickering heads-up display in my vision, pain got washed away immediately, and when my heart rate kicked up, I got calm and clear. There was no reason to discount my instincts.

I paused at the foot of the stairs and listened. The steps were old wood, bowed in the center and reinforced here and there with old metal braces; they would creak like hell. The hallway behind the door was about twenty feet long, and there was another door that led to Garces's office. I was standing there, judging the physics and the chances I'd be heard, when the steel door swung open and a skinny, short man with his long black hair tied into a tight, thick braid stepped out onto the landing.

For a second we stared at each other. *"¿Qué la cogida?"* he said, taking half a step backward.

I put my gun on him, moving fast, my old augments giving me an adrenaline-sick edge of speed.

"Aqui," I said, using one-third of my usable Spanish and gesturing at the floor. *"Aqui."*

He nodded, raising his hands up like an ass. Never do anything you aren't ordered to, I always told Remy. Don't give shit away—if someone forgets to tell you to put your hands where they can be seen, keep your fucking hands where they'll do you some good. He started coming down, muttering with each step something I couldn't quite catch. Watching him, I cheated my way to his left, and when he was a few steps from the floor, I reached out, took hold of his ankle, and spun him crashing to the ground.

Remy was suddenly there, one boot on the poor guy's neck, his massive double-action revolver pointed at the guy's head. Startled, I dashed forward and gave Remy a shove, knocking him off balance and sending him stumbling into the wall, his heavy gun making him lean. I hooked one hand into our new friend's collar and dragged him behind me as I stomped after the kid.

"Why the *fuck* do I have to always *remind* you to not just fucking *kill* every fucking body?" I hissed. Remy was hunched over, staring up at me from around his own shoulder, his cannon aimed at the floor. It was a ridiculously large gun, heavy and loud, but it would put a fist-sized hole in someone's chest, and Remy was attached to it despite the fact that bullets for it were rarer than clean water these days. His hair hung in his face and he made no attempt to move, to challenge me. He just stayed hunched over as if expecting a kick, and shrugged awkwardly.

"That's what we *do*," he pointed out.

"Fuck," I sighed, looking back up the stairs. "Maybe it would be nice to ask our new friend here what's behind that door? How many men up there?"

He nodded, slowly straightening up. "Sure, okay, Avery."

I stared at him again, my prisoner just waiting politely for our attention to swing back to him. Remy disdained caution, because Remy thought he knew how he was going to die, and he thought the knowledge made him immortal in every other situation. Until his augments popped, he figured he was protected by fate. And no matter how many times I told him he was an asshole for thinking that, he was never convinced.

"Okay," I finally said, letting my guy drop to the floor and turning to put a boot on his chest and my gun in his face. *"Hola, muchacho,"* I said, gesturing up the stairs. *"¿Cuantos?"*

He grinned, again putting his hands up by his face to signify that he wasn't a threat. I didn't need his hand gestures to know *that*; he'd already shown me his belly and asked me to scratch it. *"No mas,"* he said eagerly. *"No mas, senor."*

I nodded. *"Gracias,"* I said, smiling back. His tan face lit up and he looked like he was going to keep talking, so I leaned down and smacked my Roon into his forehead just hard enough to knock him cold—the rusting augments in my head made such precise adjustments easy enough. I straightened up and gestured at Remy to precede me up the stairs.

"Don't be an asshole," I warned him as he slipped past me, all youthful energy and grace, sinews and adrenaline.

"We *are* here to *kill* Garces, right?" he whispered back. "We're not just going to be rude to him, call him some names, right?"

I started up the stairs behind him. As I'd suspected, they creaked and wiggled under us like it was going to be the last thing we ever did. "Shut up and keep your eyes open," I suggested. "When you have the urge to be an asshole, ask yourself if I can still beat the shit out of you. If the answer is *yes*, think twice."

Teaching the kid was hard work.

He reached the sagging balcony and stepped to the right, pushing himself against the fragile railing and raising his cannon. I stepped to the door and put my hand on the handle, glanced at the kid, and then pulled the door open in a sudden, smooth lunge. Remy tensed and then relaxed, shrugging.

I stepped in front of him and took the lead. The door led to a short hallway of warping wood slats on the floor and pockmarked drywall on the walls. Two doors on the sides had been boarded over crudely, leaving just the big, heavy wooden door with the shotgun slat at the other end to worry over. It made sense to limit the approaches; Potosí was not exactly a stable little city, and Garces hadn't become one of a dozen or so tiny chiefs in it through glad-handing and arranged marriages—a direct assault on his offices wasn't out of the question. If his guards weren't all local simps who couldn't be trusted to raise an alarm, the hallway would have been an effective way to bottleneck intruders and poke a gun through the slat, raking them with fire from behind the door, which I expected would be steel-plated on the other side.

We paused just outside the door, standing with our backs against the opposite walls, and looked at each other. Putting a finger up to my lips to forestall Remy's traditional approach of Extremely Loud and Shoot Me if You Can, I reached over and gently pressed down on the door handle. It moved easily and unlatched with a soft click that sounded like a shotgun blast to my ears. Wincing, I froze and waited to see if the door was going to explode, but nothing happened. I took a deep breath, my HUD flickering in my vision, all levels green, and pushed the door inward, stepping immediately to the left, gun out but held low.

Feeling Remy step in behind me, I took in the room. It was a nicely appointed office and almost felt civilized; Potosí was the definition of the sticks, but this place was old-school: wood paneling on the walls, a stained but thick and sound-swallowing red carpet on the floor, the opposite wall dominated by two huge floor-to-ceiling windows. The left wall was all bookshelves, empty, the sunburnt outlines of books still staining the old wood. In front of the empty shelves was a massive wooden desk, dark stain with deep scratches, flat and empty. Two men sat on my side of the desk in old, busted-up plush leather chairs, the upholstery blistered and bursting. One was a huge blob of a guy, pale white with dark red hair, a face made of freckles and sweat. The other was almost as big, dark tan and with glossy black hair spilling back over his shoulders like a wave of ink, a thin pencil mustache adorning his upper lip.

Behind the desk sat Manuelo Garces, who ran half of Potosí with all the imagination and verve of a drunk pissing on his shoes.

He was about my size, and ten or fifteen years younger. He wore what passed for a nice suit in these shattered times, and his head was close-shaved and sported a few scabs where an unsteady hand had cut him. He was a good-looking kid, his face round and happy, symmetrical and balanced. He didn't look like a guy who'd come up in the slums of Potosí, slitting throats and stealing anything not nailed down, a guy who'd survived the breaking of the System and the civil war that had left Potosí and everything around it for ten miles or so a scab of destruction. He looked like a kid I would pay a thousand yen to run messages for me.

In my peripheral vision, I saw Remy step in after me, shut the door quietly behind him, and then step forward and right a little, getting out of the door's way in case someone unexpected came in. When he just stood there with his ridiculous gun held down by his crotch,

I relaxed. The kid liked taking chances and sometimes caused trouble.

I looked at Garces. He had his hands under the desk.

"I'm not here to kill you," I said. "So don't pull that boomstick out unless you want to piss me off." Then I glanced at his two guests. "You two aren't on my list of chores today, so you have a choice here: You can jump out the window, or I can shoot you both in the head. You've got five seconds."

They both stared at me for a beat, then looked at Garces, who shrugged his eyebrows at him in the international gesture for "I don't give a fuck." The redhead looked at me.

"We'll go without a fuss—"

"You'll go out the window," I said, affecting boredom, playing my role like I'd done a million times before. "Or you'll stay here forever." We weren't that high up—they might break a leg, they might get messed up, but the drop wouldn't kill them. If they made *me* kill them, I was going to make it hurt, out of sheer irritation.

In some ways, the world was easier, now. The System didn't exist anymore—except for a hunk of Eastern Europe and Russia, where Dick Marin still had a rump of the old System Security Force under his direct command. Marin—the all-digital King Worm of the Droids. He was going to fucking outlive everyone, just go on forever, a digitized brain in an avatar body, directing an army of artificial humans.

Everywhere else had just fallen to pieces. City, states, small countries, a constantly changing ocean of sovereignties. Most places were run by people like Garces, gangsters who could pay for muscle to keep the peace, or by mercenaries who'd settled down with their troops. A lot of the old army officers had set up tiny kingdoms for themselves after the army had collapsed, with their units as security. It was fucking chaos, and chaos was good for business. There were no System Pigs breathing down your neck, beaming your face across the ocean, hunting you down. There were no Vids pasting your name everywhere and telling people to report seeing you. I could throw these two slobs out the windows and no one was going to investigate, no hovers were going to rip the roof off the place and dump a battalion of Stormers into the room, and no one was going to care.

They still didn't move, so I shrugged and brought the Roon up, cocking the hammer with a dramatic click. That got them both out of their seats, Remy shifting gracefully to his left to keep Garces covered.

For a second, we just stared at each other. Then I sighed theatrically. "If you've never jumped out of a window before," I offered, "the best advice I can give you is to take a running jump—it's easier that way, instead of leaning out in excruciating increments—and protect your head."

Red still stared at me. "You're . . . not serious."

Remy laughed, a cold, sudden snort. Remy hadn't known me back in New York, before the Plague. He only knew the new Avery.

I ticked my aim downward and put a shell at Red's feet, making him jump and yelp. The pair scampered backward toward the windows and I turned to Garces.

"Remy," I called out, "make sure they jump."

Garces was relaxed, a smile on his face. He stared back at me with his hands folded in his lap. At the sound of one of the windows scraping open, his eyes flicked over my shoulder and then immediately back at me. He pushed his grin into overdrive and raised one hand to point at me.

"Avery Cates," he said.

I shrugged. "You're Psionic. Read my mind and shit, huh?"

Garces shrugged back as a pair of yowling screams pierced the air behind us, suddenly cut off. "You're the only *gringo* Gunner with a Bottom working around here." He ticked his head toward the windows. "You cost me money, there."

"Fuck your money," I said, easily, taking a seat in one of the busted leather chairs.

He took that in stride. "I'm guessing I'm down four men, too."

"Just two. The other two will live, unless they die of shame."

He nodded. I could see how he'd clawed his way to the bottom ladder of the post-System world. He was smart enough, and he stayed calm under pressure. "All right," he said, his accent subtle, giving his words a round feel I kind of liked, like every word was linked to the last by a thin line of silk. "Let's negotiate."

I shook my head. I had the Roon aimed at his face, my arm resting on the arm of the chair. "We're not negotiating. I just have a question I have to ask you before I transact my business. Something I ask everyone these days."

The office was damp, I realized. It smelled moldy. If I looked up at the ceiling, I'd probably find a deep-brown water stain, but I didn't bother looking. Garces was a two-bit neighborhood boss—the world had tens of thousands of assholes at his level now, shitheads who thought having a dozen big guys sending up tribute to you made you important. I'd known *really* important people. I'd been in the same room with them, made deals. Garces was a nobody, and I was about to remind him of the fact.

"By all means, Mr. Cates," he said, spreading his hands to indicate compliance. "If I can answer, I will. And then we can discuss who has hired you, and what it will take for you to go and kill *them* instead."

I didn't react. Every asshole in the world thought they were brilliant, that no one had ever had such a brilliant idea before. And there were probably Gunners who made deals like that, starting bidding wars, waking people up in the middle of the night to announce the latest bid, and would you like to bid higher or take a bullet to the face? But Gunners like that usually ended up dead sooner rather than later. The one thing people wanted in a Gunner was reliability. You didn't like to think that hiring me was just opening up a fucking auction.

"My question is, have you ever heard of men named Michaleen Garda, Wallace Belling, or Cainnic Orel?"

Garces squinted at me, cocking his head. "*Orel?* Everyone knows of Cainnic Orel, Mr. Cates. He has been dead for twenty years, I hear." He smiled. "Or do I hear wrong?"

I nodded. "And the other names?"

He leaned back in his seat. "Never heard either one."

I nodded again. I never expected any kind of shocking answer, but we'd traveled half the world since Hong Kong and I'd made it a standard thing, just asking. It was surprising what you could find out just by asking. I looked around the office. Chances were I was never going to have my revenge on Michaleen, aka Cainnic Orel, the most famous Gunner in the short, doomed history of the System, or on his lieutenant Belling. Both of them deserved to die, and I deserved to be the one to kill them, but I wasn't going to get any closer to that crawling around the wreckage of civilization killing little shits like Garces for pennies.

Wallace Belling had told me, three years and forever ago, that the fat times, as far as contract murder was concerned, were back. And he was right. I had more work than I could handle. The whole world was boiling, everyone grabbing what they could and riding the bull until it bucked them off, and the easiest way to skip your wait in line was to hire someone like me and delete a few people from the queue. I wasn't working Orel and Belling's legendary level, the Dúnmharú, a stupid fucking name that still made people lie awake at night with a gun in their hands, but I was sleeping indoors every night when most people were experimenting with a diet of dirt occasionally supplemented with their own fingers, and I was still alive, despite the odds. It was the best deal I was going to get, and every day I didn't get an interesting answer to my questions, I got happier with my lot in life.

Standing up, I pushed my gun into my coat pocket. "Nice place you got here," I said, walking toward the door. I felt good. My augments weren't as effective as they'd been when the military had first implanted them, making me feel like a kid with perfect balance and endless energy, but they kept my leg from aching and my lungs from burning and I slept like a baby at night, just a black stretch of peace and recuperation. I spun and walked backward for a few steps, feeling light and lively. "Too bad it's going to be someone else's tomorrow."

His sudden expression of pale horror was hilarious. "You said you were not here to kill me!" he shouted, veins bubbling up under his skin. I got the impression that Garces was a screamer, when you didn't have a gun on him. That made me feel good. Screamers deserved to be shut up.

"I'm not," I said, hooking a thumb at Remy, who stood in front of the desk with his cannon held calmly in front of him. "He is. He really enjoys this part."